MW00527458

YEARS

SIMON &
SCHUSTER

THE LIGHTNING BOTTLES

MARISSA STAPLEY

SIMON & SCHUSTER

NEW YORK LONDON TORONTO SYDNEY NEW DELHI

AUTHOR'S NOTE:

This novel contains depictions of addiction and depression. If you or a loved one
are struggling, CAMH: The Centre for Addiction and Mental Health (in Canada)
and SAMHSA: Substance Abuse and Mental Health Services (in the United States)
offer ways to find treatment and help. You are not alone.

1230 Avenue of the Americas
New York, NY 10020

This book is a work of fiction. Any references to historical events, real people,
or real places are used fictitiously. Other names, characters, places, and events
are products of the author's imagination, and any resemblance to
actual events or places or persons, living or dead, is entirely coincidental.

Copyright © 2024 by Marissa Julia Margaret Ponikowski

All rights reserved, including the right to reproduce this book
or portions thereof in any form whatsoever. For information, address
Simon & Schuster Subsidiary Rights Department,
1230 Avenue of the Americas, New York, NY 10020.

First Simon & Schuster hardcover edition September 2024

SIMON & SCHUSTER and colophon are registered trademarks of Simon & Schuster, LLC

Simon & Schuster: Celebrating 100 Years of Publishing in 2024

For information about special discounts for bulk purchases,
please contact Simon & Schuster Special Sales
at 1-866-506-1949 or business@simonandschuster.com.

The Simon & Schuster Speakers Bureau can bring authors to your live event.
For more information or to book an event, contact the Simon & Schuster Speakers Bureau
at 1-866-248-3049 or visit our website at www.simonspeakers.com.

Interior design by Ruth Lee-Mui

Manufactured in the United States of America

1   3   5   7   9   10   8   6   4   2

Library of Congress Cataloging-in-Publication Data is available on file.

ISBN 978-1-6680-1576-6
ISBN 978-1-6680-1578-0 (ebook)

For Courtney Love, Deborah Anne Dyer AKA Skin,

Dolores O'Riordan, Donita Sparks,

Fiona Apple, Juliana Hatfield, Kat Bjelland,

Kim Deal, Kim Gordon, Liz Phair,

PJ Harvey, Shirley Manson, Sinéad O'Connor,

Tori Amos, and my teenage self

One day you will ask me which is more important?
My life or yours? I will say mine and you will walk away
not knowing that you are my life.

Kahlil Gibran, *The Prophet*

PROLOGUE

"Where were you when you found out rock legend Elijah Hart had disappeared? That the talented yet troubled musician had taken a rowboat into the stormy waters off Iceland's south coast and never returned?"

The radio DJ's voice rumbles through the air in seventeen-year-old Hen Vögel's bedroom. "I was right here," she says to her walls.

"Maybe you were returning home from work when you learned the front man of the multiplatinum-selling husband-and-wife duo the Lightning Bottles had been declared dead," the DJ continues. "Maybe you were on a first date. Or a last date. Or driving in your car with the radio on." Hen shakes her head; she has never done any of those things.

"How did you feel when you realized his miraculous voice had been silenced forever?"

DJ Grüber does this every year. In case the emotions are fading, he tries to stir them up. But Hen doesn't need stirring. The difference between thirteen years old and seventeen is supposed to be a caterpillar versus a butterfly. But Hen has remained stuck in her cocoon, trying to rewrite the story of her hero's demise, since the day Elijah Hart disappeared five years earlier.

She stares up into his eyes gazing out from a poster tacked to the wall above her bed. There's a permanent sunbeam stained across his T-shirt now. He's tall and lean, his hair unkempt like he just woke up. One of his front incisors overlaps the other—Hen knows the details of Elijah Hart's face the way she knows the curves of the letters in her own name—and his left canine points out a little, so when he smiles he looks a bit like a vampire, but not in a dangerous way. It's just that you find yourself wishing he were immortal. His eyes are ocean green, but with a ring of yellow around the iris that makes them look blue at the right angle.

"Ladies and gentlemen, boys and girls, I'm DJ Jon Grüber. But you probably already knew that, didn't you?" Hen turns her attention back to the radio show and sighs. Why do adults always try to act so cool? DJ Grüber isn't cool, he's fifty. He plays a clip of himself announcing the news about Elijah's disappearance, his voice in December of 1994 not quite as cigarette-smoke raspy as it is five years later. *Icelandic authorities are reporting . . . the boat has turned up empty . . . no sign of the body . . . vigils being held around the world . . . I hate to be the one to have to tell you this . . . little hope for survival at this point . . .*

Hen flops backward on her bed and wraps her arms around herself in a lonely sort of hug. She remembers the days that followed this terrible news. The television images of Icelandic search and rescue boats. Helicopters, divers, a splintered rowboat on a black sand beach, a shoe and a waterlogged leather jacket washing ashore. There was the revelation that Elijah Hart had made one phone call in the hours before his disappearance—to his estranged best friend and former bandmate, Kim Beard. Exactly what was said during that call had never been confirmed; Kim Beard wasn't what anyone would call a reliable witness. Elijah's body never turned up, but as the days passed, his death became a given. No one could have survived for long in such cold and tumultuous water. Except—

Hen sits up and meets Elijah's two-dimensional, ocean-eyed gaze again. "How am I supposed to solve the mystery of you when I have no one to talk to?"

A scratch at her bedroom window is all that answers. A soft *meow.* The stray calico she feeds is on the sill, and when Hen lets him inside, he winds himself around her ankles like a friendly, furry serpent. She reaches into her pocket and pulls out a treat. He takes it from her hand, then licks her palm once with his pink sandpaper tongue before trotting off to the corner where she has set up a bed for him with old army blankets she found in the attic. She leaves the window open, lets the cold air flow into the room. Maybe it will finally jolt her into action.

"We lost a rock god in 1994, five years ago today," DJ Grüber growls from the radio. Hen winces. Elijah wouldn't want to be called a god. He was mostly affable in interviews—but say the wrong thing and a shadow would pass over his splendid face. "If you're not a hero, or an icon, or a god," Barbara Walters had once asked him, "who are you, then, Elijah Hart?"

"I'm really just a session musician," he'd replied, gifting her one of his seductive grins as Barbara visibly melted. Elijah had turned to Jane Pyre then, looking at his wife the way he always did, as if he saw a pyramid full of hidden wonders, not an angry-looking woman in a plaid miniskirt and 20-hole Doc Marten boots. "It's Jane I'm more interested in."

Barbara had looked at Jane too, tilted her head, and asked, "Okay, how would you define your husband, Jane?"

"I wouldn't," she had replied. Hen remembered liking that answer. It's what Hen would have said too, had she been lucky enough to be sitting there in Jane's place. But it had only cemented Jane Pyre as unknowable, obtuse. Not especially likeable. How had someone like Elijah Hart ended up with someone like her? It was yet another mystery about him.

Now, DJ Grüber's voice edges its way back into Hen's consciousness. "To mark the fifth anniversary of the loss of Elijah Hart from this world, here's what we're going to do . . ." Hen leans forward, holds her breath, hopes he might say, *We're going to tell you incredible news: our hero has been found!*

"We're going to listen to some tunes, relive some hard moments, share some memories," DJ Grüber says instead. Same old same. Hen stands. She crosses the room to her desk, where she reaches down and touches the closed drawer, the place where she keeps a secret that could change everything, if only she had the courage to let it out.

"Friends, I hope to hear from some of you today. Call in. The lines are open. Let's remember what we loved about the Lightning Bottles. Let's dive deeper into the brilliant musical legacy of Elijah Hart and remind ourselves he's never really gone. But first—"

The DJ plays a recording of Jane Pyre's voice giving the single statement she made after her husband disappeared. "He's gone," Jane said. It was the day after the search for Elijah had been called off, the sea too wild for rescuers to traverse any longer. The rock star's wife—now his widow, really—had stared into the cameras and microphones with eyes like storm clouds. Icelandic police had just released her, having questioned her extensively and determined she held no culpability in her husband's misadventure—even if the court of public opinion gave a different verdict. "I loved him." Her brittle voice broke in two, then turned defiant. "And he was mine. *My* husband. The love of *my* life. So give him back to me. Let me grieve in peace."

It had been all wrong, of course. The fans wanted comfort, for their grief to be validated. They didn't want to be told Elijah Hart had never belonged to them. Not when every word he sang felt like he was shining a searchlight into the loneliest parts of their souls and saying, *I'm here, I found you, you're going to be okay now.*

Jane Pyre didn't speak to the media again after that. And she guarded his legacy like a warden. There were rumored to be unfinished Lightning Bottles songs in a vault somewhere, and because of her, the world would never get to hear them. She released an album of remixes that was nothing but a slap in the face to fans. And she never wrote another song—even though Elijah had insisted they were collaborators and had even gone so far as to hint that *she* wrote the majority of their music and lyrics, not him. No one had believed this while he was alive, and they certainly didn't after he was dead. Jane Pyre was a succubus, nothing more. A talentless fake.

Hen had always had a hard time believing Elijah could be so wrong about someone, though. Had he really handed his heart over to a fraud? There had to be something about Jane that had caused him to fall so irrevocably in love, right? Hen tumbled this question around in her mind constantly but never landed on anything tangible. If Jane Pyre wasn't who the world said she was, she had never offered an alternative, even when given chance after chance. She was as elusive and mysterious as a creature who lived at the bottom of the ocean—and only Elijah, perhaps, had ever truly known her.

Hen opens the desk drawer. Inside is a small wooden box. Her late opa whittled it for her out of wood from a fallen ash tree when she was little. *You can keep your special things in here,* he'd said. At the time, it had never occurred to Hen that her life would shrink as she got older. She filled the box with pebbles and feathers, then forgot all about it—until she finally came to possess something she needed to keep safe.

She opens the box and there it is. Her treasure doesn't look like much. Just a crumpled piece of lined paper she handles like it's the Hope Diamond. She runs her index finger along the creases, carefully coaxes the paper to bloom. What is revealed? Pencil drawings depicting a man and a woman, a story told in a comic-style grid. "The Secret Adventures of Adam and the Rib" is drawn across the top of the page in letters that mimic the shape of spray-painted graffiti. A hand-drawn character matches each name: Adam has hair to his collar and slightly hunched shoulders; he is lean-limbed and handsome, even in pencil. Rib has thick-lashed eyes and a familiar frown. She is wearing a short plaid skirt and lace-up boots.

To Hen, there are only two people these characters could be: Elijah Hart and Jane Pyre. Adam and his Rib, which is exactly how the world saw them.

Hen runs her finger along the pencil grooves. The first square in the grid shows Rib sitting in front of a computer, typing out a list. The names of alternative rock bands flow onto the screen:

1. The Disintegration
2. L7
3. Concrete Blonde
4. The Smiths
5. The Vaselines

6. Pixies
7. Jane's Addiction
8. Sonic Youth
9. R.E.M.
10. Babes in Toyland

In the next square, Adam sits at a desk in front of his own computer, and Rib's face smiles out at him from the screen. "Weirdo," says her speech bubble—but there are hearts in her eyes. Next, the two characters are surrounded by musical notes, letters tucked into envelopes, mixtapes, song lyrics, everything flying through space.

Then a phone booth, with Rib inside, Adam drawn in a thought bubble above her head. Rib in a car, driving across a map of North America to Seattle, where she stands alone outside a bungalow surrounded by firs, pines, cedars. There is a racehorse inside her chest instead of a heart. You can feel how nervous she is. How expectant.

Finally, she ends up in Adam's arms—and Hen can almost feel it, what it must have been like to be held by him.

But, one last square. A sad ending. Adam is alone, words about love and loss creating an ocean in the space separating him from the cartoon woman. Rib tries to reach out across the chasm but almost falls in.

Poor Elijah. It's all Hen can think each time she unfurls this page. And she feels sorry for Jane Pyre, too—and wonders if she's the only person in the world who ever has.

DJ Grüber has put on a song, and it drags Hen away from the drawing and back to reality. The Lightning Bottles' first-ever and still most popular hit, "My Life or Yours," never gets old. "The bass and drum intro grabs you by the throat, doesn't it?" Grüber says, as Hen nods her head over a musical intro that builds from mellifluous to incandescent. "A full and unprecedented thirty-eight-second opening, very radio unfriendly, and yet that didn't stop it from becoming the most requested radio song of the decade." Grüber chuckles while Hen wishes he would just stop talking and let the song play. Instead, he keeps up his chatter, weaves it through the lyrics and melody. *You asked if I'd die for you / I didn't know what you meant / but the words were all there for me / from a prophet, heaven sent.*

"He was singing about his mother, of course," Gruber says, his tone somber. "We all know that now, because of the Kim Beard lawsuits. His mother, and some lines she used to read to him when he was a child from the well-known mystic poetry book *The Prophet*."

Still gently clasping the piece of paper, Hen sinks back down to her mattress and listens with her eyes closed. Some great songs make it feel like a spell is being cast, and this is one of them. It never fails to enchant Hen, to lift her up. She's soaring now, and nothing can touch her. "And here it is," the DJ says. "One of the most famous choruses in all the world. Sing it with me, folks . . ." Hen can't help it, she does. *Baby, don't cry / 'cause we're all gonna die / might as well just get high . . .*

"A call to inaction for the MTV generation," Grüber says. "Sung by one of the most transporting voices in the music world."

Once the song is over, he takes a call. A man shares his feelings about Elijah's voice, describing it as "a roman candle that flares up in the distance when maybe you thought you were the only person left on the planet."

A cold breeze from her open bedroom window ruffles Hen's hair and she sits up, reaches for the telephone that sits on her bedside table. She can do this. She *will*. Today is the day. She dials before she can overthink it, and as the phone rings, tries to plan out what she'll say. *I want to share a memory—but it's more than that. I was one of the winners of your call-in contest, back in 1994, when the Lightning Bottles were in Berlin for what no one knew was going to be their last public performance.* And Hen would feel proud, nostalgic as she remembered the way the radio station had created a temporary concert hall out of an old, underground water-pumping station in Berlin for the occasion. For one night only, it was a hidden lair for the truest of Lightning Bottles' fans, the ones who had dedicated themselves day and night to waiting by the radio, phones tucked into laps, handsets cradled in tensed hands, poised to call in at the right moment. Reportedly, fans had flown to Berlin from around the world only to sit crouched in hotel rooms, radios on, waiting, intent on possessing one of the golden Lightning Bottles tickets.

"Hello? Can I get your name, please?"

"Henri—Henrietta Vögel," she stammers to the receptionist. "I go by Hen."

"I'm placing you in a queue, Hen," the voice says. "You'll be live, on-air to share your memory of Elijah Hart in about forty-five seconds."

Hen's palms are slick. She distracts herself by continuing to imagine what she'll say. *I had to lie to my mother about where I was going; she would never have let me go to Berlin. By the time I got to the city I was late for the show and led to the only seat left—at the very front, but off to the side of the stage with a poor view. Elijah and Jane were standing at the top of a staircase, waiting to go on. I could see them. They were arguing. Elijah kept trying to hand Jane a piece of paper, and she kept shaking her head. I thought maybe they were arguing about the set list, but then she pushed him away and started to cry and it seemed more serious than that. Finally, she did take the piece of paper, but she crumpled it up. She threw it into a trash bin at the bottom of the steps. As the two of them went onstage, I darted over and grabbed that piece of paper from the trash. I put it in my pocket—and I've had it ever since.*

Grüber's voice is loud and sudden in Hen's ear. "Who do we have on the line, and what do you want to share with us on the anniversary of the loss of Elijah Hart?"

She can't speak.

"Hello? Do we still have you on the line?"

"Um. Hi. Well. So. It's just that—um. I think he might not be . . ." *I believe Elijah Hart is still alive, and that he's using street art to send out messages.* She slams down the receiver. She can't do it. Her story would sound like the lie of an obsessed fan. And besides, this isn't just her secret. It's Elijah's—and Hen knows in her heart there's only one person in the world he would want to share it with. And that person is Jane Pyre.

DJ Grüber has put on a song—"Watching Us"—to cover up the abrupt silence on-air. Unlike "My Life or Yours," this one gets right to it, a quick guitar riff and then Elijah's voice, singing, *I give you all my sweetness*

but my love comes out a scream . . . Take my flesh, my bones, my body, as he's
watching through the screen . . .

"Hen?"

Startled, Hen hides her secret drawing in her fist, crumpling it the way Jane Pyre once did. Her mother is standing in the doorway.

"Are you alright? I heard a bang."

"I'm fine, Mama. I just dropped something."

Anja is wrapped in the blue bathrobe she always wears, but her hair is wet and brushed back. She's showered, a good sign. This has been happening more often lately, but the steps Hen's mother takes into the world are so small that Hen, at the precipice of adulthood and longing to fly away, can no longer find hope in them.

"Will we maybe walk out to the edge of the driveway today?" Anja asks, and Hen tries not to grimace. The edge of the driveway—at this rate, her mother will make it into town by the time she's ninety.

"I'm listening to something on the radio right now." Hen hears the dismissiveness in her tone, sees the ripple of hurt in her mother's eyes, feels sorry, but not enough to say so. "Maybe later, okay?"

"Of course. And maybe you could also go to the market and get me some noodles and cheese. I'll make käsespätzle. Would you like that? It's Saturday. We should do something fun."

Noodles and cheese. A fun Saturday night. Despite the open window, the air in the room feels suddenly oppressive. In the past, when Anja would send her on errands, Hen would rush to the market as fast as she could, afraid that by the time she got home her mother would have retreated back into the place inside her head that made her ask things like, "Did the cashier touch her earlobe, did she scratch her nose? Did you see any men on the streets, tying their shoes?" Hen has had to remind her mother hundreds of times that the Berlin Wall fell years ago now. *The Stasi are gone, the neighbors are not spies, Mama.* Sometimes her mother will say, *No, that can't be true.* Other times, she will tell Hen that she knows the Wall is gone—and that's even more reason to be cautious. *There is nothing to protect us now, vögelchen.* Little bird. Hen's mother was fed propaganda like porridge, along with everyone else in East Germany. But not everyone took it as literally as she did. There is no help for people like her, the ones who don't know how to move on. No one even wants to believe that people like her mother exist.

"Yes, Mama. I'll go later, okay?"

Once her mother is gone, Hen crosses her room to the wall that faces the window. Here, she has set up a milking stool she took from the abandoned barn on the property next to hers, and a bunch of old buckets. It's the closest she has ever been able to get to a drum kit. She sits on the stool and picks up her drumsticks. The music from the radio is still filling her room, and Hen begins to play along, pumping her foot up and down on an imaginary bass pedal and hitting one of the buckets so hard it almost falls over. She can't believe she actually called into that radio show. Had she really been about to tell her story live, on-air?

As the music keeps playing, she can see herself at fourteen, fifteen, sixteen. Concocting more lies to tell her mother so she could return to Berlin, always with the drawing tucked into her pocket. Elijah Hart did the art for the Lightning Bottles' second album, and it was as if the cover and liner notes had been decorated in graffiti. In a few interviews, he expressed his interest in street art. And so, during her visits to Berlin, Hen sought to understand what Elijah loved so much about this form of expression. Why had he made the title, *The Secret Adventures of Adam & the Rib*, look like graffiti spray-painted on a building wall? Had he ever done this in real life? She wanted to know him, to understand him, to connect the piece of art she had of his to something real in the world.

Until finally, she made a connection beyond her wildest dreams.

Graffiti allowed a person to be somewhat famous, but in secret. You could plaster your work across apartment buildings, emblazon it on subway cars—and if you were careful enough, no one would know it was you.

But Hen had known.

She taps at her drum-buckets, loses herself a bit more in the music, closes her eyes—and she can see it in her mind's eye, among the ubiquitous layers of graffiti and art coating Haus Schwarzenberg alley in Berlin:

those soft but certain pencil-like strokes, done in paint. The brightness of
the title, emblazoned across the top of the poster. It looked like the cover
of a comic book—one called *The Secret Adventures of Adam & the Rib.*

Shock had frozen Hen in place. She had looked up and down the alleyway, wondering if anyone else saw what she saw. But of course no one
did. She was the one who had the piece of paper in her pocket. The only
one who knew what this meant—what this could be. What it *was.*

The poster had been decoupaged to the brick wall with thick swaths
of glue. It was not enough to say the style of art on the poster was similar
to the drawing Hen had in her possession. Not enough to claim some
of the details as the same. The character on the poster was a replica of
Adam, there was no question. Never had Hen felt so elated—and then,
all at once, never so alone. She didn't want to be the weird girl with the
shut-in mother anymore. Having a secret this huge made her long for a
friend more than she ever had before.

*I believe Elijah Hart is still alive, and that he's using street art to send out
messages.*

And I wish, more than anything, that I had someone to tell.

Hen keeps playing her fake bucket drums, can at this point almost
believe they're not made of plastic. She feels a sudden sense of power;
the music does that for her. If she can conjure a drumbeat from thin air,
what else can she conjure? It's such a great feeling, the moment of being
swept away by a song. The way music can make it feel like anything is
possible.

The song ends, and in the beat of silence that follows before the DJ
speaks again, Hen hears a car's engine outside. Startled, she drops her
drumsticks and rushes to the window. No one ever comes out here. She
hears the solid *clunk* of a car door slamming, the creak of an opening
trunk, leans out the window to see what's going on next door.

A small field separates the two properties, and in the distance, a
woman wearing large, dark sunglasses, her hair tucked up under a black
flat cap, walks back and forth between the car and the house, carrying
luggage. The month before, there had been a flurry of renovations done

next door. Hen's mother had watched out the downstairs window, her face creased with worry as a delivery of sleek, simple furniture arrived. But then nothing happened. The house sat, dressed up for a party no one seemed to be coming to. "They're probably going to sell it," Hen said to her mother. "We might get neighbors—it will be fine. Nothing to be afraid of."

The woman carries a suitcase, then a duffel bag, then what looks like a small safe. She comes back outside empty-handed and looks around. Is she from town? Likely not. Even from a distance, Hen can see she's dressed in shredded jeans, combat boots, a leather jacket. No one from town dresses cool like that. A gust of wind blows the cap from her head, revealing mahogany hair in a Cleopatra-style bob—and Hen is struck by powerful déjà vu. She leans farther out the window, watching as the woman bends to retrieve her hat. Her sunglasses slip from her face, then fall to the frost-crunchy grass. The woman retrieves them and walks— no, *stalks*—back toward the house, barefaced, bareheaded. Hen leans so far out she has to clutch the window frame so she won't fall.

Could it be?

Those maroon-painted lips. That scowl, as if even the wind is trying to get her. But now she's out of sight and Hen can't be sure.

Of course it wasn't Jane Pyre, she tells herself. But she flings open her bedroom door and runs down the stairs two at a time, desperate to be certain. She's got her shoes on, is almost out the front door, when her mother comes out of the living room to ask where she's going.

"To the market, of course, like you asked me to," Hen lies. "And . . . I might go bird-watching," she adds, pulling binoculars from their peg beside the front door. What a stupid lie. She's seventeen, not seventy-five. But her mother believes her.

"Be careful!" Anja calls out, following her daughter. But she stops at the threshold, as if halted by an invisible barrier. She waves goodbye to her daughter and closes the door.

Hen runs. Soon she's hidden in the group of trees outside the window of the renovated house next door. She lifts the binoculars to her eyes, brings them into focus. Black countertops, stainless steel appliances, wide-planked wood floors, stark white walls. And then—there she is, the woman Hen saw from her bedroom window, like a mythical sea creature caught in focus in the middle of an expanse of ocean that is really just a kitchen. Hen zooms in on eyes that are like gray flint, then lips so matte her lipstick looks tattooed on. Dark hair hanging in thick curtains beside sharp cheekbones.

It's really her. It's Jane Pyre.

As if sensing the presence of a spy at the window, she turns. Hen drops the binoculars and squeezes her eyes shut, clinging to a childish belief that if you can't see a person, they can't see you either. She watches vapor trails and shadows dance across the backs of her eyelids. They become threads on a spool, a story, a spell. *Something is finally happening,* Hen thinks. *I am finally getting unstuck.* But when she gathers the courage to open her eyes, the kitchen is empty. Jane Pyre is gone.

PART ONE

BERLIN, GERMANY

DECEMBER 18, 1999

Jane Pyre understands only basic German, but anyone would have known that the young man wearing the Marvel Boys shirt, standing behind her in the car rental agency line at Berlin Tegel Airport, has recognized her—despite her cap and sunglasses—and called her a piece of shit. She resists the urge to give him the finger in case someone takes a photo and she ends up in a tabloid. No more of that.

"Fräulein?"

Jane steps up to the counter and hands her ID and credit card over to the clerk, who calls up the booking file for Janet Ribeiro without a flicker of recognition. Soon, she's walking away from the desk with the keys to her rental car.

The German farmhouse she purchased has a name: Asche-Aussicht. The real estate agent told her it meant "Ash Lookout." Jane likes that. *I'm not a phoenix from the ash, I'm a ghost, I'm a gash, and soon I'll be—* The lyrics to a potential new song stream into her mind, unbidden; she presses her hand to her forehead as if trying to stanch blood flow. The last melody she ever wrote is a constant earworm. It would have been a good song, she knows. But there had been no words back then to add to it, just the haunting, nameless tune. *I'll be the stardust on your pillow / the sand that burns your eyes / When the hit of morning comes / waking lonely your surprise . . .* Jane shakes her head and the words disperse.

She dumps her luggage into the trunk of a dark-blue BMW 3 Series, gets in, turns on the ignition, and is immediately assailed by the sound of a gravel-voiced DJ saying her dead husband's name. Jane hears German words like *legendäre musiker* and frowns. She hates it when people talk about him. Which, she supposes, is like saying she hates the wind. There's nothing she can do about the fact that, even five years after he disappeared (*died*, Jane reminds herself; *he is dead, not just missing*), Elijah Hart is still a worldwide obsession.

The DJ is talking to a caller now, and Jane feels a stab of jealousy at the easy tone of their voices as they discuss her husband. Everyone seems to think they know the details, the truth of their love story, their rise to dizzying fame, their equally spectacular crash. But only Jane knows what really happened, and all her secrets have crystallized inside her like mosquitos in amber. What would it be like, she wonders, to call into a radio station and just start talking?

But Jane would never.

A song begins. It's "My Life or Yours," their most popular song. His voice rises, reverberates, touches her core the way it always did—but with this song, she can hardly bear it. She struggles to focus on the road. Jane has grown used to meandering California highways and the traffic that comes alongside the spectacular views. But here, cars shoot past at top speed and she feels vulnerable. Then the song ends and the voice of a caller unsettles her even more. A young woman, her tone uncertain, halting, says a few words before slamming down her receiver so hard Jane winces. She takes one hand off the wheel and spins the dial away from the station.

Elijah always said finding the right music was the key to solving anything, and although she knows this isn't actually true, she still channel surfs hopefully. Eventually she lands on heavy metal. It's not her favorite genre, but she's suddenly certain Elijah would say it was the perfect type of music for driving into unfamiliar territory. It almost makes her happy to feel so sure of this—as if he's there in the passenger seat, playing with the tuning dial himself.

She misses him so much. It never goes away.

The roundabouts are confusing, the German signs unfamiliar, but the chaos of the music does indeed help. Soon, the frenzy of the highway is behind her and Jane is winding her way past farms and fallow fields. Here is her exit: an unpaved road, black mountains in the distance, a glimpse of a lake with flat waters mirroring the sky that, for just a moment, flashes her brain back to images of black sand, divers and helicopters, a much stormier body of water.

Focus. The road.

Tall, slender trees wave from the gravel shoulder. The song on the metal station switches, and she recognizes the band: it's La Dure, the French punk-metal band the Lightning Bottles opened for the first time they were in Europe. Right here, in Germany. It takes her breath away a little, to hear the lead singer's voice—Maxime. So different from Elijah's, not even close to as good, but it's also joyous, full of mischief and adventure. Jane always liked it.

At the crest of a hill, she stops thinking about Maxime's voice, because she has spotted the farmhouse she's only previously seen in photos. But something is wrong. There's another roof—a neighbor. Jane frowns. A *close* neighbor. Hadn't she carefully explained to the estate agent that she wanted to live somewhere very remote, that the possibility of not seeing another person for weeks on end was perfectly fine with her?

The gravel under her tires pops like broken glass as she pulls up in front of her new house. The faded concrete exterior is covered in creeping vines that have browned and crisped in the December air. A wooden terrace on the second story is constructed of wood aged to a pleasant patina. Ash trees are everywhere, as expected. There is the decrepit barn, and beyond that, a field laid out like a threadbare green carpet. Then everything disappears into fog.

Jane turns off the engine, opens the car door—and thinks she hears the drum solo from the Lightning Bottles' song "Watching Us" somewhere in the distance. She can't be sure it's real; her music follows her everywhere. After such a long car ride, her knee aches. It's the scar from an old injury that plagues her every day, still burns incessantly—much like her grief. She wishes she could say she's gotten used to either.

She unloads her luggage from the car into the front vestibule of the farmhouse, then comes back outside to look around. In the distant valley, past the field, lies a village that must be Woolf. A gray concrete observation tower seems to stare at her from the field with curious, broken-window eyes. And then—the back of Jane's neck prickles. It feels like a warning. *Someone is watching you.* She looks toward the neighboring house but doesn't see anyone there. Maybe it's abandoned. She can hope. It looks neglected, though not entirely so. No one is watching, she tells herself. This feeling of being observed is simply one she carries, always, the way, on holidays, survivors of war hear missiles and gunfire instead of fireworks.

A gust of wind blows her hat from her head, her sunglasses fall off, and Jane swears under her breath, then gathers up her things and heads for the house, fast. *You're stomping,* the ghost of Elijah whispers in her ear. She suddenly imagines herself gray-haired and time-faded, wearing a gabardine raincoat and hiking boots, tramping through the somber landscape. She could get a walking stick. Wear strange hats. Scare any children who might happen by. *Jane,* Elijah whispers again. *That's not you. You'll never disappear the way I did.* She tries to ignore the voice. The ghost of Elijah is not always a welcome thing. He never seems to want the same things she does.

Inside the farmhouse, Jane looks around and decides she likes it. Especially the kitchen. The walls are painted white with the barest hint of pewter. Black countertops are set off by stainless steel appliances. Everything is new and fresh and reminds her of nothing, nowhere. Jane and Elijah's homes in LA were beachy and bohemian. Candles dripping down wine bottles, instruments everywhere. His family's home in Seattle had oak cabinets, homey clutter, vinyl albums spilled across the living room floor. A happy place, but only if you squinted, covered one eye, didn't look too closely. This place is a blank canvas, and that's good.

Her telephone rings; it's black plastic with a rotary dial, mounted to a wall near a window. *Ring. Ring. Ring.* And then the person hangs up and calls again. This means it's Petra, her manager, using the code they agreed upon so Jane will pick up.

"Hey."

"All settled in? You doing okay?"

Jane can't help but smile. "I've been here about five minutes. I'm fine, so far."

"Remind me again why you're doing this?"

"Because I'm finished," Jane says. "I'm exhausted."

"You're twenty-seven years old—"

"I'm a widow and a has-been with a trick knee."

"Oh, stop." But Petra's tone is as gentle as ever. "You think the world is going to forget about you, but it won't, no matter how much you want it to." She pauses, perhaps waiting for Jane to agree. "Anyway," Petra continues when Jane stays silent. "I'm calling with a little good news, actually. It's about Kim Beard's latest attempt at an appeal." Kim Beard is Elijah's former best friend, his ex-bandmate. A lot of people hate Jane, but Kim probably hates her most. For the better part of a decade, he has claimed the Lightning Bottles stole some of the lyrics for "My Life or Yours" from him. He has sued, lost, appealed, lost again.

"Frivolous and vexatious, given the history," Petra says. "It won't go ahead. And if he tries to sue you again, it will be considered harassment. It's over."

"I'm sure he'll find a way," Jane says, unable to garner any joy from this news. She knows this particular feud will never end.

"The last Marvel Boys album was a flop. Maybe he's running out of money for lawyers."

"Okay, great," Jane says, trying to inject some happiness into her voice for Petra's sake. "Thanks for letting me know."

"Just keep answering the phone when I call, okay? Otherwise, I'm showing up at your door. It's Christmastime. You shouldn't be alone."

"I'm *fine*. And I'm sure Ramona will have something to say about you coming to Europe, considering you have a newborn at home. How is he?" Jane welcomes the topic switch, anticipates the way Petra's voice will change when she talks about her son.

"He's perfect. Overwhelming. He doesn't seem to require sleep. I could use a few nights incognito at a rural farmhouse, frankly."

"You can come visit in the new year," Jane allows. "As long as you don't try to convince me to come back."

"No promises."

Jane wonders, not for the first time, what she did to deserve Petra, not just as a manager but also as a friend. In her worst moments, when she's certain she deserves all the vitriol sent her way, she reminds herself that Petra, a genuinely good person, cares about her. "Listen, I already miss you too," she says. "But I was running out of ideas for disguises when we met for lunch. Elvira, Mistress of the Dark, drew the wrong sort of attention."

As Petra laughs, Jane feels the back of her neck prickle again, the way it did outside, earlier. She turns toward the kitchen window—and fights back a gasp when she sees someone really is out there: a teenage girl, half-hidden in the trees, spying on Jane through a pair of binoculars. "What the hell," she mutters.

"Everything alright, Jane?"

The girl has dropped the binoculars and squeezed her eyes shut. Jane steps closer to the window to peer out at her. Her hair is pale and fluffy, soft-looking, like dandelion seed or the inside of a milkweed pod. She is so close, Jane can see a light purple dusting of acne scars marring her chin. She has a strange sort of half smile on her face.

"Hello? You okay?"

Jane backs away from the window. She can't tell Petra about this— she'll be on the next plane to Berlin. And the girl looks as harmless as it's possible for anyone hiding outside a window with binoculars to look. Jane just needs to get rid of her—then deal with her dismay. This farmhouse isn't isolated at all. Jane will need to find somewhere else.

"I have a lot of unpacking to do, that's all. I should go. We'll talk another time." Jane hangs up and returns to the window, presses her face to the glass. The girl is gone—but are those shoes peeking out from under a cedar bush, just a few feet away from the window?

Jane pulls her combat boots on and goes outside, moving along the edges of ash trees and unruly cedars until she sees her, barely concealed, trembling.

"Just come out," Jane says. "Come on. I know you're there."

The girl steps forward, brushing twigs from her pale hair. Her curious, attentive eyes are the purple-blue of a forget-me-not. She's not wearing a coat; the skin on her arms is mottled with cold, furred with gooseflesh.

"Is it really you?" She speaks in English, but with a German accent. There's something familiar about the girl's voice.

"No," Jane says unconvincingly.

"It *is* you." The girl's eyes grow wide with excitement. "You're Jane Pyre. I can't believe it! In my town, of all places. *Why?*"

"None of your business."

Now the girl rolls her eyes—and Jane hears her mother's voice. *If the wind changes and you're making that face, Janet, your beautiful features will be stuck that way forever. Do you want to lose your looks?*

"You always say that to people: 'None of your business.'"

"Please, just get off my property or I'll call the police."

"Oh, come on."

Jane turns and starts to walk away.

"Wait! I need to talk to you!"

Jane doesn't stop.

"Really?" the girl shouts. Jane speeds up. "You're not going to bother to listen to what I have to say to you?"

"Nope!" Jane calls over her shoulder.

"You're as bad as everyone says you are!" the girl shouts—and it's as if she actually expected something different from Jane. "You never deserved him! It's your fault he's gone! You didn't take care of him! You were the only one who could, and you didn't!"

This hurts, actually. Jane wasn't prepared for this, not today. She speeds up again, making mental calculations as she does. She can drive back to Berlin, get a hotel room, call the estate agent. Scratch that, she'll find a new one, someone who can procure her the sort of property she wanted in the first place. An actual hideaway. A little privacy, for fuck's sake.

"Why won't you listen to me; what's *wrong* with you? Why are you like this?"

Jane is almost at her front door now.

"If he had never met you, things would be different! The world would be a better place! He would still be here! You should have just left him alone! *You* should be gone, not him! You're a horrible person!"

Jane opens the door, closes it, locks the dead bolt, lets her body slide to the floor, presses her back against the door and her hands against her ears. But it doesn't matter, she can still hear the words. *You should have left him alone!* Jane closes her eyes and tries to imagine choosing a different path. *If he had never met you, things would be different!*

It's no use. She can't. There was no other way. In Jane Pyre's world, all roads led to Elijah Hart.

STOUFFVILLE, ONTARIO

1989

Janet Ribeiro was the most talented musician in her church. She could master any instrument. Drums. Piano. Guitar. Violin. Her voice wasn't bad, either—she had played the starring role in several church musicals. "The Lord has given our Janet a gift," Pastor Morris always said. This made Janet's mother, Raquel, glow with maternal pride. It also made her even more horrified when she caught her daughter violating the electric guitar the church had loaned her to practice for an upcoming "Rock 'n' Roll Hymn Sing" with an unfamiliar and evil-sounding song.

"What is that music?" Janet's mother had shouted. "Those are certainly not the songs you learned at church!"

"It's Romeo Void," Janet said. "New Wave. It's for *fun*. I can't always play hymns if I want to be a musician."

"You're not going to be a musician. You're going to Bible college to become a youth minister. This is how you'll use your gift. Campfire sing-alongs!"

Raquel said this as if it weren't ridiculous, as if they had agreed to it. Janet thought about shouting back that she would rather die than be a youth minister or ever participate in another campfire sing-along—but she had decided long ago that "turn the other cheek" was the only useful takeaway from her many school-enforced read-throughs of the Bible.

"Right. Sorry. Of course I'm not going to be a musician," she offered, hoping for peace. But Raquel would not be placated. Hearing Janet sing music about liking someone better if you slept together instead of glorifying God was the last straw for her—the second-to-last straw having been used up during the Hudson's Bay catalog incident.

At first, Raquel had approved of Janet's modeling for the department store. Physical beauty was another one of her daughter's God-given gifts—and besides, they needed the money. But then Janet forged a parental release form so she could pose in a Wonderbra shoot that paid double what the rest of them did.

"Do you know what people think of us now?" Raquel had cried when one of the church elders' wives discovered the catalog under her son's mattress, the pages of the bra ad suspiciously sticky. "It's bad enough I'm a single mother!"

"How is it *bad*? It's not your fault Dad left, it's mine!"

Her mother had pressed her hands to her ears at this. Raquel told people Janet's father, Alphonse, had moved away and died. She told Janet that although the Bible said all lies were sins, some falsehoods were necessary. Really, Alphonse had just been a nobody—at least that was what Janet always told herself to take away the sting of his prolonged absence. He'd lost his job as a welder because he was sloppy, always late. He pushed Raquel around, called Janet names, seemed to blame them both for the failures of his life until finally, one day, an eight-year-old Janet packed him a bag.

"Get out!" she'd said, channeling the mature, self-righteous anger she had seen on the afternoon soap operas her mother watched. "We don't want you here! All you do is embarrass us! And you're *mean*! Get out, and don't come back!"

Janet was a little surprised when her father actually did what he was told, slamming the door of his rusty old truck and peeling out of the driveway with more vigor than she had ever seen in him. She felt triumphant about the power she wielded, but only until they had to sell the house because the little he brought in when he actually worked was what paid the mortgage. Still, even in a smaller rental house, things were better without her father around.

Until Raquel took up with God. There was soon no limit to the things

they could be ashamed of. Single motherhood, department store cata-
logs, the wrong kind of music.

Now, Raquel strode across the room and wrestled the vacuum cleaner
out of the closet so she could begin vacuuming the already pristine beige
carpet. Watching her mother frantically vacuum made Janet wonder, not
for the first time, if she had been switched at birth. When Raquel was finished, the living room would look like it had crop rows running across it.

"Pastor Morris is coming here," her mother said over the din. "It's
not just that evil song you were singing in your room. Some of the kids
at school have been saying things. About you."

"All they do is say things about me, Mom."

"And whose fault is that?" Raquel shouted as the vacuum roared.
"Who posed in her underwear? Who listens to the devil's music and
draws strange pictures of women with their hair on fire in her notebooks?"

Janet swallowed a retort and went to sit on the couch. Raquel's fury
would pass. She just had to wait it out. No, actually, it wasn't her fault she
needed to get a job modeling so she could help her mother, who barely
earned enough as a receptionist at a local veterinarian's office to make
ends meet. Not her fault that she loved music—all kinds of it—and that
ever since she had started listening to her little clock radio alone in her
room at night, she had hungered for music with loud guitars and pounding bass the way she imagined other teenage girls yearned for boys or
pop stars—or, in the case of the kids at the tiny, church-affiliated school
she attended, Jesus Christ. Not her fault that after the Hudson's Bay catalog had been discovered by that creep John Mahew's mother, the girls at
school who had once been her friends then started whispering behind
her back that she was a slut, even though none of them had any clue
what that word meant, except maybe in the context of Mary Magdalene.
Not her fault that Ruthie, her best friend since kindergarten, didn't talk
to her anymore, had broken off their friendship with a note shoved in
Janet's backpack saying she wasn't so sure about her old friend's "scruples" anymore. Most of the time, Janet told herself she didn't need a

friend who used words like *scruples*—but she missed Ruthie, and that was the truth. Janet had imagined they would be friends forever, the kind of friends who were different but shared a past, a bond akin to sisterhood.

It hurt to think about. Janet shook her head to try to loosen the sad thoughts, cast them away, but the sharp back-and-forth movement made Raquel even angrier.

"You look possessed when you do that! Stop that right now!"

So, Janet folded her hands in her lap and thought about Elijah Hart instead. A smile played across her lips as she imagined the boy she had met online when she set up the BBS chat room using the old Commodore 64 and modem the vet had passed on to Raquel—to give to "that smart daughter of yours"—when the clinic had upgraded computers a few months before.

"Better, Janet. That's so much better. The pastor will be here any minute." Raquel wrestled the vacuum cleaner back into its closet home as Janet drifted off into a world that was half-fantasy, half-real, all hers. Raquel didn't know what a modem did, so she had no way of knowing that the innocuous machine in the corner of their living room was Janet's portal to the fledgling internet—and a whole hidden life full of possibility.

BBS CHAT ROOM "STILL LIFE IN STOUFFVILLE"

Welcome, BBSers. System Operator (SysOP) requires a bit of information about you before she'll allow you in her chat room or game zone. Yes, I'm a girl, and I don't take any sexist shit. No I will not tell you my measurements. Thank you in advance. This is mostly a place to chat about music. Be nice. I get to decide if I feel like banning you.

INTAKE

What is your
Full name: Elijah Hart
Birthday: March 19, 1970
Please choose a user name

... —— ...

User name chosen: Eli72

05/12/89

03:11 am

Eli72: Hello? Anyone there?

SysOP: Hi.

Eli72: Hi. I didn't expect anyone to be awake.

SysOP: Insomnia.

Eli72: Me too.

SysOP: What kind of music do you like?

Eli72: Whoa, that was fast.

SysOP: It's a music chat room.

Eli72: Maybe we should get more acquainted first. I'm Elijah.

SysOP: I go by Jane. Nice to meet you. What kind of music do you like, Elijah?

Eli72: I like all kinds of music.

SysOP: Glam rock? Metal?

Eli72: I mean, metal is not my first choice, but I can find something to like about any kind of music.

SysOP: Hmm. Even New Kids On The Block?

Eli72: NKOTB take their cues from the Beatles. What's not to . . . if not like, at least admire?

SysOP: Ok. Top ten favorite bands, then?

Eli72: That's a big question.

SysOP: This is not a test.

Eli72: But I get the sense if you don't like the bands I choose you'll kick me out of here. Admit that if I say my favorite band is Warrant, I'm out of here. It's totally a test.

SysOP: :)

Eli72: Can we start with you? Favorite bands?

SysOP: Sure. In no particular order . . .

1. The Disintegration
2. L7
3. Concrete Blonde
4. The Smiths
5. The Vaselines
6. Pixies
7. Jane's Addiction
8. Sonic Youth
9. R.E.M.
10. Babes in Toyland

Eli72: You had that ready to go.

SysOP: Of course I did. I've been getting into some New Wave lately, but that sort of feels like a separate list.

Eli72: It's a great list. Most people I know are a lot less original.

SysOP: What music do most people you know like?

Eli72: The Melvins, Mother Love Bone, more Melvins.

SysOP: Do you by any chance live in Seattle?

Eli72: Correct.

SysOp: But you don't like those bands?

Eli72: I guess. They're fun. But I like what you like better. Music that sounds . . . like the person who wrote it HAD to. Does that makes sense?

SysOP: Completely. As if the song was a compulsion, an urge. Ok, so, your list, then?

Eli72: Still not ready. :) Let's talk more about you. Do you play any instruments?

SysOP: I can play drums, guitar, piano, violin. I would love to learn bass. You?

Eli72: Drums, piano, guitar, bass, pretty much anything. Are you in a band?

SysOP: Yes.

Eli72: Cool! Tell me more!

Eli72: Are you still there?

SysOP: I was trying to find a way to make myself sound cooler than I am. But it's no use. I'm in a church ensemble. Christian rock, to be exact.

Eli72: I'm sure there are cool things about Christian rock.

SysOP: I'm sure there are not. And my mom is super strict. I'm running out of places to hide the albums I actually like listening to. Last month she found Jane's Addiction's *Nothing's Shocking* under my mattress and had a meltdown.

Eli72: Ah, bummer—but yeah, I can see how a strict mom might not love that album cover. To be honest, I'm over the whole naked-or-half-dressed-woman-on-album-covers thing. Sexism is getting really old. But "Jane Says" is SUCH a great song, right? Plus, that's your name. Which is cool. Negates the uncoolness of the Christian rock ensemble. ;)

SysOP: Thank you. :) And yes, it's one of the best songs ever. The alternative "Stairway to Heaven," dare I say?

Eli72: Hmm. Interesting. You're right, it's got classic written all over it. I wonder what an alternative classic will look like in twenty years though. The point is sort of for it not to become classic, right? It's not that accessible.

SysOP: What's the point of music if it doesn't live on, though?

Eli72: I don't have a huge problem with the concept of music for music's sake—but maybe that's shortsighted, I don't know. So, does your Christian rock ensemble have a name?

SysOP: Oh god.

Eli72: The band's name is "Oh God"?

SysOP: Ha! No. It's just so embarrassing.

Eli72: I'm the drummer in a band called the Marvel Boys, if it makes you feel any better.

SysOP: Why are you called the Marvel Boys?

Eli72: Not really sure. Something to do with comic books. We've all been friends since we were toddlers. Our lead singer, Kim, he thought of the name. Probably while drunk or stoned.

SysOP: Try being in a band called . . . Samson's Mullet.

SysOP: Hello?

Eli72: I'm sorry.

SysOP: You were laughing.

Eli72: So hard I spit water all over my desk and had to go get a paper towel.

SysOP: Can we talk more about *your* band instead? Please? What's the genre, the style?

Eli72: I'd say we're post-punk metal funk. Maybe. But I like it when things are hard to define.

SysOP: Me, too. Like the Pixies. Rock-alternative-metal-punk? And the Cocteau Twins! Dream-garage-soul? I love it when a band has a sound I haven't heard before.

Eli72: Yeah. Our band is loud. Maybe that's how to define us. We used to play house parties every weekend and people slam danced so hard the floors caved in.

SysOP: Come on. Really??

Eli72: OK, that happened once and it was a pretty crappy house. But still.

SysOP: Caving in a floor is pretty rad.

Eli72: I actually find it kind of weird when everyone is partying and no one is really listening to us. Wow, I sound about 80 years old, don't I? I swear, I'm a 19-year-old guy.

SysOP: If it makes you feel any better, I took the bus to Toronto and went to a Pixies concert last spring—and shushed the people standing next to me. At a club show.

Eli72: I like you, Jane.

SysOP: I WANT to say I like you, but you haven't given me your list of favorite bands yet so the jury is out. :)

Eli72: This is stressful! You have exquisite taste in music and I feel pressured to live up to it.

SysOP: Exquisite. Whoa. Relax. It's just music. No pressure.

Eli72: Music is everything. I thought we'd sort of established that.

SysOP: You're pretty intense, Elijah.

SysOP: Hello? Don't be mad. Intense is not a bad thing.

Eli72: I wasn't mad. I was thinking. And I've determined I need a day to come up with my list for you. Meet me on here tomorrow at the same time. OK?

SysOP: Ok . . . weirdo. :)

Eli72: Till tomorrow at . . . what time zone are you in?

SysOP: Eastern.

Eli72: I'm Pacific. OK, 9 pm my time, midnight yours?

SysOP: See you.

(X) to Exit to Main Menu, (?) for Help

Your selection is?

05/13/89
01:59 am

Eli72: Hi.

Eli72: Hello? Jane?

Eli72: You there?

(X) to Exit to Main Menu, (?) for Help

Your selection is?

09:06 am

SysOP: Hi.

SysOP: Elijah?

(X) to Exit to Main Menu, (?) for Help

Your selection is?

09:16 am

SysOp: Hello? Is there anyone named Elijah in here?

Malkie47: Nope, it's just me.

AlaskaGold1: And me.

Malkie47: Chattin about G N' R, because they fuckin rule. I'll fight anyone who says *Lies* is not the best album ever made, and "Used to Love Her" isn—

<<<<<<<<SysOP has terminated your access>>>>>>>
(X) to Exit to Main Menu, (?) for Help
Your selection is?

05/14/89
02:11 am

Eli72: Hello?

SysOP: Hi. I'm sorry about last night. I got in trouble for something and my mom unplugged the computer.

Eli72: That's okay. I'm just glad you're back. I thought I'd lost you.

SysOP: Nope, I'm here. So, your list?

Eli72: I want you to know this is the REAL list. These are my true favorite bands.

SysOP: As opposed to?

Eli72: The bands I tell my friends I like so they won't try to find my CD collection and set it on fire.

SysOP: Don't joke, my mother actually did that once.

Eli72: Sacrilege!

SysOP: Ok. So . . . go!

Eli72: In order . . .

1. The Disintegration
2. R.E.M.
3. Pixies
4. Sonic Youth
5. The Vaselines
6. Jane's Addiction
7. Helen Sear
8. Cocteau Twins
9. Dinosaur Jr.
10. L7

SysOP: Good list, Elijah.

Eli72: Thank you. Wow, that felt great.

SysOP: Typing out your list?

Eli72: Finally admitting to someone how much I love R.E.M.

SysOP: I love them, too.

Eli72: I know. One reason why I already like you so much. And the Helen Sear didn't throw you off? You never ban folkies?

SysOP: She's great. Plus, she's Canadian and so am I. :)

Eli72: No one knows I listen to her except my mom.

SysOP: Your biggest secret is that you like Helen Sear?

Eli72: I wish.

SysOP: Well anyway, it's official. I like your taste.

Eli72: I like yours too. Obviously. We have some crossover.

SysOP: You can stay. :)

Eli72: I'm glad. Except I'm kind of exhausted. I had band practice for like six hours tonight because we have a club show on the weekend. Kim is convinced we're not tight enough. I can't feel my arms.

SysOP: A Seattle club show. Exciting!

Eli72: I guess. Not as exciting as chatting with you, but I'm wiped and I'm afraid I might type something stupid. Same time tomorrow?

SysOP: Of course.

(X) to Exit to Main Menu, (?) for Help
Your selection is?

05/15/89

01:32 am

SysOP: Hello?

Eli72: Hi. Are you hot? Can you describe yourself? What are your measurements?

SysOP: Elijah? What. The. Hell. **[logged out] [X]**

01:59 am

Eli72: Jane?

Eli72: Hello?

Eli72: That was my idiot friend Kim, NOT ME. He stayed at my place after band practice and started looking through my shit without my permission when I fell asleep. I would never ever say anything like that to you. I'm so sorry.

(X) to Exit to Main Menu, (?) for Help
Your selection is?

ELECTRONIC MESSAGE TO SYSOP

From: Eli72

Jane, this is Elijah. That was my friend, not me. He's an asshole. Please, chat with me again. I miss you.

—Elijah

ELECTRONIC MESSAGE TO ELI72

From: SysOP

I know it wasn't you. But I don't like the idea of other people being able to read what we write to each other. It freaks me out.

ELECTRONIC MESSAGE TO SYSOP

From: Eli72

Why don't we start writing letters, then?

May 17, 1989

Dear Jane,

I've never written letters to anyone before. I hope they're not boring. I don't have much to say about myself—I'm just so curious about you. How did you get into music? And I don't mean church music. :) What was the first album you ever bought? You said you wanted to learn to play bass guitar; are there any other instruments you wish you could learn? Do you write songs? I admire people who can write great songs. I've already told you how much I love Helen Sear, and it's her voice, for sure—but also her songwriting. All her songs are like stories, in the best way. The emotional payoff is always so great.

I like R.E.M.'s lyrics, too. More obscure, but just as good. I always find myself writing down my favorite lyrics of theirs, and thinking I might try to write my own. But I never do. I prefer to just admire good lyrics.

Anyway, tell me more, Jane. About you. Write back soon and tell me anything, everything.

> *Yours truly,*
> *Elijah*

A full week passed before she received his first letter. She checked the mailbox every day, intent on getting to it before her mother did. When it finally arrived, she raced up to her room, breathless, clutching it to her heart. *Dear Jane . . .* She read it over and over and felt like a new person. No more Janet, a name she had always hated. It was amazing to her the difference dropping just one letter made—almost like writing a song and finding that a single note could make the melody come together. He had drawn little pictures across the bottom of the page, pencil-sketched images of a teenage boy she assumed was a composite of him: shaggy-haired, wearing a Disintegration concert tee, playing a guitar in one image, behind a drum set in another. He also drew a record player, with albums by his favorite artists stacked up beside it. She noticed a few of her favorites, too. She cut out that drawing and stuck it in the corner of her mirror. Since she covered the pages of almost all her notebooks with drawings and doodles, her mother assumed she had drawn it herself.

> *May 24, 1989*

Dear Elijah,

R.E.M. is so good. Not just the lyrics, which are great, but Michael Stipe's voice. It's so unique, it should be its own emotion. Like, you should be able to say, "I'm feeling a little stiped today" and everyone would know what you mean.

The Smiths' The Queen Is Dead is how I got into music. Morrissey's voice! So gloomy it's almost . . . joyous. Does that even make sense? I think this is why I'm an insomniac now. I'm used to staying up late because I would wait for my mom to go to bed and then listen to the radio at night. I never wanted to miss what the DJ might play next. Depeche Mode, Cocteau Twins, Pixies, Billy Bragg, Jane's Addiction.

What got me into playing music was the Pixies' Surfer Rosa—that album is EVERYTHING. I HAD to learn those songs so I wouldn't have to wait to hear them on the radio anymore. I taught them to myself and now I feel like I can play almost anything. Even though it turns out Frank Black is a jerk—did you hear he threw a CHAIR at Kim Deal during a concert? Why doesn't she quit already and start her own band?! But I'll always be grateful to the Pixies.

Bass guitar is really the only instrument I can't play that I'm interested in right now. I guess I also wish I could sing better, but that's not really an instrument I can learn. My voice is my voice, and it's just okay. Do you ever sing?

I do write songs, but no one has ever heard them except me, so I'm not sure if they're any good. Remember when we chatted online, and you said something about songs that felt like an urge? I've thought about that a lot. I get a sort of agitated feeling when a song wants to come out. Writing songs can be a little painful sometimes, to be honest. Then again, I'm not sure I'd trade the feeling of finishing one for anything.

How did you get into music? Exactly how long have you been in the Marvel Boys? How did the club show you were telling me about go?

Write back soon.

Jane

PS: You're a good artist. I like your drawings. Is that supposed to be you?

June 5, 1989

Dear Jane,

I'd love to hear you play, hear your songs. I'm sure they're really good. I bet you have a great voice. And I agree with everything you wrote, every single thing. Let's start using "stiped" as an emotional descriptor.

You make me feel stiped, by the way.

To answer your other questions: my mom got me into music. She's a folkie, and that's where the love of Helen Sear came from. We used to listen to a lot of Harry Chapin (speaking of storytelling in songs!), Melanie, Joan Baez. I would sing along to her records, which is embarrassing to think about now because I have a super weird singing voice, which I suppose sounds great when you're singing along to Melanie or Joan Baez, but not awesome when you're singing along to rock or punk. My mom taught me to play piano to go with my singing. I never really stopped with music after that.

I can't imagine singing something I wrote. How do singer-songwriters do that? Don't they feel totally exposed?

The Marvel Boys have been together for four years now. The club show was okay. Kim was a bit fucked-up and fell off the stage. Someone started a food fight with the cold cuts from the greenroom. I think the Seattle scene could best be described as an endless sleepover jam session with Ritalin party favors.

What's it like in your town? What are your friends like, what do you do for fun?

Also . . . I could teach you to play bass.

Except after I wrote that down I looked it up in an atlas, and Stouffville, Ontario, is about 2,400 miles away from the Seattle 'burbs where I live. Kind of far to go for guitar lessons. Sadly.

Have to go. Band practice.

Yours,

Elijah

PS: Yes, the character in the drawings is supposed to be me. I'm glad you like them. I'll send you more.

Jane and Elijah wrote each other multiple letters per week. Jane always managed to get to them before her mom did; she couldn't risk her mother finding Elijah's letters; they were too important to her. She was on her best behavior, worked extra hard at school, never missed a church band practice, pretended to throw away all her contraband CDs—which she really just hid in an old packing box in the basement, removing them only when her mother wasn't home.

Dear Elijah,

Stouffville is so boring. And my mom is so strict that I'm stuck at home a lot. Or at church. I think Seattle sounds awesome.

> *I'm counting the days until I turn eighteen (just under a year) because I'm planning to get out of here. I have no idea where I'll go—somewhere, anywhere, would be better than this town—but I've always dreamed of moving to Europe. Somewhere cool, like Amsterdam or Paris. Maybe somewhere in Germany. Where would you go, if you could go anywhere? What would you do, who would you be? I want to be a musician, if that's not obvious. I'd love to be in a band that's not just a church ensemble, get paid to travel the world and do what I love. I think being famous would be amazing. Everyone would want to know you, but you'd only have to spend time with people you wanted to be around and do things you wanted to do. Everyone would love you, because they loved your music.*

> *Wow, I've never told anyone that before. I don't know what it is about you that makes me want to answer all your questions, and more. I'm usually pretty quiet around people.*

> *Why do you think you have a weird singing voice? Aren't the best singing voices a little unusual? I bet your singing voice is stiped. :) And I'd love to hear you sing someday so I can decide for myself.*

> *I have to go to now, Samson's Mullet calls! But more soon, as always.*

Jane

The spring of 1989 turned to summer, then fall. Jane and Elijah kept writing letters. It was hard to define what Elijah Hart was to her. A friend? A pen pal? More? But whatever he was, Jane knew it was important.

Dear Jane,

Months ago, when we first started writing, you mentioned you'd dreamed of moving to Europe. To be honest, I'd never really thought much about Europe in general—no one I know even has a passport, let alone me—but because of you, I took an interest. You're right, it would be so cool to live somewhere over there. A place with history, personality. And now that the Berlin Wall has fallen, I'll admit I'm getting a little obsessed with Germany. It actually makes the evening news my dad always falls asleep in front of at night interesting. The wall was dismantled by accident, did you know that? Some government official messed up what he was supposed to say in a speech, and the next thing everyone knew, people were rushing through the gates. All those years of control, and then no one could stop freedom from happening when it did. COOL.

Do you think the world is pure chaos or that things happen for a reason? Do you believe in fate? Do you believe in anything?

Yours,
Elijah

PS: Here's a photo of me instead of a drawing. It was taken at a Marvel Boys concert a few weeks ago. Maybe you could send a photo too. I would love to be able to picture you. Then maybe I could draw you too. :)

Elijah,

I never believed in fate until I met you in my chat room. I hope that doesn't sound too weird. Other than that, I don't know what I believe in. Maybe that seems odd given that I go to a religious school and I'm in a church band—but I have a hard time swallowing Bible stories because I always find myself wondering why the women are all either mothers or . . . whores. There's no in-between, and I know that's not real. Which means the rest of it can't be real either.

I do believe in music, though. That it holds some kind of power. I remember reading something once about a rumor that Led Zeppelin sold their souls to the devil for one great song—and half believing that could be true. What do you think?? Is "Stairway to Heaven" sell-your-soul-to-the-devil good? Can songs be magic spells, or curses, or both? If I've ever felt rapture in my life, or like a miracle could be possible, it didn't happen in church, it happened in my room, when I was hiding under my duvet, listening to a new song on my Walkman or the radio.

Now, about Berlin. I wrote a song yesterday because I can't stop thinking about it either. The lyrics (enclosed) were inspired by the minister at my church giving a sermon on the "miracle" that apparently happened in Leipzig, not too far from Berlin. He said the reason the Wall fell is because thousands of people in that city prayed for it. I went to the library and read some newspaper articles about it, and he was so wrong. It wasn't prayer, it was protest! The activists just happened to use a church as their starting point, their shelter. Maybe some of them prayed, who knows. But that's not why they were there.

The song I wrote is about the difference between miracles and force of will. It's called "Miracle Monday." There's music, too. I recorded myself playing it on my guitar, and that's enclosed on a tape. And finally, I'm sending a school photo of me. Try to ignore the stupid uniform. Yellow is not my color.

x, Jane

———————

Dear Jane,

I'm nervous, but here goes. I loved your song so much I wrote a bassline for it. I played your guitar track on my boom box while recording myself playing the bassline with a tape recorder. But . . . something happened. I started to sing. And as I think I've told you, I never really sing anymore. The quality is terrible, but I think it's okay otherwise. And that you should hear it. I hope you like how I arranged it and that I didn't take too many liberties.

Sending this before I lose my nerve.

Yours,
Elijah

PS: I hope it's okay to say this, but you're really beautiful. I drew you. As you can see, we're together in the picture at the bottom of this page. I'm teaching you how to play bass. I hope that really happens one day, Jane.

Dear Elijah,

Forget about my song, your voice is incredible!!! It's like if Robert Plant and Leonard Cohen had a baby with Joni Mitchell and Helen Sear. Which, I know, is not even possible. But how in the world could you think you're a bad singer? Who told you that??

I wrote another song, it's on the enclosed tape. I feel like I have a secret superpower now, which will make every song I write better—because from now on, no matter what, every song I'll ever write is going to be for you to sing.

x, Jane

PS: I liked the drawing of you teaching me to play bass. I hope that really happens, too.

• • •

A sharp rap at the front door of her house brought Jane back to the present moment, in her living room with her angry mother. Raquel ushered Pastor Morris in; his feet left yeti-like prints on the recently vacuumed carpet. He had left his shoes on, and Janet marveled at the way her mother managed not to react to this. He sat down and said *no, thank you* to coffee, even declined her mother's famous lemon-lavender bars. This was serious.

He got right to it. "Janet, the children at school have become concerned about some letters they found in your backpack." Jane's mouth went dry. She glanced at her mother, but Raquel had her arms wrapped tightly around herself and was focused on the minister.

"What was anyone doing looking in my backpack? That's my private stuff—"

"It is the job of the entire community to care for the herd. When sheep go astray—"

"We are people, not sheep," Jane interrupted, but he spoke over her.

"*When sheep go astray*, they must be led back to the correct path. Now, Janet, I'm going to play something for you." He had brought a small tape recorder with him, pressed play. "Perhaps you'll listen to a true authority on the matter of the music you can't seem to quit."

The voice of a concerned-sounding man began to explain that heavy metal music was satanic, that some bands embedded evil messages into their songs. "The devil's evil intent gets into the teenager's brain by osmosis," the man on the tape explained. "Especially when the music is played backward." He proceeded to play a Black Sabbath song in reverse, and it sounded like gibberish. Janet couldn't help it: she laughed.

"Janet!" her mother exclaimed. "Stop laughing right now!" She turned to the pastor. "That boy," she began, and Jane's heart sank. "The one she's been writing to. He's a *very* bad influence."

"I think it's time to pray for her soul," Pastor Morris said to Raquel.

•   •   •

December 1, 1989

Elijah,

My mom found out about our letters. She's never going to let the mail come to this house now before going through it first.

Can we start talking on the phone instead? If you call me at the number below any Wednesday between 7–9, my mom will be at choir practice. I'm so sorry. I know it's long distance. But I really want to stay in touch.

Jane

Elijah called Jane that Wednesday night, and every Wednesday after. Then Raquel figured out that the boy from the letters was calling, and she started unplugging the house phone and taking it with her when she went out—no matter that Jane pointed out she had no way to call 911 if there was ever an emergency. "Go to the neighbor's, then," Raquel said. "Go outside on the front lawn and scream."

Jane took handfuls of change to the pay phone in town instead.

"Hi, it's me."

"Jane."

His voice was her favorite thing: soft but confident, his words punctuated by thoughtful pauses, easy laughter. They talked about the songs Jane was writing, what Elijah was playing with his band, what they were both listening to, music scenes in the Pacific Northwest, which centered around a sound called "grunge" and a musical movement called riot grrrl.

If Elijah's mother, Alice, answered the phone instead of him, she would say, "Hi, Jane" so warmly, Jane felt like they had met. Sometimes his dad would answer, too. His name was Moses and his voice was somber, so unlike Elijah's and Alice's that Jane asked Elijah about him. "What's your relationship like with your dad?"

"Oh." The question caught Elijah off guard, she could tell. "He's quiet. He's a dad. You know."

"I don't, really. Mine left when I was eight. He was pretty much the worst."

Elijah cleared his throat. "I'm sorry."

"It's fine." Jane sighed. "I wish I had your life, though."

"It's not perfect."

"Why not?"

It was as if he hadn't heard her. "Hey, I miss your songs, you know?"

"I miss your singing voice," she agreed. "And I have an idea. I'm going to rent a PO Box, so we can keep sending our songs back and forth, keep working on our music. What do you think?"

"I'd love that," he said. "I really would."

Our music. She'd said it, and now it existed. Their music was something special, and Jane knew it.

Late in the winter of 1990, Elijah told Jane the Marvel Boys were going on a small tour of Washington State and Oregon, and that it might be hard for them to talk on the phone regularly for the next month. "I'll call when I can," he said, sounding regretful, a little worried. "And I'll miss you a lot."

The idea of a month without their weekly phone calls and exchanged tapes filled her with something like panic. A month felt like a lifetime. She was only seventeen. A month was a huge chunk of her life. But all she said was, "That's so exciting! I can't wait to hear all about your tour when you get back."

Jane began x-ing off the days until he came back in her school agenda, but this felt too pathetic, so she stopped. Still, she kept track of the days in her mind as she moved through a life that felt gray without Elijah. She tried to work on her songs, but nothing came together without Elijah to sing them back to her. She tried to read, but nothing held her interest. Late one night, she dug out the old modem from the closet and set up her BBS chat room again—feeling disloyal as she did so, but also determined. Elijah already had a band, and she needed to find one too. But no one interesting showed up, just the same guys who wanted to talk about G N' R.

It had been thirteen days since he'd been away when the telephone rang on a Wednesday night; Jane's mother was at choir practice and had stopped taking the phone with her because lately, her daughter had shown few signs of rebellion—and had been strategically leaving Christian rock tapes lying around the house. As soon as Jane picked up the receiver and heard the music and loud voices in the background, she knew.

"*Jane.* I'm so glad you answered. I know we didn't arrange anything, but I had to hear your voice." He sounded different—tired, his voice a little hoarse.

"Hey," she said. "I'm glad you called. How are you doing?"

A long silence. "Better now. I really miss you, Jane." She twisted the phone cord around her fingers, gazed at her smiling reflection in the kitchen window.

"I really miss you too," she said.

"How is it possible for two weeks to feel like forever?"

She laughed, agreed. "So, where are you calling from?"

"A pay phone at a bar in Spokane. We're here for sound check."

"And the tour is going well?"

"It's going" was all he offered. "How are things with you? What have you been up to?"

She thought about lying about parties and friends; she had done it before. But this time she couldn't. "Elijah, the truth is, my social life . . . isn't exactly great." She explained what she hadn't before, revealed the parts of her life she'd left out in their letters and calls. "I wanted you to think I was someone more interesting than I am. But I'm not. You're a big part of my life. The biggest part, probably. It's kind of embarrassing, but I feel like you need to know the truth. Two weeks without you has been really hard because . . . you mean a lot to me. You might even be the best part of my life." Her heart was racing. What if she scared him away?

"Wait," he said. "You think you're not interesting because you don't have a lot of friends in that town you're from, the one you're planning to leave the first second you can? Jane, I think you're the most interesting person in the world."

"Even though you're . . . kind of my only friend?"

"Friend?" he repeated.

"Friend," she said firmly, not exactly meaning it. "We haven't even met yet, Elijah."

"Not yet," he replied.

Then someone called his name in the background and he said he had to go, but that he would call her the following Wednesday if he could. And if he didn't, he promised he'd be thinking about her.

When Elijah got back home after the tour, he mailed her a tape right away. It read "A Song for Jane" in black block letters. After she picked it up from the PO Box on her way to school, she carried the tape around with her all day, waiting for the moment she could pull her blush-pink duvet over her head, press her headphones against her ears, and listen.

"Hi, Jane." He had never spoken on any of the tapes, just sang. She sat straight up, surprised, the duvet falling away from her body. "This is cheesy, but I think we should tell each other everything, just like you did on the phone when I was in Spokane, so . . . here it is. While we were apart, I had this song in my head the whole time. I can't write the way you do, I'm definitely no poet, but . . ." He trailed off. "I can sing for you. And I know you'll like it."

It was "Unchained Melody" by the Righteous Brothers—frankly, the last song she would have expected him to choose to sing. A recent romantic blockbuster movie starring Patrick Swayze and Demi Moore had made it popular—and the point of liking alternative music was that you didn't listen to anything considered mainstream. Yet Elijah's voice turned it into something else entirely. She felt like he was speaking directly to her, about her, even. She wondered as she listened if there was anything his voice couldn't do. It was alchemical, spellbinding—and it was for *her*.

She listened to the song over and over and came to a realization. She was in love with him.

But when she called him the next day from the pay phone booth in her town, she felt shy. "I loved the song" was all she could manage.

"I loved singing for you," he said. "And . . . Jane? I know those weren't my words, but I meant every one. I've never felt this way about anyone."

Jane felt like she was experiencing a miracle—but still, she tried to be reasonable. "We haven't even met yet," she said.

"Imagine if we did," he said.

"I do, all the time."

She waited, thinking he might finally ask her to come visit.

Instead, he said her name again. "Jane?"

"Yes?"

"I just told you I loved you . . ."

"You did? I didn't realize."

"Well, I mean, I told you I meant every word of a song I sang to you about a guy who is basically like, *you are my everything*, and I guess I'm kind of wondering how you feel about that . . . ?"

"I feel the same," she said quickly, then started to laugh. "Of *course* I do. I was dying without you."

They were going to figure it out; she knew it. For now, this was enough. They'd meet someday, and it would be perfect. The start of the dazzling, music-filled life she had always dreamed of. Elijah was the one.

STOUFFVILLE, ONTARIO

1990

The spring of 1990 arrived, marking one year since Jane and Elijah had found each other in the ether of the internet. Jane had been temping at the vet's office where her mother worked, saving money she told her mother was for her college tuition but was really for the escape she was planning the second she finished high school.

How can I be so in love with a person I've never even met? she wrote more than once in her diary during that year. How can I love someone who only exists in my heart, in my head?

"A guy from Sub Pop saw the Marvel Boys play and asked for a demo," Elijah told her one afternoon on the phone. Sub Pop was a popular, if perpetually broke, independent record label in Seattle. He explained how the demo would have to be made at the Marvel Boys' expense, which was going to clean out all the band members' bank accounts—but once it existed, the label would help with distribution and publicity. "I guess it's exciting," he said. "A step forward for the band."

"You *guess*? A demo is huge," she said, but her heart was sinking. She had been hoping the Marvel Boys weren't a permanent thing for Elijah, that the endless sleepover jam party he described as the Seattle music scene, one he didn't seem especially enthused about, would just fizzle out. Every time he sent a song she had written back to her, his voice made it so good it felt unreal. Every song was better than the last. They were great together. They had a future. Except maybe she was the only one of them who believed that. Maybe she was wasting her time.

"Kim thinks we need to start planning another tour," he said.

She could no longer hold it in. "So again, we won't talk for . . . what, another month?" She was angry, she realized. Hurt.

"Jane, I never said I was—"

"No!" She had never been mad at him before, but she was now, and it had come on fast, like a clap of thunder. "When are we *ever* going to meet?" She hated how needy she sounded, but she did have a need. For *him*.

"I don't know," he said, and he sounded miserable. Her stomach swirled and plummeted. What had she been doing, all this time? Why had she been bothering? This was not first love. It wasn't even real.

"I have to go," she said.

"Wait, Jane. *No.* I just . . . Look, this place doesn't feel like the right one for you. For *us. Shit.* This isn't coming out right at all."

She waited, silent, for him to try to put it another way. "I don't know how you're going to feel about me when you meet me in person," he tried. "I'm scared, I guess."

"Don't you think I'm scared too?"

"You shouldn't be. You're perfect, Jane."

"I'm not. No one is."

"I'm a mess."

"You are not! I know you. I *love* you. Saying you're a mess is an insult to my intelligence."

"I need a little bit more time, okay? I don't want to screw this up with you and me."

"What is that supposed to even mean, more time? You tell me you love me, but you can't possibly!"

"I do, I swear. Jane, you have no idea—"

"And, what, I'm supposed to stay here and just . . . wait for you to sow your wild oats or whatever it is you need to do?"

"No. It's not like that at all. Wild oats—Jane, no."

Jane rubbed her eyes. *Sow your wild oats*, where had she even heard that, one of her mother's soap operas? "Then what is it like, Elijah?" Her voice was quiet now, her anger still there, but contained.

"What if you coming now ruins it?" he said, his voice equally low. "Ruins us. You don't know what you mean to me, Jane. But what if I'm not good enough for you?"

"Yes, I do know what I mean to you. Because you mean that to me. And there is no way you are not good enough. No way in hell."

She waited for him to take it all back. In the silence that followed, she felt every inch of the 2,400 miles between them. She also felt all the differences. He was scared, and she wasn't. He wasn't mature enough for a serious relationship, and she was. It had been this way the entire time, she just hadn't wanted to believe it.

She hung up the telephone and felt helpless tears slip down her cheeks as she walked home. She told her mother she was sick and went straight to bed.

She didn't call him for weeks, during which time she actually did feel like she was dying. Her mother took her temperature, fed her chicken broth, let her stay home from school, took her to the doctor twice. But the truth was that she wasn't sick, she was heartbroken.

In her bed, Jane listened to his voice, soft and romantic, singing their love song to her. *It's just a corny love ballad*, she told herself. He hadn't even written it himself.

Since she wasn't really dying, she couldn't stay in bed forever, so she finally made herself get up, eat, and become one of the living again. She'd get over Elijah. She'd avoid all memories of him and it wouldn't be that hard, because actually, he didn't really exist in her day-to-day life. She would not check the PO Box. She would forget him.

Except she couldn't. Every day she would pass the pay phone booth and double back, stand in front of it and force herself to back away. *He doesn't want you*, she told herself. *He doesn't love you.* But the day she finally went to the post office to close her account for the PO Box, there was a letter waiting.

Dear Jane,

I'm sorry. I really do love you and I want you in my life. For real. Right now. Anytime.

   You know my address. I'm ready when you are.

                                        Always,
                                        Elijah

That night, she woke up agitated, anxious. She wrote him a letter back, asking him if he really meant it, when she should come, what their plan was, exactly. But then she crumpled it up and stared down at it. She made a decision. Her high school graduation was coming up, but what was the point? She had fulfilled all the academic requirements, but her life was not here in Stouffville, and it certainly wasn't at the college her mother had forced her to apply to.

   The next morning, after Raquel left for work, Jane took her mother's neglected suitcase with the broken wheel from a closet and packed it full of all the clothes she liked. She put her mixtapes in a plastic grocery bag to listen to as she drove. Raquel had carpooled into work that day with a friend, so her rusted gray Chevette was in the driveway and her keys were on the kitchen counter. Jane loaded her stuff into the trunk, then found a notepad and pen and hastily scrawled:

Dear Mom, I'm sorry I took the car. I left some money on the counter, and I'll send more when I get a job so you can get a new one. Things with us have never been easy, but I do love you. And I know you love me. I just can't live here. I want to be a musician so badly, and I know you don't want me to, so I have to go. I hope you understand someday . . .

As she reversed the Chevette out of the driveway, Jane wondered if she'd forever miss the way her mother had placed her hand gently on her forehead to check for fever when her daughter was heartsick over Elijah. Strangely, those few weeks had been some of the best they'd ever had. *My mother loves me*, Jane told herself as she accelerated onto the highway. It wasn't enough to keep her at home, but it was an important thing to remember. She didn't come from somewhere that was all bad; it just hadn't been the right place for her. She could return someday, and she'd be a different person. Maybe even a famous person, someone everyone admired. Maybe everyone here would realize they'd misunderstood her all along.

Two hours later, she crossed the border at Niagara Falls, presenting a forged letter from Raquel giving her permission to go outlet shopping in Buffalo. The border guard barely glanced at her. She kept driving, felt her old self slipping away the farther she got. The little girl her mother had loved; the teenager she hadn't understood. The person her father had left behind just because she told him to go. The school weirdo, the "slut" who was actually a virgin. She was none of those people now: she was officially Jane. Jane Pyre, she decided, the new last name—a true stage name—coming to her like a revelation. She was heading for her destiny.

With as few stops as possible, Jane made it through Michigan, Wisconsin, Minnesota, and almost to Montana. She dreamed of a new, adult life; a sunny apartment somewhere; candles in wine bottles and instruments on the floor; and Elijah, all hers. She missed his voice more than ever now and thought many times about stopping, finding a pay phone, telling him she was coming. But she didn't. She just kept going.

Late at night, she half slept in the car, ready to wake and drive off at the first sign of danger. She got nervous every time she saw a police cruiser, in case her mother had reported her missing, but no one tried to stop her. She turned eighteen during the trip and breathed a sigh of relief because now she was her own person. She marked the occasion with a large Slurpee from 7-Eleven. She wanted to tell Elijah this, to tell him everything. And she would. Soon.

She was halfway through Montana when the car shuddered, steam erupted from the hood, the steering wheel shook, and the vehicle died. Jane got out and kicked the wheel. Her toe throbbed as she gazed up at the vast sky, then down the long road ahead. She pulled her guitar case from the trunk and filled it with as much of her stuff as she could, crammed in around the edges. She started walking. As she did, she imagined herself from a bird's eye: torn jeans, scuffed-up boots, dark hair, guitar case, the sun shining in her eyes. Mountains and horses in the background. Did she look like someone heading straight and sure toward her dreams as she trudged down that road? Or like some scared kid?

Jane hitchhiked. She took buses. She slept in her seat. Five days later, she arrived in Seattle and went straight to the address on all the letters he had written to her. She tapped at the side door of Elijah's house, then realized knocking was pointless considering the cacophony of music coming from the basement. He had been right in his assessment of the Marvel Boys. Post-punk-metal-funk.

A male voice that must have been Kim's shouted out incomprehensible lyrics delivered in staccato, machine-gun bursts. It wasn't helping her frenzied mental state. So she closed her eyes and focused, listened only to the drum's beat. *Elijah*, she told herself. *I'm here to see Elijah*. It helped, but she still wasn't sure what she was supposed to do next. Knock harder? Simply wait? Go away and regroup? She had focused so hard on her journey that she had no idea what to do now that she had arrived.

Her heart was beating in her ears, so loud that she didn't realize the music had stopped.

She looked up to see a guy staring at her from the open front door. "Hey. Can I help you?"

Elijah? Could it be? She met his appraising gaze. His hair was to his shoulders, the way Elijah's had been in photos, and he wore a Misfits tee. Elijah had never mentioned liking that band. He smelled like sweat and barnyard. Disappointment welled up. All the pictures she had of Elijah were taken at concerts, him behind a drum set, slightly blurred. She'd elevated him to mythic status in her mind. He gazed back at her, skipped over her eyes and stared at her chest. She had come all this way to tell him—to tell him what? *Hi, I love you, I can't live without you, let's start a band together, let's run away.*

"Hey . . ."

Another guy was standing behind the first one now. His eyes were green. Or blue. Both.

Jane's body came alive.

"Elijah?" she said. The stranger in the Misfits tee melted away.

"*Jane.* I thought you . . ." He rubbed a hand across his eyes, blinked, looked at her again. "I thought maybe you were never going to check the PO Box again. That you'd never get my letter. I filled out a passport application; I was going to show up in Stouffville."

"You *were*?"

"Well, yeah." He laughed. "Except I'm terrified of your mother. I called the other night, and she answered. She said, 'Jane, where are you, when are you coming home?' Then she slammed the phone down so hard I think my eardrum is permanently damaged."

"I'm sorry. I probably should have called first."

He smiled, and she noticed he had this one snaggletooth. It was so cute. He was so perfect. And he was real, standing right in front of her, close enough to touch. But then the guy in the Misfits tee inserted himself back into reality and she remembered they weren't alone.

"I saw your boots, thought you were the pizza delivery guy," he said. "So, Elijah, care to make introductions?"

"This is Kim." Now two other guys were crowded into the doorframe, staring at her.

"What's taking you so long? Who's the girl?"

"And this is Ari. And John. The band."

"Cool, great," Jane said, feeling suddenly like a fifth wheel. She hadn't imagined meeting him with three other guys standing around watching, and she felt shy and out of place.

"Guys, this is Jane," Elijah finally said. "My . . . pen pal." He winced. The guys mumbled their hellos, and Jane knew he wished he hadn't called her that. She wished he hadn't, too.

"You mean that hot Canadian chick who sent you the photos?" Kim said. "The one you're obsessed with? She looks different."

Jane looked away, embarrassed now. She knew she didn't exactly resemble the innocent girl in the school picture, or the other photo she had sent Elijah, an artfully contrived image of herself playing guitar, her long dark hair parted in the middle and flowing down her shoulders, her eye makeup dark and smudged, like she was an alternative rock version of Helen Sear. She had developed two rolls of film to get the right shot, and she felt like Kim could somehow tell this. She hated that he had seen something meant only for Elijah.

"Guys, uh . . . could we just have a minute?" Elijah said. Kim opened his mouth to protest, but Elijah said, "Don't worry, I'll bring the pizza straight down when it arrives. C'mon, get out of here." Kim cast one last suspicious glance at Jane, but then she and Elijah were alone.

Jane felt too hot in her leather jacket and T-shirt. Sweat trickled down her back. She probably looked terrible.

But he had that smile on his face again. She was mesmerized by it, forgot everything else. He stepped closer. "You're really here."

She took her own step. He smelled like Irish Spring soap, not barnyard. "Are you still scared, Elijah?"

He reached out and touched her for the first time, his right hand on her arm, his left hand on her waist, as if they were about to dance a routine that had been choreographed by the fates. "No," he said. "I'm not. I promise."

A song began forming itself in her head as she stood there staring up at him, her body tingling from the touch of his fingers on her arm, her waist. *I wanted to ask, but what if you said no? Hard to remember what I was afraid of when we dance so slow.*

"I'm so happy you're here, Jane." He added her name to the end of the sentence like a cherry on top of a sundae. She noticed how it sounded when he said it in person. *Jane.* Different. Real. A baptism. Janet no longer existed. She had left her old self somewhere in Buffalo.

They took each other in, memorized each other's faces the way they had already memorized everything else they knew about each other. They grinned like the happy, lovestruck kids they were, and when Elijah pulled Jane even closer, she fit against him perfectly. To Jane, the moment felt like jumping off the edge of a cliff into a lake of cold water and knowing at once that you would take that same leap over and over, forever, now that you knew how safe it was.

He tucked a strand of her hair behind her ear and stared into her eyes. It felt like he was asking a question that didn't have words.

"You're *here.*" His lips were so close to hers.

"Finally," she whispered back—as if she had been waiting to meet him for thousands of years, and not just one and a half. When their lips met, Jane expected a clap of thunder, a bolt of lightning—but it was just a perfect kiss. It marked the beginning of the rest of her life. Everything she had ever wanted, all in one moment.

WOOLF, GERMANY

DECEMBER 19, 1999

"You should go away," Jane says, and the words are a curse.

Elijah waves a weak hand in the direction of the ocean outside. "Yes. Let's go somewhere else. Thailand. We wanted to go there, once. Didn't we? We wanted to go everywhere, just you and me. Cambodia. Let's find a place where you can love me again."

I do love you, she tries to say. *I will always love you. Don't go.* Instead, she says, "No, not us. Just you. You need to disappear."

He takes a swig of whatever he's drinking. It's dark red, like blood, smells sickeningly sweet. "You and me, Jane." His voice is pleading.

I love you, I'll do anything, please stay, I don't really want you to go. But the words that come out of her lips are, "The only way out is for you to just leave."

His face turns to bone, then dust. Jane screams herself awake.

In the silence that follows, she thinks she hears footsteps on her front porch.

She gets out of bed and goes to the window, but there's nothing out there except the mist rising up from the valley, the Soviet-era watchtower coming into view through the morning fog. Jane pulls a sweater over the black T-shirt she slept in, one of Elijah's that doesn't smell like him anymore, no matter how much she wishes it did, and goes downstairs barefoot. When she opens the front door, she half expects the assault of a camera's flash, paparazzi lying in wait. But there is only a little wooden box sitting in the center of her front porch mat.

Jane picks up the box and examines it. It's hand-carved, softened by some kind of wood conditioner, looks innocent enough. When she shakes it, something flutters inside. She opens the box and finds a crumpled sheet of lined paper covered in pencil strokes.

When she unfurls the paper and sees what's on it, shock vibrates through her body like the gong of a bell.

The Secret Adventures of Adam & the Rib.

How can this be?

"Hello?" she calls into the fog. "Who's there? Who left this?"

She looks down at it again and knows which one it is with just a glance. The only drawing she doesn't have—and there's good reason for that. She threw it away. She didn't want it.

Her eyes skitter back down to the page. The first square of the drawing features a computer with a list of bands in block letters. It's the list of favorites she sent Elijah during their first conversation in the chat room she created when she was seventeen. How could this ever have come into anyone's possession?

She reads the story she already knows. The letters, the phone calls—then Jane in a car, driving to Seattle. His arms around her, his lips on hers. Their beginning. Even after everything, she still feels the force that drew her toward him—the way when she arrived at his door, ended up in his arms, she felt like she had dropped an anchor for the first time in her life. She was home.

"Who's out there?" she shouts. "Who left this?"

A calico cat hops down from a window of the crumbling barn at the edge of Jane's property, startling her. As she watches, he lands on an overhang, scoots down the slanted wall, and disappears into the trees.

"Hello?" she shouts. She walks down the porch steps and spins in a circle, the grass beneath her feet stiff with frost, the soles of her feet stinging from the cold.

"Elijah?" She hasn't said his name in so long that tears spring to her eyes when she does. "Are you there?"

But it's the girl from the day before, the one who yelled at her, who creeps out of the cedars.

Not Elijah.

Elijah is dead.

And Jane wants to die too. Even a moment of hoping, then having it yanked away, is enough to undo her.

"Where did you get this?" Jane says in a shaking voice, crumpling the paper into her fist.

The girl steps closer. Today she has an oversized coat on. "I was at the concert in Berlin. Your last one. I saw you and Elijah fighting. I saw him give you that piece of paper, and I saw you toss it away." There is judgment in her expression, and Jane wants to grab her by the shoulders and shake her, tell her she knows nothing, *nothing*. But that would be admitting there's anything else to know. "I took it out of the garbage. I've had it ever since."

"Oh."

"And now you're *here*, and that has to mean someth—"

Jane interrupts her. "Did you show this to anyone?"

"I have no one to show." A flicker of loneliness in the girl's eyes; Jane recognizes it but pushes away the empathy she suddenly feels.

"Could you write down your phone number and leave it on my front porch, please? My team will be in touch."

"In touch about *what*? You want me to just go away?"

"Do you know what an NDA is? There's money involved—"

"I don't want money. I want to talk to you. Just five minutes. It will cost you nothing. Please, just let me explain."

Jane's bare feet are stinging in earnest now. She wants this to be over but knows it won't be that easy. "Fine. Come inside. We'll talk in the house. Five minutes."

In the kitchen, the girl looks around hungrily and Jane feels grateful that the house is so impersonal.

"What I tell you," the girl begins. "You have to believe me."

"I don't *have* to do anything," Jane replies.

"Okay. So, I'm just going to . . ." She trails off, and Jane feels a strange sense of familiarity in the halting way she speaks—but whatever the memory is, it slips from her grasp.

Abruptly, the girl reaches into her jacket pocket and Jane wonders where the knife drawer is. But what she pulls out is just a photograph, not a weapon. She keeps it turned away from Jane at first. "When I found the clue, I knew what it was because of that." She nods toward Jane's clenched fist, where she still holds the Adam & the Rib drawing.

"What are you talking about?"

The girl draws a shaky breath. "There's a German word . . . *Shicksal*. It means . . . like, fate? Destiny. Also, it means doom, and adventure, and fortune, and . . . Just, why else would you have moved in next door if this wasn't all meant to be? Don't you believe in destiny? You of all people?"

Me, of all people. Jane shakes her head. "No. I can't explain why you took this drawing that day and then I ended up next door to you—but sometimes things are just a coincidence. When you're older, you'll get that. Okay? Life is weird, there is no plan. You picked this out of a garbage can, and actually, it belongs to me. I'll pay you for it, you will tell no one, and that will be the end."

"I think he's still alive! And using street art to send messages to you! I found one, in Berlin! I think it's for you!"

"Who are you working for? Is it Kim Beard?"

"Where would I have met Kim Beard?"

So many people hate her, so many people want to hurt her. And this is the precise way to do so.

"*Enough*," Jane says. "I won't listen to another conspiracy theory about Elijah not really being dead. Just *get out*."

Elijah used to love their fans, and he once asked Jane why she could never bring herself to feel anything for them. Why she always wanted to keep them so firmly at a distance. *They just like our music,* he said. *They're*

*like us, when we were teenagers. You remember how it was. How we felt about
the artists we revered.*

But to Jane, this was the problem. Yes, she had once been a teenage
fan who lived and breathed the music she listened to—but she had never
perceived the artists she worshipped as real people. Then she became one
of those half humans, and it scared her. She knew she might be offered
adoration by the masses, but never compassion. There was a difference.
Adulation, but never empathy. They'd eat you alive if they could, then
say you asked for it by stepping into the spotlight in the first place. This
girl would hurt her, and Jane knew it.

"Look. Please." The girl turns the photograph she holds toward Jane.
It's just an alley wall covered in paintings. "Do you see it? Take it. Look
closely."

The image features a kaleidoscope of artwork. It blurs together at
first, and then Jane begins to make out individual images: a wolf walking out of the wall. A rainbow moon. A Day of the Dead mask. Foreign
words, crude tags, and then—

The Secret Adventures of Adam & the Rib.

"*What did you do?*" Jane's voice rises with anger. "You painted this on
a wall somewhere. Admit it. You took this"—she waves her fist, the drawing still clutched there—"and you copied it onto a wall."

"It wasn't me! I can't even draw!"

Jane holds the image closer, takes every detail in. There are splashes
of color across the bottom of the painting, words in the bubble above
Adam's head that are too small to decipher.

"You need to come to Berlin and see it for yourself. Then I think
you'll understand."

Jane looks up. "That's where this is, in Berlin? Give me the exact address of where it is."

"Can I go with you? Can I show you myself?"

"I'm calling the police."

Jane crosses the room and picks up the kitchen phone, but the unfamiliar dial tone only serves as a reminder that she doesn't know which number to call to reach the police here in Woolf. Meanwhile, Elijah's ghost voice is now telling her to calm down. *She looks frightened, Jane. Be gentler with her. And what if she's right? What if I'm out there somewhere, waiting for you to find me? What if she's the only person who can show you where my message is?*

If she's right, I wouldn't be talking to a ghost.

"Are you okay?" the girl asks.

"I'm fine," Jane says. "I really just want you to leave." But the girl doesn't move. So Jane shouts, *"Get out! Now!"*

It works. The girl startles and runs like a terrified animal, and Jane feels like the monster everyone thinks she is. But she's also relieved. That was far too intense. She locks the door. But in the silence she hears a whisper she knows is not real: *Jane. Look closer.*

There's an office in the house, and she searches through the desk drawers. It has been stocked with pens, paper, various letter writing materials—as if Jane is ever going to write anyone letters. She finds a set with a letter opener and a magnifying glass, holds the glass to the image. Words come into focus.

2,400 miles was a long way to go for guitar lessons.

Her eyes blur with tears. No one else could possibly know those words. *No one.*

Unless someone stole them.

She runs to her bedroom, pulls the little safe from under the bed, and opens it. But the letters he wrote her and the drawings he made for her are all there, every single one.

Also . . . I could teach you to play bass. Except after I wrote that down I looked it up in an atlas, and Stouffville, Ontario, is about 2,400 miles away from the Seattle 'burb where I live. Kind of far to go for guitar lessons. Sadly.

The words are right there on the page. She sinks down onto the unmade bed and reads them again.

Of course she has wished for Elijah to still be alive. Every day. But he isn't. He can't be. She saw the smashed rowboat for herself, held his empty, waterlogged jacket in her hands, stood in front of the freezing, raging sea in Iceland and listened as officials told her he was gone, that there was no other possible outcome.

And, of course, she had seen what shape he was in before he disappeared into the water. He couldn't have managed to swim the length of a backyard swimming pool, let alone battle his way back to shore through the North Atlantic on a cold night.

And yet—

This cannot be real, she tells herself. All she has ever wanted is proof, but the close reality of it introduces an element she has avoided. Believing in this is dangerous. If she truly allows herself to think he's out there, and then finds out he's not, that it's nothing but yet another cruel twist of a knife from one of her many enemies, she knows she will be finished, finally and truly.

But what has her life been without him? Who is she, now that the life they had together is gone? She has tried and failed too many times to rise above the tragedy that has defined her life. Maybe it's time to stop fighting so hard.

More voices in her head now, louder than whispers, traveling to her over the anguish of time.

You will never lose me. There is nothing in the world that could ever tear us apart.

Do you promise, Jane?

I swear. No matter what happens, I'll always find you, I'll always save you.

SEATTLE, WASHINGTON

JULY 1990

During her first month in Seattle, Jane stayed at the YWCA, resolutely bussing from suburbia into the city most nights, while Elijah either came along or tried to convince her to move into his family's home.

"Just live *here*," he pleaded one rainy summer afternoon. "Just never leave." Then he stood, restarted the album they were currently obsessed with—the Breeders' *Pod*; Jane had finally gotten her wish, and Kim Deal of the Pixies had started a side project—and returned to the bed and kissed her, kissed her, kissed her.

"I can't do that," Jane said between kisses. "I can't just *stay*."

"But why not?"

"Won't your friends think it's weird?"

Every day the Marvel Boys and their friends trickled into Elijah's basement around midafternoon to begin a dusk-till-late party, filled with pot smoke, beer, inside jokes, and sometimes a bonfire and some acid tabs at the back of the Harts' yard where the lawn edged up against the stately hardwoods. It was supposed to be band practice, but that was only part of it. They were a close-knit group, and Jane watched them studiously for signs of how to get in. But she was an outsider to everyone but Elijah. And their bond was clearly a threat to his friends.

"Who cares what anyone thinks, Jane? *I* want you here. All the time. I hate it when you're not. You know how sometimes you come up here to listen to music during practice or go back to your room in Seattle? Just *stay*. I need you." She tucked herself into his embrace, breathed in his scent of soap, pine needles, and bonfire smoke.

"Your mom won't want her son's girlfriend living in the house," Jane said.

"My mom loves you as much as I do."

Alice was as warm and welcoming as she had sounded when Jane used to call from the pay phone. She had long blond hair with one white streak and grew her own marijuana in the backyard, alongside a host of other plants. She smelled of amber and patchouli, and she had Elijah's eyes, that rare green with the barest hint of blue. She smiled easily and said things like, "I just love seeing my boy so happy these days." She didn't mind that her house was always full of teenagers, that they all drank and smoked pot and never even tried to hide it, that most were high-school dropouts, including her own son. She never seemed to get worked up about anything. "I have two rules," she would say. "No hard drugs on my property. And no fights."

"What about your dad?" Jane said.

Moses was an accountant in downtown Seattle. He seemed shy, mostly quiet at the family dinners they ate as a foursome on Sundays, at a harvest table pressed up against a picture window in the Harts' split-level house. It was all so different from Jane's home with Raquel. Here, there was no order, barely any rules—except that Alice always requested a weekly Sunday dinner so they could all, as she put it, "reconnect." Those nights, Alice and Elijah talked over each other, about the music that constantly spilled from Alice's record player, or some story or other. Jane would catch Moses's eye across the table and they, the two quiet ones, would share a smile that seemed to say, *Look at those two. How did we ever get so lucky?* Or at least that was what Jane assumed was behind his timid smile. Once, when she was washing the dishes, she emptied the coffee mug Moses always drank out of and was surprised to find whiskey inside, not coffee. But just because she had been raised in a home where alchohol was verboten didn't mean Elijah's dad couldn't enjoy the odd drink, she told herself.

"My dad probably wouldn't even notice you had moved in," Elijah said.

Jane frowned at this. "What do you mean?"

Elijah just shrugged, then pulled her even closer.

"Nothing. Anyway, someday it won't matter about what my parents or anyone thinks, right? We'll get our own place. We're not going to live here forever." Jane was embarrassed by how much she longed for this. It felt unfair, when his life was so full of people who loved him, that she spent most of her time wishing they were alone. "But for now . . ." More kisses, until she felt that familiar, pressing heat in the base of her pelvis. They hadn't had sex yet. Jane had never come right out and said she was a virgin, but Elijah seemed to know. He was always gentle, patient, never wanted more from her than what she could give. "Let's dream. Where do you want to live one day? California? Bora Bora? Thailand? Back in Canada? I don't care. I'll go anywhere with you."

"An apartment somewhere," Jane murmured, eyes closed, knowing it was getting to be midafternoon and his friends and bandmates would be arriving soon, that their alone time would be over. "With sun streaming in through the windows. A big bed with white sheets . . ."

"You're so good with words." He kissed her neck. "That's why your songs are so great. I can see everything you say." He closed his eyes and let out a happy sigh. "Instruments everywhere, candles in wine bottles . . ." He paused. "But it's hardly ever sunny in Seattle, so it can't be here." He never came right out and said he was unhappy in Seattle, but he talked about leaving a lot. "A ranch, in Montana. Could you picture me as a cowboy?"

Jane stiffened. "What about our music?"

"I already said we'd have instruments all over the place. Obviously we'll spend a lot of time jamming."

"It's not just *jamming*." She pulled away and sat up while he blinked, clearly mystified by the sudden change in her mood. "Are you going to be in the Marvel Boys forever?"

"Of course not."

"Are we ever going to form a band? Like, officially?"

"If that's what you want," he said, while she wondered how it could feel like they shared the same mind, the same thoughts—and other times as if they didn't understand each other at all. She had driven across a country to be with him because she was in love with him, but it was more than that. It was about music, too. How did he not get that?

He touched her cheek, then her forehead. "Jane. What's going on inside there?"

"What do you want, Elijah? From us, from our life?"

"I want you. That's all. And everything else, I promise we'll figure it out. And I want you to stay."

"Okay," she said.

"Elijah!" Alice called out from the other side of his bedroom door. "Your friends are here."

John's and Ari's girlfriends, Tiff and Jessica, usually came to watch the Marvel Boys' practices—and a girl named Shawn was usually around too. She wasn't dating any of them. "She's one of the guys," Elijah insisted. "We've all known her forever." But she had a face like Liz Phair and a body like Debbie Harry. All you had to do was look at her, or look at the way the guys looked at her, to see that there was a bit more to it than that.

When Shawn arrived, she usually sprawled out on the couch, lit a joint, and passed it around, while Jane retreated deep into the beanbag chair she had claimed as her own, even though it always felt like it was trying to devour her, Venus flytrap–style.

Today, the joint made the rounds, and Shawn waved it, half-hearted, in Jane's direction. But Jane shook her head. She hadn't tried weed yet, was nervous about any drugs. She didn't let on that she was inexperienced, though, just pretended to be ambivalent.

Later, during a pause in the music while the band members debated adding one of their newer songs to the set list for that weekend's show at Re-bar in downtown Seattle, Shawn stood and crossed the room to stand beside Kim. She whispered in his ear, and he laughed. "That would be *hilarious*. A hot girl with a tambourine." When he talked like this—which was often—Jane wanted to punch him. "Let's do it. Right, guys? *Yeah.*" He was talking to Shawn but staring at Jane, a challenge of some kind in his eyes. He didn't like her, that much was clear. Jane had hoped the longer she was around, the more the antagonism would fade. If anything, though, it seemed to get worse. The week before, he had noticed Jane reading a Betty Friedan book she had plucked from Alice's bountiful shelf upstairs, and said, "Uh-oh, do we have a feminazi on our hands here?" He had snorted derisively, while Jane cringed—and realized the dislike wasn't just on his end. The feeling was mutual.

Now, Kim fished a tambourine from a pile of discarded percussion instruments in a corner of the basement, banged it against his hip, and laughed—but Shawn had lost interest and wandered over to Elijah's drum kit. She casually grabbed one of his drumsticks, tapped on his snare. "Hey," Elijah said, swatting at Shawn with his other drumstick. She bumped him over with her hip and sat beside him, said something in his ear that made Elijah look suddenly serious. "You shouldn't do that," Jane thought she heard him say.

Shawn just shrugged. "Whatever. I'm fine."

At house parties, Jane noticed Shawn always got spectacularly wasted—either loudly, unpredictably so, or her eyes would glaze over and she'd be in another world. The weekend before, Jane found Elijah holding back her hair as she threw up on someone's front lawn. She watched as he rubbed Shawn's shaking shoulder blades like they were broken wings. And right now, he was looking at Shawn like she was made of glass.

Jane extricated herself from the beanbag chair and went upstairs to get some water even though she wasn't thirsty. Instead of going back to the basement, she wandered outside and found Alice in the garden.

"Hey."

Jane sat down in the grass to help her press seeds into a little row of divots in the soil.

"You okay?" Alice asked.

"I guess."

Alice wiped the dirt from her hands on her smock, then pulled a joint out of the pocket. As she lit it and inhaled, Jane thought involuntarily of her own mother, who had tried to make Jane believe that people like Alice were hell-bound sinners.

"You're like family, Jane. Tell me what's wrong." Alice's voice was curled tight around the smoke.

"I don't belong here." Jane sighed out the words.

"Of course you belong here. Are you kidding me? You and Elijah are twin flames, and you know it." She held the joint out to Jane, and Jane couldn't help it: she felt her mother's judgment rise up within her. Alice shouldn't smoke so much pot, and Elijah and his friends shouldn't drink so much, or take drugs, or do any of whatever else they did. She was an outsider for a reason; this was not her world.

Except Jane had mailed her mother a letter a few days after she arrived in Seattle, and it had been returned to the Harts' mailbox with the words *Please return to sender. Janet Ribeiro's mother does not live at this address!* scrawled across it in Raquel's handwriting.

Remembering this now, Jane decided to accept the joint. Maybe she just had to try harder. She inhaled and coughed, tried again. It was better the second time.

"Did you know Elijah sang before he could talk?" Alice said. Somehow, they were flat on their backs now, staring up at the pale-yellow sun filtering through evergreen branches that waved like feathers.

"That doesn't surprise me. His voice is one of the most amazing things about him."

"The day last year I heard him in the basement, singing one of the songs you had written—that was the day I knew everything was going to be okay again. And now that you're here, it really is."

Jane's head felt full, like she had been swimming and gotten water in her ears. "What do you mean, everything was going to be okay again?"

"Life is full of ups and downs, right? And Elijah got really low for a while. It's why he dropped out of school. Teenage stuff, I guess, and just . . ." She didn't finish the thought, and Jane shook her head, trying to clear the fog. "There's nothing to worry about now." Alice made it sound like nothing. She was the only other person who knew Elijah as well as Jane did. If she wasn't worried, Jane shouldn't be either.

"Why doesn't he sing around anyone but me?"

"Oh, it's silly. Kim made fun of him, back in grade school, about his voice. Said it was girly."

"Ugh. He's such a jerk."

Alice laughed. "He sort of is, isn't he? I think Kim is just jealous of him. They've always been a little competitive. And Elijah is so . . . He's just more than Kim. He always will be. Kim doesn't like that."

"Why does he stay friends with him? Kim is never all that nice to him."

"You know how boys are. Loyal. Old friendships just stick."

Jane didn't know, not really. None of her friendships had ever lasted. Jane would watch Jessica and Tiff snuggle up on the basement couch like kittens, braid each other's hair, whisper to each other and laugh, and feel like the memories of her earliest friendships belonged to someone else.

The pot had sharpened something inside her now. The loose, hazy feeling had given way to clarity. "I wish it were different," she found herself saying. "All of it. Kim. The Marvel Boys. I wish they—" She had been about to say "didn't exist," but she pressed those words back down inside her, like seeds in soil.

"Of course you do, sweetie," Alice said. "I know what you want. The music you and Elijah play together is *incredible*. Your lyrics, his voice? Lightning in a bottle."

Something shot through Jane when Alice said that. *Lightning in a bottle.* She felt every blade of grass beneath her back and legs as she stared up at the thickening clouds above. "I want to be famous," Jane admitted. "Me and Elijah. I want everyone in the world to hear our songs." Now that she had said it, she knew how true it was. If she were famous, she wouldn't have to explain herself to anyone. If her songs were out in the world, especially sung by Elijah's transcendent voice, people would like her—love her, even. Understand her. She'd fit in. And she'd have Elijah by her side. What could be better?

"It's all going to happen," Alice said, sounding as if she could both read Jane's mind and see the future. Jane turned to look at her, to see if she was serious, but her face was in profile and Jane couldn't see her expression. Elijah was always joking about how Alice got all philosophical when she was stoned. "Don't wish these days away, though. Because they'll be gone soon enough," she said. "The seasons always change. Nothing lasts forever. Everything dies. Even us." Alice sat up then and handed Jane more seeds, her smile bright, as if she hadn't just said something depressing. "But these are perennials. This nettle will be here long after we are. So maybe some things *do* last."

Except the nettle never did grow, and Elijah said later that it was probably because Alice had been stoned—she'd planted the seeds too shallow. The squirrels carried them away.

It was August. In the basement rehearsal space, Elijah stood behind Jane and put his hands over hers, guiding her fingers over the bass guitar's strings. "Try it this way." Her body shivered at his touch, as always. She leaned in for a kiss that she never wanted to end.

They finally pulled away from each other, and Jane tried the bassline the way he had suggested. "Yes," she said. "Perfect. God, I love these mornings, making music with you."

"Same here, Jane," he said. "I really do."

She handed him a sheet of lyrics ripped from the back of her journal, the ones she had written in her head the first day she arrived in Seattle, three months earlier now. He looked down at the words and smiled, as if he knew the precise moment the lyrics had been born.

"Should we record it?"

"Sure. I'll get the tape recorder?"

He shook his head. "Hang on," he said. "I have a surprise for you."

He bounded up the steps, then returned moments later, a large box covered in brown craft paper in his hands. When she looked closely, she saw the paper was covered in drawings just like the ones from the letters he used to send: composites of Jane and Elijah playing guitar, walking hand in hand through the forest trails nearby, snuggled up in his room, listening to music.

"What's this? It's not my birthday or anything."

"No, but you had your birthday while you were on your way here, didn't you? In June. I always wanted to make that up to you. Turning eighteen is a big deal."

"Oh, Elijah, it doesn't matter. Coming here to be with you was all I wanted."

He put the box in her hands and she lowered onto a stool. "Open it," he said.

She peeled the tape off carefully so she wouldn't ruin the drawings, while Elijah waited, grinning and impatient, until the paper was gone and a Portastudio—an at-home recording device they both always talked about—was revealed.

"*Elijah!* This is amazing!"

"Just for us, Jane. To show you how serious I am about *our* music. One day we'll be in a real recording studio, but this will be a good start."

Jane wondered for a moment if Alice had told Elijah about their conversation outside, that afternoon as they planted the nettle. But it didn't matter. This was exactly what she wanted—and just what they needed.

They got to work setting it up, and soon they were recording. The morning wore on and turned to afternoon, but they hardly noticed.

You see me as I am in the afternoon glow . . . Hard to remember what I was afraid of when we dance so slow . . .

She loved to listen to him sing, loved to watch his face when he did. He looked possessed, but in a beautiful way, like his soul had gone to a place mere mortals could only dream of visiting.

But she was jolted out of the moment when she saw several pairs of feet passing by the basement window. Kim burst into the basement first, and Jane saw surprise in his eyes when he realized that Elijah was singing. "Hey, what's that . . . ?"

Shawn tumbled in behind him next—and Jane liked what she saw in her expression even less. Recognition. Pleasure. She had heard him sing before, Jane realized. A half smile played across her full red lips as she nodded her head along to the words, *Jane's* words—and this finally made Jane tell Elijah to stop singing and open his eyes. They weren't alone anymore.

"Holy shit," Elijah said, flustered. "You guys are early. What are you even doing up?"

"We're all still tripping on some crazy acid we got from Zack last night," Kim said, and laughed. "Everyone crashed at my place, but we couldn't sleep. And hey, means we didn't miss you and your pansy-ass singing voice. Haven't heard that in a while, brother." He laughed again, and Elijah looked away. Jane felt anger rising up like bile. "I didn't know you had a Portastudio now, by the way," Kim said.

"I usually put it away when you dipshits come over so no one wrecks it," Elijah said, glancing at Jane.

"Shouldn't the Marvel Boys be using it? Recording some of *our* new stuff?"

Elijah just shrugged, and Jane felt even angrier.

"Anyway, I have news," Kim said. "Zack asked us to open for Heaven Wretch at Central next week. I said we'd do it." Elijah nodded, distracted now by putting away the Portastudio and getting his drum kit set up for practice. Jane liked Heaven Wretch; they had recently released an album with Sub Pop called *Assid* that, to Jane, despite the terrible title, was startlingly good. It was getting a lot of airplay on the most influential college radio stations, and the band was gaining a following. Their shows were always packed. Their lead singer, Zack Carlisle, was a slight twenty-three-year-old with bleach-blond hair, jewel-blue eyes, and a quiet, powerful presence—to go with his arresting, guttural singing voice. He was also, from what Jane could gather, the source of most of the drugs Elijah and his friends procured so often.

Kim pulled a set list in progress from the pocket of his baggy cargo shorts, which he always wore over long thermal underwear. "Zack said an A&R rep from Geffen is probably going to be there too," he said, his tone now a study in forced casualness. Jane had noticed that in Seattle, the bands partied together, rehearsed, gigged, went to one another's concerts, wrote songs, talked about music constantly—but it was verboten to act like you *wanted* to be famous. The few bands from the area that had achieved commercial success were viewed as sellouts, but Jane could tell they were also secretly worshipped. "I think we need to practice '69er' a little more. That song needs to be tighter for the show. But we also need something new. None of our songs are standouts."

Jane carefully folded the brown craft paper Elijah had used to wrap the Portastudio box, drawing side in, until the images of herself and Elijah in their private world of two disappeared from anyone else's view. She retreated, settled into the beanbag chair, picked up the book of Leonard Cohen poetry she had discarded there the afternoon before. But she couldn't focus on the words she had hoped would inspire her own songwriting. Kim had started playing a frenetic melody on his guitar, very similar to all the other frenetic melodies the Marvel Boys songs consisted of. Jane looked up as he turned to Elijah and said, "Can you write some words to go with that?"

Elijah started spitballing, as always. The lyrics he sometimes wrote for the Marvel Boys' songs weren't really anything. *Cat, mouse, get outta my house, get up, get up, fill your mind, fill your cup* . . .

Kim shook his head. "More serious. Something *angry*. Can you write about your dad, maybe? About what a fucking mess he was before—"

Elijah hit one of his cymbals, hard, drowning Kim out. "My dad is fine," Elijah said. "My dad is . . . I don't want to write a song about him."

Kim had his eyes on Jane now. His pupils were too big, she noticed. Jane wished he would stop whatever this was. "Ah, I get it. You want Jane here to believe you're Beaver fucking Cleaver and your parents are Ward and June."

"Fuck off, Kim," Elijah said.

Something had shifted in the room. Jane felt even more out of step than usual. "Drugs then, Elijah. Why don't you write a song about the *horse* you rode in on—"

"I *said*, fuck off, Kim!"

"Hey, then maybe a song for Shawn here? Your first love. You didn't know that, did you, Jane? That these two were a couple."

Now it was Shawn who spoke up. "Kim, lay off. Leave them alone."

Jane didn't know what else to do but flee, embarrassed by the confused tears that had sprung to her eyes.

Elijah followed her up the stairs. "Wait, Jane!"

In his bedroom, she flopped down on his bed, pressed her face into his pillow. "What the hell was that?"

Elijah sat down beside her. "I'm so sorry. He had no right. I hate him for stirring this up."

"But what was he talking about?" She rolled over and stared up at him. "Was Shawn really your first love?"

He looked agonized. "It wasn't like that. It was more . . . that we tried it out. And discovered we really are just friends. I swear, it was nothing like love. Not even close to what you and I have. But . . . it did get a little intense."

"Why?" she said, her voice small now.

He looked away. "Because of some of the shit we got into."

Jane's jealousy was pumping through her body like adrenaline. Everything hurt and her stomach felt sick. But she needed to know more. "What exactly do you mean?" She sat up and drew her knees to her chest, wrapped her arms around them.

"Heroin."

Jane remembered what Alice had said in the garden, about Elijah going through a tough time. But *heroin*? "Your mom mentioned something, but she made it sound like just some harmless phase . . ."

Elijah pinched the bridge of his nose and rubbed the skin under his eyes. "It wasn't," he said. "Shawn and I—when we were dating, we smoked it at a party. Black tar heroin is everywhere around here, it's insane, like at fucking high school parties. Not that I'm trying to blame anyone else, but—" He shook his head. "I remember when we'd talk on the phone, and I knew you wanted to come here, and it all just felt so wrong. I wanted to protect you."

"You can't protect me, Elijah. You can't shelter me from everything. You need to tell me things. Like . . . what did it feel like? I need to understand."

He looked surprised by the question, but his answer came fast. "It felt like the solution to my problems. It felt *great*. Like heaven. Shawn wasn't doing so hot either. Her dad had just gone to jail again and her mom's boyfriend was hitting her, and she just needed an escape. A guy at another party taught us how to inject it, and off we went." He rubbed his forehead. "She still uses. Not all the time, but she does. Probably more than she tells me. Sometimes I think I ruined her life. That she'll never be the same. That it could kill her."

"How long were you together?"

He blinked a few times, thought for a moment.

"A couple months, I guess. Like I said, we weren't really suited for each other. We went back to being friends pretty fast. Please believe me, Jane—I care about Shawn, but not in any way that should worry you. I feel responsible for her because of this shit I got her into. I should have told you—but it's so hard to talk about. Fucking heroin." He shook his head.

Jane's heart was beating at a more normal pace now. But she still didn't understand. "Why? Why would you? What made you so upset that you felt like you needed it?"

He thought about this for what felt like a long time. "Maybe I feel things too much," he finally said. "Sadness for me is . . . I just don't think it feels the way it does for other people. Happiness can feel almost painful at times, too." He bit his lip. "I'm sorry," he said. "It's not coming out right. I sound like an asshole. And that's not everything. It's not all."

"What, Elijah? Is it about your dad? What did Kim mean by that stuff he said about him?"

Elijah sighed, and his eyes darkened again. "He's an alcoholic. Maybe you've noticed."

"I—" But Jane didn't know what to say, yet again. She *had* noticed the whiskey in Moses's cup, yes. But she hadn't thought there was a problem. And now she knew she had missed so much in this new world she lived in. No wonder no one liked her. She was totally clueless.

"It was hard—sometimes it still is, watching him numb himself every fucking day. Sometimes I feel like we haven't even met." His voice broke, and she reached out for him.

"I'm sorry," she whispered, but she didn't know what else to say.

"And I felt like I had to be perfect, for my mom. To make her happy. But I'm not perfect, Jane. You know that now. I wouldn't blame you if you wanted to leave."

"I never wanted perfection. I've only ever wanted you. And your dad seems okay now. Right? I mean, did something change? Because he seems . . ."

"What happened is, you came along." Now he smiled a little. "We had been fighting a lot, screaming at each other all the time, and I felt sure he hated me, that he wished I had never been born—but then you came. And since you got here, he's been on his best behavior. He still drinks, but quietly. He's trying to impress our company, I guess." *Company.* This unsettled Jane even more than she already was. This place was her home. She didn't have anywhere else. "You changed me too, you know," he said, touching her hand. "When I found you, it was the only thing that had ever felt *right*. Loving you was a feeling . . . that actually fit."

"Were you high the first night we chatted, on BBS?"

He shook his head. "No. I was sick. I was detoxing. I had been doing it a lot, and my mom found out—and she was trying to keep it from Moses so he didn't kill me. Alice still can't talk about it, obviously. I put her through hell. She probably should have taken me to a hospital, but she was afraid to let me out of her sight. And she should have been. That night, I honestly thought I was going to just leave here, go to Seattle, find some heroin, and just . . . keep doing it. Never come back. Die. I wanted to die, Jane. I went down into the basement and turned on my computer to find some songs to burn onto a CD—and then, there you were."

The wonder in his voice at the memory of finding her that night filled her body with lightness, began to chase away the fear, the jealousy, the miasma of all the dark memories he was sharing that felt like they were dragging her under too.

"When was the last time you did heroin?"

He hesitated. "Spokane. Our tour. That time I called you."

"I remember," she said. "You didn't sound right."

"Yeah. I ran into one of my old connections. He'd come to see a show. I did a little of what I bought, and then I went and called you. After we talked, I flushed it down the toilet. You saved me. Again. You changed my life, you know that? Finding you felt like a miracle. You don't hate me, knowing all this?"

She moved close, kissed his neck, his cheek, his lips. "Of course not." And she didn't. Now that he was opening up to her this way, she felt closer to him than ever. "But we have to tell each other everything. Always. We can't have secrets."

"I know that. I'm so sorry. I promise, there's nothing else. This is all of it."

Such unexpected joy was flowing through Jane now, and what felt like the purest, most undistilled form of love. She had brought Elijah back from the edge, without even knowing it. She had saved him—he had just told her so.

She gently pulled away from him, stood, and lifted her shirt over her head.

"Jane?" Elijah said, a half smile on his face now. "What are you doing?"

"I love you," she said. "Always. No matter what. You can tell me anything, and my love for you won't change." She peeled off her jeans, then her underwear, snapped off her bra. She walked across the room naked to put on a CD, and their favorite Disintegration song filled the room, the lead singer's voice sonorous and wild, full of the love and longing Jane felt too, all the time, for Elijah. *Eternity, until the sun goes black / I love you, I love you, I love you. World starts to crumble, no turning back / I need you, I need you, I need you. Your arms around me, your lips on mine / I want more, more, more, of this love divine . . .* All Jane had ever been told about sex by her mother was that you were supposed to wait until you got married—but she knew Elijah was the person she was going to be with forever. There was no point waiting any longer. She crossed the room again and pressed him down onto the bed by his shoulders.

"I want you."

She lifted off his shirt, pulled off his pants. It was awkward, and then it wasn't. They were naked together, and it was perfect.

Elijah held himself slightly above her body with his lean, muscled arms. "Are you sure?"

She slid under him and pulled open his end table drawer, where she knew he kept condoms. She opened the wrapper while keeping her eyes locked on his. "Positive," she said, as he took it from her hand, smoothing it over himself as her breath hitched.

"Hang on," he said. "Just wait." He kissed her lips, her shoulder blades. His mouth traveled over her collarbones, her breasts; his tongue flicked against her nipples. They had done all this before.

"*Please,*" she said. "I want to."

"I know," he said, his mouth hovering above her navel. "But I want it to be good for you. Let's go slow."

Jane's arousal was a burning-hot stone in her core, and she needed relief—but she suddenly felt self-conscious. He was so experienced, and she wasn't. She had only ever done what they had done together. What if she wasn't good at this, what if he didn't like it with her? She tried not to think about Shawn, who probably knew exactly what Elijah liked and how to do it. But then his face was between her legs and it was different than it had been—because she knew there was no end point. She could let herself go. After a little while, when she was in a frenzy of want, he raised himself up, and his hips were sharp against her thighs.

"Oh god, I want you so bad, Jane . . ."

"Me too. Please . . ." She wrapped her legs around him, guided him inside her as if she had done this before. Stars of pain erupted, agonizing little fireworks of them, but just for a moment, and then it didn't hurt at all.

"Oh my god, *Elijah* . . ."

Later, she got on top, and she realized there had never been any wrong way to do this, not with him. He moaned and said, "Wait, we should change positions again, I'm going to—" But she just moved her hips faster, tilted her head back. Her only regret now was that she had taken so long to decide she was ready for sex. What a waste. They could have been doing this all along. "Don't wait," she gasped. "*Now.*" She shuddered against him, arched her back—then opened her eyes and saw someone outside Elijah's bedroom window, staring in at them.

She sprung away from Elijah as if she'd been burned.

"Shit, I'm *so* sorry, did I hurt you? It was your first time. I wasn't gentle enough . . ."

"No, it wasn't you." Jane shook her head. "I thought I saw someone, but I think it was in my head." She laughed shakily and lay down on the bed again, aligning her body with his. Had she ruined it? No. Nothing could. They started to kiss again. The second time it was slower, gentler. But the pleasure built to the same dizzying intensity. There had been no one at the window, Jane told herself. She had just imagined that Kim was spying, for some twisted, fucked-up reason. But it was just her and Elijah—and now she knew it always would be the two of them. Jane felt confident, as their bodies moved together as if they were one, that Elijah, the man she loved, would leave behind whatever darkness was in his past because of her. They were safe now, from everything.

SEATTLE, WASHINGTON

SEPTEMBER 1990

In the fall of 1990, an aunt of Alice's died, and she was asked to go back to the small town she was from, hours away, near Olympia, for the reading of the will. She seemed nervous, flustered. "I haven't been home in a long time," she explained.

"Jane and I can come along with you, Mom," Elijah said.

"Okay. But . . ." She turned to Jane. "You know Moses can't even boil an egg. I have Betty Friedan and Erica Jong on my bookshelf but can't seem to manage to get myself out of the kitchen." Her laugh was bell-like; she didn't mind being in the kitchen, and Jane knew it. "Could Elijah come, and you stay here and stand in for me—make sure Moses gets his dinner when he gets home from work?"

Jane said she would, and Alice left a casserole recipe for her. Jane cooked it while listening to Alice's folk records. Around five, she heard Moses's car in the driveway.

"Hello, Jane," Moses said, stiff and formal, brushing the rain from his hair as he came inside.

"Hi, Moses. Dinner's almost ready."

"Okay, then," he said. He went to change out of his work clothes and was back in the kitchen moments later.

"It won't be too long," Jane said. The silence that followed was heavy and awkward. "Would you . . . um, would you like a drink?" Jane found herself asking, but then she felt a pang of guilt. No. She shouldn't have done that. Elijah had said he had a problem. But it was too late.

"I can get it myself," he said, looking relieved.

As Jane got out the dinner plates, she told herself it was probably alright. He was fine. He held down a job. Jane had never seen him drunk. It was okay. Not a big deal.

During dinner, Moses drank more whiskey, and Jane put on a Melanie record. "This album reminds me of when I first met Alice," Moses said, seeming much less stiff than before, as the folk singer's warbling voice reverberated pleasantly in the kitchen. "Hey, do you want some?"

"Oh." She was surprised. "Sure." He got her a mug. The whiskey was astringent, hot on her throat. After a few sips, it made her feel good. Not like pot, not as unnerving. This was much better, actually.

"So, how did you meet?" Jane asked, feeling a camaraderie between them, warm as the whiskey. "You and Alice?" She was glad she'd stayed back now, to get to know Moses better.

"I used to be Mormon," he said, and Jane burst out laughing.

"I'm sorry," she said. "Really?"

He laughed too. "I know. Now I'm married to Alice. Not exactly a Mormon."

She felt the thread of connection between them tighten, as she told him a little about her own Evangelical upbringing in Stouffville. "Once, our pastor came over to pray for my soul, because he said the music I was listening to had satanic messages in it when played backward."

Moses laughed. "I can definitely relate. As soon as I met Alice, I knew I could never go back home again without having to endure a public shaming." But he didn't seem bothered by this—which made Jane feel even better still. She had thought it was unusual and something to be ashamed of, that her mother had been so decisively cut from her life when she left her hometown. But Moses understood how she felt.

"Where did you meet Alice?" Jane asked him.

He smiled. "It was at an anti-war protest. I was with some people from my community, handing out pamphlets to all the supposed lost souls in Washington, DC. Then Alice walked past, and we locked eyes, and she said, 'You.'"

"She said, 'You'?"

He laughed quietly, reminding her of Elijah for the first time ever as he stared into his mug. "I never felt like I had been chosen for anything, but suddenly this magical woman had chosen me, and I guess you could say it was love at first sight." He sipped more of his whiskey. Jane sipped her own and felt wordly and mature, a sensation she had always longed for. "So I didn't go home again after that, as I said. Alice . . . she became home."

Jane got it. She felt this way about his son. As Moses talked to her, Jane realized that she had always longed to have a dad, and for it to feel just like this. The warmth inside her increased; she barely noticed how many times Moses refilled his mug. "We came back to Olympia, and then we got an apartment in Seattle so I could go to college," he said. "We used to listen to this record all the time, the one you put on there. 'The Rollerskate Song.'" Moses inclined his head toward the stereo, then laughed that quiet laugh again. "Such a silly song. Doesn't really mean anything. But I like it."

This was more than Moses had said to her, ever, in the months she had lived in his home. Jane found she didn't want him to stop talking, so she stood and filled his mug again, and he smiled at her gratefully—but after that, he got quiet. He stared out the window as Jane washed the dishes.

"I'm going to go take out the garbage," he said eventually.

Moments later, she heard a crash. She ran out of the house to find Moses on his back on the driveway beside the garbage cans. A cinder block was on the ground beside him. Alice usually put it on top of the bins on garbage day, to keep the animals out. He must have tripped over it. Jane knelt down to help him.

"I'm fine!" he snapped, startling her with the sudden sharpness of his voice. He made an abrupt, clumsy movement to push her arm away.

"I don't need help!" He scrambled up and stood, and for a moment his body wavered. "I didn't see that brick there," he said, his voice softer now, contrite. "Really, I'm fine."

"But you're bleeding." He was—his forearm was scraped, with dirt embedded in the cut. Inside, back in the kitchen, he sat in a chair and winced as Jane cleaned the wound and plastered it with a few bandages she found in a bathroom drawer.

When she was done, he stood and said, "Well, I should get to bed. Work tomorrow." He paused on his way out of the kitchen. "We don't need to tell anyone about this, do we?"

She felt disappointed because she had wanted to talk to Elijah all about sitting with his dad at the table, chatting about the past. How nice it had been. But now she knew she wouldn't.

"I promise. Our secret."

The next day, Moses had gone to work by the time Jane got up. The whiskey bottle had been put away. Nothing happened, Jane told herself. He just tripped.

Alice and Elijah came home later full of news about a cabin in Olympia the aunt had left for Alice in her will, and Jane put aside her misgivings about the night before. The house hadn't been right with them gone, and now they were back. But Elijah looked at her with concern. "Everything go okay with my dad?"

"Of course. Great. He just ate dinner and went to bed."

"I didn't even know that place was still around," Alice was saying of the cabin, dropping a bag of baked goods on the table. "We used to go there when I was a kid. It was such a good place. So many memories of my folks there." Alice's parents had been older when they'd had her, their only child, and had both passed away long before Jane moved in. "That cabin—it was almost like a member of my family. It needs work, but it's going to be *so* beautiful."

Moses returned from work, and the night was focused on making plans for the cabin. This became a new routine; Moses and Alice would spread checklists and drawings over the dinner table every night and map out the cabin's restoration. Jane thought this new purpose changed something about Moses. He seemed happier. Maybe their talk had helped, too—or maybe falling had made him realize he was drinking too much. Sometimes he would flash a smile at Jane in a conspiratorial way and she would wonder if it had all been a good thing.

Moses and Alice started going to the cabin on weekends to work on the repairs. When Jane and Elijah stood at the edge of the driveway to see them off every Friday evening, it was as if the roles had reversed and they were the parents now. Jane liked this feeling, as if she and Elijah were a married couple. Alice would reach over Moses's chest to beep the horn of the family's old Subaru station wagon as it backed it out of the driveway. Music—Jefferson Airplane, Melanie, Helen Sear, the Grateful Dead—would echo in the air behind them, and Jane would feel happiness wash over her as she stood there and waved at these people, her family. She didn't long to leave the Seattle suburbs quite as frequently; it was like Alice had said to her: nothing lasted forever, and she should enjoy these moments.

One weekend afternoon later that fall, none of the other girls came to watch the Marvel Boys' practice. Elijah's parents were at the Olympia cabin, and Jane went for a walk by herself before coming to sit in the basement, her beanbag chair positioned off to the side, near Elijah's drum kit, where she could read and doze, wait for practice to be over.

The band was working on a new song that was giving them trouble. And suddenly Jane, even in her half-dozing stage, knew what they were missing. The music ended, Elijah banged a cymbal in frustration, and Kim slammed his guitar down. "This song is a piece of shit!" he snarled. "We suck!"

"Actually," Jane ventured, extricating herself from the beanbag chair, crossing the room, and reaching for Kim's guitar on the floor. "I think if you try it like this"—she played a fast version of the tune they had been struggling with, beginning with a minor key and ending on a major, the opposite of the way the band had been playing it—"it works really well. Kind of Mudhoney-ish with a bit of Misfits punk."

Ari was nodding, already adapting with his bass to what she was playing, while Elijah kept time again on his drum kit. But Kim's expression turned darker. "Who the *fuck* asked you for advice?"

"Well, no one, but I've been sitting here, and—"

"Yeah, you *have* been fucking sitting here. Every fucking day, every time we practice, even though when I ask the other girls for a little space because we're not gelling lately, they all take a hint."

Jane glanced at Elijah. Was this true? Were the other girls told to leave? Was she really a disruption? Elijah shrugged, mouthed, *He's an asshole*. But it wasn't enough.

"You're like some kind of sycophant!" Kim continued, mispronouncing it "psycho-pant." "Why are you always *here*?"

"I live here," she said quietly.

"You're not in the band. No one fucking asked for your opinion, okay?"

"But she's right," John said, playing the melody on his own guitar.

Jane was simmering inside. Why had John stuck up for her when Elijah had not? Elijah was just sitting there, his drumsticks laid across his snare, a blank look on his face like he was simply waiting for this to be over.

"And don't *touch* my fucking guitar," Kim said, yanking it away from her.

The force of it knocked Jane backward.

"*Hey!*" Elijah jumped from his stool. His drumsticks clattered to the concrete floor. "Don't touch her, you asshole!"

"I didn't touch her! Jesus Christ, Elijah! Give me a break. She fucking fell on purpose, man! Come on."

But Elijah had Kim by the collar now. He was taller than Kim and had taken his friend by surprise.

"Elijah, calm down—Jesus, get *off* me!" Kim shouted.

The next thing Jane knew, Elijah and Kim were wrestling—and not in the playful way they normally did, like puppies in a pile. Kim was shouting and Elijah sounded like a snarling animal.

John and Ari lunged forward and pulled them apart.

"Come on, guys. Calm down," Ari said.

Both guys stood facing each other, panting and red-faced. Jane thought she saw tears glistening in Kim's eyes.

"Get the fuck out, Kim," Elijah said. "I'm done. I don't want to do this anymore. It's over."

Kim turned to Jane, who was still on the floor. "I guess this makes you happy, right? Adam's rib, getting her day in the sun. You'd be nothing without him, and you know that—so you're trying to alienate all his friends."

Jane stood up. "You're doing a pretty good job of that yourself," she said.

"You think he belongs to you, but he doesn't."

"Just get away from her, Kim," Elijah said, yanking himself away from Ari and John. "Get out." Then he turned. "You too, Ari, John. Please. Sorry. I'm so sorry."

They all headed for the door empty-handed, a funereal pall in the air after the electricity of the anger. "Take your instruments with you."

"Fuck you," Kim said, picking up his guitar and shoving it in its case. He pointed to Elijah, then to Jane, like he was trying to curse them. "Fuck you both. Forever."

And Jane couldn't keep it inside any longer. "*No.* Fuck *you*, Kim. You call *me* Adam's rib? How about you? Elijah has more talent in his pinkie than you ever will and you know it. You've been holding him back and you're not going to shine anymore without him. Are you?"

Kim slammed the door so hard behind him the entire house shook.

Seattle settled into a cold, rainy December and Kim didn't call or come back to the house. Ari and John called a few times. "There are no hard feelings," Jane heard Elijah say once, talking to John. "Yeah—it's totally cool. Yeah, we are. We have. Thanks. Good luck with the drummer auditions."

"Does it bother you?" Jane asked him after he hung up. "Not being in the band?"

"I don't want their dreams to get derailed. I'd feel guilty if that happened. And I miss John and Ari." He picked up one of his guitars and started to tune it. "But not Kim. Never."

She bit her lip, looked over at him. "So, I have an idea . . . for our band name?"

His fingers stilled on the guitar strings; he looked up. "Yeah?"

"It was from something your mom said about your voice. She called it lightning in a bottle."

He chuckled, strummed a few chords. "She's weird about my voice."

"I didn't think it was weird at all. I thought it was perfect. The Lightning Bottles. What do you think?"

He thought for a moment. "Actually, that's great, Jane." He repeated the name. "The Lightning Bottles. Yes." Then he put down his guitar and stepped toward her. "For me, it's not about my voice, though." He tucked a strand of hair behind her ear. "That's how I felt when I met you—like I'd been hit by lightning."

Just then, there was a knock at the side door. Jane's heart sank—but it wasn't Kim. It was Zack, from Heaven Wretch.

"Hey, Jane," Zack said. His eyes seemed an even brigher blue than usual, his hair a vivid Clairol yellow. He was wearing what Jane now referred to internally as the Seattle uniform: several layers of clothing that generally included ripped jeans, long johns, a T-shirt over a long-sleeved shirt, a plaid lumberjacket on top of that.

"How are things with Heaven Wretch?" Jane asked.

"Yeah, not bad, we're doing okay," he said modestly. She had heard they were on the cusp of signing with Geffen. "But we don't have a drummer. We've been through, like, five. It's my cross to bear or something. But, hey, so Elijah, I heard the Marvel Boys were having auditions too. Which made me think . . . does that mean *you're* free, man? I love your sound and style. I think you'd be a great fit, if you wanted to try out for Heaven Wretch."

"Actually, Jane and I have a band now," Elijah said. "We were just practicing."

"Oh really?" When Zack turned to her again, his smile was genuine, interested. "That's great. Cool. Jane, I didn't even know you played."

She felt shy as Elijah said, "Jane is an amazing musician. She writes our songs, plays guitar *and* bass. And I do the drums, singing, some guitar."

"That's awesome. A duo. I'd love to hear you sometime." He turned back to Jane. "What are you called?"

"The Lightning Bottles," Jane said, and it all felt real.

"That's a killer name," Zack said. "Seriously, let's jam together sometime."

"I'd love that," Jane replied. And for the first time ever, she felt like a musician—not just someone waiting for her chance.

On Christmas Eve, Kim stormed up to the Harts' bungalow and banged on the basement door.

Jane was upstairs helping Alice make turkey with bread dumplings, the family's traditional Christmas Eve dinner. She could hear Kim's loud voice, and Elijah's quiet responses, coming up through the floor.

"What did he want?" Jane asked Elijah when Kim was gone.

"They can't find a new drummer. And there's a show at Re-bar in two weeks." He popped a cranberry into his mouth. "An A&R rep from Geffen is going to be there, because of Heaven Wretch."

"Kim always says reps are going to show, and they never do. He just pretends he doesn't care."

"I know, but I think it's for real this time. Is it okay with you, Jane, if I help them out?"

"I'm not your jailer," Jane snapped, wishing her voice didn't sound so harsh. "You don't need to ask my permission."

"Just a few weeks, and then we'll be us again, I promise."

At this, Jane bristled even more. "We won't be *us* while you're playing with them? We have to turn it on and off?"

"That's not what I meant—"

She shook her head. "It's fine," she lied, turning away—because she knew it was going to have to be.

A few days later, when the band and the girls filtered in the side door, Jane left the house instead of sitting and watching practice. She walked alone for an hour, up and down the ordered suburban streets. When she reached the woods, she contemplated them but turned back, not ready to get lost. She went to Elijah's room and pulled on headphones, turned on L7 to drown out what was drifting up through the floorboards. All she could think was, *What good is lightning if all you do is keep it in a bottle?*

The night of the Marvel Boys show at Re-bar was damp and freezing, typical for Seattle in January. It was now a new year: 1991. Jane was at the house, alone; Alice and Moses were away working on the cabin. Jane had decided to skip sound check and take the bus into Seattle just before the show was about to start.

Jane went into Alice's room. She didn't usually wear makeup, but sometimes Alice would do her hair and put lipstick on her and tell her she looked like a Hollywood starlet. "My stuff is your stuff," she always told Jane, so now, Jane sorted through Alice's makeup bag until she found the deep purple-red lip shade Alice had tried on her the week before. The lipstick made her look older than eighteen and like someone else. Not a kid from Ontario. Not Janet Ribeiro. Jane Pyre. Her stage name. Maybe even her true name now. She pretended for a moment that she was getting ready for a Lightning Bottles show, painted dark purple liquid liner across her eyelids—and then startled and smudged it when the doorbell rang. No one ever used the doorbell; everyone just came into the house through the side.

She opened the front door to find two police officers, a man and a woman, standing on the porch, hats in their hands. A shock jolted through her body. "Ms. . . . Hart?" She didn't know what else to do but nod.

"There's been an accident," the man said.

"We're so very sorry," said the woman.

It had happened early that morning. Moses and Alice had been out on a winding road near the Olympia cabin, possibly heading into town, when their car had swerved for no discernable reason and tumbled down a cliff and into the inlet. "We believe your parents' deaths were instantaneous," the female officer said, as if this could possibly be considered a comfort.

"I'm not . . ." Jane began, about to tell them she wasn't the Harts' daughter. But she was afraid if she said that they'd stop telling her anything. And in a way, Alice and Moses did feel like her parents, even if she'd only known them for seven months. "I need Elijah," she said, as the horror of what had happened hit her. She felt tears at the corners of her eyes, sticking there like ice, not falling.

"Okay. We can take you anywhere you need to go."

Jane paused as she was pulling on her combat boots. She looked up. "Who was driving?"

"Moses Hart was driving."

"Was there an animal, do you know? Something he would have swerved to avoid?"

"Miss," the male officer said, shifting on his feet, looking away. "There were no signs of that, although it is possible. But there was a . . . a travel mug with whiskey in it, found inside the car, on the driver's side. Did Alice drink whiskey?"

"No." Jane's voice was sharp. "But it was morning. Moses wouldn't have been either. That's impossible. He wouldn't have been drunk in the morning. *No.*"

When she walked into the Re-bar greenroom, Elijah smiled to see her. "Hey, you're here already. Want a drink?" He held up a screwdriver that, based on the color, was clearly much more vodka than juice. She recoiled.

"I think you need to put that down. And we need to talk," she said. "Alone." Her heart was pounding, her body so flooded with shock and grief that it felt like adrenaline. Elijah's smile faded.

She pulled him into a corner, all the while feeling a sensation inside herself like she, too, was in a car plummeting down an embankment. Everything was about to change. This was perhaps Elijah's last moment of feeling like a normal person, and she was about to take that from him. Would he always associate her with this tragedy?

"Elijah . . . your parents were in a car accident," she began.

"Oh shit, are they okay?"

The tears her eyes had been holding now spilled out. She shook her head, sucked back a sob. "It was instantaneous," she said.

He sagged against the wall. "What does that . . . What do you mean?"

"They didn't make it. I don't know very much. The car swerved and went off a cliff. Maybe it was an animal." She could already tell he didn't believe this lie. His expression had changed so swiftly, his eyes had turned dark. "The police officers are waiting outside; they need to talk to you."

"Was my dad driving?"

Jane nodded. "Yes," she whispered. It was as if she had hit him. He flinched and reared back. He put his hands over his face, but when he removed them, his eyes were completely expressionless, and it scared Jane. "Let's get this over with," he said, stalking toward the door as she followed.

Outside, Jane stood beside Elijah as the officers explained terrible things to him, about his parents' bodies being in a morgue in Olympia, already identified by a member of Alice's family. They talked about autopsies, papers to be signed, next of kin, access to counselors. "Nope," Elijah said when they mentioned counselors. He backed away. "Thank you. I have to go now."

"Elijah, what are you doing?"

"I have to play this show. I can't let my friends down on top of everything else."

The officers gave him cards and numbers to call, nodded at them both sympathetically before they got into their cruiser and drove away, probably relieved to be leaving this tragedy behind.

"Coming?" Elijah said to Jane, but he had already started to walk back toward the bar, and she had no choice but to follow.

"I don't understand," Jane said, half-jogging to keep up with him. "You're going to go in there and play?"

"I'm keeping my word, at least." His voice was robotic. She felt anything but.

"Elijah, *what the fuck*? Why are you so calm?" She clutched at his arm, but he shrugged her off. "It's a mistake, okay?" she said, feeling desperate to get through to him. "Your dad wasn't drunk. It was morning. Maybe they swerved to avoid a deer—"

"Jane. You can't fix this. *Stop.*" He had his hand on the club's side door and turned to her now.

"*But, Elijah.*" She thought about the time she'd spent with Moses, how much he drank, how she'd never told anyone—how she'd poured him some whiskey herself, even joined him. Was this her fault? Could she have stopped this from happening?

"You're making it worse, okay?" His words just confirmed her thoughts.

Then he pushed open the side door of the club and noise flowed out into the dark, damp night. "You know as well as I do he drank. We talked about it. We all tried to pretend it wasn't true, even you. But it was. And now"—his voice broke and she thought he was finally going to cry, to let go of the shock and allow himself to understand what had happened. But he just shook his head and swore under his breath. Then he continued into the club, leaving Jane alone, the door almost slamming in her face. She shoved it open, called out his name. No answer. She'd never felt so alone. Alice would have hugged her; Jane would have buried her face in Alice's fragrant hair and she would have felt protected and loved.

But Alice was gone. And now, so was Elijah. She ran through the dark hallway. "Please, come back. Come *on.*" She tugged on his arm. "Let's just go. Somewhere else. Away from here." But he shook his head and wouldn't look at her.

"I'm going to play this show because on top of everything else, I don't want to let my friends down and ruin everything for them, too." She followed him deeper into the club, her breath coming in gasps, a combination of sadness and alarm—but found herself hanging back when he entered the greenroom again and approached his friends. She had by now spent endless hours with his friends. But it didn't matter. She was an interloper. An outsider. Especially in this moment. They encircled him so tightly he disappeared from her view. Suddenly, it felt like someone was clutching at Jane's throat with their hands. She struggled for breath and backed against the wall. And before she knew what was happening, Jane heard herself screaming, "You assholes!" Her anger was giving her something, at least—it was allowing her to breathe again, so she let it burn. "All of you are fucking assholes!"

They all stared at her blankly until Jane turned around and stormed out of the club, leaving one of her first legends in her wake. *Who would scream at someone like that when he had just found out his parents had been killed? What kind of a person does that?*

Jane walked in the rain, on and on, blind to where she was going, until she saw a pay phone and ducked inside. She didn't know who else to call, so she dialed her home number.

"Hello?"

At the sound of her mother's voice, Jane had to stifle a sob. She held her hand over her mouth.

"Hello?" Raquel said again. But what could Jane say to her? Her mother would have zero empathy for anyone in Jane's tragic new world. She would be appalled by all of it—as she probably should be. Jane was about to hang up, but Raquel did it first, uttering an annoyed and still-familiar *tsk* before she did.

Jane left the phone booth and kept walking, her tears mingling with the rain on her cheeks. An hour passed, then two, and she finally stopped and leaned against the wall of a building, too tired to continue.

"Jane."

Elijah stood in front of her, trembling and soaked through, just like she was. His eyes were strange, like they didn't have enough color in them. Maybe it wasn't just his eyes—maybe the whole world had lost its color. A tear rolled down his cheek, then another. She tried to wipe them away but eventually gave up. She reached for his icy hands and held them in hers, but that did no good because she was sure her hands were even colder than his.

"I told Kim . . ." His voice trembled. "I told him to get me something. I told him, 'Get me whatever I need to not to have to feel this right now.'"

"You *have* to feel this, Elijah." It felt urgent to say this to him. She pulled him close and he leaned his face on her shoulder, spoke into her ear.

"I'm so sorry. I never should have treated you that way. And you're right. It fucking sucks, but I do."

She pulled away, just an inch. "Did you . . . ? It would be okay. I mean, tonight, you just lost—"

He shook his head. "No. I didn't do the heroin. I left. I came to find you." He was crying in earnest now, his words coming out in sobs. "I won't be like my dad, even if every part of me wants to be. I won't numb myself away from the world. I swear."

"I know," she whispered. "It's okay. I'm here. It's okay, it's okay." She said this, over and over, willing it to be true.

"You're all I have now. I'm so scared."

She put her frozen hands on his tear-slick cheeks and looked into his eyes. "What are you scared of?"

"Losing you too."

"You will *never* lose me," she said. His teeth were chattering, his body shaking. "There is nothing in the world that could ever tear us apart."

"Do you promise, Jane?"

"I swear. No matter what happens, I'll always find you, I'll always save you."

They didn't go to the police station and they didn't go home. Jane and Elijah walked the rainy streets of Seattle until their clothes were wet enough to wring out like rags.

"Do you want to know why I stopped singing when I was a kid?" Elijah asked her. "It wasn't what my mom thought, not because of Kim. It was because she would always tell me my voice was a gift that would take me places. Take me far, far away, she would say." He paused. "And her eyes would get so sad when she said that. So I thought maybe my voice was going to magically separate us. Like it was a curse. And I just . . . stopped. I never told her why I didn't want to sing anymore, even when I could have. I didn't bother. I don't think I was a very good son."

"You were such a good son. You made her so happy."

"I should have sung for her more often, though. I should have made her happy, every single day. Because God knows my dad wasn't—" He shook his head, tensed his jaw. "Fucking *Moses*," he finally said. "I used to feel like we had never even properly met, never had a real conversation. He was a stranger to me. And now he always will be."

Jane thought about the night she sat at the kitchen table with Moses, sharing whiskey and talking. How close she had felt to him, how she had been sure this was what having a real dad was like. He had been hers that night, her real family—but she couldn't tell Elijah this. She could never tell him now. She just nodded and squeezed his hand, encouraged him to keep talking. It was good for him to talk about his parents. She would try to make sure he always did, so this pain didn't solidify inside him.

"And songs," he said, veering away from the painful topic of his dad and back to talking about music. "I'm afraid of those, too. Nothing scares me more, actually, than the idea of singing a song I wrote. It would be . . . just so fucking honest, you know?" He had slowed his pace, was looking down at her intently—and she saw something she knew very well in his eyes.

"You have a song inside you now, don't you?"

He nodded.

"Songs don't leave you alone. This one might haunt you if you don't let it out."

"It's about my mom," he said. "When I was a little kid, she never read me bedtime stories. She used to read to me out of her copy of *The Prophet*. I can still recite that book line by line." His eyes took on a far-away look. "*Travel and tell no one. Live a true story and tell no one. Live happily and tell no one. People ruin beautiful things.*"

"Oh," Jane said. "That's . . . so pretty and painful at the same time."

He nodded. "Yeah." His smile contained a combination of happiness and sadness—because, Jane was realizing, grief was a strange alchemy. Beautiful agony—she felt it too. Devastated that Alice was gone; struck by the wonder of ever having had her in the first place. Awash in knowledge that felt like a special secret: that she wasn't really gone. That somehow Alice was there with them, guiding them.

"She was a good mother," Jane said, wanting to find a way to convey how she was feeling to Elijah. "And good mothers—I don't think they ever leave you. I think she'll always be with you. And that means you can still sing for her, if you want to. You can still give her a song."

He hesitated, then pulled a cocktail napkin out of his pocket. "I wrote some lyrics, back at the club, before I left. I just started writing stuff down." But then he put the napkin back in his pocket without showing her, probably because he was trying to protect it from the rain. "My life or yours," he said. "Another Gibran line. *One day you will ask me which is more important. My life or yours.*" He looked down at Jane again, pulled her closer. "*I will say mine and you will walk away not knowing . . . that you are my life.*"

"She loved you *so* much," Jane said through her tears.

"She loved *you* too. She had big dreams for us, you know. She wanted everything you want."

"I know," Jane said. "I know she did. You should want it too, Elijah. No more hesitating. For her."

"Let's go to the Central," he said suddenly. "They have open mic on Saturdays."

He grabbed her hand and she followed him through the rain-swept streets. The night turned into a dream, feverish, unreal.

She knew how they looked, rain-soaked and bedraggled, like the orphans they now were, when they arrived at the Central Saloon. No one paid them much attention, and she could tell Elijah had lost some of his nerve now that they were in the crowded club. But it was too late to turn back when they stepped onto the stage.

"'Dark Shine' first," Elijah murmured, and, on a borrowed bass guitar, she played the familiar opening of a song she had written and they had practiced together many times.

When he sang, his voice was ragged and hoarse, nowhere near as good as she knew it could be. His guitar strumming was hesitant. Most people didn't even look up from their drinks or conversations. Jane wished she hadn't encouraged this. It felt like they were ghosts on the stage, just like his parents. This was just going to make things worse for him. They shouldn't have done this. His parents had just died! What were they even doing here?

After "Dark Shine," there was a smattering of dutiful applause. Someone yelled, "Show us your tits!" at Jane, and she gestured to Elijah that they should go. But he shook his head.

"Follow along," he instructed. "I'm ready. I have to let this song out, like you said."

He began to strum again, a melodic intro that seemed to her to last too long. Something wasn't right about it, but as he kept playing, she found herself gaining an understanding of the music, of what he was trying to do. People in the audience trailed off mid-conversation and watched him.

Jane joined in with a simple bassline—and then he opened his mouth and sang.

You asked if I'd die for you / I didn't know what you meant / but the words were all there for me / from a prophet, heaven sent.

With every line, his voice became stronger, more exquisite.

You wanted me to sing, I just wanted to play. / I took you for granted / had no clue you wouldn't stay.

All conversation in the bar had tapered off. Jane thought maybe the crowd was aghast by the raw emotion in his voice. It was too much. She almost stepped forward and told him to stop. He was right to have been afraid to sing a song he had written. It was *so* honest. She felt panicked as his voice became even more raw. She had to stop him from revealing himself this way—what would he have left for himself? She stepped forward, reached out. And then, it came: the moment she'd never forget. Maybe no one there ever would.

Baby, don't cry, he sang. *'Cause* . . . The pause here felt reverent. Everyone held their breath, including Jane. *We're all gonna die* . . .

She was sure that somehow, everyone in the room knew what Elijah had just lost. What they *all* stood to lose. They were all going to die someday. Everyone they loved was going die someday, too. It was awful.

Then Elijah stopped strumming his guitar and let the moment stretch. He shrugged, flashed a smile at the crowd, and sang the next line.

. . . *might as well just get high, go get high* . . .

A cheer rose up, but Jane felt shocked. Get high? She struggled to keep playing as she watched this new side of Elijah: the seductive performer, the captivating showman. He had said he was afraid of the honesty of his music, but this wasn't honesty, was it? He had battled getting high tonight and won, but now he was singing about drugs as if they weren't a demon at his shoulder.

She pulled her eyes away from him and focused on the faces in the crowd. The audience was clapping along, dancing, bending toward him like they were crops and he was the sun. There was joy in the room—and suddenly, Jane couldn't resist it, either. Out of the ashes of his pain, Elijah had written a perfect song—one about life and death, about how somehow the shattering truth of existence everyone avoided was okay. She was in awe of him, just like everyone else in that room. She loved him so much—and she loved this song, too. As she stood behind him, listening to him sing, she knew something for certain: this song was going to change their lives. Nothing was ever going to be the same again.

WOOLF, GERMANY

DECEMBER 19, 1999

In the slanting light of late morning, Jane strides across the frozen grass, up to the house next door. She lifts a brass knocker, raps with force.

The teenage girl opens the door. "Shh," she says, a worried expression on her face. "My mother is asleep."

"What's your name?" Jane says.

"Hen. Hen Vögel."

"Take me to see it, Hen. The art in the photograph, in Berlin. Please," she adds.

Hen nods. "Give me five minutes," she says. "Drive your car down to the road and wait for me there. I'll meet you."

In her car, Jane does as Hen has instructed. She waits, nervous, fiddling with the radio, then the car's seat-warming function—turning it on, then off, then to medium, then off again. Hen finally appears, with her fluffy hair and spotty chin. Jane unlocks the door for her and, when she has her seat belt on, reverses down the driveway and is soon out on the road, heading back to the city she came from the day before.

There is silence at first, until Jane turns on the radio. Loud heavy metal music fills the car. Jane adjusts the volume and Hen glances at her.

"It's not my favorite," Jane says, feeling defensive. "I just had it on for driving." She nods at the radio. "Put on what you want."

Hen spins the dial until it lands on Alt Radio Berlin, then shoots a worried glance at Jane. "They'll probably play some Lightning Bottles. Is that okay with you?"

"Of course," Jane says, forcing nonchalance. "I've played those songs so many times they don't affect me anymore." But this isn't true. The songs, all of them, have deep meaning for her. And Elijah's voice always has an effect on her. But she doesn't say this to Hen, just focuses on remembering how to get back to Berlin, on keeping up with the other drivers on the road and staying in her lane.

It takes two hours to get to the city, and no Lightning Bottles songs come on the radio. Jane thinks of questions she might ask Hen, to fill the awkward silence. Some of them are inane—*What school do you go to?*, that sort of thing. And some of them aren't. *Are you sure you aren't trying to hurt me, deceive me? Do you know what this means to me?* In the end, she says nothing, and neither does Hen.

They get to the city, and Hen suggests she go as far west as she can and find a place to park. Jane does, then turns off the car.

"Okay," she says, as if trying to reassure herself.

"Okay," Hen repeats. Jane glances at her sidelong. "Let's go," she says. "It's a ten-minute-or-so walk from here."

Berlin has changed in the years since Jane was there with Elijah, but there are still utilitarian communist-era structures on the east side of the city and mostly neoclassical apartments and various buildings on the other. An apple half and an orange half, stitched together into a city that bears a scar—but Jane wonders if everyone feels freedom a little differently here. If they appreciate it more. They must.

Jane and Hen walk west. Bicycles lean against walls and fences or in piles beside patio picnic tables. Café tables are filled with people drinking beer from froth-topped mugs, wearing coats and hats against the December afternoon's chill. Clouds of smoke and plumes of frosty breath hover above their heads before dispersing. Jane wonders all at once if she and Hen look like friends, or sisters, perhaps. She has not worn a disguise today—no sunglasses, no hat—and she realizes she should have thought of that, but not being alone feels, in a way, like its own disguise. Jane Pyre is always alone.

They follow the beacon of Berlin's TV tower, a concrete arm bisected by a tiled stainless steel orb, topped with a red-and-white-striped antenna. Hen is walking fast. Keeping up with her distracts Jane from thinking too much about the last time she was here, but she can still feel the shadows of herself, walking on this same sidewalk, standing with him, just there—not knowing their time was running out. Hen ducks down a street lined with shops and restaurants, and they enter a dim alley. Hen slows, and Jane realizes she knows this place from the photo Hen showed her back in her kitchen. Her heart rate accelerates. This is it.

The afternoon sun filters through the space above the buildings, illuminating the riot of color on the brick walls. Faces, animals, dancing figures. Words. Some in German, some in English, the languages weaving together. "God Ble$$." "*Liebe.*" "Concrete Makes You Happy." "*Donnerwetter.*" "Death to Tyrants." Spray-painted and stenciled artworks, glued-on playbills, paintings of animals, people, planets, ideas. She spots the wolf from the photograph, the rainbow moon, the Day of the Dead mask.

And then she sees what they came here for. Just one square poster, large, painted in muted gray, much less noticeable than the other paintings here—except to Jane. It's all she can see now that she has spotted it. To her, it glows incandescent. It looks like an album cover, maybe. Adam sits alone on a stool, a guitar in his arms. "The Secret Adventures of Adam & the Rib" is spray-painted in black across the top. She steps closer. In Adam's thought bubble are the words she saw through the magnifying glass back at her farmhouse: *2,400 miles was a long way to go for guitar lessons.* She reaches out to touch the poster and is disappointed at how cold it is. But what did she expect? For it to be warm, for it to feel alive?

What if someone else understands what this is? She looks around at the people in the alley. They sit at picnic tables, eating and talking, paying no attention to her or this painting. Her gaze becomes searching, but she stops herself. Elijah is not here. He can't be.

Can he?

"What do you think?" Hen says in a low voice, and Jane almost laughs. Such a simple question, with no simple answers.

"I'm not sure." Her voice is hoarse, the way it would get during the months of her life when she barely spoke to anyone. Her gaze returns to the art because it's all she wants to look at. She focuses on the smaller details now. There are tiny squares across the bottom—and these are in color. They are so small she has to crouch down to see them clearly.

The first square is a small painting of the Los Angeles coastline, a vista familiar to Jane. It's the view leading to Malibu, near where she and Elijah once lived. The painted shades are pastel, waxy, and out of focus. It reminds her of the way the smog in LA made everything look like a fuzzy scene out of an old movie.

The next tiny square features Adam and Rib standing on the board-walk in Venice Beach. He's lifting her by the waist, and she's laughing up at the sky, a champagne bottle dangling from her fingertips.

The third: Adam and Rib lying on a batik blanket, the pattern of it re-created with such perfect precision it takes her breath away. The couple is on a deck, under a star-strewn sky, fingers laced as they stare upward. "When our first album goes platinum, I'll buy this place for you," Adam says to Rib. "No matter what, we're keeping the car," Rib replies. And in the fourth square, Adam and Rib are in an orange convertible, driving away. Next, they're standing on a beach, at the top of a cliff, staring out to sea. Rib is in a white dress, Adam is in a suit. There are storm clouds on the horizon.

The final square is black as night, no stars, only stark white block let-ters: Find the last place we kissed.

"It's a clue, right?"

Jane is startled by Hen's voice. It suddenly feels wrong to have any-one with her at all—to have her memories laid out on a wall like this, too. She looks around, frantic, for a discarded can of paint. Something, anything, to cover it up with.

"This can't be here," she says, and she hears how scared she sounds.

"Hey, are you okay?"

Jane is not okay. She's panicking. It's so sudden—and it's always like this. She presses her hand against the wall as anxious thought eddies swirl in her mind. *I want him to be alive more than anything. But if it is him, if this is real, it means he did it on purpose. He left me alone, on purpose. He let me suffer all this time, and he could have done something. But he didn't.*

She tries again to breathe and hears herself gasp.

"Hey," Hen says. "It's okay. Try counting. *One, two, three* . . . breathe out—*one, two, three* . . . breathe in. Close your eyes." Jane squeezes her eyes shut against her tunneling vision. She listens to the teenage girl's voice, suddenly so mature and assured. Like she's done this many times before. "Now, open your eyes. Look around you. Tell me three things you can see."

"The brick wall," Jane says. "Snow on the ground over there. And . . ." She looks to the wall. "This poster."

Hen nods. "Now, name three sounds you can hear."

"Your voice. A bird. Someone talking, at that picnic table. A woman."

"Name three parts of your body."

"My feet. My hands. My legs."

A long pause.

"How do you feel?"

"Better," Jane says, and this is only true in that she can breathe again, and less true in that she is now embarrassed to have had a meltdown in front of a stranger. "How did you know what to do?"

"My mother has attacks like this," Hen says. "When she tries to leave the house."

"Oh." Jane feels a stab of pity.

"Why are you so afraid it might really be him?" Hen asks.

"It's not that," Jane says, but she's lying. She's terrified it might be him. But she's also terrified it might not be. She turns her back to the wall. "Thank you for showing me this. Let's go."

"Wait—that's it?"

"I appreciate you bringing me here, but I need to take you home."

Hen points down, toward the words: *Find the last place we kissed.* "This is a clue. Only you can find it."

"My lawyer will be in touch about the NDA."

"But you have to—"

"Hen, I know. But I have to do this alone. It's time for you to go home."

"No," Hen says, her voice as firm as the brick wall they're standing in front of. "No *way*. I won't sign anything." Her voice has grown loud and people are staring. "And I am not going home. Not yet."

Jane glances around. "Please, could you be discreet? If someone else finds out what this is—"

"I just want to know if it's him," Hen says in a quieter voice. "I think I deserve that, for leading you here."

"I can't risk this getting out."

"I have no one to tell."

"You couldn't even tell your best friend."

"I don't have a best friend." Hen lifts her chin, and again, Jane feels a stab of emotion.

"Your mother."

"She wouldn't understand. She's not well." Hen touches her fore-head, as if to indicate where her mother is not well—and Jane feels that stab of empathy again. Mothers are supposed to be the wind for your kite, your soft place to land if you need it. Jane never had that either—except, briefly, in Alice. This girl contains hurts Jane recognizes and some she doesn't. Some that are beyond her. But that doesn't matter, Jane tells herself. Everyone in the world has been damaged in some way. "I've kept this secret for months," Hen continues. "Why would I spill it now? I just want to *know*," she repeats. "I want to be part of this. Please."

Jane doesn't answer her. She turns back toward the poster.

"I think about it all the time, you know," Hen says after a moment. She's come to stand beside Jane. She's too close; Jane takes a step away. "How much he loved you. How everyone says you're so terrible—but you can't be that bad if he loved you as much as he did. He said in an interview once, that Barbara Walters one, that you were the reason he could sing. The reason he could be safe in the world. He said you were everything to him."

"The Barbara Walters interview," Jane repeats. "Which every fan said I forced him to do, wrote him answers on a script for. You don't believe that?"

A pause. "I never understood what the point of it would have been. So no, I guess I don't. I thought he was telling the truth. But no one wanted to believe any of it. It was weird. I did though."

Jane looks at her. "All of it?"

Hen nods. "All of it." She clears her throat. "I'm sorry I yelled at you like that yesterday. That wasn't fair."

Jane nods. "It's fine," she says. "You aren't the first."

"So?"

Jane knows she will probably regret this—but also that her life is full of regret. "Our last kiss was at the radio station, in front of the TV tower," she says. "Right before we left for the concert you were at. We were arguing—we argued a lot that day—and he kissed me, probably to try to get me to be quiet."

Hen's eyes light up. "The tower is just a few minutes away. We passed it on the way here."

"I know." Jane reaches forward, traces some of the letters on the poster with her finger. The *A*, the *R*. Their secret names—given to them by someone who only wanted to hurt them. But it took away the power. It could be Kim, Jane tells herself. He hates her enough to want to trick her. But he's also never been so nuanced in his revenge. She's not certain he would be capable of this. "So, we'll go there," she says. "We'll see if we can find anything—but then I'm taking you home. No matter what we find there. That's the deal. It has to be."

"Let's go, then," Hen says, and sets off down the alleyway. Jane notices she hasn't promised her anything as she looks over her shoulder and says, "You coming?"

"I just need a minute," Jane says. She bends down and looks at the squares across the bottom of the painting one last time. Her past, rendered in paint, plastered onto cold brick. And despite everything that happened, these memories still make her smile for the briefest of moments.

LOS ANGELES, CALIFORNIA

MARCH 1991

In Los Angeles, the coast stretched for miles, eventually disappearing into a smog that lent everything a vintage Hollywood glow, like a smear of Vaseline on a camera's lens. It never seemed to rain in California. Jane and Elijah found that sunny apartment, the one Jane had dreamed of. It was in Venice Beach, above a batik fabric store. They bought a bed with a cheap, uncomfortable mattress—but Jane covered it with pillows from Walgreens, the softest cotton sheets she could find, and a colorful spread with a mandala detail from the store downstairs. It was perfect.

"Are you happy?" Elijah asked her.

She smiled at him. "Is it even possible to be sad here? But, are you? I know it's still hard . . . you must think about your parents."

A sharp shake of his head. "I'm good. Really."

In the months since his parents' deaths, Jane and Elijah had scattered their ashes into the ocean inlet off the deck of the Olympia cabin—but the ashes had only turned to sludge in the water and sank. Jane had kept one of Alice's necklaces, a little gold circle on a chain. And she kept that tube of her lipstick, carried it with her everywhere. Elijah took some records and Alice's copy of *The Prophet*. Neither of them took anything that had belonged to Moses. They sold the cabin and the house. Elijah asked Jane to choose where they would go, and she said they should start with Los Angeles. They packed all their instruments and not much else. When his friends came to the door as they were packing everything up, Elijah didn't answer. Jane wondered if they would ever see any of them again.

One day, they locked up their Venice Beach apartment and headed for the sand, fingers linked, like always. They were on the lookout for bars and restaurants that had open mic nights or were hiring musicians. They stopped when they saw a place called the Sand Dollar. "I read about this café in the paper," Jane said. "A few bands have been discovered here."

Inside, the manager told them they could put their names on a list and come back that night for open mic. Later, Jane could tell Elijah was nervous. She didn't want to say, *Play the way you did that night at the Central*, because they almost never talked about that night. "Pretend we're in your basement, that it's just us," she said instead.

They began with "Dark Shine," but Elijah started off on the wrong key. Jane knew it and tried to overcompensate, and they sounded messy, amateurish. Then Elijah stopped playing and turned to Jane. "Let's just start over," he said, his mouth away from the mic but his words audible in the small café. Jane could have cried. Their first time playing at a bar in LA, and they were embarrassing themselves.

She took a breath, gritted her teeth, and bent over her bass as Elijah began the song again. It went better this time, but still, the audience was unmoved, barely paying them any attention, chatting and eating. Jane caught his eye, tried to telepath to him that he needed to play *the* song. He had given her the chords and the lyrics, but they had never played it again. Still, even though she had only heard it once, she knew it was great. But they hadn't named it, so she had no way to ask him to play it.

Instead, they played two others, "Watching Us" and "Six of Cups." It wasn't enough to get more than a smattering of claps as they left the stage.

They went back the next week and tried again. This time, Jane heard someone in the audience murmur, "I saw these two last week, *boooor-ing*," just before they were about to begin "Dark Shine." She could tell Elijah had also heard. He stopped, cleared his throat, stared down at his guitar. After a few beats of silence, he held his mouth too close to the mic and Jane wondered if the confident, wildly talented stage persona she had glimpsed had been just a one-night thing. Maybe he wasn't really a performer. Maybe the shock and grief had just brought it out in him.

"This, uh . . . this next song kind of means a lot to me," he said. No one in the audience was even looking at the stage, though.

The intro is too long, Jane thought as she strummed her bass along with him, playing the chords she had now memorized, to support his guitar melody. She wasn't remembering it right, maybe. Everything that night at the Central had been so sad, so heightened. This wasn't the same. It could never be. She had just imagined it being such a transcendent song.

When Elijah started to sing, a few people put down their forks. Glasses and bottles paused in front of mouths. *There's noise all around me, / I just want to sing. / Did you close your eyes, Mama? / Could you see everything?*

The words were heartrending to Jane because she knew what they meant. But somehow every person in the room seemed to understand how meaningful these words were too; Jane saw it in their faces. *Do you know it all now / have the answer we seek? / I think you'd tell me / that, baby, it's not so bleak . . .*

By the time the chorus arrived, Elijah had every single person in the room in the palm of his hand. *We're all gonna die . . .* They were rapt. He had done it again. Every song they played after that was met with loud applause.

The manager of the café came to them after their set. "We have a slot open on Sunday nights. Do you have enough material to fill an hour?"

"Absolutely," Jane said, and raced back to their apartment to write more songs while Elijah fell into bed, exhausted.

Later she went to check on him. "Are you alright?" she whispered. He didn't answer.

"Elijah, does the song have a name?" He still didn't speak. His breath was slow and even; he was sleeping.

She went back to the living room and wrote "My Life or Yours" in a notebook.

On their fourth Sunday at the Sand Dollar, Jane noticed it was more crowded than usual. On the fifth Sunday, people were being turned away at the door—and a tall woman approached after their set and gave them her card. **Petra Lakaois, Talent Manager**, it read in bold black font.

"Do you see that man sitting by the window?" she asked them. Jane and Elijah nodded. "He's a Columbia Records scout. And that man over there? He's from Virgin."

"Why are they here?" Elijah asked.

"Why do you think? Everyone's talking about the Lightning Bottles, the guy with the voice of . . . a fallen angel, I think they're saying—and his beautiful, guitar-playing wife."

Elijah laughed, ran his hand through his hair self-consciously, glanced at Jane, didn't correct Petra about the wife part. Jane felt glad. She was more than just a girlfriend. "You're kidding, right?" he said.

"What kind of joke would that be?" Petra had a frank way of speaking that Jane found appealing. "And it's not just your voice. You're both great musicians, and your songs are terrific. Especially the one with that chorus." She hums it, then sings, *We're all gonna die* . . . "What's it called?"

"We're calling it 'My Life or Yours,'" Jane said, glancing at Elijah.

"You two seem like you were born to play together. It's something very special."

Jane thought of all those months in Seattle, feeling like she was waiting for her real life to begin. And now, it was all starting to happen.

"You're going to get offers, and if you don't have someone who works for you, you could end up signing a bad deal. It happens way too much in this business."

"Offers," Jane repeated. "You mean for a recording deal?"

"That's exactly what I mean," Petra said. "Gerry over there, the guy from Virgin, he's going to tell you that guy sitting with him—his name is Brad Tarner-Dudley—wants to rep you."

"Tarner-Dudley reps a lot of bands," Elijah said, his eyes now wide. "I know that name, I've heard of him."

"He does. But he's a real dickhead."

Elijah laughed. "You don't sugarcoat stuff, do you?"

"Never." Jane liked Petra already. She could tell Elijah did too. "You can trust me." Like her words, her gaze was direct. "And that's impor- tant."

"Who else do you manage?" Jane asked.

She named a few other bands, and Elijah nodded appreciatively when she mentioned a dream pop trio he was a fan of. "I want this. I've been looking for someone like you two to prioritize. I see how great you could be, and I also see how much you love playing—how much you love play- ing *together*. It's really beautiful. A band like yours needs to be built care- fully."

"We want to do this forever," Jane said, trying to catch Elijah's eye.

"Exactly. And for that to happen, you'll need to make the right choices."

The man Petra had identified as being from Virgin had approached and was waiting behind Petra, clearing his throat and looking impatient. They arranged to meet her for lunch the next day.

"I can't . . . really believe any of that just happened," Elijah said later as they walked back to their Venice Beach apartment with their guitars slung across their backs. "*Two* scouts approached us. *Two* managers."

"Are you happy?" She thought of the way Kim always used to talk about scouts and industry people who never materialized. "I can't tell."

He rubbed his hand across the stubble on his chin. He was still Seattle-pale, even in LA. He stopped walking and looked down at her. "It's just . . . that song, Jane. It takes a lot out of me to sing. It makes me feel pretty terrible. And I'm afraid I'm stuck with it."

She looked at him closely. "The chorus," she said. "Where did that come from? It scares me a little. It makes me think maybe you *want* to do drugs."

"See, that's why I don't like it." There was frustration in his voice. "That was the worst night. I wanted a lot of things—and I had lost so much. And doesn't it bother you, Jane, that no one ever talks about the other songs?"

"No. It's a really good song," she said with a shrug. "It is, and you know it. And I'll be there, every time you sing it. No matter what, I'll be beside you."

His eyes were still troubled, but he nodded. "Maybe it'll be okay."

"This isn't Seattle," she said. "We're long gone from there. We're different here. Better off—safer. I promise."

"I'm sorry," he said, shaking his head. "Things are getting exciting for us, and I'm ruining it. We should be celebrating." He leaned down and kissed her, then grabbed her hand and pulled her toward a liquor store on the corner.

Inside, he selected a bottle of champagne from a shelf; he had turned twenty-one in March. "To toast our impending record deal—because when something really great happens, you have to toast with champagne. Or it's bad luck."

Jane laughed. She'd never had champagne before—and they hadn't had any alcohol to drink since what happened with his parents. But this was different. *Not* Seattle, she reminded herself. He popped the bottle open on the street, and they drank the champagne as they walked back toward the beach, their apartment. The bubbles went straight to her head and seemed to intensify her happiness. They were almost home when he dropped the empty bottle into a trash basket, picked her up by the waist, and swung her around while she laughed even more, lightly drunk and very happy.

"This isn't Seattle!" he shouted, while passersby stared, some smiling, some perhaps sensing a special thing about these two.

He put her down, and they sidestepped a woman on the boardwalk ahead of them. She smelled sharp, of alcohol and maybe urine, and was muttering to herself about an audition. Her feet were bare and dirty, and her eyes were hollow and sad. Jane felt a shiver of something dark as she looked at her—some kind of recognition. But nothing bad was ever going to happen to them, Jane told herself, looking away from the woman. Because the worst had already happened. Their future was bright.

Within a month of Jane and Elijah meeting Petra at the Sand Dollar and signing her as their manager, the Lightning Bottles received three recording offers: from Columbia, Virgin, and Geffen. They settled on Columbia because the executives were the most flexible on creative control, which was so important to Elijah it worried Jane a little. If he had creative control, could he cut "My Life or Yours"?

Petra set to work negotiating a deal she said would protect them the most. She lowered the initial advance on royalties amount, explaining, "I know taking less money seems counterintuitive, but it's risky to get too much up front from a record company in case your first album underperforms and they simply drop you to recoup their costs." She also negotiated a fifty / fifty deal on any secondary income and foreign deals— and then the Lightning Bottles were offered separate, smaller deals from Columbia Records affiliates in the UK and Sony in Germany.

Once the deal terms were finalized, it was time to choose a producer for their debut album.

"You're going to be one of the jewels in the Columbia Records crown, once your album is recorded and released," Alan Brosnahan, the president of Columbia Records, told them during a meeting. He had sterling-silver hair and eyes to match. His lips were thin and his smile was always tight and quick, as if he had a dozen other things he needed to be doing. But at that moment he sat at the head of a boardroom table they were growing familiar with and stretched his arms behind his head, totally relaxed as he gazed at Jane and Elijah like they were prized livestock he had just acquired. It made Jane uncomfortable. She wanted to get this part over with so they could get into the studio, where she hoped she'd feel more at home. "So, let's get to work picking the best producer we can find. They're all waiting for you in the lobby."

That day, the Lightning Bottles met Bob Rock, William Orbit, Steve Albini, Nigel Godrich, Butch Vig. At one point, Elijah asked if they'd be meeting with any female record producers, and Alan cleared his throat and said, "None that are available at the moment, no." They were told by these producers that their sound was polished and groundbreaking, transformative and transcendent. Absolutely unique. There was a lot of talk about the indie scene, which, technically, the Lightning Bottles had never been a part of. It didn't matter. They personified it, somehow. They were exactly what everyone in 1991 wanted. In the end, they chose Hamlet Garvin to produce their debut. Garvin had worked on some of their favorite albums. "Plus, he seemed like a down-to-earth guy, didn't he?" Elijah asked. "We can be ourselves around him. Right?"

Jane wondered if Hamlet only seemed down-to-earth because he told people to call him Ham and because he had crumbs in his beard. She was getting the sense that while in Seattle it had been important to act disaffected, like you cared less than you did; in LA, everyone acted like they cared *more* than they did. People became who you wanted them to be when they were in a room with you. But Jane didn't want to press too hard on all this—she just wanted the process to keep moving forward, to start recording the album, and get to what she was sure was the good part. An album, a tour. The world hearing her songs and Elijah's incredible voice singing them. The dream.

During another meeting, a few weeks later, this one with Alan, Ham, and a group of marketing executives, they were asked about their creative process.

Elijah grinned at this question. This grin was still new. The showman, the side of himself he showed to most of the people in this new world, was an act and she knew it. He was a chameleon, adapting here. And she found she didn't mind. They had been warned a few times now about the perils of fame, but if they created personas, what would the danger be? Jane wasn't sure what her persona would be yet, but thought maybe she would just be what she had always wanted: a serious musician who owed no one anything. "My girl's the creative genius," Elijah was saying. "I'm just the voice."

As everyone in the room turned to stare at her, skeptical expressions on their faces, Jane felt her cheeks grow warm. "Well," she found herself mumbling. "I mean, Elijah wrote 'My Life or Yours.' It's our best song."

"Jane, why would you say that? I couldn't have written it without her," Elijah said. "I never would have had the guts."

Alan was watching them both closely. He tilted his head.

"Elijah, I wonder if you might want to keep that to yourself—that Jane writes most of the music, the lyrics? It's impressive, of course." But his smile was strained. "Except in the rock world there's a sort of . . ." He trailed off. "I guess 'machismo' is the right word. This can't be a surprise to you two, right? Guys aren't gonna want to be screaming lyrics while head-banging in their pickup trucks to songs that were written by a woman."

"We don't care about those guys," Elijah said, dismissive. "The headbanging-in-trucks guys are not our target audience."

"Those guys buy a lot of albums," Alan said, his tone light but his expression steel. "We do tend to like to cater to them."

Elijah frowned. "We're more serious than that," he said.

"Yes, well, real serious artists guard their process," Alan said. "Right, Ham?"

"Oh, sure," Ham said, nodding sagely. He generally spoke directly to Elijah, rarely even looking Jane's way. And suddenly Jane felt like the girl in the basement again. But she wasn't, she reminded herself. This was *her* band, too. She forced herself to stop shrinking, pressed back her shoulders, sat up straight. Alan looked at her, but then away. No one else did. "You can say and do one thing, be one thing in the public eye, and let the background be completely different. And Alan is right—we don't want there to be any issues straight out of the gate. But don't sweat it right now, Elijah. We'll figure it out. For now, let's just make a great fuckin' album, right?" He nudged Elijah with his shoulder, slapped him on the back. Jane felt like an observer, like she wasn't even in the room.

That same week, their advance money came in and they went to dinner with Petra to celebrate. "Do we need, like, a financial adviser or something?" Jane asked her. Petra was starting to feel like the only person, other than Elijah, she could really talk to.

"Don't forget you have to save some of that money to pay for the record," Petra said. "And your video for your first single."

"What if we don't want to make a video?" Elijah asked, signaling the waiter for more champagne. Recently, every day seemed to hold a reason to celebrate, and they were drinking a lot of it. "I can't imagine us on MTV along with Madonna and Michael Jackson, really. It seems a bit weird."

"Alan will have other ideas," Petra said. "Your creative control clause doesn't mean you get to opt out of a video. Meanwhile, my advice is: caution. If you want a house, for example, rent, don't buy."

"We love where we live," Jane said. "We don't need a new place."

"Maybe a cool car though," Elijah said with a smile.

Jane laughed. "You don't even drive."

"I know, but how great would it be to be driven around in a convertible by the most beautiful woman in town?" He squeezed her thigh and pulled her close.

"Enjoy your new life," Petra said. "But stay grounded, okay? You have each other. You're luckier than most." There was a note of caution in everything she said to them during those early days.

It was a time, especially from the inside, when the industry felt like it was shape-shifting. There was a groundswell of alternative music that didn't fit into any of the current musical molds. Independent artists were snapped up by the major labels as tastes moved from slickly packaged pop to something grittier. The consensus, Petra told them, was that the Lightning Bottles would ensure Columbia was ahead of the new, unconventional trend—even if it was a trend that was proving difficult to pin down. Geffen had Heaven Wretch, their friend Zack's band, and there was a lot of buzz about them. Their album would be out soon, and Petra suggested the public's reaction could serve as the harbinger of what might be to come for Jane and Elijah.

One night, after Jane and Elijah made love on their cheap, uncomfortable bed, they brought their mandala blanket down the boardwalk to the beach and watched the stars come out. Then they heard the sound of someone a few feet away, urinating on the sand. As the sharp smell reached their nostrils, Elijah said, "It might be nice to live in a beach house. And not have to walk to the beach? I mean, we have the money now from the advance. Even with what we need for the album and video, if we do one, and the money for Petra, we have enough. Plus what we have in the bank." *From my parents.* He always left that unsaid. From the sales of the properties they had owned, from what they had left behind for their son. Jane had tried to encourage him to talk about his parents, for a while. But he never wanted to. "I know we love our place but . . ."

"But you're right," Jane said. "We'll do what Petra advised—rent, not buy. Let's start looking for a house." She felt something brush against her consciousness then, a tingle of unease. There had been a time she had told herself the sunny apartment of her dreams with Elijah was all she wanted in the world. Now, her world felt like it was full of moving targets, her dreams becoming elusive now that she was living them.

A few days later, Petra introduced them to a real estate agent who took them to see a house in Malibu that had apparently once belonged to Joan Didion. They signed the lease on the spot and moved in their belongings—a few bags of clothes, some books and albums, their instruments.

When Jane went into the bedroom, she saw a piece of paper tacked to the wall beside the bed's headboard. She saw that it was one of Elijah's drawings, a title scrawled across the top. *The Secret Adventures of Adam & the Rib.* She laughed aloud at this—it was clever. It was how everyone treated her—what Kim had once called her, too. But it made her feel good that Elijah could make something beautiful out of it. It took the sting away. *Someone* saw her, knew her, loved her—and he was the only person who mattered right now. And anyway, soon they would have an album out and other people would see her too. She knew it.

In the drawing, they were lying in their new bed, talking.

"When our first record goes gold, we'll buy this place," the Adam character said. "When we play our first sold-out show at Madison Square Garden, we'll stay at the Ritz. I'll fill the tub with champagne for you."

"No matter how rich and famous we get, we'll keep the Impala, though." Jane's smile widened even more as she read this. They both loved the car they had just purchased, a vintage burnt-orange convertible that gave a rude cough when she started it. Elijah said it sounded like Tony Iommi at the beginning of Black Sabbath's "Sweet Leaf," that the car had its own personality. They were always driving off into sunsets together. Increasingly, Seattle felt as far away as another galaxy, another lifetime. *This* was what Jane had wanted, she reminded herself. She didn't need to keep wanting more and more—even the heights of fame here in this drawing, they didn't actually need all that. And Elijah's drawing was a reminder of that—of who they had been back when they first found each other. They were still those people on that piece of paper. They always would be.

On their third week at Sunset Sound, as the album slowly took shape, Ham suggested hiring session musicians to expedite the process. "Given how excited Alan and the rest of the label are about the album, you want to get it out there. Before the next shiny toy comes along."

"We like to record all our own instruments," Jane said. "That's how we've always done it. It's important to us. And it won't take that much extra time just to do it ourselves."

Ham chuckled at this, like an indulgent parent. "Yeah, I'm sure it won't take extra time to do all the work yourselves, honey. Right." He turned away, and his linebacker frame blocked Elijah from Jane's view as he spoke to him.

"I know a great drummer who could take some of the heat off you, Elijah, man. I know you think you can do it all, but you're new at this. And newbies are always trying to be heroes. You'll burn out. We need to keep you limber, preserve that voice. When you sing on this album, I want you to be at a hundred percent. A thousand. You're the everything here. The golden ticket."

"I'm not the golden ticket," he said. "That's dumb. Jane and I are a team, and we do all our own instrumentation. Give us a chance to do it the way we always have. Hold off on the session musicians for now."

Ham stood. "Whatever you say, boss." But he gave Jane a hard look as he left the room—as if somehow it was her fault he hadn't gotten what he wanted.

A few more weeks into the recording process, Elijah had an all-day doctor's appointment—the label was giving them physicals, making sure they were in prime condition for whatever lay ahead—and Jane came into the studio on her own to rerecord a bass track she hadn't been happy with from the day before. There was a little envelope in her guitar case, and she opened it to find a drawing from Elijah, of her sitting on a stool with her guitar, music notes flowing around her. You're going to nail it. Love you, E. She tucked the paper into her pocket as Ham arrived, an irritated expression on his face already. She knew he'd been hoping to take the day off.

After the first time she rerecorded the track, he said, "Okay, are we good?"

"You didn't even play it back."

"That's because it was fine when we did it yesterday."

"I'd like to try it again, please. I'll tell you when it's right."

After lunch, she arrived back in the recording room to find Ian Munroe, one of the label vice presidents, sitting with Ham at the controls. "Dark Shine" was playing—but it didn't sound right to Jane.

"Is something the matter with the speaker?" she asked.

Ham turned up the volume and shushed her.

"Incredible," Ian said when it was over. "Gritty. Real. I can see why everyone is so excited about this."

"But that's not how it sounded yesterday," Jane interjected. "It's all wrong."

"It's different, I know. I mixed it to sound that way," Ham said, delivering his words in an exaggeratedly slow manner, as if speaking to someone he considered unintelligent. "There's a lot of buzz right now about the Seattle sound, and we want to capitalize on that."

"But we don't want to have the 'Seattle sound.' We want to have *our* sound."

"You're *from* Seattle though, right?"

"Well, I'm not. I'm Canadian. And we're not grunge," Jane said. "We don't even really understand what that is."

Ham laughed at her. "Honey, you aren't anyone." Then he checked his watch. "Late lunch?" he said to Ian.

Jane waited hours for Ham to return. But eventually she knew he was done for the day. All she could do was give up and go home.

"Okay, go. Sell yourself to me."

Jane couldn't even remember whose party it was, whose Beverly Hills mansion they were at this time, or why she had thought it was so important to come here at all. It was June, and despite Ham's doubt that they could record all the instruments themselves, the Lightning Bottles had finished recording their self-titled debut album. The album was in post-production now—and Alan, the label's president, had explained their work was actually just beginning. It was now time for Jane and Elijah to get out and meet people in the industry. It was going to be fun, he insisted. But weeks later, all Jane felt was tired of it. She was holding out hope that they would meet interesting new people who would widen their circle. People to talk about music with and maybe even collaborate with in the future—only what it really felt like was her long nights waiting alone in a BBS chat room. No one interesting showed up.

"Excuse me?" she said to the man who had cornered her. He was wearing a leather motorcycle jacket with no shirt underneath. A surfboard with a shark bite out of it was tattooed across his chest. The only good thing about the conversation was that he had a bottle of champagne in his hand and kept refilling her glass. "Who *are* you?" she asked him.

His expression soured. "This is my house," he said. "I'm Lynden Axworthy. Manager of Blip 99? The Quarterbacks? Jaymee Steele? And now, the Marvel Boys. Heard of them?"

She couldn't tell if he was being sarcastic or not. "No clue. Nope." She backed away, spotted Ham alone by an outdoor fountain, draining a tumbler.

"Hey, have you seen Elijah? Or Petra?"

He staggered to the side at the sound of her voice, then peered at her with bleary eyes. "Petra, huh?" He spit a piece of ice on the ground and she stepped back, repulsed as his spittle sprayed her arm. "You know she's some sort of dyke, right?" He looked triumphant, as if he had just delivered information Jane didn't already know.

In the platform combat boots she was wearing, Jane was at least an inch taller than Ham. She looked down at him and said, "Yeah, and she has an awesome girlfriend. People do a lot of things to hurt other people, and themselves. Petra choosing to be who she is and love who she loves isn't hurting anyone. Now, excuse me, I just need to go find—"

"You're a real bitch." The hatred in his words stunned her into silence, froze her in place. "You know that, right? Everyone thinks so. You're so fucking *pushy*."

"That's not true. I'm doing my job. The album is important."

She made to turn away from him but he reached up and took her shoulder in his stubby fingers. His hand was warm, nauseatingly damp. "Elijah went into the pool house with the guys from the Waverunners and their groupies, sweetheart." The Waverunners were a popular surf rock band. "You're right about one thing, Jane Pyre." The way he said her name made it sound as fake as it was. She pulled back, shrugged his hand away. "People do a shitload of things to hurt themselves, especially in this fuckin' town. So you'd better keep a closer eye on the poor guy. We're trying to release an album, and you're right." He made his voice high, as if trying to imitate her. "*It's important.*"

Then he lurched away and Jane stood still, absorbing his cruel words, delivered with such casual ease. *Everyone thinks you're a real bitch.* She hoped he was wrong about that, but she knew he was right about one thing: they *were* trying to release an album. And she had lost track of Elijah.

Her eyes swept her surroundings, looking for the pool house. She saw a long, low structure with lit-up windows and walked toward it, heart racing. *You'd better keep a closer eye on the poor guy,* Ham had said. This was part of her job—to take care of him. She had promised, the night his parents died. Sometimes it felt to her as if she had promised Alice herself.

She pushed open the pool house door, calling out his name. The lights were glaringly bright, and there was an acrid, chemical smell in the air. A young woman sitting on the couch was holding a blue glass pipe to her lips. She stared at Jane with wide eyes, her pupils like black holes.

Jane recoiled. "Have you seen Elijah Hart?"

Some of the members of the Waverunners were throwing a basketball at a wall-mounted net in one corner. Their eyes were as vacuous as the young woman's. "Yeah, he was here, I think," one of them said, frenetically dribbling the ball, throwing it to his bandmate, who threw it back fast, bounced up and down on his heels.

"He was, but he left," said another guy. "Yeah. Yeah." Then he laughed at nothing and Jane left, slamming the door behind her.

"Idiots," she muttered. She finally found Elijah in a home theatere buried in the bowels of the house, watching a movie about deep-sea diving on the huge screen. His eyes were half-closed as he reclined, oblivious to Jane's entrance. She stood still, watching him. Eventually, he turned his head and smiled to see her.

"Hey! There you are!" His words were slurred. "I was so bored I came down here. Just me and my friend Stoli here." He lifted up a vodka bottle, took a swig. "*Nashykh mam*. I just learned that from some pretentious guy upstairs." He waved a hand in the direction of the party. "It means 'to our mothers.'"

"I was looking for you everywhere," Jane said.

"I hate these parties," he said. "All the posturing and fakery."

"Ham told me you were in the pool house, with the guys from the Waverunners."

"Yeah, for like a minute. Those guys are meth heads." Elijah laughed, until he saw her face. "Jane. What's wrong?"

"You'd never do that, would you?"

"Jesus, Jane, no. I would never do meth. Come on. Come here. Sit down with me."

"I just want to go home. I don't want to be here anymore."

He looked at her more closely. "Did something happen?"

She hesitated. "Ham . . . he wasn't all that nice."

"What did he say to you?"

"It's fine. I just want to forget it. But I want to leave."

He stood. "Okay, sure, you don't have to ask me twice. Let's get out of here, go home and listen to music and make out." He grinned, and despite her bleak mood, she smiled back.

But as they walked up the basement stairs and into the front entrance area of the house, Jane heard a familiar voice that made her freeze. Kim, John, and Ari, and their new drummer—a guy who went by the name of Git, for no discernable reason—were being ushered through the front door by a clearly excited Lynden.

"Shit," Elijah muttered. "I heard they signed with Geffen, but . . ."

"They did?" This was news to Jane. "Where did you hear that? I just thought they had a manager now." She gritted her teeth as Kim's voice rang out. He had spotted them.

"*Brother!*" he called out. "Old buddy, old pal! The man with the voice of an angel!" He spoke in a breathy falsetto, laughed as if he had just told a hilarious joke. Then his gaze flicked over to Jane. "And the devil herself. The rib bone, still hanging around."

Petra had materialized; she slid her arm into Jane's.

"You all know one another, then," said Lynden, shooting a judgmental little frown at Jane.

"They were just leaving," Petra said.

Lynden was holding yet another bottle of champagne. As he popped the cork, some of it sprayed on Jane and she was reminded of Ham spitting out his ice. She just wanted to go home, take a long, hot shower, and never, ever go to one of these parties again. But Kim was still watching her. He laughed at her stricken expression, grabbed the champagne bottle, and held it up. "You're not gonna stick around and celebrate with us? We just signed a deal with Geffen. We're gonna be rock stars too. We're selling out right along with you. Guess you two led the way."

"Good for you guys," Elijah said. "Congrats, Ari. John." Ari and John nodded uncomfortably.

"Congrats to you guys too," Ari said in a low voice.

"Okay, let's go," Petra said. "Are you two alright?" she asked when they were outside. "That seemed really tense. I guess there's bad blood between you, being former bandmates and all. It didn't end well?"

Elijah shrugged, but Jane knew he was rattled. "Just a lot of water under that particular bridge," he said.

"Of course." Petra glanced back at the house. "From now on I'll make sure we know in advance if they're going to be at any of the parties or events you go to, okay?"

"Sounds good, Petra." Their car had arrived. When they were settled into the back, Jane realized Elijah had brought the bottle of vodka with him.

"Want some?" he asked her. She shook her head. He drank it in silence and looked out the window as they left Bel Air behind. His silence made her think of the way Moses had been when he drank.

The bottle was empty by the time they got back to Malibu—and Jane felt empty, too.

The next morning, Jane told Elijah what Ham had said to her at the party. He was hungover, tense and moody. But still, he picked up the phone immediately. "Elijah, no, what are you doing?"

"Fuck this. I'm calling Alan."

"Please, don't. We're so close to being done with the album. Just leave it. I needed to tell you, that's all." What she had wanted was for him to say it was okay, that no one else thought she was who Ham had said she was—not to try to fix it. She knew, deep down, the problem Ham had named couldn't really be fixed.

But Elijah already had Alan on the phone.

"You sure you can't just grin and bear it, Jane?" Alan said, his voice crackling over the speakerphone. "The album is *so* close to being done."

"That's exactly what I sai—"

But Elijah interrupted her. "No. We're done with him. I mean it, Alan."

By the end of the call, they were getting a new producer to finish off the album—and Jane had the sense she had made a new enemy in Alan. She tried to shake it off, but even weeks after the scene with Ham and his subsequent firing, she couldn't let go of the word he had called her. She could feel it like a tattoo. *Bitch.* So damning. It could become a brand so easily. All you had to do was defend yourself, defend someone you respected, hold back a smile, not laugh at the right joke. And with Kim in LA now too, she had a feeling her reputation was just going to get worse.

But when they found a new producer named Ricky Washington to help them finish the album, things began to look up again. Ricky had produced the Disintegration, one of their favorite bands, and had a reputation for coming into projects late and turning them around.

There was still a lot of talk about the "Seattle sound," but Ricky agreed that they should shine in their own way. "I don't want to add to you," Ricky said as he mixed. "If anything, your sound needs to be stripped down *more*, so it can become as big as it should be. You don't need any sound gimmicks—that voice of Elijah's is going to do all the work for you." He turned to Jane. "And your lyrics are stunning, all of them. Poetry. I know it's not public knowledge that they're yours—but they're really good. Different. No macho bullshit."

She glowed with pride at his compliment and stopped regretting the fallout with Ham. Everything was working out the way it needed to.

"Rumor has it you aren't easy to work with, Jane," Ricky said to her one afternoon in the studio, as they were nearing the album's completion, mixing and finalizing the last song. His British accent softened the comment, yet it still sent a chill through Jane. "But I quite like you."

Something twisted inside her at his words. *Rumor has it.* But she lifted her chin and smiled at him. "People like you are the only ones who matter to me, Ricky," she said, and tried to convince herself this was really true—that she could choose who mattered most to her and build walls to keep all the others out.

LOS ANGELES, CALIFORNIA

AUGUST 1991

Later in the summer of 1991, their album complete now, the Lightning Bottles were slotted into an industry showcase at Sin-é, a tiny café in New York City's East Village that was known for breaking out alternative musical acts.

After the Sin-é show, a bootleg of "Dark Shine" that had been recorded that night by the sound tech surfaced. That was when talk circulating about the Lightning Bottles and Elijah Hart's haunting, otherwordly voice became more than just hearsay.

In August, Jane and Elijah played another showcase at a record store in Santa Monica called Danny's. When they pulled up in their burnt-orange Impala, there were a few dozen people gathered outside in the parking lot—and to her surprise, and Elijah's, most of them asked for autographs. They pulled scraps of paper from their wallets, smoothed receipts against their hands. "I don't even have a pen," Elijah said with a laugh, as someone produced a Sharpie.

"Dark Shine" was then put on an industry compilation released by Columbia that started getting play on various influential college radio stations. At their next record store showcase, a security guard positioned outside the store rushed over to guide them inside when they arrived. "Here they are, the next big thing," the record store owner proclaimed.

That September, Jane and Elijah were on their way home from a planning meeting at the label when a song they recognized came on the radio.

"Hey, wait." Elijah turned up the volume; the radio DJ spoke urgently, excitedly, over the song's opening bars. *Here's the Seattle grunge band everyone is talking about . . .*

The song was "Seems Like We're Golden" by Heaven Wretch. Jane remembered the tune from some of the club shows the Marvel Boys had played with the band. Zack's raspy, growling voice, the jarring yet strangely sweet melody. It made Jane feel nostalgic for a place she was sure she had never even been, and also had a relentless drumbeat, a race car engine of a guitar tune, an all-consuming underpinning of a bassline.

"Zack's voice," Jane said. "It feels like a giant shrug and a punch in the face at the same time."

"Yeah." Elijah nodded his head to the beat. "Man. *That* is a good fucking song."

After that, the Heaven Wretch song was everywhere. It was called the theme song of an apathetic generation. *Seems like we're golden, and we couldn't care less*, sang Zack. He sounded so angry, but also like he couldn't give a shit about anything. It was, Jane had to admit, very Seattle. But not in a bad way.

As predicted, Seattle became ground zero for what everyone, inside the recording industry and out of it, called a musical revolution—and Jane couldn't believe it.

"Zack isn't even from Seattle, you know," Elijah told her. "He lived in Aberdeen." But none of that mattered.

"He must be so thrilled," Jane said. But in interviews and paparazzi photos they later saw, Zack actually appeared befuddled, slightly alarmed. He looked small in his many layers of clothing, which were so unnecessary in LA, but which he wore nonetheless. Plaid shirts and long johns that teens everywhere soon adopted as their uniform, too.

The tone in the planning meetings about the Lightning Bottles' debut album started to shift even more. Heaven Wretch was brought up constantly.

"I'm not going to jump all over the stage," Elijah said. "Wreck our instruments."

There were rumors that Zack and the rest of the band partied hard, were into heavy drugs. They were known for destroying the stage after their shows, had even done so on a live television comedy variety show. Instead of finding it strange or off-putting, the public just couldn't get enough of it.

"That's not us," Jane agreed.

"*Can* it be you, though?" Alan asked.

"Is that a rhetorical question?" Elijah snapped.

The meeting had been arranged to discuss the direction of their music video for their debut single, but it got derailed again when Elijah and Alan disagreed on what the single for the video was going to be.

"'Dark Shine,'" Elijah said.

Alan spoke over him. "'My Life or Yours.'"

"It can't be that one," Elijah said.

"Your girlfriend doesn't look so sure." He turned to Jane. "That's what I like about you, Janie." She gritted her teeth at the unwanted nickname. "I can read the thoughts on that gorgeous face of yours. And frankly, you look pissed."

But suddenly, despite her annoyance, Jane felt torn between loyalty to Elijah and the truth, which was that she *was* pissed. While she knew the song was an emotional one for him, it was a powerful song. A song that got noticed. It more than made sense for it to be their lead single if they wanted the album to chart. Alan held her gaze for a moment, his expression calculating. "Unless you'd rather it be one of *yours*." The way he said "yours" made her cringe inside. It had somehow become a source of shame, her songwriting.

"Of course not," she said.

"Jane, no. He's right—one of your songs needs to be our lead single," Elijah said.

"Could you *please* stop calling them mine? The songs—they've always felt like ours, anyway. I write them for you—for your voice. And we can't even tell anyone I wrote them, so maybe you need to get used to talking about them in a different way." She heard how loud her voice was in the room, heard Ham's voice in her head. *Everyone thinks you're a real bitch.* She tried to tone it down. "It's not about what's mine or yours. It's about what's right for the album. You see that, don't you?"

"Jane," Elijah said in a low voice. She knew he was worried about the way the song made him feel, she *knew* that—and she also knew she had promised to protect him. But this was everything they had ever wanted, in their grasp. She let out a frustrated sigh.

"Listen," Petra interjected. "I know 'My Life or Yours' is compelling as the lead single, but this is not the kind of album that will hinge on one song. Maybe we can brainstorm for a bit, then regroup and talk about this tomorrow?"

Alan shook his head. "I'm going to New York tomorrow. We're sorting this out today."

The two men stared at each other across the boardroom table, and Jane could almost feel the tension crackling.

And then, all at once: "Fine," Alan said, leaning back. "'Dark Shine' can be the first single. I have two conditions, though. 'My Life or Yours' is not a B-side. You can't do that to me, and I have a feeling you're going to try." Jane nodded and looked away; she would have put money on that being Elijah's next move, too, actually.

"What's the other condition?" Elijah asked, his tone flat.

"I want the video to be styled like a live concert. We'll do a Lightning Bottles set at an LA club—the Roxy, somewhere like that; the team will sort it out. We'll recruit fans for the video there and then do it all again."

"Fans?" Elijah repeated. "We don't have fans. No one knows who we are."

"First of all, that's not exactly true. People are talking about you. A lot. And second, this is LA; people will show up to anything they think is an audition—".

"We don't want to play to fake fans—"

Alan held up his hand. "They'll be your true fans by the time the show is over. Especially when you *play the fucking song.*"

Elijah stood up. "No," he said. "You can't do that. Show me on our contract where it says you get to dictate our set list during our live shows."

Alan stood too, making Jane feel small and insignificant in her seat. "It's not in the contract," he said. "But it is in your best interests."

Jane felt two things at once: a sense of foreboding and also an unsettling, almost disloyal sense of excitement. Elijah could fight this all he wanted. This obstinance was surely left over from their days in Seattle, when you were supposed to succeed by making it look like you didn't want to. It would pass, he'd get over it. He had to. Because they were not in control of their destiny—not exactly, not anymore. But those who *were* in control were making exciting plans for them—plans like a show at the Roxy. A music video. Buzz. All this was the dream. And Elijah would start to understand that soon. Once the album was out, he would stop acting like this wasn't really what he wanted. Because who wouldn't want all this?

Jane and Elijah pulled up to the Roxy in their Impala to find a lineup of potential audience members already snaking around the building. "They're not really here for us," Elijah said, frowning and looking away. "They're only here because the label is recruiting them."

Jane turned off the engine. They sat in silence as it cooled and ticked. "But they *are* here for us, Elijah. And I don't understand why you're so resentful." She had been gazing out the windshield, but now she turned to him. "Why are you starting to act like you don't want this, now that it really might happen?"

He rubbed at his jaw with the palm of his hand; the sunlight caught the stubble on cheeks he hadn't bothered to shave for the performance— or maybe it had been on purpose. "It's not that I don't want this, it's just—" He reached out and touched her cheek, ran his finger across its smoothness. "I'm scared, I guess. Because . . . what if the album comes out with all this fanfare, but no one likes it?" She raised her hand to his, held it against her face, felt the warmth of his fingers.

"Remember how scared you were before I came to Seattle?" He nodded. "You're doing it again. And you don't have to. Of course people are going to love you. The way *I* love you."

"You love me?" He tilted his head and smiled.

"Of course I do."

Then he took his hand away from hers and reached into the pocket of his leather jacket. He pulled out a little baggie and held it up. She recognized magic mushrooms; there were little stems and bits in the baggie that looked like dirt. "You don't need those," she said quickly.

"It's not a big deal. Really. I used to take 'shrooms before every Marvel Boys show—and the truth is, I don't really know how I'll feel performing sober. Maybe that's part of what I'm afraid of too."

"That was different. You were a drummer. You're singing today. You shouldn't be *on* anything."

"Yeah, but what if I freeze? What if I can't do it?"

"What if you do that and then you want something stronger?"

"Jane. Try to relax about this. Your mom, your church, the way you were raised, it made you afraid of *everything*. But none of this is dangerous." She didn't say anything. "It's just a plant," he said. "But if it upsets you, I won't."

"It's fine," she said. "Go ahead. You're right. I'm making too big of a deal out of it."

Inside, the Roxy was a hive of activity. Everyone moved around them with a sense of urgency. Jane was hustled off to hair and makeup, but she wiped away the red lipstick they put on her and replaced it with the maroon-purple shade from the little golden tube that had belonged to Alice. Soon she would have nothing left of it. But still she swiped on more, deepened the shade until she felt like she was wearing armor.

On the stage, techs buzzed around them, adjusting their mics. Sound techs made final adjustments to instruments and amps. Then it was just the two of them in front of a crowd of strangers. Elijah sat beside her on a stool, a mic in front of him and a special percussion pedal near his feet. Jane held her bass, already feeling hot under the lights.

The moment Elijah's voice vibrated through the air, though, Jane knew it didn't matter if this crowd of fans had been recruited or not. They really did love him. When "Dark Shine" ended, Jane looked out at the crowd and met the eyes of a woman in the front row who had been dancing wildly to the song, her arms above her head. She froze when Jane looked at her. Her eyes grew wide and she turned to her friend. Jane could see the words *She was looking at me, she was looking at me!* form on her lips. It felt so good to provoke that reaction in a stranger.

There was a long silence before "My Life or Yours," but then Elijah let out a little whoop and started to play. As he sang the chorus, he shook his head and howled at the stage lights as if they were the moon. His voice was at its best. It made her think of the first time she heard it, when he sent her the tape in the mail. *We're all gonna die*, he cried out. In the audience, hands raised above heads like they were in an Evangelical church. The crowd sang along to the simple chorus lyrics like nothing else mattered. *We're all gonna die . . .*

A shrug of his shoulders, and then Elijah turned it into an offering to his people. He had been there, he had seen it, he was there to say it wasn't that bad. He was promising them everything would be okay, just the way she always promised him that. *Might was well alllllllll just get high.* She found herself harmonizing, joining in with her own voice, almost as if she had been moved to do so by something beyond her control. She understood that every moment of her life so far had been leading up to this one, and the next one. The next. It was all about what was next. She had listened to music, gone to concerts, played songs with Elijah in his basement, recorded them in a studio, waited, and waited, and waited—but now *they* were the music. They were everything she had ever wanted to be. Because of his song. God, she loved this man on the stage beside her.

When the song ended, there was a moment of stunned silence. Then cheers came at them like a tidal wave, lifting her off her feet. Wait, no, it wasn't a tidal wave, it was her partner, her love, his hands on her waist, spinning her around, kissing her, putting her down, and grinning at her before pulling her to the edge of the stage where they stood together, clasping hands and bowing theatrically.

Jane let her eyes roam the crowd, taking in row after row of cheering new fans, until she reached the back—which was when she spotted Kim Beard. He was illuminated, made devilish, by the red of an exit sign. But then she blinked and he was gone.

BERLIN, GERMANY

DECEMBER 19, 1999

It's easy to find, now that they're looking for it. Jane and Hen had walked past it earlier that day but hadn't noticed it: a poster made to look like a concert handbill, glued to the metal of a *Berliner Zeitung* newspaper box in front of Berlin's iconic TV tower, on the sidewalk in what is almost the exact spot, Jane is sure, where she and Elijah pulled up in a chauffeured car on a cloudy morning in 1994. They stepped out onto this same sidewalk and headed upstairs to be interviewed by the DJ at Alt Radio Berlin.

"He must be exhausted," the DJ said to Jane after the interview, as the Lightning Bottles prepared to leave and go get ready for their concert at the converted water-pumping station. "All the touring, the fame—singing the way he does. He must be so tired." Jane hadn't known what to say to this. Yes, Elijah was tired. But he had also been high and practically nodding out from heroin during the interview. She knew there was a time when she had been too naïve to notice, but surely the DJ wasn't. Out on the sidewalk, as she and Elijah had waited for their car, they had started to argue. She remembered his pinned pupils, his frail form. "Could you just . . . stop yelling, maybe?" he had said to her. And then, he had grabbed her face in his hands and kissed her, hard. For just one second, it felt the way it used to. But his lips were cold and his hands were, too. He wasn't strong enough, or maybe he just wasn't interested enough, to kiss her for long.

Jane keeps staring down at the poster on the newspaper box, lost in her memories. What would she have done differently if she had known it was the last time they would kiss?

Is she going to get a second chance?

The poster reads:

LIVE, TONIGHT!

AT THE MARKTHALLE:

LA DURE

WITH SPECIAL GUESTS . . . *GREAT FREEDOM*

Jane turns to Hen. "We played the Markthalle in Hamburg in 1991. It was our first show in Europe. We opened for a French punk band called La Dure."

Hen nods, she knows. "Do you think the next clue might be at that concert hall, then?"

"Maybe."

"But either way, it's probably in Hamburg. Right?"

Jane doesn't answer. She's still trying to process that there is a *next*, that this is happening at all—that it's possible to survive going back in time, experiencing the memories she held at bay for so long and living to tell the tale. There's a bar across the street, a blinking neon martini glass on a sign, and Jane knows how easy it would be to go into that bar and find more answers at the bottom of a glass. But instead, she reaches into her handbag and feels the poker chips that swim across the bottom— months of freedom from addiction at her fingertips, almost a whole year of recovery. She wonders, if Elijah really is still alive, what state he's in. If he has been able to find ways to resist the pull of his demons. What it would mean, what she would do, if he wasn't.

"It's the weekend," Hen says. "I'll call my mother and tell her I'm staying over at my friend Clara's. Clara loves to bird-watch and does not really exist, by the way." She rolls her eyes, then turns and marches across the street toward a graffiti-covered pay phone booth. Jane stays where she is, planted to the sidewalk, staring down at the poster again, a poster advertising a concert in Hamburg that happened in 1991—long before Jane learned she was so destructible. Dangerous hope tugs hard at her heart, and she reaches into her bag to touch the sobriety chips again.

Hen returns. "Okay, done," she says, her tone blithe—and Jane realizes she has forgotten to insist that it's time for her to go home. Her expression is expectant; there is happiness in her eyes. Hen seems so certain that every-thing will be okay—and it reminds Jane of the way she used to be once. She thinks of that word Hen used that morning in Jane's kitchen. *Shicksal.* She doesn't realize she has said it aloud, but Hen smiles and nods.

"Exactly. Fate. Destiny."

But Jane also remembers that Hen used the word "doom." This girl has no idea, really, what this journey might have in store.

"Come on, Jane, let's go. Do you remember where you parked?"

And yet Jane still lets her follow along because releasing her would mean releasing any hope that she wasn't just heading straight toward more heartache and loss.

As they drive away from Berlin, Jane asks Hen to get the map out of the glove box.

"I think it will take two hours to get to Hamburg," Hen says. "Actu-ally, the way you drive, probably three." She turns on the radio—and they both fall silent as Lightning Bottles' music fills the car. Hen's hand hovers over the volume knob.

"Should I . . ."

"No, it's okay. Turn it up. It's a good song. I don't hear this one on the radio all that often."

"Yeah, it's kind of a deep cut."

The song is called "Your Old Self." It's a B-side from the Lightning Bottles' second album, *Your Heart, Your Soul, Your Spirit, Your Mind.*

As Hen nods along to the music, Jane finds herself saying, "I wrote it about Elvis, you know."

Hen glances at her. "You wrote it."

"Yeah, I did."

"But it's from the perspective of a man, clearly. *And I know I'm not the man I used to be, but you can't even look at me . . .*"

"A woman can't write from the viewpoint of a man? And also, does every song have to be *about* the person writing it? Sometimes songs are just stories about other people."

"So . . . it's true, then, that you wrote most of the songs? He tried to say that, a few times—especially during your Barbara Walters interview. But everyone said—"

"That I put him up to it."

"Right."

"And you said in Berlin that you believed *him*."

Hen was thoughtful. "And I guess I do. I don't see why he would lie—why you would ask him to. But now that we're talking about it . . . I *don't* understand why you didn't fight it more. Why do you just go along with the things everyone says about you? Why didn't you stand up and insist that they were your songs?"

Jane switched lanes. "Do I go along with what people say about me? Why do you think that—because I don't bother to argue with every stranger who thinks they know who I really am?"

Hen bites her lip. "Fair enough, I guess. But maybe it's so hard for people, accepting that you wrote them . . . because it means also accepting that Elijah didn't contribute as much. That it wasn't really him we were listening to."

"That's not true," Jane says, now vehement. "Imagine what it might be like to write a song for Elijah Hart to sing. The creative jolt that would give you. It was amazing. It changed my life." This is more than Jane has said to anyone about how it felt to be creative partners with Elijah Hart. And the world didn't end when she told her own story. It actually felt good. "Those songs were for him," she says. "And I wrote them with him. They wouldn't exist without him. It's not one or the other, his songs or my songs. We were . . . a single organism. We only worked together." She has been holding her breath, and she lets it out.

Several miles of highway unspool beneath the car's wheels, like gray tape stuck to the hills, before Hen speaks again.

"What do you mean, it's about Elvis? The song?" They're passing a field dotted with sheep.

"There was a vote in 1992 about a stamp Elvis was going to be on," Jane says. "An actual government-sanctioned vote. Did the American people want the *old* Elvis on the stamp, or the young one? They voted for the young one, and I couldn't stop thinking about it. What Elvis became, because of fame—and how no one wanted to remember him any way other than perfect. They wanted him frozen in time."

Elijah's voice is on the radio, singing the words: *You don't like the way my eyes looked back then, do you? But you should see them now, through you . . .*

"It's weird, to know this."

"It's weird to know what the song is really about?"

Hen shakes her head. "No." She looks out the window, then back at Jane. "Certain songs, I felt like he was talking to me. I think everyone in the world who listened to them must have felt the same."

Jane nods. And she knows now this is precisely why she has never come out and tried to insist on anything. Not even years later. *I felt like he was talking to me.* That's what everyone wanted. No one wanted to think it was Jane Pyre's voice in their head. And she certainly didn't want to have to be the one to tell them.

The song is over; a commercial comes on.

Jane changes lanes again, and the subject. "What other bands do you like—other than the Lightning Bottles?"

Hen looks shy as she leans down and unzips the backpack at her feet. She pulls out a tape. "I'm really into PJ Harvey lately. Do you know her?"

Jane nods. "Of course. Which album did you bring?"

"I have two." She fumbles in her bag again. "*To Bring You My Love* and *Is This Desire?*"

"The first one," Jane says.

"Are you sure? I think her most recent album is seriously underrated."

"Okay, put that one on, then."

Hen inserts the tape.

"Good driving music, right?" Hen says. "Better than death metal."

Jane laughs. "Agreed. I think Elijah would have liked it, too."

"I bet we could listen to the radio for hours and never hear any PJ Harvey," Hen says. "I get so sick of the radio sometimes. All these so-called alternative bands that get tons of airplay, most of them . . ." Hen trails off, searches for the right words. "Deeply unoriginal," she finishes, as PJ Harvey whispers to them about the wind and the whales.

"Deeply unoriginal is exactly right," Jane says. "Back when Elijah and I were first starting out, there was all this excitement about the burgeoning alternative scene. But I find it all—just so very disappointing now."

"The Offspring. Sugar Ray. *Disappointing.*"

Jane nods and turns up the PJ Harvey. "Do not mention Sugar Ray or I'll get that song in my head for the rest of the day. I hate music like that."

Hen glances at her. "Okay, but," she begins—and Jane knows what she's about to refer to. "That album of remixes you put out? That was kind of the worst, too."

"I had my reasons" is all Jane says.

"What were they?"

Jane enjoyed talking about music with Hen. It was refreshing. She even liked talking about writing songs for and with Elijah. But the years after Elijah disappeared, the choices she made when she was falling apart, are not moments she can talk about with anyone. So she just shakes her head, once, and they listen to the rest of the PJ Harvey album in silence.

After the last song plays, Hen asks, "Which song was your favorite?"

"The perfect day one. Something about Elise?"

Hen nods. "I could imagine Elijah singing it."

"Me too," Jane says. "I really could." She accelerates on the highway, wanting to get to Hamburg faster, wanting to find out what's next. To find out if he's real—if she'll ever hear him sing again. Meanwhile, Hen puts on the second PJ Harvey album and leans back in her seat. Eventually she falls asleep, and Jane has to wake her when they reach the city.

•   •   •

The sun is setting over Hamburg when they arrive. The sky above is indigo streaked with pink, and the same colors reflect back at them in the slow-flowing waters of the Elbe River. Hen is bleary-eyed and quiet; she seemed embarrassed when Jane woke her up, as she wiped a tiny smear of drool from her cheek. Jane's knee is sore from all the walking in Berlin, then the hours in the car, but it doesn't matter—she still presses on, knows she can't get to her destination fast enough.

As they walk, Jane keeps an eye out for somewhere to stop and buy sunglasses and a hat to disguise herself, but she soon forgets this task as they walk deeper into the city and her memories begin to rise around her again. They cross a bridge and the staid nineteenth-century architecture of downtown Hamburg begins to morph into shops, restaurants, and clubs. They're in the entertainment district, getting closer to the Markthalle.

"Why are there pictures and statues of the Beatles everywhere?" Hen asks.

"The original Beatles lineup used to play a lot of club shows here," Jane says. "Brian Epstein discovered them here. It's a legend now, I guess." They pass a collection of Beatles statues in a parkette. "George Harrison got deported for being underage. He was only seventeen. Like you."

They have arrived at the club where the Lightning Bottles played with La Dure in 1991. They walk around the building twice but don't find anything, not even a single graffiti tag. There are no acts of street art vigilantism anywhere at all. The restaurants and cafés that crowd against it all have clean walls, too. "This neighborhood was so different before," Jane says. "It was much seedier back when we were here. I bet any graffiti is immediately cleaned up."

She feels worried—what if Elijah left something, but it was removed?

"Can you think of anywhere else? On the poster in Berlin, it said 'special guests Great Freedom.' What did that mean?"

Jane thinks, tries to remember more. "We went somewhere after the show, with the guys from La Dure."

"Where exactly? Can you remember?"

She closes her eyes. She thinks. And after a moment, she can see the street signs. "An intersection," she says. "Lauthanze and . . . Große Freiheit."

"That's it!" Hen says, excited now. "*Große Freiheit* means 'great freedom' in German. We need a map." She pulls Jane into a corner store. When they're certain of their destination, they rush off toward it. And soon they are there: the corner of Große Freiheit and Lauthanze.

But it's different. The building that existed in 1991, when Jane and Elijah arrived in Hamburg to support La Dure on their tour, is gone. Jane turns in a circle, wonders if she has it wrong. But no. She's at the right spot. This is the intersection, plucked from a memory that is still so vivid, even after eight years. The best moments of her life. Everything else is here, the hotel on one corner, a restaurant on the other. But the building she, Elijah, Maxime, and his bandmate ducked behind, has been torn down. There's a little parkette there, a statue of John Lennon, a bench. Jane still scours every surface with her eyes—but there is nothing that looks even remotely like an Adam & the Rib painting or a clue of any kind.

"I can't find it. There's nothing."

"You're sure this is the right place?"

"I am. But . . ."

She and Hen walk up and down the street twice, go around the block, search building walls, newspaper boxes, garbage cans, benches, any surface they can find that could contain a painting. But there is no Adam artwork anywhere.

Jane feels deflated. And she can't ignore the ache of her knee any longer. "It's getting late," she says. "We need to find a hotel."

"Not yet," Hen says, pleading. "Let's not give up."

"Hen, we have looked everywhere. We're not giving up. We can try again tomorrow."

But just as she says this, a flash of orange and purple paint on a building wall across the street catches her eye. A sudden beacon. She was looking for a poster, and this is not that at all. It's just an arrow on a brick wall, outlined in magenta spray paint, filled in using a purple-white shade that seems to pulse and to glow. Jane knows these colors well, even if she has lived a lifetime since they stained her clothes and fingertips.

"We need to follow that arrow!" Jane says, invigorated now, the pain in her knee and her heart forgotten as she rushes toward it.

The first arrow leads to another. It's in the same colors, glows just as bright as the other arrow in the ever-darkening evening. Then a third one, pointing them down an alleyway. The space they enter is so tight, Jane and Hen must both turn sideways rather than walk straight in.

"There!" Hen calls out, elated. "I see it!" Like the poster in Berlin, this one is also affixed to the wall using thick layers of clear glue. Jane feels her way along until she's touching the glue, then presses herself back against the opposite brick wall so she can see the poster properly.

It is vivid with color, just like the arrows that led them here: "The Secret Adventures of Adam & the Rib" title is painted in the same neon yellow and electric purple.

"Wow," Hen breathes. "This one is *awesome*."

There are four drawings in comic-grid-style boxes, all done in neon. The first features Adam and Rib holding cans of spray paint up to a brick wall. Rib's spray can is spewing out tiny letters: *There is nothing to us that is less than love.*

The other panel features a pink pill with a heart pressed into it. It's broken in half, held out on a palm with a broken lifeline across the skin. Jane has to look away from this. She needs a minute to compose herself. This image brings guilt, deep shame—that sense of failure that chases her everywhere. *Deep breaths*, she tells herself. In through her nose, out through her mouth, and she is ready to look at the artwork again.

But just then, a jarring and familiar sound interrupts the silence in the alley.

Click, whir, click.

"Hen, come here—"

A man with a camera advances on them down the narrow passage. Jane whips off her jacket and throws it over Hen's head as she hustles her in the opposite direction.

"We have to run, once we get out in the open," she tells Hen. "Take as many turns as possible so we can lose him. Don't look back."

"Jane! Jane Pyre!"

"Get the hell away from us!" she shouts. But the camera continues to click and flash.

"Give us a smile, Jane Pyre," the photographer shouts in a German accent.

She gives him the finger instead.

LOS ANGELES, CALIFORNIA

OCTOBER 1991

The day the Lightning Bottles were scheduled to shoot the video for "Dark Shine," Elijah walked out onto the deck of the Malibu rental house. Jane was sitting with her coffee in the October morning sunshine, watching the ocean's waves pound the shore. She turned to see him holding a garment bag. "What's this?"

A shy smile spread over his face. "I was in Venice Beach yesterday, while you were at the hair salon with Petra." Jane had had her dark hair cut into a blunt Cleopatra-style bob. It was the first professional haircut she'd ever gotten—back at home, Raquel would trim Jane's hair, and she had cut it herself when she moved to Seattle, but never this short. She still wasn't used to the feel of the Santa Ana winds against her neck. "I saw this in the window of a thrift shop, and I had an idea."

Jane stood and unzipped the bag. Inside was a vintage lace dress, gently yellowed to a shade that matched the sunbeams falling across her bare feet. "Elijah, it's so beautiful. It reminds me of the dress Marilyn Monroe wore in *The Seven Year Itch*. Is it for the video? I thought the stylist gave us our outfits already."

"Yeah. Wedding outfits. A tux for me and a wedding dress for you that looks like we're trying to re-create a Guns N' Roses video. I couldn't stop thinking, why would we fake it?"

"Well, it's a video . . ."

"I know, I get that, but I don't want us to have a fake wedding, ever. It feels like it will cheapen the real thing."

Then Elijah pulled a rumpled, blue velvet smoking jacket from the bag and said, "This is for me to wear. And the dress . . . will you wear it when you marry me, Jane? Today?"

Jane had always associated marriage with the church, her past. She knew she and Elijah would always be together. In a way, she thought of the night his parents died as the night they were married—because it was the night she knew they would be bound together forever. But now she realized how sad that was and could see how important to him this was.

"Should I get down on one knee?" Elijah asked.

"Oh my god." She laughed. "Please, no. You don't have to do that."

She kissed him, let the dress dangle from her fingertips and drop to the ground, where it landed like a puddle of silky, lacy butter. "But maybe you could do something else . . ." Elijah slid the straps of her white tank top down her shoulders, took off the black silk shorts she had worn to bed, looked at her body in the early-morning light as if he had never seen it before. It was always like this with him.

They made love on the deck, to the sound of the ocean and the seabirds overhead. After, she said, "Of course I'll marry you. A thousand times, yes. Whatever you need, whatever you want, I'll do it."

When she put on the dress later, a small slip of paper fell out. It was an Adam & the Rib drawing. In it, Adam was kneeling and asking Rib to marry him. She kissed him and said *yes*. Jane wondered if that was how he had wanted it to go, or if he was happy with the way things were. She tucked the drawing away with the others, memories piled on memories. Or maybe not memories at all: maybe a story that was part fairy tale, part real life, and all theirs.

They drove their Impala out to Point Dume in their wedding clothes. The day had become overcast and rainy, a rarity in LA that Jane thought made the day even more special. It didn't even matter that when the lace dress got wet, the fabric started to give off a chemical smell.

The officiant, who doubled as their witness, was a lawyer named Brenda whom Elijah had found in the Yellow Pages. She met them in the parking lot. She was wearing a raincoat, a navy pantsuit, and high heels, which she took off, discarding her nude hose socks before walking across the wet sand in her bare feet.

After they exchanged their vows to be together forever, to love each other through any storms—and Jane tried not to think about how un- necessary this felt, to her at least, to make these promises she always lived and breathed anyway—Brenda read from Elijah's battered copy of *The Prophet*, the one that had once been Alice's. The words were about creating space in their togetherness, but Jane found herself wrapping her arms around Elijah, leaning her cheek against his rain-damp velvet jacket, wishing to erase any distance between them at all. She decided then she liked the idea of a secret marriage, a promise made between them that they didn't have to share with anyone.

Jane Pyre and Elijah Hart were not as famous that day as they were poised to become, but a family of tourists hiking the dunes in the misty rain couldn't look away from them. Not really knowing why, they took a photo of the newlyweds standing with Brenda by the water, looking out to sea as more rain clouds rolled in.

The newlyweds drove straight from the beach to the sound stage in West Hollywood that had been turned into a replica of the Roxy. It looked exactly like the club where the fans had been recruited, but it felt nothing at all like the real thing. "You were right," Jane said to Elijah. "It's all really fake. I'm glad we did what we did this morning." He smiled and kissed her cheek. Then they walked carefully around cameras, cords, and lighting towers toward their dressing room, as sound techs bustled around the stage and assistants were sent on errands, each one more urgent than the next.

The craft services table was stocked with éclairs in various exotic flavors—because apparently, Petra told them, *éclair* meant "lightning." Alan had loved that idea and had had the pastries flown in specially from a bakery in Paris.

"Doesn't it seem a bit silly," Elijah said, plucking one of the desserts from the table and holding it between two fingers. "I mean, it's essentially a cream puff. That's not very rock 'n' roll."

Petra just laughed. She said, "Even rock 'n' roll isn't all that rock 'n' roll. You'll find that out today. It's going to look like a wild, rad concert—but for you guys, it's work."

In their dressing room there were more éclairs, juice, water, vodka, and champagne. Elijah poured some for Jane and tapped his flute against hers. "Happy wedding day, Mrs. Hart."

"Ha *ha*," she said. "I love you, but I'm not taking your name. Maybe I should start calling you Mr. Pyre."

"Hey, I like that," he said. "Has a nice ring to it."

As she drank from the flute, the bubbles tickled her nose. She felt light and happy, bathed in the glow of the secret knowledge of their wedding.

But then there was a knock at their dressing room door that felt urgent, jarring.

Jane experienced a flicker of panic when she saw the serious look on Petra's face; she flashed through possible tragedies. But Elijah was here with her. Her mother didn't speak to her. Jane had no one left to lose.

Petra got right to it. "Kim Beard is threatening to sue."

"What?" Jane burst out, while Elijah stayed silent, his expression inscrutable.

"He's saying he wrote 'My Life or Yours' with Elijah, that a portion of the intellectual property rights for the song rest with him. He's delivered notice to the label and us via his legal team that if the song is on the forthcoming album and the lyrics are released along with it in the liner notes, he'll sue both members of the Lightning Bottles, the label, and the song's publishers. He'll move to freeze any collective accounts so no publishing royalties can be released. There's a cease and desist demand, too. He's trying to stop you from playing it at all, from now on. I know it sounds dire, but he's trying to scare you."

Jane thought of the glimpse she had caught of Kim during the practice concert at the Roxy. How had he even gotten in? Where was he getting all this power, this confidence? She turned to Elijah. "It's not true, is it? That he had anything to do with the song?"

"Of course not!"

"But why won't he leave us alone? Why would he make something like this up? It's *evil*."

"Kim's not evil," Elijah said with a bitter laugh. "He's just a dick. And he's petty; he always has been. He's mad that we're not friends anymore. Mad because he thinks you took me away from him. Mad because I chose you over him."

"But this is more than just petty!" She turned back to Petra. "Can he do this to us? Can he really stop us from playing the song?" Her heart was racing. Kim was going to ruin this for them.

"Don't forget, anyone can sue a person—or threaten to do so. Anyone with the means can get a good lawyer and use this kind of official language to intimidate. Just because it sounds alarming doesn't make it a true threat. Like I said, he's trying to scare you. He doesn't have the power to stop you from doing anything." She continued to speak to them reassuringly, but something was bothering Jane. She turned to Elijah.

"Does he know what it's about, what it means to you? Does he know this is the exact way to hurt you?"

"He knows," Elijah said.

"But how?"

"From Shawn, I guess."

"You still talk to Shawn?"

"Jane." He raised an eyebrow. "*You're* my wife. She's my friend."

"Wait, am I missing something?" Petra said, looking back and forth beween them. "Wife?"

"We were going to tell you," Elijah said. "It just happened this morning. And we don't want anyone to know, okay? This is just for us."

"Understood. Congratulations," Petra said with a solemn nod. "I will not let Kim Beard ruin this day for you, okay?"

Elijah rubbed his eyes and jaw. "It's just so fucking frustrating."

"I know. But don't give him an ounce of power. Got it?"

"I guess we need a lawyer," Jane said.

"I've already called Martika Assad. She's got a great reputation; I've worked with her before with another client and she's the best in the business. Plus, she's got the capacity to take this case on. She can meet with you once the video shoot is over."

"And we can still play the song?"

"Until it's proven otherwise in court—which it won't be—you can do what you want."

"What about the freezing of the royalties?" Elijah asked.

"Unfortunately, he *can* do that—but it will be temporary. We'll discuss it more when you meet with Martika, okay? Try to put it out of your minds for now. Today is a big day."

When she was gone, Jane poured herself a vodka. It surprised her, how fast she drank it, how she immediately poured more. Elijah was drinking, too.

"Nothing like someone threatening to sue you to ruin your buzz," he said, tipping more vodka into his mouth. She didn't laugh.

Kim Beard was not harmless, and Jane knew it. He was dangerous. He wasn't going to give up until he took something from them—and Jane felt the sudden urge to mark their territory in some way. "Elijah . . . if it's really our song, we have to claim it. Don't you think? We can never, ever let any doubt be cast on the fact that it's ours and no one else's."

He hesitated, but then she saw a glint of steely resolve take over his expression. "You're right," he said, and she could breathe again. "Let's go call Alan. I'm sure there will be no problem at all swapping out the songs for the video—especially considering how badly he wanted us to do 'My Life or Yours' in the first place."

But he hesitated at the dressing room door.

"It's yours, Elijah," she said firmly. "Don't lose your nerve. He can't take it away."

"It's *ours*," he said, grabbing her hand. "No more fighting it. Come on, let's go."

LOS ANGELES, CALIFORNIA

NOVEMBER 1991

DJs would talk about it for years, some for the rest of their careers: when the Lightning Bottles' first single, "My Life or Yours," debuted on radio stations, phone lines were jammed within moments with listeners calling in, frantic, needing to know, *what is this song, who is singing, where can I get this single, this album?* It was already charting on radio weekly Top 40s before the album was even out.

And the frenzy only increased when the video was released on MTV. Now the mysterious singer had a face, and it was the face of Elijah Hart. Those dreamy ocean eyes, the rakish smile, the messy hair. And Jane Pyre, his partner: silent, mysterious, beautiful. The world wanted more of them; how could it not?

The day the Lightning Bottles' self-titled album released, six weeks after their first single debuted on radio stations, a month after the video first aired on MTV, Jane and Elijah were scheduled to make several afternoon record store appearances. But then Petra called.

"The album is already sold out at every one of the stores you were going to appear at. And you may already be a little too popular for record store appearances. The label's marketing department thinks we should focus on the tour now. If people want to see you, they can buy concert tickets."

Jane was delighted—and surprised to see that Elijah was dismayed.

"How long will the album restock take?" he asked.

"A few days, at most. They're quadrupling the run. This is good news. An incredibly strong start."

But he was still frowning. "Just . . . I know the way it feels when you're excited for an album. I remember this happened to me with Disintegration's *Squeeze Me*. They had sold out of it at the only record store near me. My mom drove me to Olympia to get it, but there was a supply issue and that album didn't do as well as their others. The fans got tired of waiting. Is that going to happen to us?" Jane had noticed that ever since Kim Beard had threatened to sue them over the origins of "My Life or Yours," Elijah had become more ambitious. It was a relief to her to feel his drive increase, begin to match hers.

"Elijah, don't worry. 'My Life or Yours' is one of the most requested songs on radio stations all across the continent and charting at number one on most pop and rock airplay lists. If anything, I think the scarcity of the album is fueling fans' desire for it. None of this is going to be taken away from you."

"What are we supposed to do today, then?"

"Just relax today, enjoy all the good news, and I'll see you later at the release party at the Python's Apartment." The Python's Apartment was an exclusive club on the Santa Monica strip owned by an actor named Mikey Churl. He was most well-known for his role in a Disney fantasy franchise of movies, or perhaps for his debaucherous lifestyle—which was apparently why he opened a club: to keep these habits out of the prying eye of the public and the press. His commitment to privacy also meant it was a good place for celebrities to hang out, and the Lightning Bottles' album release party at that club was the most coveted invitation in town.

"Should we go out anyway?" Jane asked him. "It is a bit anticlimactic to just stay home, right? We could drive by some of the record stores. See some of the fans for ourselves? Make this feel more real to you."

Elijah agreed, and they drove down Sunset first, toward Dave's Records. There was a line of people all the way down the street. They passed by Dyzzy on Vinyl, Permanent Records, Mono Records, Canterbury. All had fans lined up around the block.

"This feels all wrong," Elijah said as the Impala inched forward in the traffic. "People should have access to our music."

Jane had hoped the outing would lift his mood, but it seemed to be doing anything but.

In Long Beach, there was a traffic jam in front of a record store called Into the Groove. They parked across the street and Elijah drummed his fingers on the dash as their single came on the radio. But he turned it off, which further disappointed Jane. "Elijah, come on." She couldn't keep the frustration out of her voice now. "This is supposed to be a great day."

"I know, I'm sorry. I just imagined all this so differently. I finally started to want it, but it's just so . . ."

"I get it. Me too. But I have an idea." She pointed across the street at the record store. "See the way the building has a flat roof? Kind of like a stage? What if we go up there and play a few songs?"

"We don't have our instruments," he said, still glum. "And can we even do that?"

"It feels like the precise sort of thing Alan would get behind. I bet all Petra has to do is call him and it'll happen. Come on." She slid across the seat toward him, nuzzled against his shoulder. "Imagine how you would have felt that day you couldn't get the Disintegration album, if they had played an impromptu live show on the roof of the record store . . . ?"

She could feel the idea taking root within Elijah. When she looked up at him, he was growing animated, his eyes lighting up.

Within an hour, it was officially a go. A team of security guards had arrived at Into the Groove, a small team of roadies, two amps, a mic, Elijah's Fender Stratocaster, his custom percussion pedal, Jane's Rickenbacker bass.

"Alan would do anything for you at this point," Petra told them. "You might want to start thinking of bigger things to ask for, actually."

Other SUVs had now pulled into the parking lot. Alan was there, and their producer, Ricky, their marketing and PR teams, and someone from legal, just in case. They didn't have a permit, but the word was the police who had caught wind of this were just as excited to see the Lightning Bottles play as everyone else.

As they waited at the back of the building, their instruments now set up on the roof, Elijah looked at Jane thoughtfully, as if weighing what he was about to say. Then he pulled a little baggie out of his pocket. "Mushrooms, again?" she said, trying to keep her tone light. He was happy. He was good. She didn't want anything to change that. Still, her smile faded when she saw the tiny pills. "What are those?"

"Ecstasy," he answered. She looked closer. The pills were tiny, pink with purple hearts pressed into them. They looked like candy. Elijah pressed down on one with his thumbnail and it snapped in half, breaking the little heart in two on his palm. "Take half. Do it with me. *Trust* me, Jane."

"Where did you get them?"

"Same guy I got the mushrooms from."

"I don't like that you have a drug connection here in LA."

"Jane, these are hardly drugs. They're . . . hallucinogens. They're fun."

"You said that last time. At the video shoot."

"And I was *fine*. Remember?"

"This seems a little more serious, though. It's not a *plant*."

"Jane." He kissed her, slid his hand up her back, under her shirt. "We're rock stars now. You can take a half an Ecstasy pill and it's not going to kill you. Have fun with me. Please."

All at once, she wanted to. She wanted to let go of always having to be the responsible one, fully let go of Janet Ribeiro and her church-heavy upbringing. Of always having to worry about him, about everything. He wasn't the only one who was feeling like this huge day they had been waiting for was anticlimactic. She wanted to feel something—she wanted to feel everything. Jane watched as he swallowed his half-pill dry. He held out his hand again, and she took her half.

But when she swallowed it, she was immediately overtaken by fear and regret. "It's okay, Jane, really," he said, keeping his eyes on hers. "You'll be fine."

"Will it be . . . right away?"

"Nah. About half an hour. It'll probably kick in right when we're in the middle of playing."

"What have I done?"

Elijah laughed. "You're cute, you know. I'll take care of you. Come on."

Elijah took her hand. They sat on the concrete, leaned against the wall of the record store building and talked as they waited—for the concert to start, for the drug to kick in. Finally, Petra came around the corner and told them it was time to climb up the ladder and start the impromptu show. Jane's heart raced with nerves—but the fear was only temporary and morphed quickly into excitement, elation. Elijah watched her. "Feeling good?"

She nodded.

"Then let's go."

There were startled, exuberant cries as Jane and Elijah appeared on the rooftop of the record store. They picked up the guitars that had been hidden behind an air duct. Elijah grabbed his mic. "Hey!" he shouted down. "We're sorry there aren't enough albums to go around today. That fucking sucks!" A wild cheer rose up from below. "Maybe this will help make it better."

When the Lightning Bottles launched into "Dark Shine," a heaving mosh pit started in the parking lot as if they had hit a start button on a frenzy. And Jane suddenly felt a happiness so complete it was tangible and real, like a ladder she could climb up. Elijah started messing around, playing a Disintegration cover—"Show Me," one of their favorite songs—and she played along easily because she knew the song by heart, and because in this moment, she could do anything. The Disintegration cover was greeted with more wild cheers, more slam dancing from the fans below.

Then Elijah turned to Jane and gazed into her eyes for what felt like a long time, with ever-widening pupils. Then he turned away, took the mic in both his hands, and adopted a wide stance, like he was about to take a physical hit.

She had heard him sing thousands of times by then, but it was different with this drug coursing through her veins. It felt like she was witnessing a true miracle. She closed her eyes and listened to him, and everything else fell away. As he started to sing "My Life or Yours," she felt a pulling sensation, like the song was being wrenched away from them—but this wasn't a bad thing. It felt like freedom. She opened her eyes and saw the song like a balloon on a string. It was slipping through his fingers and taking to the sky.

When he sang "We're all gonna die," the crowd below sang along, their voices rapturous—as if they weren't singing about the saddest reality of being alive. And suddenly, that was no longer what the song was about. The sadness floated above them and then it was gone. Jane stepped toward the edge of the building and looked down at the crowd. She felt what they felt. This song wasn't about the night his parents died anymore, or even about actual death. It was about being high and having fun. About being young, the world at your feet. It was about knowing life contained devastating truths—but you didn't give a shit because you felt immortal, and that made it true.

Elijah stopped singing and the crowd below kept on going; they had the lyrics to the chorus already memorized. When it was over, Elijah turned to Jane, his pupils black holes now, all the green-blue almost invisible. He let go of his guitar and it hit the ground with a thud. He stepped toward her, grabbed her face in his hands, and kissed her in that fervent, passionate way of his. After watching him perform, this was such a turn-on. He was *hers*. She lifted one leg and wrapped it around his waist. The crowd cheered louder. "What a rush," he said into her mouth. "What a high."

And then he lifted her off her feet and spun her around. Journalists had arrived, and Jane knew there were dozens of photos being taken of them in that moment. She could see them imprinted on the backs of her eyelids. She looked up at the spinning, sunset-streaked sky and wanted to stay this way forever, twirling around with her husband, on the roof of a record store. High, but just enough to be happy, not afraid.

• • •

A few weeks later, Jane and Elijah stood backstage at the Markthalle in Hamburg, watching La Dure, the punk band from France the Lightning Bottles were opening for, warm up.

"They're good," Elijah said into Jane's ear. "Really heavy, but they can carry a good tune, too. And their singer is great."

She watched the way the singer vamped across the stage, shaking his long blond hair, and she nodded in agreement.

"I can't believe we're on tour," she said. "This is so . . ." She searched for the word and didn't find it. Back in the US, their album was continuing to climb charts, but they were in Europe for a month, cutting their teeth by opening for a punk band.

"Wondrous," he whispered back.

"Exactly that."

"The Disintegration has played on that stage, Jane."

She wrapped her arms around his waist, put her ear against his chest so she could hear his heartbeat, even in the musical din. It was faster than usual. "The Clash."

"New Order."

"The Pixies."

"Iggy Pop."

"This is the dream."

Once the show was over, Jane and Elijah tumbled backstage to the sound of the crowd roaring for even more of them. Maxime, the lead singer of La Dure, with his golden eyes and shaggy blond hair, looked like a French surfer, but in punk clothing. He approached, patted them both on the back. "That was our best show ever. You two are *magic*," he said. "I wish we could tour more with you, beyond Hamburg—but we're lucky to have you for a few shows, anyway. Okay, now, what do we need here, what do we want? Vodka, beer, champagne, cocaine?"

Jane laughed nervously, and Maxime caught her eye. "Booze, then," he said. He led them to a table filled with bottles, and once they had drinks in hand, he paraded them around the room, making proud introductions. Everyone they met raved about their performance, used words like *transcendent*, terms like *once-in-a-lifetime*. And none of the guys from La Dure seemed to mind that the Lightning Bottles had stolen the show. Everyone was thrilled to be in the presence of the next hottest thing in the rock world.

Hours later, the tempo of the party dipped a little. Jane and Elijah sat on a couch in the corner; Elijah was doodling on a napkin, an image of Adam and Rib in an airplane and then on a stage taking shape while Jane watched, a little bored, then added some drawings of her own.

Maxime approached. "Let's get out of here," he said. "I must show the Lightning Bottles a good time. It's my duty." His voice was jokey-solemn, but his expression turned thoughtful as he glanced down at the napkin. "You like art? Come with me; let's get you out of here and into the real world, while you still can. While not every single person recognizes your faces."

As they snuck out the back door of the venue, Jean, La Dure's drummer, caught up with them. "Hey, not without me!"

They all waited as Maxime retrieved a backpack from the band's tour bus. Jane could hear the sound of metal clanking inside as he pulled it onto his muscled back.

"Where are you taking us?" Elijah asked. Maxime had a bottle of vodka in his hand and he handed it to him. Elijah took a long swallow, and handed it to Jane.

"To do something we've done for fun since we were young punks growing up in Pigalle," Maxime said. "To make you immortal."

They ran through the cobblestone streets, their voices bouncing off the buildings. Eventually they ended up in a back alley with a blank swath of brick wall, behind a building at the corner of Große Freiheit and Lauthanze. Maxime opened the backpack to reveal several cans of spray paint. There was a glass bottle in the bag, too, and he lifted it out, laughing. "Ah, my lost bottle of Chartreuse. I wondered where this had gotten off to." He unscrewed the cap, took a long pull, and passed it around. "Another secret to immortality," he said with a wink. "Although

I can't remember why. All I know is a bunch of French monks have kept the recipe secret for hundreds of years, and only two people in the world at any given time know what's really in it."

The liquor was sharp and smooth at once. It made Jane's head feel as if it had been spun into another galaxy. "*Whoa*," she said, passing it back to Maxime.

Elijah sifted through the paint cans in the bag, while Jean explained the plan: "Maxime and I have a signature tag. Here, we have the space to make it very big. But we have to be fast, just in case someone catches us. It's a hefty ticket, maybe a night in jail."

Maxime passed the bottle of Chartreuse to Elijah, who drank it deeply, then passed it to Jean. "You can try too, but let us show you how to do it," he said. "Prêt, Jean?"

He put down the bottle and the two shook their cans, then moved together over the wall like they were dancing a choreographed routine. Up and down, sideways, up again. The sound of the paint spraying out of the cans was the music they danced to. Jean outlined letters in magenta, Maxime filled them in with a pastel purple that glowed in the night. The letters *K-I-F-F-E* emerged, looking like they were bubbling out of the wall.

"What does *kiffe* mean?" Jane asked.

"It's really just our tag, but it means . . . more than 'like' but less than 'love'? You might think of it of a lover." Jane was sure he glanced at her fast, then looked away. Her body felt one single jolt. She had never been looked at that way by anyone but Elijah.

"There is nothing to us that is less than love," she said to Maxime. He just smiled.

"Want to try?"

Jane shrugged off her leather jacket and handed it to Elijah, who folded it over his arm. Her white T-shirt glowed in the night, and she got paint all over it, and her ripped black jeans, as she sprayed a big *J*, loopy and fancy, so it almost resembled a treble clef. Elijah had taken a can now too, was weaving a neon *E* into her electric-purple *J*. They were clumsy at first but soon got the hang of it and moved together just as

easily as Maxime and Jean had, the letters representing their names melt-
ing, blending, blurring together, glowing in the night like a beacon. *We
were here. And you don't know who we are.* She began the arc of a heart on
one side of the letters, and Elijah did the same. They met in the middle,
laughing with delight.

"*Magnifique!*" Maxime said, clapping them both on the back, his voice
loud, boisterous with drink. "There you go, Jane Pyre, Elijah Hart. Now
you really are immortal. Isn't that the very point of art? You will be gone,
but this will be here—unless someone paints it over, but even then, there
will always be traces, until this building is dust. Until the world is dust."

They traipsed through the city, and Jean and Maxime did more tags,
but Jane and Elijah left it at just one because that felt like enough. Every
time they heard a siren, they ran, laughing, like children causing mischief.

When they had finished the vodka and the bottle of Chartreuse,
their steps began to weave. Elijah's eyes were half closing and his words
were slurring as he staggered alongside Jane, singing an Iggy Pop song
about being a passenger riding through the city's backside.

"I should probably get him back," Jane told Maxime, stumbling a
little too. "We had *a lot* to drink tonight."

"Yes, and I think Elijah had most of that bottle of vodka and much of
the Chartreuse on his own. I'll help you," Maxime said.

"How do you seem perfectly sober?"

"Ah. Because it is not my first time becoming immortal."

By the time they arrived at the hotel—an Art Nouveau building, near
the river—Jean had disappeared somewhere along the way, saying he had
a German girlfriend to meet. Maxime helped Jane get Elijah upstairs, past
a disapproving doorman who shook his head.

They half carried Elijah from the elevator to their room, laughing
when they almost dropped him on the carpet. Once he was deposited on
the bed in their suite, Jane pulled the blankets over him and kissed her
husband's forehead.

She walked Maxime to the door. "You made it an unforgettable night,"
she said. "Thank you."

He smiled at her. His pupils had dilated in the dim hotel room so that the gold of his eyes was barely visible. There was a drop of neon paint on his cheek. "It was my pleasure. You two are both true talents. Your husband's voice shines bright—but so do *you*, Jane. He is the lightning, but you are the bottle. And, I must say, you are very beautiful."

Jane realized that Maxime was about to kiss her. But she gave a small shake of her head, murmuring her thanks for the kind words. She wouldn't do that to Elijah. She couldn't even really imagine kissing anyone else—even if she did wonder what it would be like to kiss someone who didn't love her, someone who simply wanted her. Maxime looked back at her one last time in case she had changed her mind, but she just shook her head again.

Inside the hotel room, she undressed, showered, and slid into bed beside her sleeping husband. She wrapped her arms around him and dreamed of Lightning Bottles' song lyrics spray-painted across the seven wonders of the world. Of their initials, *J* and *E*, tangled together forever, a blazing neon secret.

HAMBURG, GERMANY

DECEMBER 19, 1999

Jane and Hen run through the streets of Hamburg, taking random turns until they can no longer hear the footfalls of the photographer behind them or the click of his camera.

They stop in front of a café. "Go into the restroom," Hen instructs, firm. "Keep your face covered with your jacket. I'll handle this."

Jane hears Hen speaking in German to the waiter as she crosses the restaurant. A little while later, there's a tap at the door. Jane opens it tentatively to find Hen holding two coffees and a paper bag. She points to a back exit. They walk outside together into the darkness of a quiet alley.

"What did you say to him?"

"That my friend had a nosebleed. Are you hungry? I got pastries."

Jane can't remember the last time she ate. The pastry is soft and tastes of cinnamon and sugar. A few people pass, but no one looks at them. They stop walking eventually and sit on a bench near the water. Jane breathes out—not with relief, not exactly. She turns to Hen, whose face is alight. She doesn't seem rattled at all.

Jane sips her coffee, needing the caffeine boost, telling herself, as she often has to, that that's all she needs. She hears footsteps and looks over her shoulder, but it's just a young couple out for a stroll by the river. "I wish we could go back to that alley." She releases a frustrated sigh.

"Of course we have to," Hen says in that matter-of-fact way of hers. "What do you mean, you wish?"

"No," Jane says. "We can't go back. I have to get out of Hamburg. No one can know about these paintings. I'll get a proper disguise and come back. I'll take you home first."

"You know I don't want to go home yet."

"You do not want to be involved in this anymore."

"I already am involved."

Jane shakes her head. "It's just better I handle this on my own. It could define you for life, being photographed with Jane Pyre. It might have already."

"I don't care about that."

"Your friends—"

"I don't have any friends."

"Your mother, then."

"What about her? All I have ever done is protect my mother. Being away from home has made me realize I can't do that anymore. I have to live my life."

"This is not your life, Hen. It's *mine*."

Hen was silent. Jane thought maybe she had gotten through to her— until she spoke again.

"You just don't get it, do you? You never have."

"What's that supposed to mean?"

"It's why people don't like you. Elijah cared about the fans; he made us feel loved. *You* make us feel like we don't matter. Like we weren't even allowed to grieve him. And whether you like it or not, I'm in this. I'm the one who found the first clue. I can't just walk away and pretend none of it happened. He's not just yours, you know."

Jane bristles. She sounds like Kim. "And he belongs to *you*?"

"I'm not just some nobody!"

"I didn't say that."

"But maybe it *is* true, right?" She's suddenly deflated. "I've never been anywhere or done anything." There's such sadness in her voice that Jane feels guilty. "I love music more than anything, and drumming best of all, but do you know what my drum kit is? I set up a bunch of old milk buckets in my room. I tap on them quietly so I don't wake my mother. Can you imagine? Probably not. You've only ever had the best instruments, haven't you?"

"Hen, I—"

"I know it's sad, okay? But those stupid buckets feel real to me when I play them, when I listen to my favorite Lightning Bottles songs, when I hear Elijah's voice, or you playing guitar or bass. I play along and pretend I'm in your band." Her voice breaks, and a sob escapes her lips, and all at once, Jane can see it: Hen, sitting in her poster-lined bedroom. The upturned buckets in the corner. And also, Jane sees herself at seventeen. In her bedroom back in Ontario, door barred by a chair, headphones covering her ears, listening to the music she loved so much, her fingers brushing against her guitar but not playing any notes in case her mother heard. Young Jane is feeling the music. Living the music. Being the music. Waiting for her real life to begin. Jane can't get rid of her. Hen is right; she's part of this now.

"What's wrong with your mother?" Jane asks after a minute, her voice soft.

"My mother has been stuck in her own paranoid world since the Berlin Wall fell. She's too scared to leave the house."

"But why? I thought the dismantling of the Wall was a good thing for everyone?"

"I guess it's hard to understand unless you lived it. What being fed propaganda your entire life does to you. Most people knew it wasn't true, that the Wall had no reason for being. But what if you believed it? My mother did." Hen puts her face in her hands for a moment but then draws a long, shaky breath and sits up straight. "I feel for her," she says. "I love her. I want her to be well again. But I can't fix her."

Jane understands not being able to fix a broken person, no matter how desperately you wish you could. But even though she understands, she doesn't know how to comfort Hen. Should she reach for her, pat her on the arm, hug her? Elijah would know what to do in this moment, Jane is sure of it.

"I called my mother from that pay phone in Berlin, but she didn't answer. She never answers the phone. I left a message on our machine, explaining I wouldn't be back for a while. I said she was going to be on her own and that I was okay, and she had to believe that I was."

"Don't you have school?"

Hen snorted softly. "Really? Come on."

"School is important. Your future . . ."

"All I know of the world I've read in books or seen on television. I want to live a real life. I want to go places, and be someone—someone else. This is my chance. Don't you see that?"

"Yes." Jane nods. "I do, Hen. I get it."

"Okay, then," Hen says, relief in her voice. "So, I'm staying with you. Stop threatening to take me home. Let me help you."

Jane nods, allows herself to feel a little relief, too.

"I'll go back to the alley and look at the painting," Hen says, standing. "You stay here. I'll come back and describe exactly what I see. And I promise, if I see any sign of the photographer, I'm out of there. I was raised by a woman who thinks everyone is a traitor or a spy—I know how to be paranoid."

The December night gets darker and colder. Jane's hands, wrapped around her cold coffee cup, begin to numb. But just as she's starting to feel concerned, she sees Hen in the distance, rushing back toward her.

"Okay, so the art in the last square is sort of weird," Hen says, sitting back down on the bench beside Jane. "It's a platter on a table with . . . like, pastries on it?" She searches for the word. "Éclairs," she says. "At first I thought they were little hot dogs, but I think they were éclairs."

Jane smiles. "Elijah was never very good at drawing food."

"And there was a little card beside the platter. It said . . ." She thinks for a moment. "Something like, 'These have been flown in specially from Paris, France.'"

"Éclairs," Jane says. "Éclairs from Paris. They were at our video shoot. He thought they were so silly. But, *lightning*—that's what the word *éclair* means in French. The head of our record label, Alan, basically our boss, had them flown in from Paris."

"Paris," Hen repeats.

"Yes." Jane stands, drops her coffee cup into a bin, looks down at Hen. "That's it. He wants me to go to Paris next."

She hasn't spoken of Elijah in the present tense since he disappeared into the ocean—but she has done it now, and it feels right. After all, he is no longer a ghost, and she is no longer alone.

LOS ANGELES, CALIFORNIA

JANUARY 1992

By January of 1992, the Lightning Bottles' debut was one of the fastest- and highest-selling albums of the decade. It went gold within a month and platinum by the new year, the million copies it had sold so quickly meaning the Lightning Bottles were overtaking some of the biggest names in the music business with a sound that everyone said they had never heard before. As the buzz around them built and towered, the Lightning Bottles returned from their teeth-cutting shows in Europe— where they had opened for La Dure and a few other European punk and alternative bands—and focused on rehearsals for their upcoming North American tour in support of the already wildly successful album.

But rehearsals had to pause for a day so Jane and Elijah could go do the last thing they wanted: visit the Santa Monica courthouse for the *Kim Beard v. The Lightning Bottles and Columbia Records* pretrial conference.

They arrived in court in an SUV driven by a chauffeur—they hadn't been able to drive the easily recognizable Impala since the day of the album's release. A crowd had gathered on the sidewalk in front of the courthouse, spilled out onto the road, and were ushered behind block- ades by police officers. Many of the crowd were wearing Lightning Bot- tles T-shirts, holding up the album. One or two were wearing Marvel Boys T-shirts, though. Elijah gripped Jane's hand so hard it almost hurt.

"It'll be okay," Jane said. "This conference is going to give us reassur- ance that Kim can never touch our work, or either of us, with his lies. It'll be over soon." She couldn't tell if she was getting through to him. She felt nervous, too, but worked hard not to show it.

"There are two security guards waiting for you at the rear entrance," Bev, their driver, said as she drove around the back of the courthouse. She spoke into her headset, then looked at them again. "You need to get out of the car and walk to the door now. Okay, *go*."

Outside, they were hit by the flash of cameras, so many that it almost felt physical. Jane flinched and pressed herself against Elijah, unable to hide her alarm. A chaotic swarm of voices came at them from every direction.

"Elijah! Jane! Over here!"

"Elijah, what do you have to say about your former best friend's lawsuit?"

"Elijah, did Kim Beard really help you write your hit song?"

"Jane Pyre! Why don't you ever smile?"

The next day there would be photos everywhere of Elijah in a ragged vintage tuxedo jacket, a Smiths shirt underneath, and Jane in a red-and-black plaid miniskirt, black crop top, leather jacket, and cherry Doc Martens that climbed all the way up the backs of her calves. They clung to each other's hands as they ran for the courthouse. Elijah looked sweet and terrified. Jane just looked angry. As they reached the door, a loud voice rose above all the others: "Is it true you got married in a secret ceremony on a Malibu beach before you left for Europe? Why didn't you tell anyone?"

Petra was waiting for them inside.

"Are you two okay?"

"Why are they asking if we got married?" Jane asked. "How does anyone else know?"

She grimaced. "Shit. Sorry—I was going to tell you. Some tourists took a photo of you two on that beach when you were getting married, then recognized that it was you and sold it to a tabloid." She shook her head. "I hate that you found out the way you did. Especially today. There was nothing we could do. And it's not negative press—it's kind of nice, right?"

"It's fine," Elijah said. "Jane, really, it is. We have other things to focus on." His eyes had drifted past them, down the hall. Kim, Ari, John, Git, and Shawn were standing in a loose knot. Shawn was dressed all in black, like she was attending a funeral. Her hair had grown out since Seattle. It hung long and lank on either side of her face. She wore minimal makeup and she looked like one of the supermodels who were suddenly everywhere—like Cindy Crawford combined with Kate Moss, gorgeous and strung out at once. That familiar jealousy hit Jane, a vestige from the shy teenager she had been in Seattle. *You aren't her anymore,* she told herself. But today, she felt like it.

As they passed the group, Kim called out, "How ya doin', brother?" His chestnut-brown hair had already been long in Seattle, but now it hung nearly to his waist. He had on a black baseball cap, backward, and a Butt-hole Surfers T-shirt, a suit jacket pulled over it. Meanwhile, Shawn gazed at Elijah, lifted a hand, and waved so briefly it was barely noticeable—unless you were watching her, which Jane was.

"Come on, guys," Petra said. "We need to get in there." They moved off down the hallway toward the boardroom, where Martika was waiting at a long table.

"So, you both understand what today is, right?"

"I could use a refresher," Elijah said. "I've never been sued before." He tried to smile, but it faded fast.

"A claim conference is essentially both counsels presenting their views to an arbiter, who will decide if the case has enough merit to go to trial. Most of the time they do go forward, so the case can be officially closed one way or another. Your recounting of the evening in question, Elijah—that while you were distraught about your parents, you wrote a few lines of lyrics down on a napkin, that Kim was procuring drugs, but then you left to go find Jane, that you sang the new lyrics for the first time to a tune you made up on the spot, is more than believable. But there is of course the issue of whether or not Kim Beard was involved in the writing of those lyrics you wrote on the napkin before going to Jane. That's a little harder to prove definitively—but it comes down to reliability."

"It sort of sounds like you're already talking trial," Elijah said. "I don't want a trial. I want today to be it. I don't want to have to rehash it all ever again. This will be bad enough. The origins of the song are painful for me. As you know. As I've said over and over again."

Some of the personnel for the label were starting to arrive. They all nodded at Jane and Elijah before taking their seats.

"I promise, a trial will be easier than you think," Martika said in a low voice. "And I cannot stress this enough: it will be important so it can be established irrevocably that you own this intellectual property. That the song was indeed your creation."

"Which it was," Jane says. "I was there."

More people enter the room and Martika lowers her voice further. "You have nothing to worry about. That night at Re-bar, after you left, Elijah, the Marvel Boys trashed the stage and were kicked out of the club. Every witness Kim Beard could call, anyone there with him that night, was incapacitated by alcohol, potentially drugs. I've already got witnesses lined up who will corroborate all this at a trial, should it go there. And then there are the countless other witnesses who saw you two perform at Central Saloon later that evening, who spoke with you afterward and can confirm you were both upset but seemed sober. That you both drank only water that night. Who wouldn't, after their parents had been killed in a drunk-driving accident?" Jane looked away from her, suddenly ashamed. But just then, Kim and his crew walked in. When he saw Jane he started humming the tune of "Oh Yoko" under his breath. She narrowed her eyes at him, felt like a teenage girl in a basement again. But so what if he thought she was Yoko? John and Yoko had loved each other—and they had been true artists, together. She kept glaring at him until he finally looked away.

A dimunitive woman with pure white hair and large glasses entered the room. She sat down at the head of the table and looked at each person, one by one.

"Okay, shall we get started?" she said, glancing at her watch. She seemed completely unaffected by the fact that there was a media circus outside, and she was in a room full of nouveau famous rock stars.

Kim's lawyer, Tom Appleton, a middle-aged man wearing a sharkskin suit, stood. He circled the boardroom table twice, as if winding himself up. "Before the Lightning Bottles even existed," he intoned, "there were the Marvel Boys. They recently released an album that is experiencing great success, too." Jane hadn't listened to the Marvel Boys' album, and she didn't plan to, ever. She already knew what it likely contained: probably a dozen or so songs that all sounded the same, featuring average instrumentation and Kim Beard shout-singing lyrics he had hastily rewritten after Elijah left the band. "The album has already sold a hundred thousand copies and is well on its way to going gold," Appleton said, his tone smug—as if being one-fifth toward anything could be considered "well on its way." Meanwhile, the Lightning Bottles album was charting faster than any other album that decade. Its current platinum status had left the Marvel Boys well behind.

But Appleton continued to detail and inflate the Marvel Boys meager accomplishments. "And no one even knew the names Elijah Hart and Jane Pyre, no one had heard of the Lightning Bottles, until they released a song that Kim Beard wrote *with* Elijah, his best friend since childhood, during a very tragic moment in his life—a moment when many witnesses say Jane Pyre, the woman who supposedly loves Elijah, screamed at him before abandoning him."

At that, Elijah leapt from his seat, his chair falling to the floor with a clatter.

"No, you will not fucking go there, man!" he shouted at Kim's lawyer. Then he turned to his former friend. "And *you*, Kim," he said, his voice low and menacing now. "How fucking dare you? You fucking owe me. I wrote all your goddamn songs. It is not the other way around."

"Sure it is, Elijah," Kim said calmly, but Jane could tell he was rattled. Elijah never lost his temper. In fact, Jane had only seen it happen one other time: the day the Marvel Boys broke up.

Martika stood and put her hand on his arm. "Please," she said firmly. "Just sit down. Let me do my job."

The arbiter frowned at Elijah. "One more outburst, Mr. Hart, and I will simply end this and send you to court for the trial."

He ignored her. "My mother, the woman this song is about, told me life wasn't always going to be fair," Elijah said. "And she was right—but I didn't know *how* right until today."

"Enough!" The arbiter stood. "I meant what I said, Mr. Hart. But you chose to continue your tirade. We're done here." She turned to Martika. "Don't say I didn't warn your client, Ms. Assad. Kim Beard's claim versus the Lightning Bottles and Columbia Records will go forward. And, as per the initial claim document, no publishing royalties from that particular song will be released to any party until the claim is settled." Her heels clicked on the polished concrete floor as she beelined for the door, but she looked back over her shoulder once before she left the room, her gaze landing on Elijah. "My granddaughter isn't going to believe it when I tell her I met you," she said.

The door banged shut and she was gone.

Kim stood. Now he and Elijah faced each other from either end of the boardroom table.

"See you in court, brother," Kim said.

"Stop fucking calling me that."

"Okay, pal."

The room emptied out and Elijah slumped back down at the table. Martika began to speak, but he interrupted her. "Please," he said. "Let's just schedule a meeting. I can't talk about this right now. I just want to be left alone." He looked up. "Petra, you, too. We'll talk later. I just want to be with Jane."

Once everyone was gone, he put his face in his hands. *"Fuck."*

Jane wished he hadn't sent Martika and Petra away. She had no idea what to say to him, how to comfort him. "That fucking song is going to kill me." She touched his back. His body trembled beneath her fingertips.

"Elijah, no. Remember when you sang it on the top of the record store? That was beautiful, it was *amazing*. You let it go that day, do you remember?" But he just shook his head—and she realized she had been high that day, likely having her own experience separate from his. "I promise," she said, trying a different angle. "It's not just you in this. It's *us*. Together."

"I still don't know if I can handle it. It's too dark. It chases me."

"It's not just *dark*, though. It's an exquisite song. And your mom would have loved it. She wouldn't want you to hate it so much. She would say something good came out of something bad."

He sighed and shook his head. "Let's just get out of here."

They left the courthouse through a side door and were about to hop into the waiting SUV when Elijah paused and looked up. She followed the direction of his gaze and saw Kim Beard outside the courthouse, speaking to a crowd of press.

"Don't," Jane said, pulling him back toward the car. "No more looking back when you don't have to. Especially not at him."

But Elijah grabbed Jane by the hand in an abrupt movement. "Come on," he said. "We're the main attraction here. Not him and his shitty band. And we have some happy news. Right? It just broke today. Plus, we have our side of the story to tell."

For some reason, this idea terrified her. She had grown used to sitting in silence, in their meetings, in their world. But there was no stopping him as he leaned into the SUV, which had a bar that was always stocked, grabbed a bottle of champagne, and popped it open. "Let's go." He pulled her along with him. His fingers dug into her arm, and it hurt a little. As they approached Kim, a murmur began. He kept talking, but soon, all the reporters had turned away from him and toward Jane and Elijah.

"Hello," Elijah called out, waving the bottle of champagne. "So, whatever he's telling you is bullshit. Don't listen to Kim. The song at the heart of this dispute, 'My Life or Yours,' is a very personal song to me. It's about my mother." It felt like he had pulled a pin on a grenade. Did everyone really need to know the depths of the pain that had inspired the song? But he kept talking, oblivious to Jane's chagrin. Kim, meanwhile, tried to shout something to the reporters, but when they ignored him, he stormed away. "I wrote it the night she was killed by a drunk driver." His choice of words surprised Jane. And the media was going to jump on this, she knew it. They'd find out it had been his father who was driving. She squeezed his hand, trying to signal him to stop, but it was no use. "My mom, Alice, was beautiful and kind. She had long blond hair and she looked like Helen Sear and she liked to smoke weed." He allowed a grin, the one that would become famous, launch a thousand, a million, instantly lifelong crushes. "She made me—and Jane, here—feel loved all the time. She made it clear we were the most important things in the world to her. She taught us about life, and she taught us about philosophy, and she helped us believe in ourselves. There is only one person in the world who could have written those lyrics, and that person is *me*. My mom didn't even like Kim. She fucking hated him. Any questions?"

"Why is Kim Beard saying he helped write the song, then? Is it true you were together the night you wrote it? Is it true you and Jane were fighthing?"

"Kim Beard can't write lyrics that go beyond the surface." *Flash, flash, flash*, went the cameras. "The Marvel Boys album is already out—take a listen, if you want. What song on that record would make anyone think Kim could be remotely capable of contributing to a song about love, loss, and compassion? What about his persona suggests that at all?" *Flash. Flash. Flash.* Elijah pulled Jane forward. "Anyway, we don't want to talk about Kim. We heard that the news is out about our wedding. We're really happy. Right, Jane?" He raised the bottle of champagne again, held it to his lips, passed it to her. "Every single day feels like a celebration with my brand-new wife. And we're just getting started." Jane felt like an animal frozen in headlights. Was this what fame was, putting yourself and your secrets on display? What about the songs, the stories she was okay with telling—the made-up ones, the fantasies, the legends? Elijah bent to kiss her temple but she stared ahead, willing this moment to be over. *You wanted this*, she reminded herself. *You wanted to be famous. You wanted everyone to know your name.* But it had always been her songs, her words,

Elijah's voice, that she imagined people would be interested in. Not their past, not their relationship.

Each camera's flash seemed to reveal another truth to her. The song she had fought so hard for Elijah to claim, because she knew it was the key to their fame—now it felt like it was going to be their undoing. *Flash.* She felt suddenly certain they wouldn't survive if their world of two was constantly crowded out by other people. *Flash. Flash. Flash.*

"Smile, Jane," Elijah whispered as the reporters shouted out questions. She tried, and she failed. When the photos ran the next day, the commentary would be that Jane Pyre didn't look very happy for someone who had recently married Elijah Hart—that maybe, she wasn't happy at all.

LOS ANGELES, CALIFORNIA

FEBRUARY 1992

The Lightning Bottles went out on tour in support of their wildly successful debut album, traveling from one city to the next with such speed and regularity that they often lost track of where they were. Taking mushrooms or Ecstasy before each show had become regular practice for Elijah, and Jane joined in once in a while, but mostly she just drank. He insisted it helped him be a better performer—and Jane couldn't argue with the fact that he was electric onstage. It was an exciting, exhausting first month on tour, a blur of cities and fans, parties and music.

Then the 1992 Grammy Award nominations were released, and the excitement increased. The Lightning Bottles were up for Album of the Year, Record of the Year, Song of the Year, Best New Artist, Best Music Video, and Best Alternative Music Album. Heaven Wretch was also nominated for many of those categories—and the Marvel Boys had been nominated for Best Alternative Music Album, too, although Jane and Elijah tried to ignore this fact.

When they returned to LA a few days before the awards show—they were taking a short break for the Grammys and a few appearances on late-night talk shows before heading back out on tour—Elijah called Zack to congratulate him, and Jane overheard him on the phone.

"Yeah, fuck them," he said, and she could only assume he was talking about the Marvel Boys. "So, you're doing okay? You sound a little . . . yeah. I get that. Yeah. We should do that. See you at the awards, man."

"Is he alright?" Jane asked when Elijah hung up. She was remembering how kind Zack had been to her, that day back in Seattle when he had been looking for a drummer and they had told him they'd formed their own band. "We never ended up jamming with him."

"I said that too. We'll set it up. He seems a little worn out from all the attention," Elijah said.

Jane almost said she was too, but she bit the words back. It was *so* Seattle, to say you didn't want it. And she did, she reminded herself. They were stars, living the dream. They were Grammy-nominated musicians.

Later, a huge bouquet of lilies arrived at their house; Jane nearly gagged at their cloying, funeral smell—and the card made her feel even worse. "Brother: Hope my song brings in lots of hardware for you. Can't wait for the paycheck." Jane threw them in the trash outside before Elijah saw them.

"Do you think we'll actually win anything?" Elijah asked Jane as their limousine crawled through the perpetual LA gridlock the next day. "As cheesy as this sounds, it really is just such an honor being nominated, isn't it?" His smile was shy. It was a relief to Jane that although he sometimes acted like a stranger onstage or when he talked to the media—which Jane, since the excruciating experience outside the courthouse, always felt skittish about now—their fame was not changing him. He was still her Elijah.

"It is," she agreed. "I can't believe this is happening, that this is us."

"Oh, come on, you can." His smile grew wider. "You always knew we'd be famous."

She laughed as he poured her a glass of champagne. "Okay, you're right, I did." She looked down at the flute, with its innocent-looking bubbles that always tickled her nose. On tour, Jane had moved past champagne, though. "I think I need something stronger," she said. "I'm nervous."

He rummaged around, pulled out a bottle of tequila. "Tequila is supposed to be like . . . an upper," he said, pouring her a glass. "Although I wish I had some actual uppers." He pulled two baggies out of his jacket pocket. "But I've got 'shrooms, if you want. Or some Ecstasy. I know you liked that . . ."

"Once," she said. "I liked it *once*. And there is no way I'm going to the Grammys high. You shouldn't either."

"I'm not a lightweight like you, though."

She laughed it off, threw back the tequila, and poured more as he swallowed both mushrooms and a pill, washing it down with a vodka-and-tequila mixture he coined as his signature cocktail: the Golden Grammy.

That night, the Lightning Bottles did end up winning, and big, in almost every category they were nominated in except Best Alternative Music Album, which went to Heaven Wretch, and Record of the Year, which went to Natalie Cole. In truth, Jane felt relieved by this—Record of the Year was awarded to the production team, too, and that would have meant standing onstage with Hamlet Garvin.

She was sure she had never been happier—but then the show's host, a well-known actor-comedian, made a joke about her. "Did you notice that those beautiful little butter flowers on your bread plates during dinner were still a little frozen, too cold to spread?" he said. "That was on purpose—the caterer wanted to see if butter would melt in Jane Pyre's mouth." It was just a joke, and not a very good one, but it still embarrassed Jane.

"You just have to smile more," Alan, who was sitting at their table, leaned over and said. "Try it sometime."

"Congratulations," Bono whispered to Jane later, patting her arm as she moved past him from her seat to accept the award for Album of the Year. "You two are absolutely electric." This was all that mattered, Jane told herself. Recognition from artists like Bono was the stuff of dreams. But she still couldn't get the joke about her frosty personality out of her head. And she did feel frozen. In the bright lights onstage, as they accepted their awards, she now wondered if she should stand there smiling or if that would just look weird. Then she stumbled and nearly fell on her way up the stage steps to accept the Best Music Video award, and she realized she had had too much to drink. She was grateful that Elijah remembered who to thank. All she could do was nervously murmer, *Thank you, thank you.*

When they accepted their last award of the night, the one for Album of the Year, Elijah looked out into the crowd, grinning. He pulled Jane close, his arm slung around her shoulders. "Here we are again," he said. "Sick of us yet?" Laughter, cheers. "Listen, we're so grateful. And we know what it's like to be music fans." He then found the cameras, stared into them, spoke to the people watching at home—the ones, Jane knew, who he felt really mattered. "We *are* music fans." When Heaven Wretch had won for best alternative music album, Zack had taken the microphone and mumbled, "Thanks . . . I guess?" before wandering back to his seat and getting lost along the way, obviously intoxicated. But Elijah, no matter that he had been drinking too, had even more hallucinogens in his system too, was perfect.

He turned to Jane. "And you, Jane. I want to thank you. For the music, the songs. *Everything.*" She didn't know how to respond. He wasn't supposed to even hint that she wrote their songs, was he? *Smile*, she told herself, *just damn well smile.* She did. "Thank you back," she said to her husband.

He kissed her as if the cameras weren't there. She was the one to pull away first—because she felt something in the room shift then, felt an almost palpable sensation of envy flowing her way. Everyone wanted Elijah Hart—but the moment he looked at Jane Pyre, he belonged only to her. Suddenly this felt dangerous. Jane put her hand on her husband's chest and whispered, "Okay. That's enough."

As Jane and Elijah returned to their seats, a commotion broke out. From the back of the auditorium, Jane heard shouts.

"You fucking frauds! You thieves!"

It was Kim. Security was upon him quickly, and he was escorted away before the cameras could fully catch what was happening. But still, it shook her.

"Don't worry, he's just jealous," said Michael Stipe, who was sitting nearby. "You should be flattered. Really, Jane."

"Oh, sure," Jane said. "I am." She smiled so big she was sure she looked slightly unhinged. But she was talking to Michael Stipe. This was what she had always wanted. "Who cares about him anyway?"

And she found she really didn't care about Kim. What she did care about was getting another drink—it had been hours. The after-party couldn't come soon enough.

"Hey, guys," Zack said later, at the after-party. His expression was listless. "Congrats on all the awards."

"And to you," Jane said. "Can you believe we're Grammy winners? I feel almost crazy even saying it." She was feeling better now. She had a martini in her hand, and the vibe at the party was more relaxed than the awards ceremony had been. Annie Lennox had come over to meet them. They had chatted more with Michael Stipe, and Elijah had even told him about their letters, the way they had wanted to turn "stipe" into an adjective. Tom Waits had sidled up to Jane at the bar and complimented her guitar playing.

"Well, maybe?" Zack said. "Like, is any of our music the big fucking deal everyone is making it out to be, or is it just because we're from Seattle and someone, somewhere decided Seattle is where it's at? Plus, I'm from Aberdeen. It's kind of fucked, right? I mean, sorry. I don't mean to insult you or anything. I just . . ." He trailed off, but his cynical tone was like a splash of cold water on Jane's mood. She stared at Zack as he shook his head and licked his lips, seeming lost in thought now. His lips were cracked and dry. His blue eyes were even brighter than usual, his pupils barely visible, like pinpricks in the middle of his irises. He wore his customary layers, despite the fact that the room was hot, crowded with people. "I'm gonna get out of here. Just wanted to make sure to say hi to you guys."

They watched him go. "He's in bad shape," Jane said, but Elijah just stared into his empty glass.

"So am I. My drink is empty." He saw her face. "Come on, forget him and his sour Seattle mood. Let's get refills."

Jane lost track of how many times they returned to the bar, lost track of the night altogether after that—until later, when she was in the bathroom and she heard her name spoken outside the stall. Suddenly she was sober.

"That Jane Pyre joke? I know. Totally. Like, she looks completely miserable, all the time."

"If Elijah Hart wanted to make out with me, I wouldn't care if we were on the stage getting a Grammy or in front of the pope. How do you think he stands living with her? Do you think it's, like, one of those fake relationships?"

Enough. Jane flushed the toilet and pushed open the stall door, but the women hadn't noticed her yet.

"I heard she's a total bitch. She had their first producer fired for some petty reason no one really knows. And look at how crazy she's driven Kim Beard. Poor guy. Jane Pyre is bad news."

Jane's footfalls in her combat boots were heavy as she approached the sink to stand beside the women, who she recognized as a pop star and someone who might have been her younger sister.

"Oops," the younger woman said.

Jane didn't speak. She washed her hands slowly and deliberately, looking from one woman to the next. They were afraid of her, she realized. She scared them. She took out her lipstick and reapplied it carefully while the two women stood, too mortified to move. Then she left without a word—and felt a tear slip down her cheek when she was back out in the hall. *Shit.* She wiped it away, grabbed a martini from a tray, and went to find her husband.

Jane awoke the next morning to a horrible headache and a mouth that felt dry, putrid. She groaned and rolled over. Elijah was asleep on the bed beside her, fully clothed, a cigar in his hand, a scorch mark on their sheets and mattress.

Jane staggered from the bed and walked down the hallway into the living room, holding her head.

But they were really there: four golden gramophones, shining bright in the morning light that flowed in through the window. Jane walked over to the awards, picked them up one by one, forgetting about her headache as she caressed them with reverence.

When Elijah got up, they started drinking again. "Hair of the dog!" Elijah shouted, possibly still drunk. "Besides, this life is too good not to celebrate properly, right, Jane? Let's forget about everything else and just be happy."

Except that day, an article surfaced about Jane Pyre that wasn't flattering. Lip-readers had caught what she had said to Elijah onstage—"Okay, that's enough"—and rumors set fire. First one gossip magazine, then another.

> *Does Jane Pyre really love Elijah Hart? Is she using*
> *him to get famous? Is she as coldhearted as she seems?*
> *Anyone catch her face after that joke?*

"It doesn't bother me," Jane insisted—but that was a lie. It felt just like it had when she was growing up in Stouffville. Like no one understood her.

There's just something about her, one article read, *that's hard to put a finger on, but it's just not pleasant.*

The Lightning Bottles always saved "My Life or Yours" for the encore in their shows; the anticipation would build throughout the concert until a rapt crowd sang the chorus of their hit song, thousands of voices becoming one.

We're all gonna . . .

All Elijah had to do was hold out the microphone. Fans called it a transcendent experience, compared it to religion. Elijah was a minister, passing around an offering plate every night. He gathered up adoration, energy, stayed on a high for hours—but sometimes Jane found herself feeling a little emptied out after their shows. Especially after their concert in Toronto, when she had a ticket and a backstage pass sent to her mother—and Raquel never showed up.

"Forget it, Jane," Elijah said. "You have me. We're the only family either of us need." He would say this more and more, especially as it became clear that the public adored him and didn't feel the same about her. And that was true, they were family, still the twin flames Alice had always said they were—except some nights, she felt she could barely reach him. He was always on something during their shows, and it set him apart from her. She would drink to try to keep up but could never seem to catch him. It worried her sometimes, the depths of their partying. The blackouts she experienced with increasing frequency. But they were fine, she told herself. They weren't like Zack, for example, who had overdosed in a hotel room in Las Vegas and was now in rehab. Or the Waverunners, destroying their teeth and their skin on meth and acting like it was normal. They would stop partying so much once the tour was over and some semblance of normalcy returned. They would go back into the studio to record their second album, and Elijah would feel like hers again.

In June of 1992, near the end of the North American tour, after nearly six months on the road, the Lightning Bottles played to a rapturous crowd at an amphitheater in San Bernardino, California. Most of the crowd of almost sixty-five-thousand fans held up lighters, turned themselves into a constellation, all gravitating toward Elijah and his comet of a voice. But when he opened his mouth to sing their final song, nothing came out. He held up the mic and the crowd filled in the lyrics—and no one noticed except Jane.

Their tour doctor diagnosed him with severe vocal cord strain, said the only solution was vocal rest and that they should cancel the last few shows on the tour. At first, Elijah thought it was funny. He wrote Jane Adam & the Rib comics instead of speaking. Since their night with La Dure in Hamburg, he had added graffiti-esque details to his drawings. But he got bored, fast. The tour had been a blur of excitement, and now their house just felt quiet. Jane pulled dustcovers off furnuiture, lit candles, but it felt all wrong. It didn't feel like home anymore, and she wondered if from now on she was only going to feel at home in hotel rooms, or tour buses, or sleeping in the seat of a plane.

"Should we move?" she asked Elijah. "Should we go on a trip?"

Elijah just shrugged, as listless as she was.

So Jane asked Petra to find them a new place to rent. Since the royalties for "My Life or Yours" were still tied up in Kim's dispute, the trial date several months away in a backlogged court system, they had to be careful with money. But they chose a more tony address in Beverly Hills, a place with a proper security gate and a private pool rather than a beach. Jane tried to use the time after they moved to write songs, but Elijah's damaged voice rattled her. For the first time in her life, she had writer's block. She listened to music instead. Her favorite recent album was from a band called Hole, an album called *Pretty on the Inside* she would scream along with, hoping to loosen something inside herself enough to start writing again. It didn't work.

Then the Lightning Bottles were invited to tour with a traveling alternative, punk, and metal rock festival called Söckdologer. Elijah gave his voice a few more weeks of rest, and Jane still worried about how lethargic and low he seemed. But when they met up with the tour in Oregon, against the backdrop of mountains and redwoods, all the fresh air, Jane felt nothing but optimistic. They were given a luxurious yurt to sleep in, filled with the soft light of lanterns at night. It was romantic and exciting—except some nights, Elijah didn't come back to the yurt at all. She'd find him in the morning, passed out in some backstage area or other. He seemed to find the bands who partied hardest to hang out with and, as usual, Jane couldn't keep up—or maybe she just didn't want to.

She brought it up one morning, and he snapped at her, reminding her all at once of Moses, shouting at her after he fell on the driveway. "Jesus, get off my case! You're not your judgmental mother, so don't act like her." She flinched at his harsh words, and he immediately apologized. "I'm sorry," he said. "I just have a really bad hangover. I shouldn't have said that. I'll tone it down."

But he didn't, and their petty little arguments became more frequent and more serious.

In August, La Dure joined the music festival tour for a few of the West Coast shows, playing on one of the side stages. When Jane saw them in the lineup, she was excited. But Elijah didn't seem as thrilled. It was late afternoon when Jane spotted Maxime and his bandmates arriving. Elijah had smoked a joint with the members of a ska band from Detroit and was sprawled on a backstage-area couch, eyes half-closed. Jane was sitting nearby, as bored as she always was, waiting for nightfall, when they could go onstage and play.

"Hey!" Maxime's eyes lit up when he saw them, but Elijah barely opened his eyes. "What are you doing now?" Maxime asked Jane. "Want to walk around with us, check out some of the other bands?"

"We don't go out there. We always get swarmed."

Maxime gave her his sunglasses, then swiped a battered fedora from one of the passed-out guys in the ska band. "There you go. No one will know it's you. Tuck your hair up underneath. Perfect. Let's go."

Jane had the best day. She drank frothy beers from plastic cups, watched some great bands play—the Jesus and Mary Chain, Lush, Rage Against the Machine, Luscious Jackson. It was getting dark by the time she returned to the staging area, arm in arm with Maxime and Jean, and Elijah was still on the same couch. But now he was awake, and alone, and glowering.

"Where were you?" he shot at her. The smile faded from Jane's face.

"We were just . . . walking around." She took off the glasses and fedora.

"Did you steal Alec's hat? He was pissed."

"She borrowed it," Maxime said lightly. "She needed a disguise. How are you, man?"

"A little tired, man. It's been a busy year. Come on, Jane. We're due for sound check."

Elijah's reaction had unsettled her, but the day with her friends from

La Dure still stuck with Jane as they traveled to the next city with the music festival—even if it was never repeated, and she demurred when Maxime asked again.

One night in their yurt, she began strumming her guitar and, for the first time in months, wrote a song. It was called "My Lost Bottle of Chartreuse," and when she played it for Elijah, he said it was good.

"We should practice it a little more and then add it to our set," Jane suggested.

Elijah gave her a long look and Jane couldn't tell what he was thinking. But then he nodded and said, "Sure, whatever you want." After they had learned the song, he put his guitar down and stood. "Hey, I told the guys from Dinosaur Jr. I'd hang out with them today." And he left her alone.

He returned drunk and boisterous. His breath was sour when he kissed her. Jane poured some vodka and water into a red plastic cup to bring with her onstage, and he watched her, then stepped closer and said, "Maybe you want some Chartreuse."

"Maxime is a friend," she said in a low voice.

"You wrote a fucking song about him."

"Not *about* him. About that night we spent with them in Hamburg."

"Yeah, but what about that line. *You looked at me like you wanted me, and I wondered.* I can't believe you want me to sing that."

"Elijah, it doesn't mean anything. It's a *song*. And we need to try out some new material. We can't just keep playing the same songs over and over."

"You know as well as I do that songs mean fucking everything. Nothing is *just a song*, Jane." And he stormed away. She didn't see him again until their set was about to begin. He didn't even show up for sound check. Just before they were about to go onstage, she felt him behind her. She turned—and she knew. His eyes looked like Zack's did, with pupils as tiny as pinholes.

"Elijah, what the fuck?"

He ignored her, walked onstage. "My Lost Bottle of Chartreuse" was on their set list, but she tried to signal him not to play it. It was a bad idea. He did it anyway. When it came to the line *You looked at me like you wanted me, and I wondered,* he changed it to *You looked at me like you wanted to fuck me, and I wanted you to.* Jane almost dropped her guitar. She went back to their yurt after the set and waited for him—but he didn't return until the sun was coming up. He barely said anything before he passed out, and Jane spent the next few hours sitting beside him, watching him, checking if he was breathing. When he woke up she told him they were done with Söckdologer, that she wanted to go home. Wordlessly, he packed his bag and followed her to the door.

"How often have you been doing heroin?" Jane asked him when they were back in LA. Her heart was racing and she felt sick.

"Just that one time," Elijah said. "And I'm so sorry, Jane. I was an asshole."

"I understand jealousy," Jane said. "You know it happens to me too."

"You know I love only you. I'm sorry, I really am. I've just been so stressed. The tour, everything, it's been a lot."

"Please, listen to me. That felt like a worse betrayal than anything. You were addicted once; it could happen again."

"I'm fine," he insisted. "It was just the one time. Please, come here, Jane?" He patted the couch beside him, opened his arms to her. She was upset with him but still found him hard to resist. "I won't do it again," he said when she was close.

"I won't let you," she said.

Late one night, in their LA home, Jane woke up to use the bathroom. She pushed open the door to find Elijah in there, slumped on the closed toilet. He sat up abruptly when he heard her, and a canister dropped out of his hand, blue and white pills scattering all over the floor.

"It's just something to help me relax at night," he said, his words thick and slurred.

She picked up the canister and read it. "Elijah, these are barbiturates. Where did you get them?"

"From our tour doctor. It's fine. I had trouble sleeping sometimes, on tour. I needed them."

"We're not on tour anymore."

He didn't say anything.

"Why didn't you tell me?"

"I don't know. Because it's nothing."

"These are addictive. They aren't good for you."

"Not sleeping isn't good for me either."

She looked at him closely. "You don't eat, you're too thin—and your voice . . . it just went that time. Plus, the way you acted at Söckdologer. Maybe it's because of these."

"My voice went because I was exhausted. You're right, I need to eat better, I need to rest more. And Söckdologer . . . I was jealous. You know that. Let's just put it behind us."

She flushed the pills down the toilet. "Jane. Don't."

He sounded so agonized—and she knew it was about the pills. She knew she needed help with this. So she called Petra. Her partner, Ramona, was a naturopath, and Jane asked her to come over. Ramona suggested that Elijah take a concoction of skullcap and melatonin, that he drink teas made of various powders and roots to help him sleep better. Jane began to cook the way Alice had. Casseroles covered in cheese, stews, big salads. She watched Elijah carefully, and he did seem better. She had lost sight of him during the blur of the tour, but it was okay now.

"But still, he's not himself," she confided to Petra. "He's the same as when we got back from the tour. He's just . . . flat." She clasped her hands together, wrung them like wet rags. "And I'm not writing again. I have, like, two songs for our next album. We're just not *us*."

"Back before you were famous, what sort of dreams did you have together?"

Jane thought for a moment. "We wanted to travel. All over Europe."

"And you were happy when you toured there, right?"

"Some of our happiest days."

"Go back. Take an actual vacation. Why not . . . rent a house in Barcelona? Go to the Amalfi Coast or France. Rent an apartment in Paris. You can go anywhere, do anything. Take the break, take the rest. Take the chance for a change of scenery—just the two of you. I think it will help with your writing."

Jane talked to Elijah about it, and he agreed a trip was a good idea. They chose Paris and flew out the next day.

PARIS, FRANCE

DECEMBER 21, 1999

Hen had never been on a plane before and seemed alarmed by the idea, so Jane said they'd drive to Paris, stopping halfway at a hotel for the night. The halfway point is Cologne, where they shop for disguises before checking into their hotel. Jane isn't going to make the same mistake she had made in Hamburg. She will not be recognized this time. They buy wigs, hats, sunglasses, fill shopping bags with them, and load them into the trunk of the BMW.

Jane checks in *Bunte*, Germany's most well-known celebrity gossip magazine, but no pictures of her skulking in a Hamburg alley with a teenage girl have been published. Not yet, anyway.

They arrive in Paris on December 21, four days before Christmas. The city is even more lit up than usual, the lights colorful and festive. Jane had almost forgotten about the holiday and thinks of Hen's mother, alone at home. She considers saying something, but what is there to say? Hen made her decision, and really, it isn't Jane's business.

Hen is entranced by Paris, pressing her face against the window of the car as more and more monuments come into view: the Eiffel Tower, the domed roof of the Panthéon, the vivid stained glass rose windows of the Notre Dame cathedral, its skyward-pointing spires. But Jane tries to keep herself immune to the city's charms. After all, she'd once sworn to never return here.

The December sun is sinking early, inching the city toward the golden hour it wears so well when they reach their hotel. Turrets, domes, flags, awnings. "No building in Paris is plain," Hen says admiringly. "I love it here." Jane wishes she could feel the same—delighted, a first-time visitor to Paris, taking it all in, no bad memories to grapple with. But this place was not kind to her.

They check into a small hotel at the edge of the Latin Quarter, where Jane hopes they will go unnoticed. They put their bags in their room, then return to the street, where they find a small, out-of-the-way café to have dinner. Hen orders hot chocolate and a croque monsieur. Jane has the fish of the day and finds herself ravenously hungry. She wishes she had ordered what Hen did.

Despite her childlike ordering, Hen looks older tonight. She decided to disguise herself too, has her hair in a low ponytail, under a flat cap, is wearing black-framed glasses and bright red lipstick. Jane is in a long dark wig and fedora, no makeup. No one has looked at her twice.

Once their plates are cleared and the bill is paid, Jane suggests they go see if they can find the hotel where she and Elijah stayed. "There are so many places to look for the next clue in this city, but it's a good enough start," she says.

Elijah feels close here. Her memories and recollections thicken. She finds herself searching the faces of every person they pass on the sidewalks for someone who looks like him. Her heart aches when no one resembles him, when everywhere her eyes search proves fruitless. The hotel is still there, but there is nothing on its walls, nothing in the nearby alleys, no clues, no sign of an Adam poster at all. Is she chasing a dream, she wonders? Or worse, a cruel hoax?

Hen is watching her. "I have an idea," she says. "I saw a Christmas market on the way here, and there was a Ferris wheel. What if we go ride it? The view might help you think about other places around the city where Elijah could have left something, places you went together." She looks shy. "And it will mean I get to see everything, this entire city."

The little gondolas on the wheel at the holiday market Hen leads Jane back to look like glowing Christmas tree ornaments. The spokes of the

Ferris wheel are the color of France's national flag, shining bright in the night. Jane and Hen take their seats, the door of their gondola cabin closes, and the wheel begins to move.

Which is when Jane realizes Hen is trembling.

"This thing seems pretty rickety," Hen says, squeezing her eyes shut. "Are we sure it's in good condition? Definitely safe?"

"I assume we're perfectly safe. None of these gondolas have ever fallen off, to my knowledge."

"Maybe I should have mentioned I'm afraid of heights," Hen says. "Except I didn't actually know it, because I've never been up this high." As she clenches white-knuckled fists in her lap, Jane searches for a way to comfort her—but all she can think about are the sentences Hen has just uttered.

Maybe I should have mentioned I'm afraid of heights.

Except I didn't actually know it, because I've never been up this high.

"Hen, could you give me a beat?"

"Excuse me?" Hen cracks one eyelid open.

"Drum." She points to the metal bar in front of them, in the middle of the car. They have risen to the top of the ride now and the city is spread out before them. The spokes, and the wheel, all that endless iconic charm—but Hen keeps her frightened gaze inside the teetering car, while Jane focuses on the song forming in her head. "Please," Jane says. It's starting to feel urgent—and she hasn't allowed herself to feel this since Elijah disappeared. After all, what was the point of writing songs if Elijah wasn't there to sing them? But suddenly, writing this song feels just as important as finding him.

Hen opens her other eye. She unclenches her fists. She taps gently on the bar so the car won't shake too much, and Jane hums along, then brushes aside her self-consciousness and lets herself sing softly. The tune, the words, take shape. *Maybe I should have told you I was afraid of heights. You were looking for someone to save you, I just hated lonely nights . . .*

Her stomach swoops as the Ferris wheel ascends, descends, as Paris comes in and out of view. She sings. Hen keeps time.

"I like it," Hen says when she stops. "It's a *great* song. You're good at this."

"I thought we had established that," Jane says, and she smiles. She feels lightheaded, elated. She hasn't done this in what feels like a lifetime. But the ride is over. The attendant opens the door, and Jane says to Hen, "Let's go up again?"

"No way." Hen hops out of the gondola. "That was terrifying. My worst idea so far. Let's go buy a map instead."

They find one in a corner store, then sit down on a bench. Jane unfolds it, squints to make out the details in the dark.

"Wasn't there a restaurant where you two played one night, where you sang Christmas songs? I remember reading about that once," Hen prompts.

Jane nods, and the food she ate earlier is now making her queasy. "Yes, we did."

"That was the night you got arrested, right?"

Jane squints down at the map, avoids the question. "It was here." She points to an intersection in the 6th arrondissement. "I don't know if the café still exists, but we can go and look around."

The café is not there; it's a clothing store now, and the neighborhood is much tonier than Jane remembers. The walls in this neighborhood are clear, mostly. The odd graffiti tag, but most have been scrubbed, painted over. There is one mural on a building's exterior wall, but it is a commission, features brightly colored images of children with schoolbooks following a teacher like obedient ducklings.

A poster on a telephone pole causes Hen to stop walking. Jane's heart flutters with excitement, trepidation—but it's an actual concert poster, not one made by Elijah's hand.

"La Dure!" Hen exclaims. "They're playing a concert tonight." Her eyes are alight with excitement. "We should go. Don't you think?"

"I'm not sure why we would," Jane says, hesitant, but also drawn to the way her past is intersecting with her present.

"Oh, come on. Let's find the club. *Please?* The only other concert I've ever been to was . . . well, yours."

"We're not dressed for a club concert."

But Hen points to a brightly lit shop window up ahead, the display filled with vivid minidresses and sequined miniskirts. The store is called Femme Sauvage, and Jane knows it will have what they need, so she says, "Fine," and walks toward it, opens the door. "Okay," she says. "Choose something to wear." Hen's eyes light up even more.

Jane finds a black skirt, frosted with dark sequins. High boots. A long jacket. There is a fuchsia wig on a hatstand and thick-rimmed glasses on a stand by the register, and she gathers all these things up in her arms.

Hen steps out of a changing room in an orange miniskirt, a matching orange fuzzy jacket over a white T-shirt. She finds white high-top sneakers, a wig that looks like Baby Spice's pigtails. Jane can't help but laugh. "A real club kid," she says. "All you need is a backpack and a candy pacifier."

They buy the clothes, wear them out of the store. Jane has almost forgotten, in the fun of the impromptu shopping trip, what she is doing here in this city—but the night makes her remember. She's chasing the beating of her own heart, the core of her existence, with no clue how to find it or if she ever will. But she's *almost* having fun—maybe she even is. They buy makeup at a drugstore and she helps Hen with hers in a café restroom, paints her lips the same dark color as hers usually are.

"Wow," Hen says, gazing at herself. "I've never looked like this before."

At the club, the doorman only gives them a passing glance, doesn't ask for ID, just the cash for the tickets. They walk through the door and into the darkness, the heat of the room already oppressive. As they pass a bar, Hen veers off, away from Jane, who follows, says nothing as Hen orders herself a Kleiner Feigling. She asks for a water for herself and then stays as close to Hen as she can as they press their way close to the front.

The opening band comes on: a trio of women who remind Jane a bit of Lush. She becomes absorbed in the music and doesn't notice that Hen has wandered off to the bar again. This time she returns with a blue cocktail in her hand and Jane has to bite her tongue, stop herself from saying, the way her mother might, *Are you sure that's such a good idea, Hen?* She is not the mother here, she reminds herself. Hen can do as she pleases.

When the opening band finishes, the floor in front of the stage fills up, and Jane and Hen are pushed back, closer to the bar—which is when Jane feels hands on her shoulders. She flinches, hard, and someone's drink spills across her shoulder blade. She turns to see two men standing behind them, each holding out drinks. Hen is delighted, her maroon-painted lips forming a smile. "She's too young for you," Jane finds herself saying, pulling Hen away while Hen says, *"Hey!* I am old enough to take care of myself!," and the men call out to her in French.

Even over the music and the laughter and the loud chatter, Jane hears the looseness in Hen's voice, smells the alcohol on her breath. She doesn't know how much more of this she can handle—not because she wants a drink right now or because any of this is tempting her off the wagon; Jane knows she will make it to 246 days of sobriety when the sun rises the next day. It's something else that's bothering her: the fact that she's now responsible for Hen. Jane isn't good at taking care of people. Bad things happen to people under her watch.

The stage lights begin to pulse, the small crowd roars, and Jane pushes them closer to the front again. "Let's just watch the show," she says to Hen. "Come on."

When the music starts, Jane relaxes. You can't think too much when music like this is playing. For the duration of the concert, she tells herself she will give her mind a break. From all of it. From Elijah, and whatever message he may have left for her somewhere in this city. She tries not to think about what the messages may mean. That he's still alive—and that he has been the architect of these years of her agony—or that he's still dead, and the clues are just a cruel trick. All she can do now is listen to this music she used to know and love. To a person singing it who was a part of her past.

Hen stumbles into her, spills some of her drink, which she then

gulps back—just as Jane sees that Maxime is watching her. He looks a little different. Maybe a bit more like an artist, a bit less like a punk rocker.
He's wearing a black T-shirt, black jeans, his hair is longer than it was
years ago. He breaks her gaze and she wonders if she imagined him looking at her at all. He riffs on his guitar and cheers rise in the crowd. The
room is getting hotter and her thick-rimmed glasses are fogging. Jane
removes them and wipes them on her blazer—then looks up in time to
see Maxime back at the edge of the stage, watching her again. This time,
there is no mistaking it. He tilts his head, and the stage lights flash hard in
time to the beat. She puts her glasses on again and backs off a bit, pulling
Hen with her. Did he recognize her? Did she want him to?

"Jane?"

She turns to Hen. Even in the dim of the club, Jane can see how pale
she looks. Her eyes are glazed. "I don't feel so good." Jane puts her hands
on Hen's shoulders and guides her toward the back door.

"Come on, steady, you'll be okay," she says, her hands firm on Hen's
back until she gets her outside.

"Oh god," Hen says, doubling over, groaning, then retching. Jane
passes her the water bottle she's still holding; Hen gulps it down.

"I'm *sorry*," she says, wiping her mouth. "I've never had more than a
sip of wine before. I shouldn't have done that. I just . . ."

Jane shakes her head. "It's okay," she says, removing her glasses and
putting them in her pocket. The magenta wig is making her head sweat,
so she takes that off, too.

"Oh god, I'm so stupid," Hen says. "I just wanted to know what it
was like to be drunk—and it's terrible, horrible, how do people *do* this?"

Jane finds herself chuckling. "Are you okay to walk a little? Here,
have some more water. Let's go out to the road, we'll get a taxi back to
the hotel. We'll have a big breakfast tomorrow. That'll make you feel better. You're young enough that that's the only hangover cure you'll need."

Hen just groans in response.

Back in the hotel room, she collapses into her bed, her lipstick and
makeup staining the pillowcase. She looks younger again, like herself.

Jane places a glass of water beside her. She makes sure she is on her side before she falls asleep, sets one of the wastebaskets on the floor beside the bed.

She leaves her a note, just in case she wakes up.

Jane returns to the club, goes around to the back, and bangs at the door. Eventually, a burly man in a leather vest opens it. He says something in French, and Jane uses the French she learned in elementary and high school to the best of her ability. "Maxime, s'il te plaît. Dites-lui qu'une vieille amie est là pour le voir, à la recherche de sa bouteille de Chartreuse perdue."

Maxime appears at the door within seconds. "There you are. Come on." He drapes his jacket over her shoulders because she's forgotten to wear one, lights a cigarette, offers it to her.

"Are you hungry? Are you thirsty? Do you still have a taste for Chartreuse, then?" She can hear the words she wrote, for Elijah to sing. *You looked at me like you wanted me, and I wondered.*

"I don't drink anymore," she says.

"Not even wine?"

"No." She keeps her voice firm.

"Understood. Coffees, and we will walk. You still drink that, at least?"

"Of course. I'm not dead."

He laughs and leads her into a late-night café, orders them tall, steaming cups of milky espresso to go. Coffees in hand, they walk through the city. It is well past midnight, but Paris at this hour is anything but asleep.

They make a bit of small talk. He tells her what La Dure has been up to, talks about art. "I don't paint on building walls anymore," he says, glancing down at her. "I paint on canvases now and have had a few gallery shows." He shrugs. "Growing up, I guess. I have less of a taste for the idea of being arrested. But I do still have a taste for street art." He slows, looks down at her. "Do you?"

Her throat has gone dry. She holds her coffee cup to her lips, but it is empty now. She just nods, not trusting herself to speak.

His expression is thoughtful. "I've been waiting for you to come here, to Paris," he says after a moment.

"You have? Why?"

"A street artist friend told me about a piece. A month ago now. He took me to see it—and I felt this great sense of familiarity in those two figures, the woman and the man. I never forgot a single detail of that night with you two. It was magic. Wasn't it?" She nods. She hasn't forgotten either. "I remember he was making you drawings, at the concert after-party. When I saw how similar this was, I thought about contacting you, but I didn't quite know how to put it."

"Is this art by any chance signed 'Adam'?"

"You know, then," he says, relieved. "You already know, so I don't sound crazy."

She shakes her head. "You don't. Could you take me to see it?"

"Of course," he says. "We'll walk? It's about ten blocks from here, I think."

As they walk he points out other little works of art, pauses every now and then to show her something.

"This is one of my favorites." It's a flock of birds on the side of a building that look like they're made from origami paper, about to fly or blow away.

Next, he shows her rows of dancing figures in black and white, painted between the second- and third-story windows of an apartment building. He tells her these are painted from photographs the artist takes of people at concerts and at raves. "He waits for the moment—you must know the one, Jane, when the music has you in its grip and you are not of the world." She nods, stares hard at the image of a woman dancing with her eyes closed, her feet bare—and thinks it's beautiful but also invasive. "Did the woman know someone was taking her picture?"

He raises an eyebrow. "Good point. Probably not."

They walk until they reach stairs leading up to Montmartre. Here, it is quieter, the Sacré-Cœur closed, empty of its daily prayers. The Moulin Rouge has let out for the night; its red lights are dimmed.

Down a cobblestone alley, around a corner, and then, on the side of a building, a splash of orange. Jane rushes toward it. It's the very same shade as their old Impala.

It's done in the style of a vintage movie poster. Adam and Rib are driving off into the sunset. Rib has a scarf on, but the wind is unraveling it and it looks like it's about to blow away, straight out the side of the wall and into the real world. Two guitar cases are in the back seat of the car, and music notes flow all around, like dandelion seeds, like wishes.

But this is not a scene that really happened. This is an escape to a place they never found. In the back seat, a handbag spills out its contents. Jane peers at the objects: Lipstick in a gold tube. Concert tickets to see Adam & the Rib at various shows, but no names or cities on any of them. There is nothing in this painting that leads her any further on her quest. Is it a dead end?

"It's beautiful," she says—but that's all it is.

"You had that car. He talked about it."

"He loved that car, even though he didn't drive."

"I've been asking around," Maxime says. "Trying to find out who did this without drawing too much attention. Everyone is looking for the next Banksy, or wants to *be* the next Banksy, so no one thinks my interest is too unusual, not yet."

"What have you found out?"

"There's another, Jane. Here in Paris. But it's not . . ." He hesitates. "Not as pleasant as this one."

She's torn between relief that there's one more clue—and dread. "Things weren't pleasant with us, when we were here," she says. "It was one of our worst times."

"I know," he says. "I saw the news." There are questions in his eyes, but she has gone this long without talking about it and knows she won't now. She shakes her head slightly, and he doesn't ask.

"It's a little far from here," he says, "but we could take a taxi."

Jane's eyes are back on the vivid orange of the Impala, the idea of how happy they could have been. *Should* have been. She doesn't feel ready to face the truth—to look at the darkness of what really happened head-on.

"No," she says. "Not tonight."

Moments pass in silence, and then he pulls a pen and a piece of paper from his pocket, writes down an address, and hands it to her. "You'll find it there," he says.

She slides the paper into her pocket. "Thank you."

"Jane?"

She looks up at him.

"I want to ask you something." He steps closer, and she can smell him. Whiskey and smoke. "Was the song 'My Lost Bottle of Chartreuse' about me? I wanted to ask that other time I saw you, but . . ." He shakes his head. "It wasn't the right moment."

"Yes," she says.

"Yes, it was about me?"

"Yes, Maxime. It was about you."

He recites a line. "'You looked at me like you wanted me, and I wondered . . .' I *did* want you, you know."

Her cheeks grow warm. "I know," she says.

He laughs gently. He is now very close to her. She likes how she feels under his gaze. "Can I kiss you?" he asks. She hesitates—but then she finds herself tilting her face up to his.

He pulls her up toward him with strong arms, covers her mouth with his. Not a soft kiss—but not too hard, either. It is as she imagined it, this kiss. Because she has imagined it.

As they kiss, Jane realizes that not all roads lead to Elijah Hart. There were others. There still are.

Maxime's hands are in her hair. It feels good. She lets her mind go blank and her body fill with the starry heat of a first kiss. But finally, she puts her hands against his chest and pulls back slightly.

"Let's go to your hotel room," Maxime says.

"That won't be possible. I brought a friend. She's . . . sort of my charge. A teenage girl."

"Right. You were with her at the concert. She seemed very drunk. You're not a very good babysitter."

Jane laughs. "She's my neighbor. It's hard to explain."

"Then don't explain anything. Just come back to my place."

"I can't," she says.

He drops his arms from around her, but he's not angry; Maxime isn't like that. He takes one step away but still looks at her like she could be back in his arms in an instant, kissing him, if she wanted to be.

Jane touches her fingers to her lips. But the kiss has made her more certain than ever: there are other paths she could choose, yes, but only one she will ever want. She looks at the poster again, at their happy, could-have-been life. Driving off into the sunset together. She would do anything to have the possibility of that back.

"I'm sorry."

"There is nothing to be sorry for, Jane. I knew him too—I knew both of you. What you had was special. You were two sides of the same coin, I think. Meant to be."

"When you saw us at the concert in Oregon—"

He shakes his head. "That wasn't him. Don't talk about it—you don't need to."

"Thank you, Maxime. Really."

"Jane." He steps close again. "I might not love you like Elijah. But I see you."

"I know that."

"We could kiss again?"

She laughs softly. "Not a good idea. This time I might not be able to stop." This widens his smile, is a gift to him. "I should get back to my hotel. But, Maxime?"

He touches her cheek. "You don't have to say it. This secret is safe with me. I will not tell a soul, I promise. And maybe, someday . . . I'll see how it turns out. I'll see you two happy again."

She wants to believe this could be possible. She closes her eyes, and for a moment, she does.

Instead of a kiss, she hugs him goodbye.

As she pulls away, the tender moment is broken by a flash.

"Jane Pyre! Who is your Parisian friend?"

She runs, but the flashes of the camera are as relentless as always. And this guy is fast. With her sore knee, she can't run fast enough. She slows to a stop. "Smile for the camera, Jane!"

She finds herself reaching for the lens, ripping the camera away, and smashing it to the ground with a force that surprises even her.

PART TWO

PARIS, FRANCE

In Paris, no one paid Jane much attention. If anything, she felt she fit in well with the cool, aloof attitude of most Parisians. She noticed the women here were unsmiling too, their heads held high, their style effortless. In LA, she and Elijah couldn't go anywhere without being recognized and sometimes even mobbed.

One morning, while Elijah slept in, she found the café where Sartre had composed *Being and Nothingness*. She stood still for a moment, wondering what it might have been like if she had gone to college instead of becoming a rock star. Who would she be? But she was still on the right path, she told herself. She went inside, got a syrup-thick espresso, and drank it at the counter.

She walked to the Seine and followed it to Montparnasse, where she found a vegetarian restaurant called Aquarius; she and Elijah had recently stopped eating meat. She bought two pressed tofu sandwiches, ate hers as she walked. Elijah was awake when she got back to the hotel. He was wearing a white robe, drinking his coffee in a seat by the window. He smiled when he saw her, and she had that coming-home feeling that had been absent for so long.

"You're back," he said. "I missed you. You have mayo on your cheek." He stood, dabbed it off with his finger, kissed her. "I love you, you know."

"I love you too." She told him about her walk, about a restaurant she wanted them to try later, was relieved when he ate his sandwich fast and said he was still hungry. His already lean body had developed newly sharp angles that would sometimes surprise her in bed as she ran her hands over him. It would feel like touching the body of a stranger, like she was missing someone who was not even gone. But today, he was back with her. Slowly but surely, Paris had brought them back. She had written two songs so far. "It was such a good idea to come to Paris for a break," she said, and he agreed.

Later, they went to dinner at the restaurant Jane had found. There was live music, and they sat close to the stage and watched an ethereal folk singer, her voice a gentle, compelling murmur, do covers of Édith Piaf, Melanie, Helen Sear, Dalida. The manager discreetly brought over a complimentary bottle of champagne and welcomed them to the restaurant, asked if they wanted a table in a more out-of-the-way location or even a back room.

"We're happy here," Elijah answered. "We're really enjoying the show." He glanced at Jane, then at the manager again. "Hey, so . . . maybe we could go up there, play a song or two, later on? Surprise your patrons?"

It was Christmas Eve, so they played covers of "Blue Christmas," "White Christmas," "Last Christmas." Elijah was playful, making Jane laugh on the stage. She watched him and saw Elijah, sitting at the kitchen table with his mother, listening to records, throwing back his head and singing along.

After they finished their impromptu set, the folk singer took the stage again. She reminded Jane a little of Alice; she sang in a dreamy way that was mesmerizing and strange—and Jane liked it, but after the joyful rush of their little performance, something about the music made her start to lose her energy.

"Should we go soon?" she asked Elijah.

"Let's just watch the rest of her set. I want to tell her what a great job she did, and then we can go."

He chatted with the folk singer and one of the waiters for a little while after she finished performing. "We're going to go outside and smoke a joint," he said to Jane. "Want to come?" She was a bit irritated but told herself not to be. They were having a great night. She nursed a final drink as she waited. Soon, they were arm in arm, walking back to their hotel through a gentle snowfall, and Elijah was waxing poetic about how beautiful it all was, what a beautiful night it had been. Jane thought Paris might be her favorite city in the world.

Elijah was in the shower; Jane was rooting around in her bag, looking for a negligee she had bought the day before, with stockings and garter belts. She could find only one stocking though. Finally, she gave up her search for it and just put on the negligee. She wanted to keep the good feeling going, wanted to keep connecting with Elijah. She checked herself out in the mirror, then walked over to the bathroom and turned the knob. But it was locked. She jiggled it.

"Elijah!"

"Just a sec!" he called out.

Something about his voice. Something wasn't right. She used more force and the ancient lock gave way, the door flinging open.

At first, she wasn't sure what she was seeing. Why was the missing stocking tied tight around his arm? But then, through the shower steam, she saw the needle in his skin. He startled at the yelp she hadn't realized she'd let out and dropped the needle. A bit of blood sprayed across the wall. A crime scene.

"What the fuck, Elijah?"

"Shit. I'm *so* sorry. I thought the door was locked."

"You're . . . sorry? Sorry that you didn't lock the door?" It was almost laughable, how small that word felt in the face of this. *Sorry. Sorry. Sorry.* She put her face in her hands. "Oh my god."

"Jane, really, it's . . ." But there was nothing for him to say.

She stepped farther into the bathroom. The back of the toilet tank was open. As he flailed around, searching for words, failing to find them, she looked inside the toilet tank and saw two balloons. She reached in and pulled them out, held them dripping in her hands. They were the size of her palm. Each was heavy. She pinched one. It was powder-filled.

"Heroin," she said. "Right?"

He could do nothing but nod.

"For how long? And don't lie to me."

"Not since Söckdologer. Really."

"But why? Why now? I don't understand. We were so happy here . . ."

"I know." He looked miserable.

She saw a lighter on the floor, a spoon on the counter. She could suddenly hear her own voice in her head, speaking calmly and lovingly, promising to take care of him, to protect him from everything. And meanwhile, had Elijah ever really promised her anything?

"Where did you get it?"

The folk singer . . ."

"She's the one who gave you this?"

He looked ashamed now. "No. But I saw the marks on her arms, so I asked her. It was one of the waiters, the one I went outside with."

Now her anger was a white-hot flare. She had been sitting there the whole time, sipping her drink like an absolute fucking fool. They hadn't been smoking a joint, they had been doing heroin. She spun away from him. He followed her into the bedroom.

"Where are you going?" He had his eyes on the heroin she held and the hungry look of longing in his eyes made her want to scream. She grabbed a long jacket of Elijah's and shoved the balloons into the pockets.

"Hey, *wait*—" His voice sounded as desperate as it had when she had flushed his pills back in LA. She buttoned the jacket up over her negligee and pulled on her combat boots, stomped back to the bathroom, and picked up the syringe, just in case he had more around somewhere.

"Jane, *please*."

She slammed the hotel room door against his voice pleading with her to stay—to stay because she had his *drugs*—and stormed down the four flights of stairs to the street. She retraced her steps back through the city, the glimmering lights of Paris now a lurid reflection of her incandescent rage.

At one point, she stumbled and fell on the sidewalk, tripping over the laces of her untied combat boots. Her knee was now bloody but she kept on going, on a mission, seeking vengeance.

She arrived back at the café and peered through the window. The waiter sat at a table with a group of the other servers, counting his tips. The friendly manager was at the bar, writing things down in a ledger. Did he know one of his staff was an addict, a dealer?

Jane was about to go in and confront the waiter when she saw *her*, sitting on a bench across the street, appearing to be half-asleep. The folk singer, nodding out, her blond hair falling in front of her face.

"Hey! Hey you!" Jane pulled the balloons of heroin out of her pocket, the syringe. The woman looked up at her, confused, spaced-out. "You bitch." Jane hated that word but needed to say the worst thing she could think of, spat it at the woman again and again, her voice growing louder and louder. It wasn't the singer's fault, she knew that. But Jane couldn't stop herself. She felt unhinged. "You want these? You want these fucking drugs?" The singer just stared at her, as if unsure of who she was or where she had come from.

Jane kept screaming. The manager stood at the door of the restaurant, watching the scene. Then he went back inside and picked up his telephone. Soon, the flash of a police moped's lights lit up the night, the low whine of a siren pierced the air.

The paparazzi followed soon after. And after that, a new spectacle: Jane Pyre, arrested in Paris for possession of heroin with the intention to traffic.

PARIS, FRANCE

DECEMBER 22, 1999

Bang, bang, bang.

Jane had been up for most of the night, tossing and turning, but finally fell into a disturbing dream in which she went to see the next Adam painting. It was around the back of the Palais de Justice, painted onto a wall, the purest black. Jane touched it, and it sucked her in like a black hole. Then the banging sound—knocks on the door. Clearly not part of her dream. Hen is still snoring softly on her side; she hadn't moved since the night before.

Jane, fully awake now, approaches the door. "Ne nous dérange pas, nous dormons," she says, assuming it is housekeeping.

"C'est la police. Ouvre la porte."

The door has a judas window, and Jane slides it open, peers through the peephole, sees two uniformed police officers standing with a member of the hotel staff.

"What do you want?"

"Open the door."

Jane wonders if she should refuse and call Petra or Martika for help. But what has she done wrong? All her supposed crimes happened years ago. Behind her, Hen is stirring.

Jane opens the door. "What can I help you with?"

Hen, sitting up now, is still wearing her outfit from the night before, mascara pooled below her eyes.

"Are you Henrietta Vögel?" one of the officers asks her.

"Yes, but what's it to you?"

"Your mother, Anja Vögel, telephoned a television station in Paris when she saw images of you with Jane Pyre last night, outside a club. She said you had been taken."

"Taken?"

"Kidnapped," the other officer says, looking from Jane to Hen in confusion.

"She's my neighbor," Jane says, although she knows it's far from a proper explanation.

"I'm here of my own free will," Hen says. "And I'm an adult; I can make my own decisions, anyway. I told my mother I was going on a little trip with my friend here. She's overreacted." Hen turns, opens a drawer, and takes out her wallet, holds up an ID card. "I'm eighteen," she says. "You see?" She points. "I turned eighteen yesterday."

"You *what?*" Jane says.

She ignores Jane's surprise that it was her birthday and she didn't say anything. "I can make my own choices." One of the police officers looks at her identification, then confers with his partner. Jane still feels mystified. And when an image of Hen's mother flashes into her brain, she is struck by a wave of guilt.

The police officers finish conferring and hand Hen back her ID. "You really do need to call your mother," one of them says.

"And you may be hearing from us," says the other, turning to Jane. "She was a minor when she left with you. We have to figure out if that still means charges can be laid."

"My mother is not going to press charges!" Hen exclaims. "I'll make sure."

As the police officers prepare to leave, the hotel manager begins pacing, agitated. "I must ask you to please leave my hotel," he says. "I do not want this business here, whatever it is. Police here, this sort of attention." He waves his hands around. "And now, photographers in the lobby, disturbing our other guests!"

Shit. "We'll go," Jane says. "Just give us some privacy to pack up. Please, could you try to get rid of the photographers?" The manager nods and the police officers seem placated enough to depart.

She closes the door behind them and turns to Hen.

"I didn't know it was your birthday yesterday."

"That's not what's important here," Hen says. "What's important is that we need to see Elijah's next message. But how can we do that with a million photographers following us?" Jane can tell Hen is starting to panic. She is almost as invested in this as Jane is. Her guilt increases when she thinks about the fact that she has already seen Elijah's next message. And she hasn't told Hen about it.

"I've evaded the press before, and I can do it again. But, Hen . . ."

"I'll call my mother, okay? But I'm not a child. And I told you—I'm not going back. Not yet. I want to stay with *you.*"

She says it as if Jane is leading her on a journey that has a guaranteed happy ending. As if she has no idea who Jane and Elijah actually are. Which, Jane reminds herself, she doesn't. And if she sticks around, she's going to learn that soon enough.

"Hen . . . I went back out last night, after you fell asleep." But she finds the truth clenching up inside her like a fist.

"You went back out and what?" Hen looks alarmed.

"Just for a walk," Jane says, evasive now. Maybe it's time to start keeping things to herself again. Hen is starting to depend on her—and Jane is a terrible caregiver. Look at what state Hen got into last night. And on her birthday!

"I went out for a walk, and a photographer saw me, that's all. That must be what started all this—the photographers at the hotel."

"Oh," Hen says, but she frowns, looks at Jane closely, as if she doesn't quite believe her.

NEW YORK, NEW YORK

JANUARY 1993

The newspaper headlines after Jane's arrest in Paris revealed that most people had suspected it all along. Look at the way she stumbled up the stairs at the Grammys. The way she's always so silent—probably too high to speak. Her erratic, domineering professional reputation. And Kim Beard—who seemed like a great guy, just a fun-loving musician—had been utterly destroyed by her. She stole his best friend. She may have stolen his music. Everyone knew what she was really like. No surprise at all that she was also an addict.

Some journalists made an attempt to find her family and reported that her mother, Raquel Ribeiro, had nothing to say about her—except this: "Jane Pyre is not my daughter." That was one of the headlines—along with a favorite that ran in a few publications: JANE THE JUNKIE.

Jane had stayed silent during and after her arrest, refusing to speak to police detectives, until Martika had arrived in Paris to help her post bail. In a hotel room suite after Jane was freed, Martika asked her what had happened the night she was arrested. "I don't think it matters," Jane said. "What really happened—no one will care."

"A judge will care," Martika said. "And *I* care. I need the facts or I can't do my job. You don't want to end up back in jail for this, do you?"

Jane thought of how she had felt during her two nights in a Parisian jail cell: Like her insides had been scooped out of her. Like her life had become a nightmare. Like she had lost everything. But there was something else she had felt: shame. She knew she hadn't actually done anything wrong, at least not legally. But she had broken the most important promise she had ever made. *I will take care of you, Elijah. I will always keep you safe.* Yet again, she had missed the clues. And now, all the world had to say about any of it was that *of course* she was a druggie, of course she did heroin, of course she was unhinged. She hadn't even had a beer before she met Elijah, but she had been painted as a drug-addled hellion.

Jane took a deep breath and told Martika what had really happened—the restaurant, the folk singer, finding Elijah doing heroin in the hotel bathroom. Her reaction, her arrest. "So the drugs were his," Martika said. Jane had been staring down at her empty hands, squeezing them together, wringing them out, but now she looked up.

"Can you get me cleared of these charges without my having to admit that?"

"You're saying you want to perjure yourself."

"What's the alternative? Elijah being charged with possession, intent to traffic? You see what will happen, right? The stories everyone will tell. That I'm trying to ruin my own husband, blame him for my sins. And I don't want to do that to him. I'm mad, but I still don't."

"We need Petra," Martika said. Jane had never seen her rattled before—and she knew why. Because Jane was right, and Martika had to realize that. She could tell the truth, and she would ruin herself even more.

"Just tell me what the defense could be," Jane said.

"If what you say is true, that the folk singer was using, she'll want to protect herself. She's not going to want to testify that you were trying to sell her drugs, especially if it's not true. Also, the waiter was arrested yesterday for speeding, and drugs were found in his car. You bought the drugs from him. You had no intention to traffic—and you did not bring the drugs across any borders. I'll ask for your sentence to be a large charitable donation. The children's hospital in Paris could use it. You'll be fine."

Jane nodded, then stood.

"Thank you," she said. "You can go now."

When Elijah found out what Jane was doing, he was beside himself—or so Petra reported to Jane, who wasn't taking any of his calls. "He won't let you take the fall for him," Petra said.

"He has no choice."

"He's going to rehab. He's checking himself in for sixty days. He wanted me to tell you that. He said when that news breaks, everyone will know it was him, not you. And he can deal with the consequences. He wants to."

Only, that wasn't what happened. His trip to rehab was painted in the media as Elijah having crumbled under not just the pressures of fame but the realities of being married to Jane Pyre. A group of concerned fans wrote an open letter to Jane Pyre, published in *NME*, imploring *her* to go to rehab and set Elijah free, to stop forcing her husband to carry the weight of her addiction himself.

"You need to give an interview," Petra beseeched her on the phone. Jane had told her to stay in LA, not to come to Paris; she wasn't needed. "Come on, Jane. Your background isn't at all what anyone says it is."

"It's true that my mother disowned me. Right? So who is going to corroborate my past?"

"Before you came to Seattle, you were a wide-eyed innocent. You were in a fucking church band called Samson's Mullet!"

"No one will ever believe that, and you know it."

"We can get the minister from your church to corroborate. Ministers don't lie!"

Jane actually laughed at this, but it quickly turned into a sob. "My minister thought I was evil incarnate. He would come to our house and pray for my soul. Please, Petra, just leave it. Things will only get worse if I try to defend myself. Besides, rock stars get arrested for drugs all the time. I'm sure it will blow over."

She heard Petra sigh. "You know it's not the same," she said. "That it won't be the same for you. Think about Marianne Faithfull. Being caught with the Stones, doing drugs, wrapped in that fur rug—it ruined her. She lived on the streets."

"Fuck, Petra. You're not really helping."

"You know I'm always honest."

"Well, it's not 1967. It will go away. Martika is going to make it go away. I just need to get through this." She paused. "And I'm glad Elijah is going to rehab. I can't help him with this—he needs real help. Nothing that I can give him." Her voice broke, and she made an excuse to hang up the phone before Petra heard her crying.

Jane didn't know what to do with herself when she returned from Paris, her sentence exactly what Martika had argued for: a large charitable donation to a children's hospital. TRASH PYRE, read one headline, with a photo of her leaving the airport looking haggard and strung out, when really she was just tired and sad, filled with an ache that had only ever been soothed in one way: making music with the man she loved. But with Elijah in rehab—it had been three weeks now—she had no outlet. And she couldn't leave her house because every time she did, she was photographed. No one ever said she looked sad—they said she looked angry. No one ever suggested the dark circles under her eyes might be from worry and lack of sleep—they said she was hungover from her latest binge. No one ever said her weight loss was because she was too heartbroken about Elijah's betrayal, too empty inside without her livelihood, too distraught about the state of her marriage, to eat very much.

Elijah sent letters, but they didn't help. They were always Adam & the Rib drawings, but these didn't cheer her up the way they usually did. Each scene from their past or a rose-hued future, each entreaty to forgive him, landed on her front step like a dead thing. She couldn't forgive him. Because it wasn't him she was angry with anymore. She hated herself for letting him slide—and her shame threatened to swallow her.

In February, when she and Elijah had been apart for a month, she got a call from the management team of a top-charting Irish-born singer named Fiadh Connelley. They wanted to know if Jane would play guitar for Fiadh when she sang at the legendary folk-rocker Hal Cohen's up-coming tribute concert at Madison Square Garden, celebrating his thirty years in the music industry. Jane said yes and booked a flight.

Alan called Jane himself when he found out.

"You know who she is, right?"

"Of course I do," Jane said. "Who doesn't?" Fiadh had sold four mil-lion copies of her most recent album and had won a Grammy for her cover of a famous song, but she had refused to accept it because the artist had just been accused of raping a groupie. Jane reminded Alan of these facts.

"That *alleged* rape was back in the seventies. And it was never proven in court, Jane. Anyway, your public relations image is not great right now, as I'm sure you know. I think your PR instructions were to look like you're thriving—not consort with toxic waste?"

"Geez, Alan. She's a person, you know."

"Be that as it may, I don't want you to do this. It's unwise. Rock stars are rock stars—but you've taken things a little too far."

She thought about what Petra had said to her, when she called her in Paris. "Have I? Wasn't Keith Richards once charged in Canada with the exact same drug charge as I was? Except all anyone talks about is that he was having a dalliance with Margaret Trudeau?"

"Well then, have an affair with a politician's wife. Do something sexy. Just not this."

"I'm hanging up now. I have a flight to New York in a few hours."

"Wait— Jane, come on. I care about you, do you realize that? You and Elijah, you're my favorites." She gritted her teeth. Of course they were. Their debut album had almost gone double platinum at that point. "Don't associate with Fiadh. I'm begging you. Did you see what she did on *All Night Saturday?*"

"Who didn't?" A few months earlier, Fiadh had done a live spot on a comedy variety show that always featured the hottest actors as hosts and the most popular musicians as performers—Jane and Elijah had appeared on the show just before the Grammys. Fiadh sang her hit, the cover song, then produced a painting of St. Francis of Assisi and set it on fire before singing—or at least, starting to sing; the fire alarm and subsequent evacuation of the building put a stop to things pretty fast—a protest song called "Holy War."

"She burned that painting because it had belonged to the Mother Superior at the Catholic high school she went to," Jane said. "And this was Fiadh's abuser—"

"Her alleged abuser," Alan interrupted. "Never proven. And who goes after a nun?"

"Who goes after a teenage girl?" Jane countered, but Alan just sighed.

"You should take my advice, Jane. You're going to regret this. A fucking nun, Jane. People love nuns. And the entire *All Night Saturday* studio had to be evacuated. It was the only time in history the show did not go on."

"Jesus, Alan, who cares? No one was hurt. Except Fiadh, obviously. I'm sorry—*allegedly* hurt. She was speaking out against child abuse. And I'm doing this. You won't change my mind."

Hal Perry was an icon, a staple of the early folk music scene and then an electric-rock pioneer whose poetic, lyrical songs had been covered by hundreds of artists.

"Did you know we're two of only five female artists in a roster of twenty? Fecking bullshit, if you ask me," Fiadh said to Jane at the first rehearsal, rubbing a hand over her stubbly head. "That's why I asked you to join me. I don't need the remaining members of Booker T and the goddamn MGs backing me up, thank you very much."

Fiadh was tiny, just over five feet tall, but she had a fierce presence. She had shaved her head just as she started to get famous, much to the chagrin of her record label, who didn't know what to do with a woman who refused to conform to beauty standards. And for what it was worth, she was beautiful—even more so without hair. She also spent most of her time pissed off about one thing or another. Jane liked her a lot.

On the night of the performance, Jane and Fiadh hovered backstage at Madison Square Garden. Without Elijah beside her, Jane felt like she was missing a layer of skin. But she didn't have too much time to worry before the head sound tech did a final mic check and they were being hustled through the curtain.

A platinum-selling country singer named Karl Kristie was emceeing the event. "I'm real darn proud to introduce this next artist, whose name to me means courage, integrity . . . fire itself!" The crowd cheered, or so Jane thought. "Ladies and gentlemen, Fiadh Connelley—with special surprise guest Jane Pyre of the Lightning Bottles on bass guitar!"

Fiadh was going to start off by singing a tender ballad called "Girl from the West," one that Cohen had recorded with Johnny Cash back in the seventies. It would be quiet at first, but about halfway through, Jane would play louder, and Fiadh would turn the soft longing in the song into desperate, howling passion. Since it started so slow, they needed the crowd to calm down before they could start.

But the crowd didn't calm down. The cheers grew louder—and then Jane realized the sound she was hearing wasn't a cheer at all.

They're booing, Jane realized as she got the frantic signal from the head tech to begin playing.

Jane began playing. But Fiadh turned to her and sliced her hand through the air for her to stop. She walked over to Jane and stood on her tiptoes to speak into her ear. "Do you know the song 'Holy War' by Joe O'Shea? The one I was trying to sing on *All Night Saturday*?"

Jane nodded.

"Will you play it with me? You don't have to."

"I want to," Jane said firmly, picturing Alan's chagrin.

"Let's turn our backs while I sing and you play guitar, then walk off stage without turning around. Deal?"

This was something Cohen was known for doing on a whim at concerts; he might have, if he felt like it, played entire concerts without once turning his face to the thousands of adoring fans who had come to see him. And no one had ever thought it was rude. He was a beloved male artist, entitled to treat his fans however he wanted—and Jane knew in her heart that doing this with Fiadh wasn't going to be greeted with a shrug, the way it was when Cohen did it. But maybe it would reveal the sexism, the double standard of it all—maybe, she told herself, it would start an important and necessary conversation.

Fiadh grabbed the mic out of its stand. They both turned their backs. She ripped out her earpieces and threw them to the ground, and Jane did the same. Now she wouldn't be able to hear the head tech anymore, which was a good thing because he did not look happy.

Fiadh began to sing.

Until we are all equal, we've got a holy war. Until no one is first and no one is last, it's an all-out war.

Her voice was so powerful, it rose up over the shouts. The veins in her neck pulsed; Jane could feel her voice vibrating up through her feet, thrumming in her legs, in her chest—just the way she felt when she was beside Elijah. *People, we've got a war,* Fiadh sang, her fists clenched around the mic. She made the word "war" into a battle cry for everyone, any-where, who had ever been hurt. Jane didn't know how the crowd was reacting because she couldn't see their faces, but she knew there were no more boos, and no more cheers, either. Only stunned or maybe, just maybe, reverent silence. The song ended and Fiadh grabbed Jane by the hand, the way Elijah always had in the past. They bowed and ran offstage.

The backlash was swift. Photos of Fiadh and Jane with their backs turned to the crowd, then running offstage, hand in hand, appeared in newspapers across the country, with headlines like, TOXIC TWOSOME or HITTING ALL THE WRONG NOTES. After the *All Night Saturday* incident, Fiadh had become one of the most hated women in the music industry—but Jane Pyre was a very close second.

Every day there seemed to be another article about how awful Jane Pyre was. Mostly, Jane could ignore them. But then one evening as Jane was sitting down to dinner alone at home, she saw a headline splashed across *Creem*: HART-THROB ELIJAH'S FIRST LOVE SPEAKS OUT ON WHY JANE PYRE IS WRONG FOR HIM.

Shawn. Of course.

> *Shawn spent a great deal of time with her, back in the day. "And, honestly? I have no idea what Elijah sees in her. Unless I'm missing something, she's not a very nice person. We spent a ton of time together, and we could have been really close if she had allowed it."*

Jane frowned. Something wasn't right about this. This didn't sound like Shawn.

> *"But there's something wrong with her. I mean, look at those cold, dead eyes of hers. Is she feeling anything? Hard to tell," Shawn muses, suddenly looking very sad—and even more beautiful than usual. "I worry about Elijah. I'm not surprised to hear he's in rehab. Living with Jane Pyre would drive anyone to substance abuse."*

Kim put Shawn up to it. He had put these words in her mouth, and Jane knew it. Because Shawn had barely paid attention to Jane, back in Seattle. It had made Jane's simmering jealousy of her even harder to bear. But Kim—he was another story. He was a textbook narcissist, looking for someone to vilify in order to fulfill his insatiable need for attention and validation. He was using Shawn to feed his vendetta—and this made Jane furious. Maybe if Jane had been a bit more mature back in the day, she and Shawn could have been friends. She took responsibility for that. But it was Kim who had taken her teenage feelings of jealousy and turned them into a feud. And that was despicable.

Before she fully knew what she was doing, Jane ran the magazine through the lit candelabra that sat on the table before her. The fire alarm went off, and the security guard on duty at the time rushed in to help put out the blazing pages of the magazine—and then, later that night, sold a statement to a tabloid about how Jane had set a fire on purpose. The tabloids the next day had renamed her JANE PYRE-O.

Elijah was holding one such tabloid the next evening when he knocked on his own front door. Jane opened it to find him standing there in the twilight, a backpack over his shoulder. It had been forty-five days since she had seen him last. His hair had been trimmed, and he looked like he'd aged in the time he'd been at rehab. It had been the longest they'd been apart since Jane had first stepped into his arms back in Seattle. She was still sad, but as soon as she saw him, she felt consumed by joy and relief.

"What are you doing here?" she whispered. He dropped his backpack and opened his arms. She stepped into them, collapsing against his chest. She should have been pushing him away, she told herself—but all she wanted was to be in his arms. "Why are you back so early? Weren't you supposed to stay at Passages for sixty days? It's only been forty-five."

"You were counting?"

"Of course I was." She pulled away and looked up at him. "I felt dead without you," she admitted.

"Come here." They sat down on the couch. "I felt dead without you too, but, Jane . . . don't you see? We can't go on like this. And you know it."

Jane's heart felt like it had seized in her chest.

"Are we over?" she whispered.

"What?" He sounded stricken. "Oh my god, no! That's not what I meant. Jesus. No." He grabbed her, held her tight, released her gently, and looked down at her. "Jane, I adore you. You are so talented, so amazing, you are the reason for everything I have. *You are everything.* But you let people say these things about you, let people believe them. And I can't stand it."

She blinked at him. "You think I have any control over what people say?"

"You lied in court. You said it was you. I need to take responsibility for this. *I* did it, not you."

"And you went to rehab—and people still think I'm the addict. There is nothing we can do or say to change that."

"We haven't even tried! Come on. When people say shitty things about you, it hurts me too. When people talk to me and ignore you—it makes me want to—" He shakes his head. "It just makes me hate all this so much. It makes me want to obliterate myself with drugs, Jane. This is one of the breakthroughs I had in rehab, with my doctor. Everywhere we go, *you* are the most interesting person in the room. But no one seems to care. They look to me—and it's terrifying, okay? And depressing."

"Are you saying you get high because everyone hates me?"

"I mean, that's part of it. And the fact that everyone calls me this musical genius, and it's not what I ever wanted. I'm singing your songs. I wanted that—to sing your songs and watch people love you. To be one of your many admirers."

"Oh, Elijah, who cares?" But she did care. She had wanted that too—to be loved, to be accepted. It felt silly now, a girlish dream. "People say things about me. They hold me to a higher standard than you. They want me to be the villain; it's just easier. It feels better for them. We can't change the way the world is."

He didn't say anything. He looked away, out the window at the ocean. "I missed it here," he said. "I just want our life back—but I want it to be different. We need to fight this, Jane."

She felt lonely and afraid—and exhausted. "I just want our life back too," she said. "More than anything." There were tears in her eyes, but she wasn't sure what kind of tears they were. He was here, and that made her happy—but he had left rehab early, which made her scared. She moved away from him a little, then stood, suddenly filled with a need to put a little distance between them, to get some perspective.

"What else did your doctor say? Tell me more about your recovery."

"Will you sit? Please, come here." She did, but cautiously, still keeping distance between them. "I did that thing where you take a personal inventory. It was painful—but it made me realize so many things. I'm a people pleaser, which is why I put up with Kim for so long. I want to avoid conflict. That was because of my dad. I never unpacked anything after my parents died—and I needed to. I'm sorry, Jane." He leaned toward her, looked into her eyes. "That was painful for you too. I forced us to sweep it all under the rug and never properly deal with it. And I don't want to do that now. I want us both to find enlightenment and true connection, and how can we do that when we let the public control the narrative about who we are?" There were lines beside his eyes and around his mouth she was sure hadn't been there before he went to rehab. He kept talking, about the hard truths he had mined during therapy, the realizations he had made. She was always looking for shades of the teenager she had fallen in love with, to reassure herself that he was still there—but what she realized now was that Elijah had grown up. And that wasn't a bad thing. In fact, all she could think was, *Finally*. She hadn't realized she had been waiting for this.

"Jane?" He leaned closer. "Can I . . . ?" The way he asked permission to kiss her made her stomach swoop, her chest fill with birdlike flutters.

"Yes," she murmured. After a month, her physical need for him felt ravenous, insatiable. In seconds, she had pushed him down on the couch and straddled him. But she grabbed his wrists and pinned them, pushed him away one last time.

"You're straight now?" she said, clamping her thighs around his hips. "No more sneaking around, no more drugs? I just need a yes or no."

"Yes, I'm straight now. No, I will not be sneaking around anymore. I swear, you're the only drug I need," he said. She loosened her grip on his wrists and he stroked her hair, her shoulder, her collarbone. "Hey. *Hey*. Relax. It's still me. It's still *us*. Just breathe." He wiped some tears from her cheeks. His touch was so gentle. She let him lower her to the couch, and then he began moving his gentle kisses down her body. He kissed the center of her chest. "You're everything," he said. "Your heart." He kissed lower, her solar plexus. "Your soul." He kissed all the way around her rib cage. "Your spirit," he whispered. Lower. "Your mind. All I need." A song was in her head. *Your heart, your soul, your spirit, your mind.* It would end up being the title track of their next album.

But now, in this moment, she laughed, gasped with pleasure. "That is *not* where my mind is, Elijah."

"Really?" he said, laughing too. "Because that's exactly where my brain is located."

They stayed in bed for two days, just enjoying each other, not talking about anything other than the moment. But eventually Elijah turned to her, a serious look in his eyes.

"Jane, I called Barbara Walters," Elijah said. "We're giving a live interview, in two days."

"You *what?*" She sat up. "But . . . let's just move forward."

"I told you, it's part of my recovery. Enlightenment, connection—coming clean so I can *be* clean. I need this. Please, Jane."

"Okay," she said. "Yes, Elijah. If you need to do it, we will."

It didn't feel right to her, but saying no to him now, when she had just gotten him back, this new version of him that seemed to know what he needed to be safe, to be clean, this person who wasn't going to rely on her alone, would have felt even worse. "We'll do whatever you need," she said. *Even if it's the last thing I want*, she did not add.

"If you're not a hero, or an icon, or a god," Barbara Walters said, "who are you, then, Elijah Hart?"

"I'm really just a session musician."

Elijah spent the interview trying to tell his story, their story—trying to explain that he was the one with the drug problem. Except he could only go so far, couldn't say that Jane had lied in court—and Barbara had the court transcripts from Paris. She finally told Elijah gently that it was lovely that he was trying to defend his wife, but she was only interested in the truth.

"Jane, is it true what Elijah is saying—that you write most of the songs?"

And somehow, she couldn't say it. "We collaborate on our songs," Jane said.

"Except for 'My Life or Yours,' which Elijah wrote about his mother."

"Jane wrote the bassline," Elijah interjected.

"How nice," said Barbara.

It became clear to Jane that the narrative she had allowed to stand was all anyone was ever going to believe about her. After the interview, fans said the way Elijah appeared to be trying to give his wife all the credit for their art was nothing but disturbing. That obviously Jane Pyre was not the genius behind the Lightning Bottles' captivating song lyrics—because all you had to do was watch Elijah talk about their music to know that. *He* was full of passion, and Jane Pyre looked like a robot. And the way he kept looking over at her for approval—she must have put him up to it. The poor man. Why had he ever married her? PYRE PROPA-GANDA, read one headline after the interview. STOCKHOLM SYNDROME? read another, above a picture of Elijah and Jane coming out of Sunset Sound, the recording studio, each one of them alone with their thoughts, both looking exhausted, a little bit sad.

Jane peered closely at the photo, taken when neither of them had been aware anyone was watching—but the truth was that people were always watching them. She did indeed look unhappy, but Elijah looked worse. In that unguarded moment, he appeared miserable. Jane kept watching Elijah when he thought she wasn't, and she saw the way his eyes would take on a faraway look. An expression of longing for some-thing that was not her—because she was mere feet away and he could have reached out to her if he wanted to. But more and more as time went on, he didn't.

PARIS, FRANCE

DECEMBER 22, 1999

In the hotel bathroom mirror, Jane applies several layers of the wrong shade of foundation, garish pink blush, a silver wig, and reading glasses. Hen puts on a pink wig and sunglasses. They pack their bags and bring them to the hotel room door.

"Hen . . ." Jane begins, standing still in front of the closed door.

"What is it? Are you nervous? You've evaded the press before."

"It's not that. It's just . . . I've been thinking about your mother. How upset she must have been, to be without you on your birthday. How worried she obviously is. She called the police, Hen. And you said it yourself, she's not well. With Christmas coming up in a few days—"

Hen interrupts her. "Please, don't."

"It might be time for you to—"

"I said, *don't*. We just have to focus on getting out of this hotel. Finding the next clue. Then I'll go to a pay phone and I'll call her, okay?"

Jane goes out the back door, Hen out the side. They meet in the alley behind the hotel. Jane has the piece of paper from Maxime, with the location of the next Adam & the Rib drawing, but she doesn't need it—she has the address memorized.

"I was thinking perhaps there might be something near the courthouse, where my trial was," she says. "I had a dream about the courthouse last night, and it occurred to me it could be a good place to look." The lie

rolls off her tongue, but Jane has forgotten how impossible it is for someone like her to have secrets at all. As they approach a newsstand, Jane sees
her own face on the cover of a tabloid. She hopes Hen won't notice, tries
to distract her, but she's too late. Hen stops in front of the newsstand,
her eyes wide.

"There's you. What is all this . . . ?"

Hen begins gathering up the papers, all with photos featuring Jane
and some of them featuring Hen herself. Jane feels like a child caught in
a lie. She pays for the stack of papers and follows Hen to a park bench,
because there's nothing else for her to do but watch this unfold.

"Oh my god," Hen says, staring at an image of herself, doubled over
outside the club while Jane rubs her back. It's hard for Jane to tell how
she's feeling. Mortified but maybe also important, a little bit famous. She
flips a page, and there are the photos of Jane and Maxime in a passionate
embrace. Hen looks more closely as Jane's heart sinks. "Is that the guy
from La Dure? It is, isn't it?" She reads some more, then looks up at Jane
again. "You *attacked* a photographer?"

Jane turned on her cell phone that morning, and it's ringing in her
handbag now. Three times, a hang-up, and then more rings. Petra, likely
full of questions about what in the hell is going on. But Jane lets it ring
until the phone goes silent. She wonders if this is finally the time when
Petra will decide she's done for good with the train wreck that is Jane
Pyre.

"Could you please just throw those away?" Jane says.

But Hen is looking back down at the photos of Jane and Maxime
kissing.

"I thought Elijah was the love of your life."

"You can't possibly understand."

"Why, because you think I'm just a kid?"

Jane considers telling Hen the truth. That she doesn't think she's just
a kid at all, that she thinks she's smart, and brave, and mature beyond
her years. That she's grateful for her. And that she loves Elijah beyond
all measure, but that love is often complicated. She can't say those things

though. She has to set Hen free. She can see this already, doesn't even have to look at the next clue to know it's time. Jane has put off this reality, but the next part of the story is too bleak to bring anyone else along for the ride. It certainly didn't have a happy ending the first time—and there's no reason for it to now. How can she possibly fulfill the fantasy of yet another dazzle-eyed fan who just doesn't get it?

Hen looks panicked. "What if Elijah sees this and thinks you don't love him?"

"We aren't characters in a movie, Hen!" Jane snaps. "Please, can we just go?"

She knows she's treating Hen badly, and yet, with every step she feels almost more at ease. Pushing people away is just what Jane does.

They reach the Palais de Justice, and the poster is precisely where Maxime said it would be. Behind the courthouse, beside a dumpster. But Jane still walks around for a bit and pretends she doesn't know exactly where to find it.

Maxime was right; it's not pretty. Unlike the rest of Elijah's works, this one is ugly and stark. The first square features a bathroom, a toilet tank, a male arm with a needle stuck into it, the shadow image of a horrified Rib standing in the doorway. *In which Rib takes the fall for Adam* is written in black paint across the bottom of the image.

"What does it mean?"

Jane doesn't answer Hen.

Rock bottom? is painted in stark, black block letters above an arrow, pointing north. Then the words: *No. Not even close. We had to go somewhere else to reach our rock bottom.* At first glance the arrow appears to be simply painted black, but when Jane looks closer, she sees that it is textured. She touches it. Tiny grains of sand, thousands of them, not really black, but the darkest shade of gray. She knows exactly where these grains of sand came from.

"Jane?"

Jane turns to Hen. "Yes?"

"Does this mean . . . that what he said about the drugs being his is true?"

Jane nods, but she sees doubt mixed with disappointment in Hen's eyes. She turns back to the wall.

"Can I ask you one more question?" She continues on before Jane can answer. "You've talked a lot about the songs you wrote—but you've never once talked about 'My Life or Yours.' I read all the articles about the court case between your band and Kim Beard. Kim claimed he helped Elijah write it. And Elijah said in interviews that he did write that song—that it was about his mom. But . . ." Jane closes her eyes. She isn't ready for what she knows is coming. "Did Elijah lie? Does part of that song really belong to Kim Beard?"

She could tell her the truth. All of the truth. There could be one person in this world, other than Elijah, who knows everything. But why would she do that to Hen? It has been enough of a burden for Jane to carry this complicated truth inside her for so long. So she just says, "Of course not. Elijah wrote that song himself. Kim Beard is a liar."

Hen seems relieved. "I thought so," she said. She takes one last look at the wall before turning away. Her optimistic expression is back. "So, what's next? Is it Iceland?"

She looks so hopeful. Doesn't she understand? Iceland is a black hole, a dark pit of memories so bleak no one should have to relive them. But Hen thinks everything is going to turn out okay—because, Jane knows, Hen doesn't see Jane or Elijah as real. They're characters to her. She just found out something distasteful about a man she has revered—but she is able to cast it aside and keep on believing the story she tells herself about him. The entire point of celebrity is for people to be able to project their hopes, their dreams, their fantasies, onto canvases. Their unrequited love, their rabid hatred. Celebrities aren't real people. Jane knows this, because she is one.

LOS ANGELES, CALIFORNIA

MARCH 1993

Jane decided that if she couldn't be the solution to Elijah's addiction issues—if, actually, she and her irrevocably tarnished public image were part of the problem—she could call in outside help to keep him sober. Because he slipped a few times after coming back from rehab. He didn't hide it from her, and Jane thought maybe she was supposed to feel good about this. Instead, she just felt complicit. She had promised him she would keep him safe, promised herself this, too. But she had failed. She was failing. She hired a personal trainer and a dietician, a reiki master and a guru. They did cleanses and went on healing, yogic retreats for long, seemingly endless weekends during which the time stretched interminably and they ran out of things to talk about. Without their instruments to rely on, a dull silence often fell between them at night. And to be honest, the silence sometimes just made her want to drink.

Meanwhile, in public, the rumors still swirled. People said the reason Jane and Elijah never went out to parties or events anymore was because Jane had Elijah at home, locked in a drug den. One tabloid even posted pictures of a dungeon they claimed existed in the musicians' California home. A particularly unhinged tabloid article suggested Jane Pyre was a witch who had cast a spell on Elijah Hart to keep him with her.

"I'm so used to it," Jane said. "Can't we see it as sort of funny?" She held up a magazine photo of a brick-layered basement with shackles on the wall, lifted an eyebrow at her husband. "I mean, we *could* get some handcuffs . . ." But he didn't even smile.

"You know how I feel about this, Jane. It breaks my heart."

And it makes you want to get high, to hide away from it. She felt a surge of frustration. She said she didn't care—but of course she did. It hurt her, too. But she had started to resent the fact that it had become all about him and his reaction to it. "There's nothing we can do about it," she snapped. "Maybe it's just time to ignore it. No more reading these articles, ever." She told Petra and their assistants to stop telling them about their press unless it was important—or positive. But no positive news ever came in.

Jane told herself that if there was music to focus on again, things would get better. She tried harder to write new songs, but the block still lay on her like a shroud. After the one song she had written when Elijah returned from rehab back in the spring—she had called it "Your Heart, Your Soul, Your Spirit, Your Mind"—and the other one she had written at Söckdologer that had made Elijah so upset with her, she had only been able to come up with two others that she knew were just mediocre. They were nowhere close to having enough material to make a new album. And it didn't help that the *Kim Beard v. The Lightning Bottles and Columbia Records* intellectual property hearing, which had been delayed due to Elijah's rehab stint, now loomed closer and closer.

The day of the trial, the media swarmed the courthouse in anticipation of the arrival of the grunge stars at the center of the most fascinating feud in alternative music history.

Elijah wore a black suit to court, and Jane wore black pants and a black jacket with a scarlet blouse underneath. The photos of herself entering court would haunt Jane—they would be used, out of context, for the rest of her life. With the crimson at her throat and the grim expression on her face, she looked like the witch people said she was.

As Elijah had predicted in the pretrial motion, the proceedings amounted to a rehashing of the worst night of his life. Tom Appleton, Kim Beard's lawyer, circled the courtroom in the same type of sharkskin suit he had worn when they saw him last, looking like he was searching for someone to take a bite out of.

"How would you describe Jane Pyre's demeanor the night Elijah's parents were in the accident?" he asked Shawn.

"She was real upset," Shawn said. But then Kim cleared his throat, and Shawn looked over at him. "She was . . . um . . . cruel, controlling, and . . . hysterical," Shawn added, shooting an impossible-to-decode glance at Jane, one so brief it almost didn't happen.

"Do you remember Elijah and Kim sitting together that night, writing lyrics together?"

"Elijah was crying for a while, and Kim and I were comforting him, we all were," Shawn said, while Jane's heart began to ache for her husband. She reached for his hand; it was cold and limp. "Then he started writing stuff down, and singing. We . . . rarely heard him sing. But when we did . . ." She cleared her throat, trailed off. "Jane only wanted him to sing for her, I guess." She was looking at Kim again. "His voice was spectacular. I loved hearing it. Even that night, it just made everything better." This was true—Jane had been there, too. When Elijah sang at the Central, even the darkest tragedy had lost its sting. She glanced at him now, wished she could find a way to convey this to him, but he was staring straight ahead, his body tensed like he was about to take a bullet for someone.

"Tell us more about the night Elijah's parents died."

"He and Kim wrote that song. Together," Shawn said. "I do remember that."

Martika cross-examined her. "You just used the words 'I do remember that.' That makes it seem to me like you don't remember certain things about the night. Am I correct?"

"No. That's not what I meant."

"But were you drinking that night, Shawn?"

"Yes."

"How many drinks would you say you had consumed by the time Jane arrived with the terrible news?"

"I'm not sure."

Martika pulled out a document. She said, "I have a copy of the bar tab from that evening. You closed out at around nine p.m., which was around the time Jane arrived with the news. Was that the point you went backstage and began to consume the beer that was freely available for the bands and their groupies in the greenroom? This receipt says you had fourteen screwdrivers before that point. Does that sound accurate to you?"

"Some were for my friends."

"But some were for you."

"Yes."

"And what about drugs, Shawn? I also have a witness who will corroborate that you called a dealer that night, and—"

Jane glanced over at Elijah in surprise just as he shouted, "Stop! Leave her alone!"

Elijah had told her Kim called the dealer. Suddenly, Jane could feel Alice close to her, see her face, the way she had looked that long-ago afternoon in the yard, when they had planted nettle seeds together. She felt this way now, as if Shawn's words had pressed a tiny seed of doubt into the soil of her mind. And it lived inside other seeds; ever since what had happened in Paris, Jane knew she didn't trust her husband anymore. Not completely. Something had broken.

There was silence in the courtroom after Elijah's outburst. Martika blinked a few times, taking her client in. During the small commotion and discussion with the judge—spurred by Kim's lawyer—about whether he should be removed from the courtroom, Jane sat still, feeling the doubt still growing inside her.

Martika asked to consult with her clients. "I work for you," she whispered, "so I have to ask—is that what you really want? You *don't* want me to try to get her to perjure herself?"

"No," Elijah said. "That is absolutely not what I want. Shawn is my friend."

"Shawn is a pawn," Jane muttered.

"That's not very nice."

She looked up. "I'm not trying to be unkind," she said. "Your friend there, she needs help. Her partner is a narcissist and a control freak and . . ." She shook her head. "She's stuck in a horrible, toxic relationship. I feel sorry for her. Her mouth is full of Kim's words. If she's your friend, maybe you should check on her—see if she's okay. I hear the stories about the groupies."

"Yeah," Elijah said, his tone as acrid as smoke. "And yet you're the one they write shitty articles about. Life is so not fucking fair."

Jane rolled her eyes. "Honestly, you're just figuring that out?"

Martika cleared her throat. "Elijah, you haven't answered the question. You really want me to dismiss Shawn Aarons? She's a strong part of our case."

"And she's not okay. And who knows how Kim will treat her if she's the one who brings this all down. I want it to be him, not her. Leave her alone."

This meant it was time for Kim Beard to testify.

"Mr. Beard," Tom Appleton asked him. "Are you saying you wrote 'My Life or Yours' with your old friend?"

"Listen, I'm not trying to take all the credit, Tom. But I did contribute—I contributed something pretty major, that should at least get me a songwriter's credit. It's all I'm asking for."

"What line did you add to the song, Kim?"

"I mean, we talked through the entire song together. He was writing stuff down, we were talking. I helped him out with the whole thing, I'd say. But that main line—I wrote that. That's what I'm here to say. I wrote that on a napkin."

"Please, could you share the line you're referring to?"

Kim grinned. "'We're all gonna die, might as well just get high.'" When he said it, it really felt like his. Jane wanted to be sick. She could believe what he was saying. That night, when Elijah sang that line, she remembered how jarring it had been for her. And every time he sang it, the way he seemed to adopt a new persona, become someone else altogether. The showman. The performer. She had Elijah's hand in hers again, but she let it drop. "It's what inspired the entire song, man. Elijah took the napkin I wrote it on with him when he left, too." Now he addressed his old friend. "Didn't you, brother? You knew it was fucking great."

Jane felt her throat go dry. She wanted a drink—and not just water. She wanted to numb herself, blind herself to the truth Kim was trying to get everyone to believe. She didn't trust Kim—but she didn't fully trust Elijah now, either. And maybe she was finally ready to admit to herself that part of her had always been surprised by that line. It did sound more like something Kim would say than Elijah.

When Tom was done with Kim, Martika stood. She began by reading a few lines aloud from various Marvel Boys songs. The puerile torrent of rhyming words sounded absurd in her mouth. She then read some lines from "My Life or Yours." "Remember," she said, "Mr. Hart's mother had just died. These are the words of a grieving son."

> There's noise all around me,
> I just want to sing.
> Did you close your eyes, Mama?
> Could you see everything?
> Do you know it all now,
> have the answer we seek?
> I think you'd tell me
> that, baby, it's not so bleak.

When she finished, Martika was silent for a minute, letting the words hang in the room—letting everyone imagine Elijah, in the torrent of his grief, writing these words. And something began to shift inside Jane. She took her husband's hand again. "I love you," she whispered, because it was still true, no matter what. "It's going to be okay." She couldn't be so sure of this.

"So, you say you helped him with this song," Martika said to Kim. "Do you have experience with loss, too?"

"I was there. I was with him. So, yeah. I'd say I do."

"Did you help with the pivotal line or the entire song? I thought just one line was in question here."

Kim lifted his chin. "I *inspired* that song, okay?"

Jane felt Elijah stiffen beside her, saw him clench his fists in his lap. She felt defensiveness rise up inside her, her standard impulse to protect the person she loved, no matter what. "She's baiting him," she whispered. "He wants everything to be about him, you know that. If he's going to double down this way, he will lose." *And even if he's lying, it won't matter.* She left this unsaid.

"Wait—so you're trying to claim the entire song now? You're saying you wrote the entire song right before the same show where you and your band were so drunk that you trashed the stage and were kicked out of the club?"

"I'm not saying I wrote all of it. But, yeah. I mean . . . none of that matters. We were drunk, so what? Music gets written while people are drunk all the time. And the song was his biggest hit. Because of *me*. End of fucking story."

"Alice, Elijah's mother . . . she enjoyed smoking marijuana, is that right?"

"Yes," Kim said.

"And would you say she was the kind of woman who sometimes liked to give advice? Was she a person you might refer to as 'philosophical'?"

"I mean, I guess so."

"Might she have said something along the lines of . . . I'm paraphrasing here but, 'we are all mortal, we will all die someday—try not to worry so much, try to let go'? Perhaps not in the exact same way, but the chorus of the song could really be an interpretation suited to a rock song of someone trying to tell their child that life was unfair, that death was inevitable—and to try not to worry so much. Right?"

"I think you're overcomplicating it, Marnina."

"Martika. And I'd prefer to be referred to as Ms. Assad, thank you. But, no. I think I understand the song in a way that you don't. No further questions, Mr. Beard."

After Martika dismissed Kim, she told the court she felt no need to have Jane Pyre or Elijah Hart take the stand at all and that she was prepared to make her closing argument.

"The work of the Lightning Bottles speaks for itself," she said, as she placed a small boom box at the center of a table in the middle of the courtroom. "This is Jane Pyre's, from when she was a teenager. This boom box traveled across North America with her, from Ontario to Seattle." Elijah squeezed Jane's fingertips and she squeezed back. "She also brought some tapes with her on that journey."

Martika pressed play. It was the first song Jane had written and sent to Elijah, the one he had sent back with his singing added in. The one about the fall of the Berlin Wall. "Miracle Monday." Jane was swept back in time. She clutched Elijah's hand as she listened.

"Elijah Hart and Jane Pyre have been making music together since they were teenagers." Martika played another melody, one they had recorded instrumentation for but struggled to find the right words for—and Jane realized it was the earliest version of the tune for "My Life or Yours." Martika had asked Jane and Elijah to dig through any archival material they could find, but she hadn't told them she was planning to play this.

"Sadly, it was only when tragedy befell Elijah Hart that he found the words for this piece of music. And with his longtime collaborator, Jane Pyre, by his side, he was able to create beauty—in the form of the lyrics we all know so well—out of this tragedy. Whereas, *this* is the sort of song the Marvel Boys are known for. Just for the sake of comparison."

It was their hit song, "Heads on Fire," which involved Kim shout-singing his usual nonsensical lyrics into a mic. Martika stopped it after the first stanza. She put in another tape, pressed play.

The opening drumbeat of "My Life or Yours" filled the courtroom. People started nodding their heads up and down to it as if they couldn't resist. Even the judge, and even Tom Appleton, started tapping his foot before quickly stopping himself. Martika let it play all the way through. Jane marveled at how good it was, how she never tired of it. The song ended and Martika let the silence hang for a moment before thanking the court and jury for their time.

After Tom made a brief closing statement, the jury left to deliberate. It didn't take them long: after an hour, they determined that the Lightning Bottles were the sole owners of the intellectual property rights for the song "My Life or Yours." Kim Beard was ordered to repay their legal fees. He stormed out of the courtroom, followed by his entourage, pausing when he reached Jane and Elijah's table.

"This is not over," Kim said. And Jane knew he wasn't lying about this—knew that no matter what had happened in the courtroom, the seeds had been planted.

But it was over for the moment, and she tried to find solace in this.

Elijah stood and looked down at her. He was silent for a long moment.

"Let's go get absolutely fucking wasted," he said.

The record company began to apply pressure on the Lightning Bottles about their second album. Jane continued trying to write songs, but they weren't like her old ones. When Elijah tried to sing them, they didn't sound right.

"If you feel so strongly about a bridge, why don't *you* write some lyrics and music once in a while, Elijah?" Jane snapped at him one afternoon when Elijah kept trailing off in the middle of a song she had written and asking her to add something, insisting there was an element missing in the composition.

He threw down his guitar, spun around, and, to Jane's shock, punched the wall. His knuckle came away bloodied. He stared down at it, then back up at her. "Fuck," he said. "What the *fuck* is wrong with us?"

He left the studio, but Jane didn't follow.

She didn't have an answer to his question—all she knew was that they had once had it all, and then let it all go. It had happened so fast. Like a flash of lightning in the distance, so exciting and all-consuming in the moment. And then . . . gone, as if it had never been there at all—leaving only the vestiges of a storm in its wake.

Ricky Washington, their producer, quit later that week. Jane was sitting in their rehearsal space alone when he came in to tell her the news. "I have a career to worry about, too, other artists who want to work with me. You two need to figure yourselves out. Call me when you're ready to make a record."

Jane left the studio and went to the Python's Apartment. She got drunk with Mikey Churl, the actor who owned it. She felt guilty at first, but then it was such a relief to have fun with someone who didn't care what people said about her—because people said the same things about him, and worse. Only he was a man. His behavior was frowned upon but also indulged.

In the weeks that followed, she became a regular at the Python's Apartment. She'd see many faces she recognized when she stopped in. Musicians, actors. A folk-pop star who had had a fairly public meltdown now pulled pints and mixed drinks behind the bar. He seemed happy. The bathrooms were set up to make drug use and sex as easy as possible—although Jane never touched drugs, just drank herself into oblivion. Martinis, shots of Chartreuse, which Mikey started ordering in for her from France by the case.

She saw Zack Carlisle there a few times, but he barely seemed to notice her, or anyone. Heaven Wretch's second album had been released and done well, but then Zack had overdosed in a hotel room in Italy while on tour. He had gone to rehab but hopped over the fence and left after three days. When Jane looked at him, she felt a cold shiver down her spine, a whisper of something she needed to see but was too drunk to comprehend. So she just looked away.

The Lightning Bottles appeared on the cover of *Rolling Stone* magazine for the second time—but in this photo, neither of them were smiling. They both looked pale and unhealthy. Jane could see her not-so-secret drinking all over her face, and Elijah looked like he hadn't seen the California sun in months. THE PRICE OF FAME was the cover line, and the article was about what their "lightning fast" shot to stardom had done to them. Jane and Elijah weren't reading their press anymore, but still Jane picked this article up and took it home. She read about the speculation that their second album wasn't going to do as well as their first, that they had only been a flash in the pan. A journalist named Jennifer Paradise wrote lines that stayed with Jane:

> It would seem that if the Lightning Bottles' well for songs about love and passion has dried up—especially assuming Elijah wrote most of their previous songs about Jane, a woman he seems to grow more distant from every day—this duo might be in serious songwriting trouble. Unless, of course, Hart can begin to show his chops even more as a songwriter and go beyond just his own dark personal experience and out into the real world.

That was *it*. The article was painful for Jane to read—but also galvanizing. She could mine the world instead of her own soul for material. Their career depended on it—and so did her future with Elijah.

So she stopped going to the Python's Apartment and started going to the studio again. She still drank, kept a bottle of vodka tucked into her guitar case, but since no one saw her do it, she could pretend it wasn't happening. She started looking for material outside of their lives to write about as she sat alone with a guitar in one of the rehearsal rooms. When she heard about a national vote to do with an image of Elvis on an upcoming stamp, her creative fog finally lifted. She wrote a song called "The Old You" and another called "Lightning Fast," which was not about the Lightning Bottles but was instead about the famine crisis in Somalia. She wrote a song called "Guillotine Rain" about the civil war raging in Yugoslavia. She wrote a song called "When's My Turn?" about Hillary

Clinton. She wrote a song about the LA race riots and South Africa's road to ending apartheid. One night, back at home, she played these songs for Elijah. When he sang them back to her, she knew they were good— maybe even great. They were on their way to another album. They were moving again. But the album was missing a love song, and this plagued her. She knew they needed it.

Elijah came back to the studio, and he brought an idea with him.

"Let's add a cover to the album. Let's do 'Show Me' by the Disintegration. Remember when we sang that on the roof of the record store?"

"God, that feels like a lifetime ago," Jane said. "But yes."

He laughed softly. "A lifetime. Yeah. But it wasn't that long, Jane. Two years." He stepped closer, looked into his eyes. "I'm still here, Jane. Are you?"

"Are you using?" she had to ask. They had been so distant, so she had no idea.

But he just shook his head. "I'm good."

He sat on a stool and played the Disintegration song, and it really was like going back in time—not just to the roof of the record store, but to the first time they had ever made love.

If you show me your secret insides, I promise you, I promise, I'll turn into art. My love, my love, my love, look inside me, promise, we'll never part . . .

The Disintegration cover turned the album around even more. Jane and Elijah decided to produce it themselves, rather than look for another producer or reenlist Ricky. The time they spent in the studio, recording over and over on their instruments, layer by layer, began to feel like old times. The work they did on sound and mixing and direction gave them both a new purpose.

Then, one afternoon, Elijah found the vodka bottle in Jane's guitar case.

"You've been drinking?"

She nodded, embarrassed at being caught—and at the fact that now she was the one hiding things.

"Jane, it's okay. Don't look like that. Come on. This is *me*." He lifted the bottle and stared at it. "Booze is not my problem, right? We can handle it. This straight-edge life isn't really for us anyway." He looked up and smiled, tilted his head. "We're still rock stars. Aren't we? It's okay to act like it, just a little."

She should have asked for help then. She should have told him that her drinking scared her—that it felt like a need. Maybe even an addiction. But she was afraid of what that would do to him. And also, she wasn't strong enough to resist.

He lifted the bottle to his lips and took a sip, passed it to her. Soon, they were kissing, entangled, and their old selves again. For better or for worse.

The Lightning Bottles were in the studio, putting the finishing touches on their album on a spring day in 1993 when the news broke that Zack Carlisle was dead. He had overdosed out on the sidewalk in front of the Python's Apartment.

Jane remembered how she had seen Zack there a few times, completely lost in his addiction. She knew she had just looked past him, grateful that he wasn't Elijah. And even now, she pushed away the reality of Zack's death, didn't allow herself to remember the way she had admired him back in Seattle—how he had been the first person in the world, other than Elijah, who had made her feel like a true musician. *Seriously, let's jam together sometime.* They never had. But she didn't let herself think about this. He was a casualty of a scene they were trying so hard to leave behind, rise above—even if in reality they were considered to be the king and queen of grunge. The truth was that Jane was still grateful it had been Zack, and not Elijah.

Later, she would wonder if this selfishness would come back to haunt her.

PARIS, FRANCE

DECEMBER 23, 1999

Jane sits in a café across from Hen. The window looking out onto the Paris arrondisement is festooned with a cedar Christmas garland woven with little twinkling lights. "Petit Papa Nöel" plays softly through the speakers. It's they day before Christmas Eve.

Jane pushes an envelope across the table.

"It's a train ticket to Berlin. You'll be able to make it home to your mother by Christmas."

Hen doesn't say anything. Jane knows this won't be enough to get her to go. She reaches into the inner pocket of her leather jacket, pulls out the crumpled sheet of paper with the Adam & the Rib drawing that started her journey with Hen in the first place, and places it on the table between them.

"I thought you might want this back, too. But also . . . it's not what you think it is."

"What do you mean?"

"*I* drew it, Hen." She gathers her breath. "It wasn't him, it was me. I made it for him. Sometimes I would add to his drawings—but it was my first and only time creating an Adam & the Rib drawing of my own. We were in London. He had stopped doing them for me at all by that point. He was very lost in his addiction. And I wasn't really any better, though I was pretending I was." She closes her eyes and can see it. The night in the London hotel, as she sat and drew, naïvely thinking a comic strip of memories would bring him back from the brink of his addiction, would bring him back to her.

Instead, when Elijah woke up the next morning, all he wanted to do was go find somewhere to score drugs. Their moments of tenderness and understanding were always so fleeting.

"I don't understand," Hen says.

"I drew this for him, but he wouldn't take it. I brought it with me to Berlin. But he didn't want to see. He needed to get high, and that mattered more than us. We argued. In the hotel, in the car on the way to the radio station. During the interview, he was high. And I was so angry. Everyone knew what was going on, but no one wanted to acknowledge it. And of course, everyone blamed me. I blamed myself, too. But what you saw at the concert, what you thought was him trying to give me something he had drawn for me—it was just me, trying to get him to take it, to see us again. But he wouldn't. And so I threw it away."

Hen blinks at her.

The waiter stops by the table. Jane asks for the bill.

"Was any of it real?" Hen asks when the waiter is gone.

"What do you mean?"

"Was it all just an act? Did you ever love him?"

"Of course I did," Jane says without hesitation. "It was never an act. Ever." She nudges the crumpled page with her knuckle. "This is my love for him. This artwork. Our songs. I loved him—I still love him—so much. I want nothing more than to find him and for everything to be perfect. But I don't think it will be that simple."

Hen takes the envelope with the train ticket and leaves the drawing untouched on the coffee-stained table.

"I thought he was a hero. I thought he was a god. I thought this story was . . . like a fairy tale."

"I know you did," Jane says.

"But he's just a person, right? And so are you."

She sounds so surprised by this, as if she actually believed something different. As if she had actually believed that Jane Pyre and Elijah Hart were magical, immortal, pure legends.

Better than anything. Better than human.

"I really wanted to meet him," Hen says, her voice almost a whisper. "But you're right. It's probably not a good idea after all."

She stands up and leaves the café without saying goodbye.

LAS VEGAS, LOS ANGELES, SAN DIEGO, SACRAMENTO, SAN FRANCISCO, PORTLAND, SEATTLE, VANCOUVER...

DECEMBER 1993

"What day is it? What city am I in?" Elijah would joke onstage, during the Your Heart, Your Soul, Your Spirit, Your Mind tour. When Elijah called out to them, the crowd would scream the date, scream out the name of their city for him, scream out their love. He would grin and start to play. Jane, beside him, kept a water bottle filled with vodka close to her at all times. She started to get tired of all the screaming.

They spent the end of 1993 and the first part of 1994 touring North America at a pace that made their downward spiral hardly noticeable. "Hey, it's rock 'n' roll," said a singer of one of the bands who opened for them—a rap/rock group from California—when he discovered Jane throwing up violently in a backstage stadium bathroom. "This is the lifestyle, this is the *life*." He offered her some vodka to clean out her mouth with. And wasn't he right? What was the point of staying sober when everyone around you acted like being drunk, being high, was perfectly fine—maybe even what was expected of you? Jane, of course, didn't fare well in the media, but behind closed doors, no one cared what she did—or maybe it was that they didn't notice. They were all doing it too.

Jane started mixing Chartreuse into the water bottle filled with vodka that she would bring with her onstage. She hardly remembered anything about that tour except that when she wasn't drunk, she was lost. And that after the shows were over, Elijah would come down from the rush of the crowd's adoration—and then he would do everything he could to stay high, including actually getting high. When they got back from this tour, she would get him clean again. That was what she told herself.

In Arizona, Elijah lost his voice again, and they had to break for two weeks while he recovered. In Argentina, in the summer of 1994, Jane fell off the stage and tore a ligament in her knee—and Elijah stumbled over to try to lift her back up again and dislocated his shoulder falling off the stage after her. At this point, they became the butt of jokes on the late-night shows they used to perform on.

Petra came to their Argentina hotel room, sat them down, and said that something had to change. That this had to stop.

"I should have put an end to this tour a long time ago. I'm very sorry. You both need help."

"No rehab," Elijah said.

"But why? You liked Passages. You did well."

"Liked it? I wouldn't say that. I left. It didn't really help me, did it? Look at me now. And I'm handling it. That was a bad night. When the tour is over—"

"But that's the thing," Petra interrupted. "The tour is taking on a life of its own. The label will keep you out there until you break."

"We're not going to break," Jane said, even though in a way they already had. But the idea of stopping the tour filled her with panic. Nothing but a black hole waited on the other side.

"Well, what else do you suggest? I mean it, both of you. This can't go on," Petra said.

"Just give us another chance," Elijah said. "We need to keep touring. We love it. Don't we, Jane?"

She didn't know what to say. She wasn't sure *love* was the right word. Maybe *need* was. A need that was beginning to feel like yet another addiction, to the constant movement, to the persistent feeding of the gaping maw of their fame.

But by the time the Lightning Bottles got to Europe in the fall of 1994, some of their shows were getting boos, not cheers. In Copenhagen, Petra knocked on their hotel room door once more—they had been fighting a lot and now asked for adjoining rooms—and implored them to pause the tour and get the help they needed.

Elijah was sick that day. He had told Jane he was trying to kick. He didn't like the booing. He knew he had to step things up. Now he looked at Jane and said, "Maybe she's right. Maybe we need to take a break."

"Fuck you," Jane said. She was drunk. It was eleven o'clock in the morning. "How about you just get yourself clean and stop losing your voice halfway through songs? I'm fine. I'm keeping up."

"What if I can't do this anymore?" he said. She stared at him—and where she knew in the past she would have felt a surge of love and empathy, she just felt empty.

"Why . . ." She trailed off. *Why did I let you get this way? Why did I lose sight of you again?* She rubbed her head, which was perpetually aching. *Why can't you just stay clean?* The album, the tour, the dizzying world they existed in. Everyone else in their world was messed up in some way, on drugs, on booze, on both, especially in the grunge and alternative scene. Zack had been the first casualty, but then Kristen Pfaff of Hole overdosed in a bathtub. Heaven Wretch's drummer committed suicide. One of the members of the Waverunners drowned while intoxicated. The list went on. If someone was still alive, that meant they were doing well, at least in Jane's mind.

Petra was looking back and forth between them, a worried expression on her face. "Okay, here's the plan. We cancel the rest of the European tour. But we don't leave on this note, we don't make last night's disaster of a show the last image your fans have of you two. I have an idea. Alt Radio Berlin has been asking you to do a showcase for ages, remember? They want to do a contest on the radio for listeners—and

I always said no, you were too big for that. But you two need a little redemption. You can do an acoustic show—it will be beautiful. It will be good for you two, to strip things down. You go to London first, to an industry party I promise won't be like all the others—there's a producer I want you to meet in London, for your next album. And then, go do the small show in Berlin, and then you rest. Together. Find a house to rent—"

"Oh, and *that* went so well when we took a rest in Paris after our last tour," Jane said, the old bitterness returning, which meant that at least she felt something. Their fame had become a curse, a knife constantly twisting in her back—but she knew their fall from stardom would be even worse for her. If they completely lost their footing on the craggy rock face they were climbing, the landing would be unforgiving for Jane. People would still love Elijah, that was a given—and they would blame Jane for however he ended up. The most hated woman in the music industry—Jane Pyre had long ago overtaken Fiadh Connelley, who had moved back to Ireland and had largely disappeared from view—would become a distasteful afterthought. She closed her eyes against the black hole she had been trying to avoid—but when she did, an image of the woman they had seen the day they got their offer of representation from Petra at the Sand Dollar café rose up in her mind. That long-ago day in Venice Beach, when they had been approached by scouts and record companies, had champagne to celebrate, had been one of the happiest of Jane's life. But she had also seen that woman and felt a chill, a premonition.

"Jane?"

She opened her eyes. "Can we have a little time to think about it?"

"Sure. Get some rest. We'll talk tomorrow."

When Petra left, Elijah stood too. He disappeared through the door to his adjoining room, closing it behind him.

Jane crossed the room and found herself gazing at a bouquet of roses on a corner table. The soft petals, layered on top of one another, protecting each other, opening when the light came. And the thorns below. She grazed her thumb along one and felt the pain. She knew if she pressed harder, she could draw blood.

And suddenly, Jane Pyre was writing a new song. *A rose is the shape of love . . .*

She slid a rose from the vase and went to the door that separated her from her husband. She could tell him about her song. Show him how in a rose, the love and pain comingled.

Except she knew it wasn't that simple. Petra was right. They needed a break. They needed rest. It didn't have to mean their career was over, and this new song in her mind was proving that to her. They could clean themselves up and go on. They just needed a little more time.

In November of 1994, the Lightning Bottles officially postponed their European tour and flew to London. The producer Petra had wanted them to meet had invited then to a party at a DJ and music entrepreneur's penthouse.

As they arrived at the door, Elijah reached for Jane's hand. He hadn't done that in such a long time, Jane startled and dropped her handbag.

"Are you okay?" she asked him, after she had picked it up.

"No," he said. "Are you?"

She shook her head, *no.* And for the first time in a while, they smiled at each other again, almost laughed.

Inside, a waiter passed with a tray of champagne. Elijah raised an eyebrow and grabbed two glasses, handed them to her, then grabbed two more for himself. "Let's make a little hay before we dry out?" he said. All she could do was nod. She wasn't anywhere near ready to dry out just yet.

The host had spotted them and rushed over. She took them around, making introductions until soon they were in separate conversations.

"Excuse me." A woman's voice, low and melodious, in Jane's ear. "Jane Pyre?"

It was Helen Sear. "Oh my god, it's such an honor," Jane said.

"The honor is mine. I've always wanted to meet you. A fellow Canadian, too! I bet we're the only ones at this party."

They found a settee with a view of the London skyline.

"So tell me, how are you?" Helen asked this as if they weren't meeting for the first time. Like she actually cared. And Jane felt sudden emotion drag at her.

"How am I?" she repeated, blinking back tears. "I'm sorry," she said, dabbing at her eyes. "I think I'm just . . . jet-lagged or something."

"Nonsense," said Helen. "You're exhausted, sick of this bullshit industry, and dealing with a partner who is circling the drain. You also drink too much, but who wouldn't, in this world?" She waved her hand around in a circle, condemning the entire room. Then she met Jane's eyes again and Jane thought about saying the word, *Help*, but she didn't. She did put down her drink though.

I know you, Helen's eyes seemed to say. She reminded her of Alice.

"Elijah's mother was such a big fan of yours. And Elijah and I are too, of course."

Helen put her hand on Jane's arm. "Thank you—but let's not talk about me. You don't have to confide anything, Jane, but I want you to know I feel a lot of sympathy for you. When everyone makes up stories about you, I don't blame you for clamming up in public. It's one thing to be the star, another to be considered the woman behind the man who is falling apart. I was with someone like him once," Helen said, and now her eyes were faraway and sad.

Jane made it a point not to read gossipy articles about other celebrities and musicians, but it had been impossible to avoid the news about Helen Sear last year: that her partner, a younger writer named Wesley Prine, the father of one of her three daughters, had taken his own life by drowning himself in a Muskoka lake.

"Some people just seem to find all the ledges, don't they?" Helen sighed. Then she leaned in closer to Jane. "Your love isn't going to save him, you know," she said.

"Oh, I know," Jane said. "I tried, and I failed."

"But it's not your responsibility to save him."

"Who will, then?"

Helen gazed out the window for a moment, then back at Jane. "Fame is such a curse. It's the price that must be paid for doing something we love this much, but still. Sometimes that price feels a little too high, doesn't it?"

Jane nodded. "I wanted this life more than anything," she said. "I thought it would be so different. I loved music, and Elijah, so much that I was sure it would be my armor—but lately, I feel like I hardly know him. He's a stranger, and music is . . ." She trailed off. "A job I barely even like anymore. How did this happen?"

"Isn't that the irony? Sometimes the best part of a dream is dreaming it." Helen tilted her head. "That sounds like a song."

Jane smiled. "You know, the very first time Elijah and I ever talked— online, in an internet chat room—he told me you were on his top ten list of favorite musicians. It's part of why I fell in love with him."

Helen laughed. The sound was deep and true, like her voice when she sang. Jane leaned toward it, was sure she would never forget hearing it. "Well, if that isn't a reason to fall in love with someone, what is? And I've seen that man on a stage." She put her hand to her heart. "My *god*."

"I know," Jane said, longing for that person again. "I don't know where that Elijah went. What happened to us. I have to do something."

Helen looked at her hard now. She leaned in. "He won't survive unless he can survive on his own. You can't be the one to keep saving him. He has to save himself, Jane."

That night, Jane went into Elijah's room and crawled into bed beside him for the first time in months. He was passed out, and she watched him sleep for a long time. "Elijah," she whispered. He didn't wake, but he threw his arm across his forehead and let out a sweet-sounding sigh. Jane felt something other than emptiness. She felt so much love for him. And she had to help him—help *them*. As wise as she seemed, Helen Sear couldn't be right. Her husband had killed himself. She had failed to save him, and he had failed to save himself. Jane couldn't let that happen to her. She had to pull Elijah back from the edge.

She got up to get her notebook. But she didn't write a song. Instead, she began to draw.

VÍK, ICELAND

DECEMBER 25, 1999

After Hen is gone, Jane stays in Paris for one more night, then flies on to Reykjavík alone. As she travels, she imagines Hen on a train, heading back to Berlin. Imagines, even, her throwing away all her Lightning Bottles posters and CDs when she gets home, trying to pretend the band she once loved never existed. It will be for the best, Jane tells herself. And she hopes Hen's mother is happy to see her—and that maybe she can find a way to move on from her fears. Perhaps losing Hen temporarily, and then getting her back, will have helped. Or maybe it will have made everything worse.

Jane rents a car and drives to Vík during the fleeting daylight hours, past craggy cliffs, waterfalls flowing down from their tops like Rapunzel's hair. Charming white farmhouses with red roofs, gray stone barns built into the sides of mountains, stocky little horses standing by roadside fences.

The house she and Elijah stayed at in Vík is abandoned now. Jane knows it had become a makeshift memorial in the years after Elijah disappeared, that Lightning Bottles fans made pilgrimages there, left flowers, photos, candles. There had been a small fire at some point, and the owner didn't bother to restore it. Jane drives up the long road toward it. All the houses in this part of Iceland look so lonely. Miles between each of them, no trees to tuck themselves into. Granite and basalt outcroppings in the background. The loneliest beauty Jane has ever seen.

She sits in the car and looks at the house. How quick, how easy, it is to go to ruin, she thinks. Just five years on and this place, which once looked so modern and sleek, appears to have been uninhabited for a century.

Jane finds herself reversing away from the house. She's not ready. Not yet.

In Vík, she goes to a bar. It is only four o'clock in the afternoon, but it's dark as night outside, the sun already setting on Christmas Day. The bar does not have a festive atmosphere, and Jane is glad. This feels like a place for serious drinkers. And she is, as hard as she tried to fight it, a serious drinker.

A waitress approaches a table nearby with a tray of shot glasses and a set of little plates. The people don't look at Jane, don't notice her at all as they eat, then take a shot together.

"I'll have whatever they had," Jane says to the waitress. The young woman explains that the shot is *Brennivin*, a traditional, very strong Icelandic liquor. And the pallid morsel on the plate is fermented shark. You eat the shark, you chase away the flavor with the alcohol.

Jane looks skeptical, and the waitress smiles.

"It's mainly for bravado, I think," she says. Jane had expected it to be something about immortality or protection from trolls.

"Bring me two of the shots," Jane says.

When it arrives, Jane picks up the tiny piece of fermented shark by the toothpick that spears it. She puts it in her mouth, chews, gives up. It's too rubbery. She swallows it down and tastes ammonia on her tongue. The two shots are lined up in front of her.

But then she hears a throat clear. The waitress is back.

"I'm just wondering . . . are you Jane Pyre?"

"Yes," Jane says. "I am."

The waitress just nods, walks away, says nothing to anyone. She fills a glass with water and brings it to Jane—and this act is such an unexpected kindness Jane doesn't know how to react.

"Thank you," she manages. She washes away the taste of the shark with the water, leaves too much money on the table, and walks out of the bar.

VÍK, ICELAND

DECEMBER 1994

After the Alt Radio Berlin showcase, Jane and Elijah flew to Reykjavík.
They had rented a house in a town on the south coast called Vík, were
going to hide away there for as long as they could.

Jane drove for hours, Elijah asleep beside her in the passenger seat as
she took in the scenery. The closer they got to Vík, the bigger the rock
formations became. Boulders were strewn about fields as if thrown by
an angry god, houses looked out of place, like they had been plunked in
the middle of nowhere. The sun finally rose fully, bright and hopeful,
illuminating the greens and the yellows of the grass on the mountains,
the white of a glacier in the distance, the stocky horses grazing in fields.

Elijah asked her to pull over so he could throw up.

In the end, Jane had consulted with a doctor, so she knew how to
handle the detox—but seeing it close-up was even worse than she'd
imagined. She had tried to stop drinking too, and her withdrawal symptoms weren't as harsh as Elijah's, but they weren't easy, either. She knew
what they were doing was risky, but she didn't feel they had any other
choice.

Walls of granite. Rivers, burbling white and frothy by the side of the
road as she drove again. A lake with islands strewn about like dropped
beads. Little fishing boats lined up on the shore. Trees, rocks, water, sky,
birds, and an ocean so cold-looking, it chilled Jane to gaze at. As they got

closer to Vík, the sand on the beaches darkened to black. It felt right to Jane. Like this place matched her soul.

The house was a modern box made of wood, steel, and glass. It was perched above Reynisfjara Beach. There were basalt stacks in the water, like rock soldiers standing sentry. Or gravestones, Jane thought as she carried their stuff inside because Elijah was too weak.

Elijah stood at a window. "Do you know what they say those are?" he asked her, pointing at the rock formations.

She didn't know.

"Trolls," he said. "I read that. Legends say they are trolls that went out into the ocean to try to pull ships to the shore. But you should never be out on the ocean too late in the night, or you'll turn to stone by the time the sun rises." He said this as if it were fact. "Now they're trapped in rock forever."

He left the window and collapsed onto the couch, wrapped himself in blankets, and started to shiver from his withdrawal symptoms.

Jane went outside. She picked her way down the rock steps, slick with mist, to the beach, stood still, and stared down at her feet. At the way her black leather boots matched the sand. She saw the path of a horse's shoes and followed them to the water's edge. Had a horse gone out into the water and transformed to rock? Were legends real?

Jane turned and looked up at the house. There was a legend inside it—and he felt *too* real. He, unlike a legend or a myth, was mortal. And so was she. She looked away, back out at the water, tried to tell herself legends were just stories people made up to make the world seem better. More interesting and magical than it really was.

That night, from the bedroom she had chosen, separate from Elijah's, Jane heard noises coming from the kitchen. A crash. A bang. When she came out, she saw Elijah in the darkness holding a bottle of something. It was red. Not wine. She could smell it, too sweet, from where she stood. It was liqueur of some kind, maybe cherry or fig. Jane had been drying herself out, had been taking gabapentin to help manage her own with-drawal symptoms from alcohol. But she wanted a drink. Even whatever sickly sweet liquid he had, she wanted that, had to fight the urge to wres-tle it from him and drink it herself.

"Where did you get that?"

"There's a cellar," he said, his words a slur. The blanket he had been holding up fell away from his body. He was only wearing boxer shorts. He looked like a starvation victim.

"Elijah, put that down. You shouldn't be drinking."

"You need to know some things, Jane."

He leaned against the counter, holding its edges as if he would slide to the floor if he didn't hang on.

She walked to the sink and poured water in a glass, held it out to him. But he didn't take it. "Jane, listen to me. Kim was right. I did steal it."

And then he sang it, his voice so tarnished, so weak, a once-beautiful thing, now ruined. *"We're all gonna die, might as well just get high."*

"No. Stop. It's too late for any of this. We just need to—"

"Keep lying? To ourselves, to everyone? Jane, we can't. Lying has ruined us. I can't. No more hiding, Jane."

"You're wasted. You aren't making sense."

She tried to take the bottle from him. He staggered away, into the living room, picked up his jeans from the floor, and pulled something out of the pocket. "He wrote the fucking hook, and I stole it."

"I'm not stupid. I know that. But I've always told myself—and you should too—that it is just one line."

"Except it's more than that. It's a curse." He held a napkin, which had probably once been white and was now slightly yellowed. He waved it like a flag. "Take it," he said. "Look."

Jane just stared at him. "No," she said.

"I want to break the curse!"

"It's not a curse, Elijah. Those don't exist. This is real life, okay? Not some dream. Not some fucking fairy tale. Just stop this. Put it down."

"Do you want to know *why* I stole it? I thought he wouldn't even care.

I thought he wouldn't remember. I thought it was mine—and it is mine, isn't it? Because *he* could never have turned it into what we did. Right?" Jane nodded, but she couldn't speak. "But it turned into something bad."

Jane could see them, at the start of their career—the way he had implored her, and everyone else, to lose the song that caused him such pain. What if she had said yes, what if she had helped him, instead of letting her ambition matter more than her love? But at this thought, something else rose up. Anger. Why had it never been okay for her to have any ambition at all? Why had he always been so weak?

He was still speaking.

"When he sued us, I thought fighting back and taking it could be payback for all the times he hurt you. All the times he hurt me. That's how I justified it. I'm sorry, Jane. I'm so sorry. I should have told you."

"I think it's too late for you to be sorry. I think sorry doesn't matter now."

He held out the napkin again, like she was supposed to know what to do with it, this thing that could ruin them—and that was saying something, considering how wrecked they already were.

"What if we ran away?" Elijah said.

"We *have* run away."

"No, but really ran away. Disappeared. Bought one of those islands." He waved a weak hand in the direction of the ocean. "Built a . . . cabin or something. And got a generator and . . . grew food. Or . . . I don't know, just survived, together. Somewhere. Thailand? Cambodia. Find a place where you could love me again. Where we could fix us." He took another swig from the bottle. "You and me, Jane." His voice was slurred and he could barely stand straight. "We could have a whole bunch of babies. We could be like . . . homesteaders or something."

"I don't want babies." This was true; it had always been true. Her anger felt suddenly sharp. There was only one thing she had ever really wanted—or maybe two. Elijah Hart. And for her music to be considered great. For it to set her apart from the world in a way that would keep her, keep them both, safe. Instead, bringing her music to the world, rising up as a famous woman, a beloved and delicate man by her side, had proven to be her downfall. Now she took the napkin from his outstretched hand, looked down at it, and saw Elijah's handwriting, some words from the song that were familiar—and then the most familiar words of all, in handwriting that did not belong to Elijah.

HEY MAN, WE'RE ALL GONNA DIE. MIGHT AS WELL JUST GET HIGH!!!!!!

She looked back up at Elijah and felt sudden clarity. She could hear Helen Sear's voice in her mind. *He won't survive unless he can survive on his own. You can't be the one to keep saving him. He has to save himself, Jane.*

"You should go away," she said. "You should go somewhere and really just . . . stop all this. Get out of this world. Hide, if you have to." She crumpled the napkin. "Don't show anyone this, don't tell anyone. Kim didn't write the song, just that one stupid line—and it's what you do with it that makes it great. You can be great again. But you have to go somewhere and . . . get better. I can't help you. You have to start helping yourself. And you can't do that with me, and you can't do that in this world of drugs and booze and fame and lawsuits—this world will eat you alive. And I . . . I can't save you." She choked back a sob now, forced herself to be strong. "I really can't. Look at me. I'm a mess too. We're so broken."

"I know you're angry. I don't blame you. I was a real shit in Berlin. You were trying and I pushed you away. Where's that drawing you made me? Can I see it now?"

She shook her head. "I threw it away."

"I'll get clean," he said. "You'll help me."

"I can't," she said. She raised her voice, shook her fist at him. The napkin was squeezed tight inside. "Don't you see? I can't help you anymore, Elijah. It's not working." She dropped the napkin on the counter, shook her head. "I can't believe you had this, all this time, and you never told me. You're so good at hiding. Just go *hide*."

"What exactly are you saying?" He didn't seem drunk now, he seemed perfectly sober. "Jane, what do you mean?"

She started to cry. "I'm saying I can't save you. I never could, Elijah. You need to save yourself."

Jane had taken a sleeping pill, but instead of waking up groggy, she sat straight up the next pitch-black morning, her words from last night, *You should go away*, playing over and over in her head like an alarm.

She got up to find the kitchen empty. The bedrooms too. The blankets on the living room floor were as flat and lifeless as a frozen lake.

Jane went outside, rushed down the stone steps. No sign of Elijah. And that was when she realized. She'd seen a small rowboat on the beach the evening before, and now it was gone. Jane walked across the black sand, toward the water, which was so icy when she reached out to touch it, she could barely stand to keep her fingers in for more than a few seconds.

Every year, on the anniversary of the tragedy, the people who had revered Elijah Hart, who had believed the songs he sang were about them, had been so certain that he and no one else had written those songs, would ask themselves: *Where were you when you found out Elijah Hart was gone?*

Jane Pyre had been standing in front of the ocean, screaming his name into the wind.

Eventually, Jane went back to the house to call the local doctor she had the number for. He called the police for her. The police searched the house, the beach. Soon, rescue divers arrived.

"He made a call from the house phone," they told her, later. "We traced the call. He telephoned his old friend Kim Beard."

Jane's broken heart sank. Please, no. Had Elijah called to tell Kim the truth, to finally admit out loud the thing Kim had been saying for years? Was that going to be his legacy and hers? Where was the napkin? She had to get back to the house and find it. Later, she did.

"Kim Beard is not a friend," was all Jane could say.

"Well, he called him."

Jane couldn't believe that she didn't even know what Elijah's last words were—and that Kim did. "What did he say?" she asked the police detective, her heart in her throat.

"He asked him for help. He said he was scared. Kim is on his way to Iceland, actually. He got on a plane to Reykjavík practically the minute he hung up the phone. He wants to be here the moment he's found."

All this felt like an accusation. *He tried to come here and help him.* Left unsaid: *Because you clearly were of no help.* But Jane knew she deserved it. Knew this really was all her fault. Knew it for the first three days of the search. Knew it was her fault when, on the fourth morning, a rowboat was found, splintered on the black sand of the farthest southern point of Reynisfjara. Farther north, a leather jacket, sodden. His. One shoe. Jane was brought out to the water each time to identify the items, confirm they were his. Two more days of searching as a storm blew in and raged, and then the search for Elijah Hart was suspended. He was declared dead. Drowned.

Jane Pyre wasn't criminally responsible for what happened, but she knew the truth. Elijah Hart was gone because of her. She'd never forget that, and neither would anyone else.

VÍK, ICELAND

DECEMBER 25, 1999

There are petrified bouquets on the lawn in front of the house in Vík. Plastic-shod photos, waterlogged and stuck under rocks or sinking into soil. Prayer candles, death lanterns, melted wax.

The door of the house hangs slightly ajar, blown open, perhaps, by the rough sea winds. Jane pulls it open the rest of the way but hesitates on the threshold. A sound, then movement inside, and her heart goes to her throat—but it's a stray cat scampering out of her sight, a black streak, then gone.

The house stands silent, thick with dust. It's dark inside, and when she flicks a light switch, nothing happens. But when she walks farther inside, she sees a flashlight sitting in the middle of the floor, at odds with everything else in the room. Not dust-covered. Shiny, new-looking. She picks it up and turns it on. It illuminates part of the room. She feels safer, now that she can see better what lurks around corners. Nothing. Blank walls. She walks from room to room until she gets to the last bedroom, the one she stayed in.

The Adam and the Rib painting is above where the bed had once been. It covers most of the wall, and it is impossible to mistake what she is seeing.

Rib is in a bed, and she looks sick, near death. Pills scattered around her. Empty bottles.

She steps closer, to see if it is a shadow on the painting or if it is what she thinks it is. Adam, but as a ghostly figure, there in the room with Jane. Words written small, on a piece of paper clenched in his almost nonexistent hand. I'm sorry. I wasn't strong enough to save us both.

His other shadow palm is spread wide open. But I'm strong enough now. And I don't want to live without you anymore.

It takes her breath away. She drops the flashlight. For the first time since this quest began Jane feels a real sliver of hope. And tears fill her eyes. He really was there with her once, during the five years she thought she had lived without him. She hadn't just imagined it to save her own life.

LOS ANGELES, CALIFORNIA

DECEMBER 1994

Jane Pyre left Iceland the day she made her single statement about her husband's death to the press. She stared out into a sea of cameras and faces—in that moment, these felt even more dangerous than the ocean itself—and said: "He's *gone*. I loved him. And he was mine. *My* husband. The love of *my* life. So give him back to me. Let me grieve in peace."

But first, she had to find out why Elijah had called Kim Beard. She asked around, but Kim had flown back ahead of her to the US. As soon as she landed in LA, she went straight to his mansion. His security team made her wait, and Jane could tell it was a typical Kim Beard power move. Almost an hour passed before they finally let her drive through the gate. She walked up to the house and rang the bell.

Kim opened it himself. "There she is," he said. "Turning up like a bad penny." Kim had always been unoriginal, had always spoken in clichés. Yet this man was somehow partially responsible for the success of her music? And the proof was on the napkin, which was in her pocket.

"Did you come here to say you're sorry?" he asked her.

"For the death of your . . . your best friend?" she said, the words heavy with sarcasm. But she couldn't deny that, for a moment, he looked genuinely sad.

"He *was* my best friend, Jane. Or I was his. I mean, I was the one he called to ask for help at the end. Not you. How does that make you feel?"

"What did he say to you?" she asked.

"Nervous about that, Jane?"

"I have no reason to be nervous. I just want to know what my husband's last words were. I think I have a right to know."

He just shook his head.

"Why do you hate me so much, Kim?"

"I could ask you the same."

"It's true," she said. "I've never really liked you. You were a real jerk, back in Seattle, from the second I got there. But I've never tried to take you down. I just don't get why you feel the need to do that to me."

He looked at her for a long moment. "He would have been better off without you. I've always thought that. Everyone has."

At this point, Jane couldn't deny that he was probably right. She looked away from him. "Just tell me what he said to you. He's gone now. Can't we bury this stupid, pointless feud? A fight over someone who doesn't even . . . doesn't even exist anymore?"

"Give me the napkin, and we're good. And I'll tell you what he said to me."

"What napkin?" she asked.

"Don't pretend with me. He told me you have it."

Fuck.

"And he was strung out and drunk. He didn't know what he was saying."

Kim stepped toward her, and for a second, she was worried he was going to hurt her. But instead he just looked down at her and said, "I'm going to keep fighting you, Jane Pyre. I'm never going to stop. Not until you admit it. I can forgive Elijah. He's my brother. He always will be. But you? Never."

"He was not your brother," Jane said. "He never, ever saw it that way. He hated you. And it is not your song. You had nothing to do with it."

"You have proof I did, and you know it."

"I have nothing. And neither do you. You can keep trying until the day you die, but there is no proof—and he's gone now anyway. His side of the story is gone too."

"That's what you think," Kim said, before slamming the door in her face.

• • •

Kim gave a *60 Minutes* interview. Jane watched it alone in her living room. He was trying to sound sincere, but that had never been his strong suit.

"He was my best friend, and he proved it that night, calling me up, telling me—" Here, his voice broke dramatically. "Telling me he loved me. Telling me how wrecked he was. That he needed help." He blinked back his crocodile tears. "He said that Jane told him she didn't want to know him anymore. That she was sick and tired of the state he was in." His shoulders shook. "I wish I could have gotten there on time. Made him see that someone in his life cared about him. But I didn't make it. I was too late to save him."

At this, Jane threw an empty bottle of vodka at her television set, and the screen broke and smoked, sparked, then turned black. But then she raced upstairs, because she had to see the rest of the interview. On the set in the bedroom, there he was again. "Kim, did he say anything else to you during that phone call? Anything that could be considered important?"

A long, shaky breath. "He told me he was sorry. That he wished he had handled things about the song differently. That he wanted to give me the scrap of credit I had asked for, because really, I deserved it. He wanted to acknowledge that we had done this great thing together."

"What do you want?"

"I don't want money, that's not what this has ever been about. It's about creative collaboration and music and . . . art. And brotherhood." Here, he gazed at the screen. At Jane. "Unbreakable bonds. He said he was sorry, and I forgive him. I forgive him completely. But her, I don't forgive."

"You're referring to Jane Pyre?"

"Of course I am."

"And why can't you forgive her?"

"Because she's a liar. She doesn't understand that the truth will set her free."

Jane put the napkin in her safe. She locked it up. And then she set about the business of destroying herself before her grief over Elijah could destroy her first.

VÍK, ICELAND

DECEMBER 25, 1999

Jane turns away from the painting of the shadow of her husband, visiting her in her lowest moment. The words *I'm sorry. I wasn't strong enough to save us both* repeat themselves in her mind.

As she turns, she sees one more painting on the opposite wall. It's the Copenhagen hotel room, the one Petra visited them in when she asked them to stop their tour. It has been re-created perfectly, right down to the room's red walls and black lacquered doors.

In the painting, Rib leans her head against the side of the door—and Adam leans his head against the other side. Jane walks to the wall and touches the paint, runs her hands over the lines, as tender as a lover.

She goes outside and picks her way down to the water, walks across the black sand beach and stands by the ocean. The waves splash her feet and wet her leather boots. A flash of color on a black rock catches her eye. She approaches and leans down, picks up the rock; a red rose is painted on it in beautiful, painstaking detail.

There are other rocks with paint on them, too. Not roses, though. These rocks have numbers on them.

95

96

97

98

99

All the years they were apart. Also, a countdown. The last rock reads, *Y2K*.

New Year's Eve, six days away—the dawn of a new millennium that many are saying will bring chaos. *Y2K*. Computers failing and planes falling from skies and humans shown to be at the mercy of technology. Jane hasn't really been worrying about it though. Every day for the past five years has felt to her like a day when the world could end—and in many ways, her world already has ended.

Another flash of color in her frame of vision: Jane sees a green glass bottle shining from where it is tucked deep into the black sand. She picks it up and spots a little scroll inside. She thinks for a moment, then breaks it against a rock, pulls the scroll out. It's on vellum and is a drawing of the converted water-pumping station in Berlin where she and Elijah played what would be their last show. The one Hen was at. In the drawing, the stage is filled with candles, and Adam is standing there, waiting.

Jane, come to Berlin. Meet me here on New Year's Eve. Unlock the door with the numbers on the rocks. Please believe this: I can be strong enough for both of us now. I can be good enough for you. I love you. Always.

—Elijah

LOS ANGELES, CALIFORNIA

1995–1999

JANE PYRE'S BAD YEAR!

After her Las Vegas wedding to Hollywood bad boy Mikey Churl, Jane Pyre, the widow of iconic musician Elijah Hart, decided to try her hand at acting. Churl was reportedly pivotal in landing her a role in *Marilyn*, a biopic about the ill-fated starlet. In the film, Churl played the role of Joe DiMaggio.

After the fairly middling movie was released, Pyre got another role, this time in an untitled Rupert Damryn action-adventure where Pyre was to play a bionic female spy. Then, Pyre reportedly suffered an on-set injury.

"It's embarrassing, really," says an unnamed source who was part of the film's crew. "She was doing a scene that took place at the top of the staircase, not even a particularly difficult action scene, and she just . . . toppled down the stairs. She was clearly drunk."

After that, Pyre apparently became belligerent on set, blaming Damryn himself for the

accident, which she said was caused by a faulty
stair railing. Damryn fired her from the film, her
marriage to Churl was annulled on the grounds
of non-consummation, and she wasn't seen in
public again for months.

Until last week, when she was spotted walking down Sunset Boulevard, midday, visibly confused and obviously high on something . . .

An annulled marriage. A failed acting career that had been a mistake in
the first place. Rumors that ranged from the ridiculous to the alarming.
That she was frigid—when really, Mikey Churl was just too wasted all
the time to have sex. That she was unhinged, which was true. That she
had had her husband killed by an Icelandic mafia that didn't exist. In the
years after Elijah's disappearance and Jane's failed marriage, along with
her joke of an acting career, Petra was the only person who came to see
her. Jane had tried to set her free many times, but she always told Jane
she was her friend—and also, still her manager. She would keep working
for her, even if her job no longer entailed setting up tours or liaising with
recording company executives.

The label kept reaching out, sending assistants over to ask if there
were any posthumous recordings that could be released. In 1997, desperate to be left alone, Jane released the remix album. She wanted people to
stop asking her if she had any music to share. She didn't. Now that Elijah
was gone, she never would.

As a 1997 New Year's resolution, Jane took up running, even though
it made her worsening knee injury flare up. One morning, the pain built
and built during her run. She got home, sat down—and then couldn't
stand up. Surgery was required to rebuild the ligament, which had by
then been torn twice.

Long after she no longer needed them, Jane found a doctor who
would refill her painkiller prescription. On the day she was photographed

wandering down Sunset Boulevard, high, she was out because she thought she had a lunch planned with Petra—but she had gotten the day wrong. She still went for lunch by herself, waited at the restaurant for Petra, consumed a bottle of champagne and several martinis, and thought that she seemed perfectly fine, perfectly composed, as she wandered home—in the wrong direction. As the paparazzi images would attest, she was a wreck. She stumbled on the sidewalk and fell. Someone who saw her said she was mumbling something about an audition.

Petra came over the next day when she didn't show up for their lunch and drove Jane to a rehab, but Jane checked herself out after a week. She began to feel certain that she did not have anything to live for. Petra called every day and eventually, Jane just stopped answering. She unlocked her door, and every once in a while, either Petra or someone she sent came to check if Jane was still alive, to implore her to eat, to drink water, to bathe.

Then came the night in 1998 when Jane heard someone inside her house and was sure a crazed fan had broken in to murder her.

"Who's there?" she called out. "Who is it?" She was on her bed in a half-lucid sleep, fading in and out of life. "Hello?"

Elijah. She was suddenly as sure of his presence as she was of her own heartbeat, faint but still there. He was standing over her bed with the saddest expression on his face. She reached out for him and was sure she could feel the warmth of his skin against her cold hands.

On her pillow, a little later, she saw a single red rose. *The shape of love.* She grasped at it. Sirens in the distance, paramedics at the door.

When she came home months later from the detox facility it was almost impossible to remember what had happened that night. She asked herself, asked Petra, over and over: *Who called the ambulance? You must have*, Petra said. *The call came from inside your home. Did anybody find a red rose?* Jane asked. Petra said she'd try to find the paramedics who came to the house and ask them. But no one remembered a red rose. Jane finally accepted that she had imagined that anyone else had been there to save her.

•   •   •

On a rainy night in 1999, Jane approached a church pulpit and stood in front of a microphone for the first time in three years. Dozens of people were gathered in the sanctuary, their backs straight against the pews, watching her. Waiting, these strangers. Witness to her downfall.

But there was a face Jane recognized. The woman from that day on Venice Beach. She smiled at Jane encouragingly and Jane felt sudden, startling hope.

She cleared her throat.

"My name is Janet Ribeiro and I'm an addict."

She did this again, night after night, until she knew it was true and she couldn't lie to herself about it ever again. She went to churches or community center basements, library meeting rooms; she repeated these words in front of strangers she knew she could trust, over and over again until she finally felt like she was winning against her addiction. Some of the other people in the group were actors and musicians and people she recognized; some were fans of the band she had once been in with her husband. But no one ever sold their stories to journalists. Jane found people she could trust. She was given little poker chips to mark the length of her sobriety. Silver: one day. Red: thirty days. Purple: four months.

Outside the meetings, the rumor mill still kept chewing on scraps of Jane Pyre. Kim Beard kept suing her, launching first an appeal of the intellectual property ruling and then a civil suit. He never stopped talking about that damn napkin.

Jane collected more poker chips. Pink, dark blue, copper. And one day, she packed them up along with Elijah's letters and drawings, and she moved away to start a new chapter of her life. Alone in Germany, with no neighbors for miles—except for Hen Vögel and her mother.

BERLIN, GERMANY

DECEMBER 31, 1999

The door of the old water-pumping station creaks open after Jane inputs the numbers *95, 96, 97, 98, 99.* She hears the sound of fireworks and celebrations outside, the distant *gong* of a church bell halfway through its twelve chimes. Then she steps inside and closes the door. The bells stop clanging. The nineties are over and a new millennium has begun—but you wouldn't know it from where she stands, at the top of a concrete staircase leading into the past.

She swings the flashlight back and forth. "Elijah?" His name echoes in the darkness. There is no answer, but she can see streaks and lines of paint along the corridor walls. She shines her light on them, reads:

"The Secret Adventure of Adam, *Alone.*"

In the first square, she sees the house they stayed at in Vík. Adam is inside, thin and sickly. He and Rib argue. He drags the rowboat to the edge of the shore and is about to get in.

You were right, Jane.

He takes off his leather jacket, his shoes, and puts them in the boat, pushes it out into the water, watches as it floats away into the angry sea. It makes Jane sick to see this—to see him going away, just as she'd told him to.

But in another square, he walks back to the house. He makes a phone call.

Help me, Adam says into the receiver. Jane closes her eyes and tears seep out. He had to ask *Kim* for help, because Jane couldn't—or wouldn't—do it. How can he forgive her for turning away from him when he needed her most? But Jane forces herself to keep going. To open her eyes again and see what he wants her to.

In an alley in Reykjavík, he gives me a passport, contact lenses. He tells me we are brothers forever. I have given him what he wants—or so I think. He promises to keep my secret, because he knows I'll die if I don't go away. He also promises he won't hurt Rib—but he doesn't keep that promise. (I'm sorry.)

Jane is the one who is sorry, who hates that Elijah felt he had no one to turn to but Kim.

But it's as if he knew she would feel this way. The next square is filled with words. Was it really that Rib didn't want to save Adam back then, or was it simply that she could not? She had done it so many times, he had forced her to do it, begged her to—but it turned out she had never been saving him. She had only been holding him out of the danger that was always lurking. The demons that never had anything to do with her, but he made her feel that way.

Another square, the letters bold: There was only one person in the world I knew would let me go. Kim. He let me go because he loved me, because he really did see us as brothers, but also because there was a part of him that wanted me gone so he could shine.

Jane walks on, reads more. It seems that Adam is gone now. There is no more "he." It is *I*. Her heart lifts. She begins to feel him close.

I travel away from Iceland, under my alias. I go to Italy, to Naples. Walk the streets there, pretend I'm someone else. I pretend I can't speak. Sometimes I try out my voice in front of a mirror to make sure it still works. It sounds different.

Jane hears something deep inside the old pumping station. She steps farther down the corridor, swings the beam out in front of her, hoping so hard. "Hello?" she calls.

Silence. She turns the beam back to the wall.

He is on a plane. Arrows on a map. He's flying back to the States with his fake passport, his disguise—which is really just his brokenness. No one recognizes him.

Newspaper headlines:

RIB MARRIES!

Jane winces, wishes she could go back in time, erase this part of her story. But there she is, standing in Las Vegas, in front of an officiant dressed as Elvis. She is holding a bottle of red wine, spilling it on her dress like blood—this really happened. It looked like a crime scene. She is laughing. But Jane knows the truth—she wasn't happy.

In the next square, he stands at the edge of a cliff, looking down at Point Dume. The next few squares are dark. A relapse. Lost time. One year, written in black.

"I'm so sorry," Jane whispers.

In the next square, he has drawn himself in the shadows of her house in LA, the night he saved her from dying after all the painkillers she had taken—the night she thought she'd seen his ghost.

I wasn't strong enough. I could only make sure she didn't die, and then I had to leave or I would start using again.

He went back to the airport, flew to France. He lived in an artists' squat. He was quiet, unnoticeable. The rock star was gone. I feel like I've been without her a thousand years. But then the ghost of her starts to talk to me, even though she's not dead. I start to believe we can find our way back to each other—but I know I have to tell her our story, the way she tried to tell it to me, back here, in Berlin.

Elijah paints tourists' portraits in Montmartre in Paris. He paints people's fences, paints the exterior of houses. Makes paintings on poster board in the artists' squat where he lives. And then, one night, he takes one of those paintings and glues it to a building wall.

Three last squares: a starry sky, but each yellow star against the midnight blue is the word I wish in the tiniest writing. The next square contains an arrow, neon and purple, directing her onward. A tiny red rose—the shape of love—on a black rock on the beach in Iceland.

When there is no more art, Jane moves forward, hears her own ragged breathing in the semidark.

She turns a corner and sees the stone platform where they played their last notes together. Pillar candles flicker. Jane turns off her flashlight. In the silence, she imagines two heartbeats in the room. They're afraid but certain, brave but terrified. They know that the shape of love has velvet-soft contours and piercing thorns, and that this is okay.

Boom. Boom. Boom. Boom.

These two hearts know each other. Have played concerts together, to sold-out arenas, to thousands of people, and also just for themselves in a Seattle basement.

And now they are finally alone again. Just the two of them.

She steps up onto the stage and for one second, she can almost hear the roar of a crowd, all gathered to adore a man they didn't really know. And to hear her, Jane Pyre. To listen to her songs, to sing her words, even if they didn't know it.

Then—a man walks out of the flickering shadows. He is a stranger with close-cropped hair and a face covered in thick stubble.

He takes a step closer.

He is tall and lean. His body is familiar.

She takes a step closer.

Closer, still.

His eyes are blue. Or green. Or both.

"Elijah?"

Still hers.

"Jane."

Still his.

He clears his throat. "I was scared you wouldn't come." His voice is thinner, softer. Like he doesn't use it much. But she can hear the man she knew. Would know his voice anywhere.

He reaches toward her as if a magnet is pulling at his hand, but then he hesitates. "Can I?"

"Please."

He touches her.

"*Oh.*" It is a gasp, a soft surprise. He is not a ghost. Elijah is real.

Now that he has been invited, he puts his hands on her waist and holds them there. She can feel his pulse through his fingers. *Alive, alive.* Elijah is truly alive. He is here with her. She puts her head against his chest for a second, to check his heartbeat, make sure she's not imagining this. She looks up, takes him in—that face she still knows so well, but five years older. She stares into his eyes and sees his soul. It is much, much older. Many lifetimes.

"You once promised you would find me," he says. His voice is growing stronger now and is full of reverent wonder. The way he looks at her, the way he speaks to her, makes her feel precious and untarnished. "But I should have promised you that too. I should never have asked so much of you."

There is a blanket on the floor near the candles and they lie down beside each other. Jane gets herself as close to Elijah as she can, the way she would when they shared a bed in his room in Seattle. She aligns herself with this new version of him, fits herself into him. "Tell me everything," they both say. "Tell me all of it, tell me more." Hours pass, their voices rising and falling. Some candles sputter out, the light shifts and fades. Maybe outside in the new millennium there are planes falling from the sky and chaos and ruin—but Jane suspects not. And anyway, it doesn't matter. If these are her last moments in the world, it's fine with her. Elijah holds her face in his hands and stares into her eyes. She searches his expression—and then she says something that is very important to her.

"255 days."

He nods. "410," he replies.

Then he begins to take off her clothes.

Later, they have to talk about it.

"Kim . . ." She still hates saying his name.

"In a messed-up way, he really was my brother for a time," Elijah says. He hesitates for a moment, as if knowing he has to get this right. "And there was nothing he wouldn't have done to separate us—you know that. Which is how I knew he would help me when I called him. But also . . . Jane, I told him to keep suing you."

"What?"

"I told him that you would eventually give in and give him the napkin, and then he could tell you the truth about me. I'm sorry—it wasn't the best plan. And it didn't exactly work." He shakes his head. "You are far too stubborn—I love you so much for that. And Kim is just a jerk, as we know. He was so cruel to you. I should have known."

"It's okay," Jane says, because it is. "I don't let him hurt me anymore."

He nods. "So, I had to figure out my own way to get to you. The artwork was just a start. I wasn't certain you would ever find it. But you did."

"Five years," Jane says, reminding herself of the time that has passed. Because all at once, it feels like no time at all.

"I had to go—you were right, Jane. I needed to totally escape our life—the fame and the crowds and the expectations—in order to survive. I had to grow up. Stop dragging you down with me. I had to get away from everything. Save myself."

She shakes her head. This is so hard to accept. "But I shouldn't have told you to go. I shouldn't have given up on you—on us."

"Jane, you didn't give up. You gave me the challenge I needed. Truly, the only solution. And I'm the one who should be sorry. You needed help, too—and I had nothing to give you. No way to save you, except to leave. Look at you—how strong you were. How strong you are." He touches her cheek, holds her chin in the palm of his hand like it's the most delicate thing. "Can you forgive me for all the suffering I put you through? I kept trying to get back to you. I thought it would be easier—but it seemed impossible, until recently."

"Of course I forgive you," Jane says. "I need you to forgive me too."

"There's nothing to forgive. Ever."

She feels safe and secure in his arms, but the sound of more church bells outside reminds her of the world. She feels suddenly afraid. "What should we do now?"

"I don't know," he says. "I don't have answers. I just need you. Us. That's all I know right now."

"I need you too. But also . . . there's someone you need to meet. It's important. *She's* important. She led me to you. And she needs to know that you . . ." She trails off, touches his cheek, his jaw, traces the contours of her favorite face. "Are exactly who she thought you were. Just as good. Just as great."

Before they blow out the candles and leave the water-pumping station, Elijah pulls a duffel bag out of the shadows. It's full of cans of black spray paint. Together, Jane and Elijah spray over the secrets and stories, the legend of Adam and Rib, until it only exists in their minds and hearts. At the bottom of his bag are two Day of the Dead masks. They put them on, cover their faces, and go out into the night. The New Year's Eve revelers who thought Y2K was the end of the world are now dancing in the streets and in the clubs as if they have survived something more than just the arrival of a new year. For a few moments, Jane and Elijah do the same. As she twirls with Elijah in the street, Jane feels happy. She holds the feelng close, in the same way she holds on to him.

They find her car and drive to the farmhouse. Her lonely bed becomes something else. Their bodies, entangled again. She looks down at him, this man who has come back to her, and she knows that what they had before, in their past, is nothing compared to what they will have. That back then, they were so young, and they were just getting started.

They make love in the middle of the night, and in the morning, before falling back asleep.

When Jane wakes up beside Elijah later, she has a moment of panic. She is afraid to open her eyes in case it was all a dream. But then he's touching her and kissing her and he is very much real. It is better than a dream.

Later, after they've finally gotten out of bed, Jane stands and walks to the window. She looks out at Hen's house.

Hen will have seen her car. She'll know she's back. "We should go over," Jane says.

They dress and walk across the property line to Hen's house.

A woman is sitting on the front porch with a calico cat on her lap. She puts down the cat and stands when she sees Jane. "I know who you are," she says—and her voice is not warm or cold, just matter-of-fact. It's refreshing for Jane, to have someone know who she is and have her existence, her name, just *be*, without judgment. This is the way Hen speaks, too. Jane has missed Hen. Her mother has the same blue eyes, the same dandelion-blond hair, but with a little gray. Then she looks at Elijah. "Don't worry. I won't tell anyone you're here." Jane can almost hear the words unspoken. *I have no one to tell.*

"I'm sorry about taking Hen with me. I should have checked with you," Jane begins.

Hen's mother just shakes her head, not as if it's all fine, but as if it's over now and what can anyone do to change the past?

"I'll go get her."

Moments later, Hen is there, clinging to the doorframe, looking out at them like a shy child. The cat is now winding itself through her legs. She picks it up and its lawn mower purr fills the air. "Hi," she says.

Elijah smiles at Hen then, and that smile of his—Jane knows what it is to have that smile directed at you for the first time. "Hen," he says. "I've heard all about you. I came here to thank you. Thank you for bringing Jane back to me. I owe you my life."

Hen steps closer, still holding the cat. She peers at him, takes him in. "You're welcome," she finally says. "But . . . what were the final frames, please? Before this part we're at now, how did the story end?"

They sit out on the front porch for a while, talking, until Hen's mother timidly invites them in. She brings them tea and then dinner, a comforting noodle dish with brown bread, a green salad. The kind of food Alice would have made. All of this is served in the living room, on wooden trays they hold on their knees while the news plays silently in the background. Russian forces are moving toward Chechnya. A little Cuban boy has been rescued from the Atlantic Ocean, the sole surviver on a migrant boat. Computer experts are still surprised over the smooth transition into the new millennium.

As they eat, Elijah tells Hen about his time spent lost and invisible in the world for five years.

"Would you do it all over again?" Hen asks. It's late by then. Close to midnight.

Elijah tilts his head, pensive. "Which part?"

Hen turns to Jane, then Elijah. "Would you start your band, release that song, if you knew everything that would happen?"

Elijah is thoughtful. "Music led me to Jane—and now I'm meeting you, Hen, and that's pretty great, too." That smile again. "If I had to go through all this again, if it was the only way to be sitting here on this porch feeling the way I do in this moment—then yes, I think I would."

He turns to Jane. "How about you?"

"I don't think I can answer that question," Jane says. "Not yet."

They're tired; the three of them are all yawning. Hen gives Jane and Elijah a flashlight, but they don't use it. They hold hands and walk back over to Jane's in the darkness after promising Hen they'll see her tomorrow.

And they will. But the next morning, they have something they need to do first. Jane and Elijah put on disguises—he a fedora pulled low, colored contacts, and glasses; she a white wig, a woolen toque, an oilskin jacket found in a closet—and they go to Berlin. They buy real drums and guitars, and they set all those up in the loft of the old barn. Then they go get her, ask her if she wants to come over and jam with them.

In bed, late at night again, Jane gives Elijah her answer. "To the question of if I'd do it again . . . if I'd choose fame. The answer is no." She pauses. "I think we need to disappear. Together this time—and for real. For good."

They wait a few more days. Then they write Hen a letter and slide it under her door before they leave, the stars shining down on them in the cold January night. They've left her some songs, and a computer with a modem, and code words to watch for when they contact her, once they're settled. They've written in their letter that it's not really goodbye—but they have to go. They hope she understands.

In the Cambodian fishing village of Kep, Jane and Elijah's days are measured by the moment the sun pokes its head above the horizon—at which point the boats can already be seen in the light of dawn, making their way out onto the ocean to bring back their haul of crab and squid—and the instant the sun fizzles into the sea and the boats are back. When night begins, they walk to the crab market to buy fresh seafood and vegetables to cook at home, or skewers from the barbecues along the water.

Elijah still likes to sleep in, and Jane still likes to wake early. She rambles alone past salt fields that sprawl the way suburbia did back in Seattle, plantations growing spicy peppercorns from trees in uniform rows, so different from the wild jungle beyond them. One day, Jane uses the peppers to make her own hot sauce. It is so hot that tears stream down both of their faces when they sample it. Jane doesn't try that again.

At the National Park, Jane always goes to the mountaintop to visit the "Little Buddha." It is carved from white marble that is slowly turning green, as if the deity is becoming one with the trees that surround him. Many mornings, Jane sits down cross-legged a few feet away from the Buddha. She sits in silence, and sometimes she grapples with fears and dark thoughts. Other times, she feels completely at ease. And then she goes home to Elijah. She is always, always happy about this.

At the end of their days, if Jane and Elijah are lucky, they sometimes catch the green lightning flash that happens in the moment the sun drops below the horizon. They have a record player, but only a few records. They play music together, but Elijah doesn't sing anymore. Maybe he's afraid someone will hear, and so is she. Or maybe it's just too painful. Jane hopes one day it won't be, but for now, it simply is.

One night, at one of the ramshackle restaurants built out over the water near the crab market, they're sharing an order of crab amok. A rom kbach band is playing lively folk music.

"Do you miss it?" Jane asks him. "Playing music for people?"

He laughs. "No, actually. Not yet. Do you?"

She doesn't hesitate. "Yes. I miss it so much. I miss writing songs. I was thinking I'd start again—not for any reason other than just . . . for me. For you. For us. You don't have to sing them for me. But what if we send them to Hen?"

He nods. "I love that idea. Let's send them to her."

"Do you think we'll stay here forever?" Jane asks, after a few moments of contented silence. He has her hand in his, is massaging her palm, running his finger up and down her unbroken lifeline.

"Probably not," he replies. "Nothing is forever."

"Except us," she says, and she knows he agrees.

Suddenly, she feels them: lyrics for a new song, flowing into her mind. She grabs a napkin to write them down.

We will stay here forever
and never
be here again.
No matter what happens
it will not be the end.

EPILOGUE

Hen999: Hello? Anyone there?

Eli72: Hi! Happy 2001!

SysOP: How was the show tonight??

Hen999: It was awesome. We were super tight. The crowd loved "Not the End," but actually, they also really got into the love ballad, "The Shape of Love." It's slower, but it still rocks.

Eli72: I really like that one too.

SysOP: And you're doing okay? Keeping it together? No bad rock star behavior?

Hen999: Ha, ha. I swear. I'm as straight edge as they come. You don't have to worry about me. One time getting drunk and throwing up is enough. I'm still not over it.

SysOP: You'll tell us if we ever do need to worry?

Eli72: If you ever need help, or need advice?

Hen999: Guys, I promise. You've both already been so helpful. But I wish you two could be at the album release party next week. You deserve to be. I can't believe it's been a year since I've seen you.

SysOP: Maybe someday. I don't think we're ready to risk going out in the world yet, even disguised.

Eli72: For now, we'll be there in spirit.

Hen999: So . . . you're happy there? Where you are?

Eli72: Yes.

SysOP: Very.

Hen999: Good. I'm glad. Hey, did you hear about Kim Beard?

Eli72: Nope.

Hen999: He's touring again. It's going to be called the My Life Is Mine tour. I can't believe you let him have the song.

Eli72: Ah well, who cares? That one line was his.

Hen999: Sure, but what's the line without the rest of the song, and without Elijah's voice? I bet no one will go. Actually, who am I kidding? People are sheep.

SysOP: Ha!

Eli72: It's a long life, if you're lucky. Maybe he'll change. Anyway, forget about him. Tell us more about you.

Hen999: Well, my mom came to our show! I was saving that up to tell you.

SysOP: Hen! That's so great. I guess the meds and therapy are working?

Hen999: So far, so good.

Eli72: You still live in Jane's old place and she lives in your house?

Hen999: Yes. Baby steps, right? I like having her close, to be honest.

Eli72: You should get some rest. Shows take a lot out of a person. And Hen, please don't forget. We may be far away, but we're always here for you. We owe you.

Hen999: You don't have to worry—my band is about 1/9000th as famous as yours. I'll be fine. And you don't, really. You've given me a lot. Let's call it even.

Eli72: Night, Hen.

SysOP: Sweet dreams.

Hen999: Goodnight, you two.

<Logout/Goodbye>

THE LIGHTNING BOTTLES SONG LYRICS

My Life or Yours

You asked if I'd die for you
I didn't know what you meant
but the words were all there for me
from a prophet, heaven sent.
You wanted me to sing, I just wanted to play.
I took you for granted
had no clue you wouldn't stay.

There's noise all around me,
I just want to sing.
Did you close your eyes, Mama?
Could you see everything?
Do you know it all now
have the answer we seek?
I think you'd tell me
that baby, it's not so bleak

baby, don't cry
'cause we're all gonna die
might as well just get high, go get high
'cause we're all gonna die
no sense asking why, just get high
'cause we're all gonna die

I run through the rain
loss chases me down
when did you close your eyes?
when did you drown?

I took you for granted
but I took you at your word
when you said my voice was magic
the truest thing you'd ever heard.

It's okay now
I'm okay now
It's gonna be okay now

'cause we're all gonna die
might as well just get high (yeah) just get high, just get high
'cause we're all gonna die
let's get high, don't ask why, just get high

My life or yours?
I don't know anymore.
Your life or mine?
This grief has no floor.
I took you for granted, Mama, took you at your word
you told me my voice was the one true thing you heard.
Doesn't matter why now
doesn't matter how
I think you'd say it's time for me
to take my very first bow

and it's okay, nothing matters anyway

'cause we're all gonna die
might as well just get high, go get high
'cause we're all gonna die
let's get high, don't ask why, just get high
'cause we're all gonna die

How did it feel?
(doesn't matter anymore)
What did I steal?
(what did I say as you walked out the door?)
Give me a choice
(I don't wanna get high)
you said my voice
(don't wanna die)
was your life

and it's okay
I know what you'd say
it's okay now
you'd say
we're all gonna die
might as well just get high, go get high
'cause we're all gonna die
let's get high, don't ask why, just get high

hey, hey, hey . . . we're all gonna die
(give me my life back)
just get high, just get high, let's get high
(give me my love back)
'cause we're all gonna die
don't ask why
(I am yours)
just get high, go get high
'cause we're all gonna die
(gonna find you)
don't ask why, never ask why

we're just all gonna die

Dark Shine

You are the sun
that makes me shine
in this bitter world of mine
I never thought I'd feel this way
Now I can't breathe if you won't stay.

Shine on, baby, shine out your love
It fits my heart just like a glove
Shine on, baby, shine so dark
I think you know you've left your mark.

You are the sun
that never shines
in this hazy world of mine
Love so strong it feels like hate
Love so perfect I know it's fate.

Shine on, baby, that dark, dark love
Give it to me now
one push, one shove
Shine it on me, your dark, your shine
tell me you'll be forever mine.

You are the sun (shine on, dark shine)
that makes me shine
(your cold, dark love)
It makes you mine
(this bitter world, divine)
Don't stop, don't hide
(let your darkness shine).

Six of Cups

You said the moon was broken
and you tossed it from our sky
Who are you to decide our fate
without a reason why?

You gave me another missing piece
and called me incomplete
You said the words so softly
you made them sound so sweet

Oh sun, oh moon, oh me, oh my
I'm nothing but a lover
Please hear my cry
Oh moon, oh sun, oh stars, oh sky
I'm looking for my Six of Cups
I feel like I could die

You said the moon was broken
you said the sky was black
but I looked right back at you and said
you know it will be back

I took away your missing piece
you are not incomplete
I said the words the way I do
they never sounded sweet

Oh moon, oh sun, oh me, oh my
I'm looking for my Six of Cups
I'll never let you cry
Oh stars, oh sun, oh me, oh my

we are the lovers now
I'll never let you die

A thousand dreams
and one is true
last night I wished you loved me
and today I know you do

Oh moon, oh sun, oh me, oh my
I'm looking for my Six of Cups
I'll never let you cry
Oh stars, oh sun, oh me, oh my
we are the lovers now
I'll never let you die

Acknowledgments

I'm grateful to you, my readers, for making it this far—or, if you're like me, flipping to the acknowledgments first and still deciding to read this book. If not for you, I would just be selling books to my parents and in-laws, and I wouldn't get to do this job I've harbored fantasies about since I was old enough to write my name.

Also: To my agent and friend, Samantha Haywood, the best partner, colleague, cheerleader, fierce negotiator, and visionary. I adore you. Thank you to Eva Oakes for the most astute read, and Laura Cameron, Megan Phillips, Barbara Miller, and the rest of the team at Transatlantic Agency, for everything else.

Dana Spector at Creative Artists Agency, for loving this book as much as I fully expected you to and working so hard to make the Lightning Bottles famous.

The team at Reese's Book Club, for changing my life and for their continued support of my work. What a dream; it never gets old.

At Simon & Schuster US: Thank you to my editor, Carina Guiterman, for wanting to work with me just as much as I wanted to work with you, and for exceeding my expectations; thanks as well to Jonathan Karp, Tim O'Connell, Sophia Benz, Hannah Bishop, Danielle Prielipp, Yvette Grant, cover designer Math Monahan—and copy editor Stacey Sakal, for the life-affirming moment of finding such lovely comments (and a crying emoji!) in the margins of your edit. I recently unearthed a high school essay wherein the teacher's remark was *very well-written, but you clearly have some serious issues with punctuation*, so your wholehearted approval is something I will always hold dear.

At Simon & Schuster Canada: To my editor, Brittany Lavery, for taking up the reins and doing an excellent job of it; Rita Silva, the best of the best; Rebecca Snodden; and Nicole Winstanley (!!!).

I'm also grateful to Nita Pronovost, Adria Iwasutiak, and Felicia Quon. (Peaches, baby. Always.)

Alan Cross: Years ago, when I first discussed this book with you, you sternly told me to "get it right." The fact that, in the end, you declared I had nailed it is an honor and compliment I do not take lightly. Thank you for your time, expertise, and access to so many musical insights.

Thank you also to Tara Maclean for the soul-level discussions about songwriting; and Kate Henderson for helping with the entertainment law details. Any errors made or liberties taken in either case are mine. (*Nashville* made songwriting look so easy; *Matlock* always made courtrooms seem so fun.)

Thank you to Alternative Berlin Tours for a comprehensive and inspiring exploration of the city's street art. (If you like street art, or are intrigued by what you've read about it in these pages, you should visit Berlin and take this tour!) And to my family, for tagging along on trains, cars, and planes across Europe as I mapped out Jane and Elijah's journey.

I'm also grateful to Kalman Magyar for helping me sort out some of the details about traveling within Europe in the nineties.

The stack of books I read as I researched the various components of this novel would pile up to my office ceiling. For helping ensure I didn't go broke/run out of storage space, I'm indebted to the Toronto Public Library system—my first stop, always, on the way to finding a story.

Thank you to Laurie Petrou for an insightful, bighearted first read. To Sophie Chouinard for planning the Iceland trip; you helped change the trajectory. Alison Gadsby, Kate Henderson, and Sherri Vanderveen—I'm so glad we're still going strong. Asha Frost: the way you hold space for my dreams is a gift. Beatrix Nagy: you've made it possible for me to keep doing this job by always calling me out in Pilates class for having "important hands"—and you've kept me humble by questioning how I can manage to keep the stories I write straight when I can't even remember how to do "bird dog." Kerry Clare: I'm so glad books brought us together. Chantel Guertin, Nan Row, Amanda Watson, Nance Williams. Old friends Liz Davis and Susan Robertson, for helping me remember my teenage self. Lauren Fox, perfect princess and total weirdo. Laurie Elizabeth Flynn, for the most encouraging and kind first endorsement of all time. Suzy Krause, because it feels wrong not to mention your name here when our books have decided to be besties. Lori Dyan, for blazing into my life like a ray of sunshine. Liz Renzetti, Uzma Jalaluddin, Bianca Marais. And, this is the part where I've forgotten someone and hurt their feelings: please, forgive me.

My family: Bruce Stapley—best dad, best hype man, best enthusiast in general; Valerie Clubine, truly the wind beneath my wings and the person who loved me just as I was during some difficult years—I miss you desperately, and now I know I always will; James Clubine, for love, support, and faith; my younger brothers, Drew and Griffin Stapley, for *almost* reading at least one of my books each. Love you anyway. My older brother, Shane Stapley, for letting me be a roadie for his band even if I probably didn't actually carry any amps, for taking me to Lollapalooza and countless other concerts, and for letting me steal your Pearl Jam tape. (But, I'm still mad at you for the Kurt Cobain T-shirt.) To Joe, Joyce, and the rest of the Ponikowski family for all their care and support.

My children, Joseph and Maia, who have grown into teenagers who occasionally like my Instagram posts but mostly think I'm the cringiest. That's the way it's supposed to be. I love you more, I love you most.

Last but not least, Joe. I'm glad our love isn't star-crossed and that we managed to find each other in this lifetime. I think you're so cool.

About the Author

MARISSA STAPLEY is the *New York Times* bestselling author of *Lucky*, a Reese's Book Club pick, and several other internationally bestselling novels, many of which have been optioned for television and translated into many languages. She has worked as a journalist, magazine editor, and creative writing teacher, and currently resides in Toronto with her family.